"Quade," she whispered.

His tortured groan rippled through her body to land in her abdomen.

"This is insane," he muttered, brushing her hair away from her shoulder as if he couldn't help himself.

"Insane?" She partially turned to meet his gaze. "We're being chased by creepy dudes with helicopters, a weirdo who can turn into a wildcat, and who knows what else. We're in a crappy old barn, it's freezing, and we're both getting turned on. We left insane several miles back. This is—I have no clue what to call this. But bite me, take my blood, and let's figure out our next move."

A dark scruff covered his rugged jaw, making him look even wilder than she knew him to be. "I'm glad you can keep your sense of humor in this type of situation," he said.

"I'm not laughing," she retorted, stretching her neck more. "You are still bleeding." Drops were falling onto her shoulder. "Stop being a jackass and bite me."

Also by Rebecca Zanetti

The Dark Protector series
Fated
Claimed
Tempted
Hunted
Consumed
Provoked
Twisted
Shadowed
Tamed
Marked
Talen
Vampire's Faith
Demon's Mercy
Alpha's Promise

The Realm Enforcers series
Wicked Ride
Wicked Edge
Wicked Burn
Wicked Kiss
Wicked Bite

The Scorpius Syndrome series
Mercury Striking
Shadow Falling
Justice Ascending

The Deep Ops series
Hidden
Taken novella
Fallen

Hero's Haven

Rebecca Zanetti

LYRICAL PRESS
Kensington Publishing Corp.
www.kensingtonbooks.com

LYRICAL PRESS BOOKS are published by

Kensington Publishing Corp.
119 West 40th Street
New York, NY 10018

All Kensington titles, imprints, and distributed lines are available at special quantity discounts for bulk purchases for sales promotion, premiums, fund-raising, educational, or institutional use.

Special book excerpts or customized printings can also be created to fit specific needs. For details, write or phone the office of the Kensington Sales Manager: Kensington Publishing Corp., 119 West 40th Street, New York, NY 10018. Attn. Sales Department. Phone: 1-800-221-2647.

Lyrical Press and Lyrical Press logo Reg. U.S. Pat. & TM Off.

First Electronic Edition: January 2020
ISBN-13: 978-1-5161-0748-3 (ebook)
ISBN-10: 1-5161-0748-9 (ebook)

First Print Edition: January 2020
ISBN-13: 978-1-5161-0752-0
ISBN-10: 1-5161-0752-7

Printed in the United States of America

This one is dedicated to Boone Brux and Asa Maria Bradley, my fellow authors, trusted friends, and energetic adventure seekers. Arctic Thunder Forever.

Chapter One

It was time to die.

Thank all the gods.

Quade Kayrs had spent lifetimes—too many to fathom—fulfilling his duty. Even when this world so far from home had changed from monotonous to pure hell for centuries upon centuries, he had done his job. Oh, he had died many times in this horrendous place. From the flashing fire to the freezing cold to the hungry creatures, many times the life had slid from his body. But as a vampire-demon hybrid, he returned to live again each time.

Until now.

He sat in his cave, the rock ice-cold against his back, watching the lick of fire at the entryway. The weak flames sputtered and died. No more fire after a millennium of burning. The world trembled, finally giving up the fight. Ready to die along with him. The sky cracked wide open outside, revealing the other world, the one he was bound to keep trapped. His enemy was there somewhere; Quade could only hope that bastard would blow up along with him.

There was no way to guarantee that fact, but Quade had done his best. If the next life gave points for suffering in this one, he was going to be a freaking god.

Not that he cared.

He had stopped caring about anything but duty so long ago. He could barely remember himself, much less anybody else. Once, there had been brothers he trusted and loved. On his home world, their bones had to have been crushed to dust by now. Even though time moved faster in this hell, they could not possibly still be alive after all these centuries.

Shutting his eyes, he let his body go limp. No more fighting. No more pain. No more anything.

He smiled, his lips cracking from the rare movement. Finally. It was over. The freezing chill washed over him, while the ground started to shake as the world prepared to explode into nothingness. Shards of frozen rock fell, cutting his legs. He did not twitch. Pain was a companion, nothing to acknowledge. The walls shook. Something howled in the far distance, something not of this world. How many worlds would crumble with this one—destruction spreading like the ripples of water from a rock across a pond? He and his brothers had played such a game in his childhood.

His childhood.

Images of his existence before this place flashed before his eyes. His brothers. His friends. The life he had once enjoyed.

Ah. It was good to let go. Would he see them again? Hope was beyond him, so he let it, too, slide away. He exhaled slowly, the arctic air ripping through his lungs.

"Um, hello?" A soft voice had him forcing his eyes back open.

He blinked. She was a vision in the corner of the cave. Sun-kissed blond hair; one green eye and one black; tiny stature. "You," he rumbled. When had he last imagined her? So long ago he could not count. An idea filtered through the fog in his brain. Before, she had looked like a demoness. Maybe that had been wrong. "Are you an angel?"

She looked around the darkening cave, her eyes wide. "Angel? No. My name is Haven." Her shoulders slumped. "You're not real."

"You're not real, either," he returned, chuckling for the first time in eons. Funny. Nothing was real. Her name fit her, because for so long, the image of her had been his only haven. "You have not come for a while."

"No." Another creature screeched far away, and she jumped. "I've, ah, been taking new medication. It has worked so far." She rubbed her arms and shivered. "I shouldn't be here."

He struggled to keep his eyes open. "Nobody should be here." Soon, the angel would disappear like before. That was all right. Though why was he imaging her in such odd clothing? Blue pants, white shirt, tall boots? "Where is your proper dress?" His imagination was odd.

Lightning cracked across the sky, propelling her toward him. "We have to get out of here."

He laughed. Full-on belly laugh. This was a good way to die. "Right. My mind wants out." His body was done.

Then she touched him, grasping his arm.

He jolted, his body electrified. What the hell? He slapped a hand over hers, feeling warmth. In the few times she had come to him through the years, the female had never touched him. Her hand felt real and fragile beneath his. So far, dying was lovely. As was she. He smiled. "You are taking me home?"

More rocks dropped, one slicing her forehead. Blood welled, and she cried out.

He blinked. She could feel pain? The beast at his core, the one long dormant, stretched awake at the fresh scent of her blood. "I do not understand."

She grabbed his other arm and tugged. "We have to go. Now."

He shook his head. "Nowhere to go." Once, there were portals to other places, ones he had ignored and purposely kept closed, to do his duty. But as his world began to die, he had searched for them; they were gone. That made sense, really. If this place was to go, it would be better if it failed to take others with it. "Sit with me." He might as well take comfort in his imagination as he left the world.

She pulled harder and then smacked him across the face. "Dude. We have to go. Now." Frantic, she looked wildly around. Then she settled, her eyes closing and her breath evening out. "I can do this." She opened her eyes, and those intriguing orbs focused on him. "Please. Trust me."

Beautiful. His last view was going to be of beauty. He liked that. "As you wish." He pushed to his feet, his bones creaking.

She took his hand and led him to the edge of the cave, staring down the jagged cliff.

He looked down as well. Maybe this was how the end would come. All right.

She tightened her hold. "Ready?"

He nodded. Then, keeping her hand, he jumped toward death.

* * * *

Haven Daly sat up in the bed, screaming silently. A trick she'd learned at way too young an age. Her heart thundered, and sweat prickled over her skin. She gasped, trying to breathe, letting the panic roll through her because she couldn't beat it. All she could do was let it take her and then pick up the pieces afterward.

She pounded her palms against her closed eyes. *No, no, no.* She rocked back and forth, trying to slow her breathing. Not again. Not the nightmares again.

Something wet her hand, and she slowly lowered it to see blood. Ouch. She frowned, gingerly probing the cut above her eye. The rock in the cave had cut her. That was impossible. It was only a dream. Had she somehow self-harmed during the dream? That was a new one. But it was the only thing that made sense.

Man, she missed her cat. She'd left him with an elderly neighbor in Portland because she wasn't sure how long she'd be running.

This time her dreams had been different. Something had pulled her in opposite directions, and she'd had to fight to follow Quade's voice. What had tried to force her to go another way this time?

Dreams sucked.

Just as her breathing leveled out, the urge to flee north took her. Not again. Her legs trembling, she stood on the clean motel carpet and tried to fight the compulsion. Dawn had yet to arrive outside, but she'd slept with the bathroom light on, as usual, so she could see.

For months, she'd been drawn north, ending up in a small Idaho town in this quaint motel for several nights. She was on the run, so that suited her purposes fine. Wallace was a sweet town with a rich heritage of mining and construction, and the people had been kind to her all week. The waitresses at the motel had learned how to make her coffee and had nicely given her a cupcake yesterday for her birthday. Even strangers on the street said hello, for no other reason than to be polite.

It was a nice place to be drawn to. Even as she had the thought, she began dressing in faded jeans, a long-sleeved white shirt, and her brown boots. After using the facilities, she pulled her long hair into a ponytail and quickly packed.

When the compulsion took her, it won. Every time.

She checked out of the hotel and ran for her battered Jeep, her boots slipping on the snow. Sparkling Christmas lights twinkled from the surrounding trees, looking cheerful despite the winter storm blasting around and the wind cutting into her. Putting the heat on full force, she drove away from Wallace and back onto I-90, once again having no clue where she was going. But she was done fighting, so she just drove, peering into the swirling mass of snow. Reaching Kingston, she pulled off, driving past a still closed restaurant called the Snake Pit, and then along a winding river.

Where was she going this time?

She'd been taking her medication, the new stuff, as well as several herbal supplements. For a short time, they had helped curb her craziness.

Unfortunately, she'd learned early on that crazy always won. The last shrink, the one in Oregon, had diagnosed her with a bizarre delusional disorder. At one time or another through her life, she'd been diagnosed with many a mental illness. Nothing had cured her, so she'd accepted there was no cure. She'd done better in Oregon, painting consistently enough that the local gallery had offered her a show. Looked like it had been a success. She'd had to leave before the big night and hadn't attended. However, her bank account, the one in Texas, was now a little fatter. That was nice.

The wind increased in power and the snow fell so thickly she couldn't see beyond the headlights. She slowed on the icy river road. Closed for the season cabins and locked guardrails protecting empty private camping areas lined the river road, while trees covered the other side. Cottonwoods, pines, and spruces, all blanketed in snow.

Where was she going?

She rubbed the cut above her eyelid. It had stopped bleeding; it must not be too deep. The dream delusion had been stronger than ever before. This time, she'd touched him. The wounded and angry man. Quade. He'd told her his name on her second visit. Why had her imagination named him Quade? She'd never known a Quade. Why was she seeing him again? It didn't make sense.

Things rarely did.

Almost on its own, the Jeep turned down a road with public access to the river for rafters. A wide, icy parking area lay empty as the snow billowed all around.

Sighing, she parked the vehicle and stepped out, watching the clouds lighten across the river as dawn arrived. Cold blasted her and the snow hit her hard. Shivering, she reached in the back seat for her down jacket, shrugging into it and zipping quickly. Her gloves were in her pocket, and she drew them on before walking toward the river. Was she supposed to look in the dark blue, freezing water?

Shrugging, she let the delusion take her. The water was fathomless and looked cold.

All right. A twig snapped, and she swiveled to see a couple of deer tramping along the tree line, their noses down as they foraged for food.

One glanced up at her and went still.

So did she.

Finally, the doe turned and bounded into the forest. Fair enough.

"Why am I here?" Haven muttered.

Another sound caught her, and she turned the other way. Beyond the brown camping sign that reminded people to pack out their litter, a rumble echoed. Blinking snow from her eyes, she tilted her head and picked her way across the icy ground toward a locked building holding bathrooms. Her coat was soon covered with snow, as was her hair.

The sound had come from behind the wooden building.

Swallowing, she let the pull take her, slogging through snow and around the building to find . . . more trees. The river wound by in cold silence, as if taking a break from its chatter before the snowpack melted to cause rapids. She shivered, rubbing her arms to warm up.

What in the hell was going on? Why was she here? Maybe her brain had finally broken completely. What now?

The sound came again. A low groan.

Her breath quickened, and her head jerked. Her legs bunched to run away, but instead of obeying her mind, they started moving toward two naked cottonwood trees. She coughed out a sob, fighting herself, but her legs had taken over. Or rather, her craziness had taken over completely.

The snow grew thicker, and she struggled through the chilly powder, fighting to stay on her feet. Finally, as she moved between two spruce trees, her delusion manifested itself fully. She had to blink several times to take in the sight before her.

A naked Quade was slumped in the snow against the trunk of a pine tree, his body unmoving, his eyes closed, bruises covering him. Snow had already gathered in his long black hair and beard.

"Well," she murmured out loud. "This is new."

Then his eyes opened. Deep and bluish-green and sizzling. "Haven," he rumbled.

Chapter Two

Quade hurt too much to be dead. Damn it. Cold tinged his skin, and his head ached. He rubbed his ear, not surprised to bring back blood on his fingers. His vocal cords, not used for anything but screaming for so long, ached as he said her name. Instinct took over, and he grasped snow, bringing it to his mouth. The flakes disintegrated in his mouth, cooling down his damaged throat.

A sound caught his attention through the wild storm, and he turned his head. Water. Planting his hand on the frozen snow, he shoved himself up and then ran toward the sound.

"Quade," the woman called from behind him.

He could not stop. Not a chance. He grabbed the branch of a tree, a real tree, and barreled around it, leaping for the rushing water. Like an animal, he dropped to his knees and dunked his head. His forehead hit a rock, and he winced, but he kept drinking. Rapidly. So much water.

Finally, when he could take no more, he lifted his head. The snowy world spun around him, and he shut his eyes to dispel the dizziness.

"Quade?"

He partially turned, acutely aware of his nudity and animalistic position. "Where?" he grunted.

The female took a step back, her already pale face turning stark white. Even her lips had taken on a light blue color. She must be freezing.

He shook his head, trying to grasp reality. Wiping water off his face, he stood again, wobbling a little. The air was lighter here. "Where am I?"

She hunched farther into her coat. "Idaho."

Idaho? Where the hell was Idaho? He smelled pine. Real pine and fresh water. The scents of his youth. Eons ago, when he had endured the ritual of the Seven, he had crossed through different worlds, but none with a name. "Who is in Idaho?" His voice, rusty and hoarse, sounded odd after all this time.

She eyed him as if he was a starving animal. "Um, we are?" She wiped snow off her face and shivered, her gaze staying above his neck.

He had opened his mouth to ask more questions when dizziness blasted him between the eyes. He went down as if struck with a club, his knees smashing through frozen snow to hit the raw ground.

"You're going to freeze." Apparently making up her mind, she kicked through the snow to reach him, grabbing his arm. "Come on. I have a Jeep over here." She tugged, an ineffectual but stubborn little thing. Heat and a new, unexpected pain flashed along his right palm, and he pressed it into the snow. Steam rose. What the hell? He lifted his hand and looked. The marking. The Kayrs marking.

It was impossible. He was not to mate. No matter what, the Seven would not mate, because their lives were not their own. They were sacrifices in the end.

She looked down at the improbable mark and shook her head. "This is an over-the-top delusion." Indecision and confusion clouded her pretty face.

He nodded, staring at his palm and the raw brand of the letter K surrounded by a Celtic knot and jagged lines. The marking a demon got when he met his mate. It should not be on his hand. "You are real," he murmured, looking up at her.

"You're not," she retorted, pulling on his arm. "Though you feel real."

None of this was making sense. He allowed her to pull him up. "We require shelter." The storm seemed to be getting worse. He tried to transport himself, taking her through time and space to the place of his youth, but his ability was gone.

"This way." Grasping his hand, the one covered in scars from the Seven ritual, she turned back toward the trees.

He followed her, his steps light. The air around him was different from the world he had just left, making breathing and moving much easier. The female was small but trudged on with determination. He liked that about her. They emerged in an icy field with a snow-covered small shelter in the middle. Was it blue?

She pulled him, her head down, her boots sliding. "Come on."

He tried to scout the area for threats, but the storm was too powerful for him to get a bead on enemies. She tugged him around the odd shelter and pulled open a door to reveal two thick chairs separated by a box. "Sit. Now," she urged.

How very odd. He slid onto the seat, which was smooth. The female pulled open another door behind him and retrieved a blanket off a long seat, which she planted over him. He clutched the material, which was soft and warm. "Thank you."

"Sure." She shut his door and ran around the front.

What an odd shelter. Would they just sit in it and stare outside until the storm passed? He knocked on the clear glass. Glass. He remembered that vaguely.

Haven opened her door and took her seat, shutting them in. A wheel was in front of her. Silence descended inside the shelter. She reached to the side of the wheel for something dangling and twisted her wrist. The shelter rumbled and bumped.

Quade froze, his chest filling.

She pulled on a knob in front of her, and heat blew toward him from vents. He dropped his head, looking inside. "There is a fire in there?" How was all of this possible? "Where are we?" He truly did not understand.

"We need to find you clothes." She looked over his blanket-wrapped body. "Nothing I have will remotely cover you." She turned back to the wheel, moved a lever between them, and the shelter began to move.

Shock filled him, followed by a chilled heat that made his heart thump harder than it had in years. Then Quade Kayrs, one of the most dangerous and feared hybrids in any existing world, fainted like a virginal maiden.

* * * *

Haven drove through the storm, her shoulders hunched, her eyes squinting as she peered into the swirling mass of white. Even so, she glanced at the man sleeping beside her. Biting her lip, she reached out and nudged him on his muscular bare upper arm. He felt real. Everything felt so real.

How could this be another dream?

When he'd shown her his palm and the striking K tattoo, she'd nearly jumped out of her boots. For years, she'd been drawing that symbol. Painting it, even.

Of course, if all of this was in her head, if she'd finally disengaged from reality, that made sense. Nothing else did.

Her car dinged, and she started, looking at the gauge. Shit. The compulsion had taken her, and she hadn't checked the gas tank. It was almost empty, and when her old Jeep started dinging, she had less than a couple of miles left. She was way too far along the river road to make it back.

Okay. She could handle this. Probably none of it was real, anyway.

She drove for another half mile until she could make out a rough snowy drive off the road. Holding her breath, she turned the vehicle and drove over bumpy ice toward the river, twisting several times and wincing when tree branches scraped the sides of the Jeep. She took a final turn and drove up to a dark and weathered A-frame cabin surrounded by snow. Nobody had cleared a path, and the cabin appeared winterized with windows boarded up.

She parked and silently debated whether to turn off the vehicle or not. It probably didn't matter. She didn't have enough gas to make it back to the main road, so she left the heat blowing on the sleeping giant before jumping out and softly closing the door.

The storm fought her, and she had to struggle through drifts of snow, but she finally reached the weathered wooden door. She bent to look at the meager lock and then removed her gloves before taking out a couple of bobby pins from her purse. Picking locks was an ability she'd learned at one of her foster homes, along with picking pockets. Both were skills she hadn't had to use in quite a while.

The lock gave easily. She pushed the door wide open and quickly moved inside, studying the space. A sliding glass door let in light from across the main room, revealing the winding river. While eaves protected the door, snow had piled high on the porch and narrow deck beyond.

The faint scent of lemons still hung in the dusty air. She moved forward and removed a plain white sheet from a cedar log sofa that faced a stone fireplace. A small kitchen lay behind the sofa with a bathroom to the right. Wooden steps with a hand-cut log railing led up to a loft, where the bedroom probably was situated.

Logs were arranged perfectly in the basket to the side of the fireplace, probably more decorative than practical, but they'd work for now. Long matches in a pretty box were next to the logs. She ducked down and started a fire, using bark for kindling. Another lesson learned in a different foster family. Gently, making sure the flue was open, she leaned in and blew on the sparking fire until it caught.

She stood up and pinched her arm. Nope. Not sleeping. Maybe in a psychotic state?

"The fire burned out in your moving blue shelter outside." Quade stood in the doorframe, his shoulders touching each side, the blanket wrapped around his hips. His chest and abs looked as if there was a steel chest plate right beneath his skin. Hard and ridged and beyond masculine. Four scars, deep slashes, cut over his heart. What had attacked him?

Man, he was tall. And broad. And seriously dangerous looking. She shook her head and tried to focus on his words. "The heat stopped in the Jeep? Yeah. We're out of gas."

He looked around the cabin and stepped inside, his eyes stark and his hair a wild mass around his head. A gust of wind sprayed snow inside. He moved closer and shut the door behind himself, his gaze not leaving hers. "Are your people anywhere near here?"

Her voice took a moment to work. "I don't have people."

One of his impossibly dark eyebrows rose. "You are a demoness, no?"

Shock and pain slashed into her so quickly, she swayed. "No. I am not a demon, nor am I possessed." How dare he? The memories of those times her family had tried to exorcise demons from her still caused her night terrors. "*You're* a demon," she snapped.

He straightened. "Well, just half."

What? She placed her hands on her hips. "Excuse me?" Was he messing with her? Or rather, was her own hallucination messing with her?

He kicked snow off his bare feet and strode toward the fire. "I'm half vampire, half demon. I assumed you knew that."

"Huh." She nodded, her shoulders going down. "That's it, then. I'm totally crazy." She'd been told she'd eventually go insane, so it wasn't a huge shock. As a delusional state, this wasn't bad. The fire was nice.

"You could be crazy," he agreed. "Most demonesses are." He glanced down, way down, at her. "But you have one black eye and one green, and your hair has some honey in it. Purebred demons have all black eyes and white blond hair." He turned toward her and dropped his head, sniffing her. "Interesting."

Her breath caught, and she took a step back. In her haste to leave the motel earlier, she'd forgotten her colored contact.

He reared up, his eyes widening. "Holy hammock. You're half *fairy?*"

Was that horror in his tone? It was worse being a fairy than a demon? Man, she'd had no clue her imagination was this good. Who knew? "I guess it'd be better to be a fairy than a demon," she mused, turning back to the fire.

"Fairies are crazy, even more so than demonesses, which is nearly impossible," he muttered, also turning to face the fire. "No logical person would ever want to be a fairy. A demoness would be preferable, though barely. Surely you know that."

"Nope." She might as well kick back and enjoy this delusion. The man did have a spectacular body, so at least she'd have something to draw. Her supplies were still in the SUV. "Why don't you go through the cupboards and look for any cans of food that might still be here? I'll get my stuff from the car." Without waiting for an answer from somebody who wasn't really there, she headed for the door.

He stopped her with one strong hand on her arm. "Wait. Is there danger here?" His palm and that tattoo heated her skin, even through her jacket. This close to him, she could smell cinnamon and more pine. How crazy was that?

She gulped. "I don't know the rules of this world. I mean, we're in my head, so there's probably no danger."

He turned to her, his eyes now a burning green. An unreal green. "In your head? I do not understand."

Her fingers itched for colored pencils. "Doesn't matter." She had to draw him. Now.

Chapter Three

Quade settled on the sofa as the female stirred the pot set into the fireplace, his long legs encased in soft material called sweats they had found in a box up the stairs. A ripped gray T-shirt covered his chest, and even though the material smelled dusty, he had never felt clothing this soft.

Firelight danced over Haven's pale hair and angled features, turning her into a goddess. Her earlier words still failed to make sense, but he had not spoken to another being in centuries, so maybe the communication problem was with him. The marking on his palm ached, and his head felt light, but being near her centered him. She had found some cans and dumped their contents into the pot, cooking for him. While the food bubbled, she drew with colors on paper—many pictures of the world they left behind—blowing up into nothingness. The female was talented.

His mate.

But it was not to be, and the truth ached through him in a lonely trail. He had been in too much of a daze to fully grasp the fact that he was not dead. This world was much like the one he had left behind so many lifetimes ago. "Where are we, Haven?" he murmured.

She spooned the contents from the pot into bowls and handed him one, along with a spoon. "I told you. It's lunchtime in northern

Idaho in the USA on Earth." Her grin warmed something inside him.

Then her words registered. Earth. Hope swelled through him. "My people called it Ertha." He was home. Really home. She had come for him, and the female, his female, had brought him back to his people. "Thank you," he said, his heart thumping. Hard.

"It's just a can of corn combined with a can of mixed veggies," she said easily, sitting next to him on the lone sofa, one leg tucked beneath the other. She smoothed her hair behind her ears. "There are more cans of vegetables in the cupboard, but nothing very interesting."

She smelled like a spring meadow in full sunshine. He cleared his throat, set the bowl to his lips, sliding the food down to his stomach. Warmth exploded there, moving out, and he closed his eyes. When had he last eaten? The memory of food was too distant. The sofa shifted, and he opened his eyes to see her dig through her pack and draw out several small beige bottles. "What are those?" he asked.

"My pills." She tipped the bottles and then lined up four differently colored small bubbles on the narrow table between them and the fire. "They're supposed to make me sane. Make it so I can't see you and places that do not exist." Her sideways glance was contemplative, her eyes deep pools of sadness. The real kind. "They're not working."

Her words struck him. Deep and hard. He halted her hand as she reached for the first pill. "Fairies can transport themselves to other worlds, and one with demon blood might be able to stay here physically while making the journey mentally." His mind had been mulling it over since she had saved him.

She jerked her hand free. "I am not a demon."

Sure she was. Half, anyway. He took her hand again, holding firmly enough that she could not break free. "Is there a reason you deny your heritage?" If he had all the facts, he could fix this. It was his duty, and one he would gladly accept.

"Heritage?" She swung toward him. "I was adopted by psychotic assholes who spent the first many years of my life trying to exorcise the demons from me and then putting me in different asylums. I'd give anything to be able to forget my heritage."

"What does 'adopted' mean?" he asked, frowning as her hand trembled in his.

She sighed. "It means that my biological parents, whoever they were, gave me up, and I was taken in by a fanatically rigid pastor and his placid wife. They figured out pretty quickly that something was wrong with me."

He shook his head, and his long beard moved with him. "Somebody left you with humans?" The idea was unthinkable. Where were her people? Where the hell were his? "Tell me that is not true."

She coughed out a quiet sob that sliced his heart in two. Maybe three. "Now I'm arguing with my own delusion."

He grasped her arms and lifted her into his lap, facing him. Both of his hands wrapped around her biceps, and he pulled her toward him. "Do I really feel like a delusion to you?" His voice, already hoarse, dropped lower in his attempt to keep from growling like an animal. Rage, one darker than he'd ever felt, heated through him, forcing his still-battered brain to focus into blade-like sharpness. Whoever had abandoned her, and whoever had hurt her, would bleed. "I am real."

She placed her palms on his chest, her head cocking. "I sure can make them up. You're all muscle. Lean and tough."

He tightened his hold until her startled gaze lifted to his. "You are not human. Demons, vampires, fairies, witches, and shifters all live on this world with you. They are just different species from humans." At least, they had eons ago. "The reason you can travel to other worlds, at least in your mind, is because you are not human. That is good. Neither am I."

"Right." Her thighs bracketed his, awakening parts of his body he'd long forgotten. "Giving in to the delusion means there's no way back." Her tone mimicked somebody else, and he didn't care who.

Decades. The female had spent her life being told she was crazy, learning to tamp down her true nature. How could he get through to her? He released her arm and slid his hand along her smooth jaw, groaning at the soft skin there. "How have you survived this?" The pain echoing in his voice made him wince.

She shrugged, her smile lopsided and sad. "I just keep trying. It's all I can do." Her eyes lightened. "Plus, I paint and draw. That helps center me, usually."

Well, at least he had a mission now. Several, actually. First, he would help her see the truth. "How about you do me a favor?"

"Sure," she said. "What can I do? Fly?"

"No. Let yourself believe me, just for a little while. What if?" He caressed her fragile neck. "Let us play what if. Just for one night?"

She blinked and leaned into his touch. "Sure. Why not?"

Good. It was a good start. Is she was able to play what if, why could not he? Pretending, just for an evening, that he could have a mate might give him memories to warm him in the years to come. He gently lifted her and set her beside him, standing up. "Do you have soap in that bag?" He vaguely remembered soap.

She pulled out a small bottle of liquid. Soap had apparently changed from squares to liquid. "There's no hot water."

Of course. He took the soap and moved to the glass doors, eyeing the clear, clean water beyond the snow. "I shall bathe in the river, and when I am finished, we are going to cut this beard and my hair." He looked over his shoulder. "Then we start playing what if, just for the remainder of this day. You and me."

* * * *

What if. She'd agreed to play what if, and once she started, Haven couldn't stop. If she wasn't human, then she wasn't crazy. However, if she was delusional, she'd gone bonkers.

While her scarred, hot-body of a hallucination bathed himself in a freezing cold river, she busied herself with cleaning up the dinner mess. A quick scrape of snow over the dishes and pot, and they were ready to use again. After stoking the fire, she piled her hair in a thick hat and bundled up in her coat, slipping her refractive eyeglasses on her nose. She'd noticed a small shed near the house when they'd arrived, and hopefully there was a generator with gas in there somewhere.

Slipping on her gloves, she opened the door and nearly walked into a county deputy.

She blinked. "Um, hi."

The man, in full uniform, appeared to be in his mid-twenties. His bright blue eyes narrowed. "I noticed the tracks in from the main road. Where's Hank?"

She plastered on her most innocent expression and glanced behind him. New snow had almost covered the Jeep's tracks, darn it. One more day, and there wouldn't have been any sign of her presence. "Hank isn't here. Said I could borrow the cabin for a while and work on my paintings. It's the perfect place."

The cop's eyes narrowed.

Oops. She smiled.

"Hank is the crankiest bastard ever born. No way would he let anybody use his cabin." The cop moved fast, turning her toward the wall and grabbing her wrist behind her back to cuff.

The sound that came from the deck defied description. Animalistic and furious. She turned her head to see a blur of muscled motion across the distance. "Wait—"

Quade grabbed the cop and threw him full force toward the kitchen wall with one hand. The officer dented the wall and fell onto the stove before rolling onto the kitchen floor. "You are unharmed?" Quade's eyes had gone from the usual aqua to a bizarre silver.

Gulping, Haven nodded.

"Good." His chin went down, and he pivoted, heading for the downed man.

"No." Haven rushed in front of him, planting a hand on his ripped abs. "Don't hurt him."

Snow matted in Quade's hair and water glistened down his hard torso. Steam rose from his skin. "He touched you."

"Yeah." She turned and bent down to feel the cop's pulse. Strong and steady. Good. "He was doing his job."

Quade crouched, seemingly unconcerned with his nudity. He reached for the gun in the cop's holster. "What is—"

"No." Haven slapped his hand. "Leave that alone." That's all she needed. For a cop to have lost his gun. The guy would never stop looking for them. "Help me get him to the sofa."

Quade looked at her, then at the cop, and finally shrugged. "I do not understand this world." He leaned down and hefted the guy into the air, striding to the sofa and depositing him.

Haven followed, grabbing a blanket to drape over the unconscious man. "Get dressed and pack up everything we need." She didn't wait for his agreement but hurried outside, struggling past the patrol car and through the storm to the storage shed. Holding her breath, she fought the wind until the door opened and then looked inside. Shoot. No generator and no gas. Only a couple of garden hoses, several deflated inner tubes, and a manual lawn mower.

Okay. What now? She looked over her shoulder at the county police car. Stealing that would be a huge mistake. Right now, the cop only had her on trespassing, and that could be explained away by necessity. But Quade had hit the officer. That was harder to deal with— if this was all real. She was starting to actually believe that it was. So, what should she do?

The mental debate only lasted a minute. Sighing, she yanked an old garden hose free and shoved herself through the snow. It had been a long time since she'd siphoned gas, but what the heck. She bit her lip and inserted part of the hose in the cop's gas tank. "Quade? I need a couple of knives," she called out.

He appeared in the doorway with two kitchen knives, wearing the too small T-shirt and too short sweats. "If there is killing to be done, I am the one doing it," he said, his hoarse voice determined.

She huffed out air in the cold. "Nobody is killing. Except for the tires. Give me a knife and then slash his tires, would you?"

He eyed her for a moment and then strode through the snow on his bare feet to hand over one of the knives. "What are you doing?" Snow gathered on his dark hair and lashes, and he studied the cop car as if he'd never seen one before.

"Getting gas." She sliced through the worn hose to make it slightly smaller. "The tires."

He frowned. "You are a bossy female."

She looked over her shoulder. "Some guys like that kind of thing."

"I do not." He said each word slowly, looking over at her Jeep. "Tires?"

Okay. The guy didn't know anything. She rubbed snow from her face. "Let's say I believe you about my being inhuman and traveling at least with my mind to other worlds—I take it you were on another world. When did you leave this one?" Her life had taken a way too bizarre turn.

"I was born around the year 600, lived about four hundred years, and then left to guard a dangerous enemy." He spoke absently, studying both vehicles intently. The snow whipped his shirt up at the waist.

She swallowed. "You're telling me that I'm hanging out with a two-thousand-year-old vampire-demon hybrid?" Right. She wasn't crazy. Nope. Not at all.

"I suppose," he murmured. "Though I lived lifetimes in that place, so I am probably older, actually."

They didn't have time for this. "Slash the tires. The four round rubber things are filled with air, and if you puncture them, the cop won't be able to follow us." Sure, he'd have his radio, but it'd take an hour for anybody to come get him, and she planned to be long gone by then.

Quade's nostrils flared, but he bent to do her bidding. "Way too bossy," he muttered.

Chapter Four

Quade held his hands before the heat as the female maneuvered what he now understood to be a vehicle down the icy roadway. Although he did not yet understand how the Jeep functioned, he would figure it out soon. Tension emanated from her, elevating his heartbeat. "If you need me to take care of an enemy, just say so."

She looked into the mirror between them again, biting her lip. "No killing. We already discussed that."

Most females in his time would've let him help. Insisted upon it, actually. "I need to find my family," he said. How, he had no idea. Now that he was home, probably, his brothers had to be somewhere. Since Haven was unaware of immortal beings, she would not know where to look for them. However, she did understand the world. "Do you have any ideas?"

"Ideas?" Her voice rose as she turned a corner and increased their speed as they drove up an icy ramp. "Yeah. Get out of Idaho, drive through Montana, and end up in Wyoming before the Idaho police chase us down." She lowered her chin, squinting into the swirling storm outside. "I had on my hat, so he didn't see my hair color—that'll make it hard to identify me. Also, snow covered most of the Jeep and my license plate, so we're clear there." She continued as if talking to herself. "I was wearing my light-refracting glasses, so my different-colored eyes weren't a tip-off."

He sighed, and the world tilted around him again. The dizziness had to disappear soon, or he would go mad. He did not like being at the female's mercy, especially since she did not know a thing about him or his people. Plus, the mating mark on his hand, even though he could never use it, made her his duty to protect as long as he could. "I am accustomed to leading," he murmured.

She glanced at him sideways. "Don't like independent women, huh?"

He blinked. "Independent? Sure. But not bossy." His hands now warm, he placed them on the sweats, which extended to his mid-calf quite nicely. "In my time, many women were leaders. Humans had a problem with that. Not us." How could he explain his position?

"I see." She looked him over. "The cop did get a glimpse of you, I'm afraid. After we're out of Montana, we need to cut off that beard and most of your hair. With some conditioner, we can save most of it above your shoulders. Maybe not quite all of it."

He would love to rid himself of the long beard. His stomach pained him. "Once we find shelter, I will hunt for supper." The area appeared rife with deer.

"Right." She drawled the words. "As soon as we hit Montana, I'll go to a drive-through. Get you some food."

Her words were so foreign he did not bother to ask for clarification. As the snow billowed down and the heat warmed his chilled body, his eyelids closed on their own accord. Hopefully when he awoke, he would be himself again and not such a lost soul. Or perhaps his soul would always be lost.

Unfortunately, the woman next to him seemed even more adrift than he in this odd new world. "Our chances for survival appear slim," he murmured sleepily.

"Speak for yourself, buddy," came her quick retort.

He fell asleep with the feel of a smile on his face.

* * * *

The big guy finally stirred next to her as she paid for their order. Haven blinked her eyes several times to keep herself awake, tucking the fast-food bag between them and driving back onto the Interstate. She had both lanes to herself in the storm, which suited her just fine.

He jerked fully awake. "Where are we?"

She slowed down a little due to the poor visibility. "Just left Bozeman. Would've stopped in Missoula or Butte, but you were out, so I figured I'd keep driving. I got hungry around seven and finally stopped at eight tonight." She reached for a wrapped burger from the bag and handed it over to him. "Here."

"Thank you." He quickly unwrapped it, looked it over, and took a large bite. His eyelids closed. Then opened again. "What the hell?" He spit out the food, coughing. "Are you trying to kill me?"

She frowned. "No. Are you allergic to gluten or something?"

"Gluten?" He tore open the top bun and lifted the patty to his nose, sniffing. "This is not meat."

"Well." She shrugged, her senses going alert. How irritated was he? The guy really was large and dangerous, and he moved like he could fight. "It's hamburger. Mostly. I did see a documentary once that said they use filler in the burgers, but it's still meat."

"Filler?" he snapped, shoving the bun back into place and handing the burger to her. "Not food."

Okay. Irritation ticked through her, but she shoved it down. "You have to eat to keep your strength."

He craned his neck, looking out the window. "What are those lights?"

"Lights. Streetlights on the Interstate," she said, bewilderment haunting her again. Was he telling the truth about his past and about who he was? It actually seemed possible. But believing him was such an incredible risk to her emotions and her mind that she just didn't want to go there yet. "You have to eat, Quade."

"Then stop the vehicle and let me catch a deer," he barked.

All righty. Her temper was about to catch *him*, and she needed a few hours of sleep. "Tell you what. I'll go to a supermarket, buy you organic food and some clothes, and we'll find a motel outside of town for a few hours."

He exhaled loudly. "I do not understand the words you are saying, female." Frustration and a healthy hint of anger rode his words. "Not one of them. Filler. Gluten. Supermarket. Motel." He threw his hands out, and one hit the window. "Rooms that move. Lights in the sky. Cops."

She drove down an off-ramp, amusement and warning battling for supremacy. "You sure get cranky when you're hungry."

He jerked and then chuckled, a deep and oddly soothing sound. "In my time, you would be called impish."

"These days I'm called a smartass." She turned and shared a smile with him, ignoring the warming in her abdomen. "Listen. I know all of this is weird, but trust me."

His eyes, that deep aqua, darkened. "I do. Always have."

Well. Okay, then. She pulled right up front at the supermarket, since most intelligent people were not out in the storm.

Quade peered through the window, his body going stiff. "What is that?"

"A store," she said, looking him over. "Try to duck down a little and just stay here. Trust me," she said again, then she jumped out and ran through the snow, sliding several times. Hopefully, the place would have some XXL clothes for the big guy. She shopped quickly, halfway afraid that he'd show up in the store and halfway afraid that he wouldn't be in the car when she returned.

Yet he was.

She piled the bags in the back seat and started the engine. "I should've left the car on. Sorry." It was way too cold.

He looked toward the bags.

"Steaks and chicken, organic, that we can cook." She drove sedately, not wanting to draw attention, even though nobody else was out.

Turning, he rummaged in the bags, his broad shoulder bumping hers. "Thank the gods." He drew out scissors and instantly started cutting his beard.

"Hey. Throw that outside," she muttered, pushing the button to lower his window.

Snow flew inside, and he made quick work of the beard and then his hair, cutting to the top of his neck. Finally, he set the scissors down.

She rolled up his window and studied him. A short beard still covered his face. "I have a razor for you, if you want it all gone."

"I want it all gone."

After about twenty minutes, she found a roadside motel that looked like it had kitchenettes. Her eyes itched with the need to sleep. After checking in, she drove around the back to find their room, which faced a snowy field that led to an industrial area. "Come on, Ace."

"Quade," he said, stepping from the Jeep on his bare feet and grabbing three bags as he went.

"I bought you boots. Size fifteen on clearance." She took the other bags and led the way to their room, unlocking the door with an actual key. The room was clean with a full kitchen over to the side. She set everything down and dug into one bag, handing him shampoo, conditioner, shaving cream, a razor, toothpaste with toothbrush, and a large bar of soap. "Take a hot shower, shave, and I'll start the steaks." She pointed to the conditioner. "Use a lot of that on your hair, and you should be able to get out most of the knots. Then more shampoo." She pointed to the bathroom.

He frowned but dutifully took everything with him. She set to cooking the steaks in a pan while also looking for a large salad bowl.

Several moments later, he poked his head out the door. "I do not know how these work. Don't. I mean, don't."

"You're learning contractions," she murmured.

"I want to sound modern." He nodded as if in satisfaction. "The devices in here? How do I work them?"

This was so weird. She turned down the burner and moved into the bathroom, instantly caught by his smooth and very hard chest. At least he still was wearing the sweats. Leaning down, she turned the knob on the shower, waiting until the spray was hot. "Twist this for hotter or cooler." She straightened and stopped cold at the wonder on his face. In his incredible eyes.

"Hot water?" He craned his neck to look up at the nozzle. "Really."

"Yes, really." Steam began to surround them, cocooning them together. She hustled out of the bathroom and shut the door. He'd have to figure the rest out himself. She set the television on a sitcom for background noise.

Humming, making herself live in the moment and not question herself or reality, she finished the steaks and set them on a plate. The bathroom door opened, and she turned to tell him that dinner was ready, but the words stuck in her throat.

He was spectacular.

Smoothly shaven, hair already curling around his ears, sharp angled face. He again wore the borrowed sweats with his chest bare and muscled and defined. That jawline. Rugged and strong, and with those aqua eyes, incredible. Beyond words. Definitely beyond this world. "The toothpaste was delicious. Can we acquire more of it?"

He'd eaten all of it?

A bubble tickled up her esophagus, and she chuckled. She bit down, trying to stifle herself. Another chuckle escaped her, and then another. She went into a full-on laugh, holding her sides. He was real. So incredible, and all these years while she'd been drawing him, he actually existed. Why that was funny, she'd never know.

"Haven? You're getting hysterical," he said, his head cocked.

She gasped for air, wiping her eyes. What was wrong with her? "You're just so good-looking," she sputtered. "Too good-looking. It's like you mixed every action hero on the screen into, well, *you*."

His dark eyebrows slashed down. Then slowly, he turned toward the television. "And *that* is you."

"What?" She coughed and shook herself, trying to be sober. She looked at the TV to see a pretty good composite drawing of herself wearing a hat next to the old Quade, the one with a beard and long hair. The announcer said there was a manhunt in Idaho and parts of Montana for the woman and her companion who'd injured a Shoshone county deputy in Idaho. It figured the cop would be able to draw. Panic caught her. What if her family saw the picture?

She moved to the set, her heart thundering. No vehicle description and no license plates. Good. No color of her hair, and she'd worn her glasses to hide her odd eyes. That was good as well, when it came to the law. But her family would recognize her. At least she'd wiped down the cabin, so there wouldn't be fingerprints.

Quade moved to her side. "What is this box?"

"Television."

"Who sees this besides us?" His voice lowered, sounding much more in command than he had so far.

She turned to look way up at him. "Everyone watching."

The announcer read from a sheet. "The male being sought had one visible tattoo, and here's a drawing." A surprisingly accurate drawing of the K marking on Quade's hand danced across the screen.

"Fuck," Quade muttered.

Exactly. She turned to start gathering her belongings. "We have to get out of here—get to another state. Wyoming is the closest, but it'll take several hours." She swung to face him when he didn't move. Instead, only his head turned toward the door, and his strong face lifted like an animal catching a scent.

The frozen window by the door blew apart with a crash louder than thunder. She screamed.

Chapter Five

He'd forgotten their smell. Molding lemons. The Kurjans. Real ones. In less than a heartbeat, Quade pivoted, putting the female behind him before gauging the threat. Two soldiers, their red hair tipped with black; yellow eyes and nearly translucent white skin. Taller than he—and for the moment—broader as he regained his strength.

Power, clean and free, ran through his veins with the comforting familiarity of a long forgotten song. One he'd missed more than he would've thought possible.

His fangs dropped and he charged, the howl from his chest raw and feral. Pure.

He hit the first soldier mid-center, propelling them both into the door, ripping it from the frame, and landing hard on the cold ground outside. Darkness shrouded them, pierced by only one streetlight in the far corner of the lot. The door skidded several feet over the ice, finally smashing into a snow-covered vehicle. Growling, he punched the male in the throat, putting enough force into the blow that his knuckles ripped apart muscle and bone, splintered through the wooden door, ice, and inches of frozen asphalt.

Quade jumped up and finished the enemy with a bare foot to the neck, effectively decapitating him.

He turned, his fist and foot bloody, to see the other Kurjan step through the demolished doorway with his arm banded around Haven's throat, her body held captive in front of him.

Quade stilled. The beast at his core coiled and bunched with anticipation. His chin lifted. "Let the female go." Only a Kurjan would hide behind a female. Some things never changed.

"No." The meager silver medals on the Kurjan's right breast showed him to be a mere foot soldier.

Haven's green eye had darkened, and the pupils of both eyes had widened. Her face was so pale as to be translucent, and a fine blue vein showed beneath the skin of her neck. She shook her head. "This can't be happening." Her hoarse voice trembled. She looked down the line of motel doors, but they all remained closed. The place must be nearly vacant.

The Kurjan leaned down and inhaled deeply. His reddish black eyebrows drew together. "Demon?" He sniffed again. "What else is that?"

Quade didn't answer. While demonesses were rare, fairies had almost been a myth, even in his time. Unfortunately, this one didn't know how to fight. How had no one ever taught her? "Let her go, and we can fight."

The Kurjan angled his head to view his dead comrade. "I don't think so." His chin lowered. "You're a Kayrs. I saw the marking on television. Who are you?" He moved closer, forcing Haven to move with him, although she finally started to struggle a little. "I don't recognize you from the dossiers we have on the family."

They had no clue who he was—that was good. "Distant cousin," he rumbled.

"Hold up your palm," the Kurjan ordered, tightening his hold on Haven until she gasped and grabbed his forearm with both hands.

Fury heated his chest, but Quade held up his palm, showing the marking. "It is Kayrs," he affirmed. His lack of knowledge about this new world was starting to piss him off. "You saw the television and knew to track me here?"

"Saw the TV, went through video in surrounding areas, and caught you on-camera at the grocery store. That was stupid," the Kurjan said, his hold such that Haven was forced up on her toes to keep breathing. "You have the marking, but this little one isn't mated yet. I can barely scent you on her." His smile revealed long yellow fangs. "She'll be coming with me. With us."

Us? More soldiers must be on the way. "You do not want war with my family," Quade warned, hoping to hell it was the truth and he still had family in this world.

The soldier shrugged, knocking Haven's head forward. "It's true we're at peace, for now, but you're unknown, and that isn't good. I'm taking you in, and then we'll decide what you're worth." When Quade stepped forward, the Kurjan shook his head. "I'll cut her head off."

Quade stepped closer, having no choice. His body thrummed with violence at the smell of Haven's fear. "You do not want to cross me, Kurjan."

The soldier looked at the fallen man again. "You took his head off without a knife or sword." He frowned. "Fangs?"

Quade angled to the left. He was stronger than he'd been on his world, probably from fighting for survival for centuries. Or maybe the other place had changed him somehow. Either way, he now possessed skills, even as he tried to regain his full strength, that were unknown to him before. "Fist," he murmured, leaping forward as fast as he could.

At the same moment, Haven shifted her weight and punched the Kurjan's groin with a satisfying thump as her fist landed. The Kurjan howled and pivoted, the momentum throwing Haven back inside the room.

Quade grabbed his arm, ripping it from the socket with a loud crack. He secured the soldier's knife from his waist, already slashing and cutting as he took the bastard to the ground.

One final stab down, and he cut the head free.

Sucking in air, his body rioting, he ran inside the room. The female was picking herself up off the floor. Good. She hadn't

seen him kill. "At least they weren't Cyst. We have to go. Get the
food. Now," he ordered.

* * * *

The female drove out of the parking lot as if the hounds of hell
were on her heels, which they seemed to be. After washing the
blood off himself, Quade ate the two steaks with his hands as
they drove, and the ache in his stomach began to disappear. He
was still shirtless and bootless, but food was all that mattered.
He reached for fruit from the bag. "You do not want anything?"

She gulped and shook her head. "Not to eat. But my pills in
my purse. I need those."

He rolled down the window, appreciating the gadgets in the
vehicle, and threw out an apple core. "I discarded the pills."

She jerked the steering wheel and regained control, speeding
up the ramp to the Interstate. "What do you mean? Where are
they?" Her voice rose.

He rolled the window back up, watching his finger on the button.
Then he turned toward her, worried about that tone in her voice.
"You said they made you forget me and not believe reality. Now
you know the full truth. I threw them outside back at the cabin."
They'd turned the snow to a light blue and light yellow color before
Haven and he had fled that scene, as well.

"No, no, no." She pounded her small hand on the steering wheel.
"You can't just quit antipsychotics and antidepressants cold turkey.
God. What have you done?"

"Cold turkey?" His body responded to her distress, tensing and
preparing for an unseen battle.

"Yes." Her grip tightened until her knuckles turned a bluish-
white. "Those pills affect body chemistry, and people need to be
weaned from them."

He rubbed his smooth chin—an odd feeling after so long. "Like
a calf from a cow?"

"Sure," she sighed. "Like a calf." She wiped her eyes and bit her lip. Then she turned and faced him, taking her eyes from the snowy road for a moment. "You had no right to throw away my pills."

He bit down a fast response that would get him punched. "I apologize. I did not realize that pills were like ale."

She studied him and then turned back to the window. "Okay. Good news is that I weaned myself off the old pills and these are fairly new, so it shouldn't be too bad."

The female had the metabolism of a demon-fairy. "Have the human pills actually had an effect on you?" he asked.

"Rarely," she said, her voice grim.

"Mayhap it is because you are not human," he offered, trying to lighten her tension.

Her sigh was heavy this time. "Mayhap," she repeated with just enough sarcasm to raise the hair on the back of his neck. "Either way, I'm going to crash a little. We have to get to another state first. Farther from Idaho than we were."

"I can drive," he said, wanting to get his hands on the wheel.

"Right." She turned the heat up and drove for several miles in silence. He could almost hear her thoughts winding through her beautiful head, but he patiently waited for her to speak. Finally, she did. "What were those guys?"

He'd wondered which topic she'd attack first. "Those were Kurjan soldiers, and they're the enemy of vampires and most demons. The attackers were decent soldiers but nowhere near the top, so they do not know who I am. Yet." It made sense that they'd seen him on that television box and then investigated. "Unlike my people, they cannot go into the sun. It makes them weak."

"I've drawn them. Dreamed of them," she whispered.

That made sense. "Have you heard of the Cyst? Dreamed of them?"

"Who are they?"

"They belong to the Kurjan religious sect and are the most deadly soldiers. They all have a thin strip of white hair on their heads and down their backs—purple, black, or red eyes," he said, wanting to hold his breath for some reason.

She nodded but didn't speak.

How frightened she must have been. "My purpose, my destiny, was to inhabit one of the two worlds that trapped their leader, Ulric, in another world, or bubble. Since my world fell apart, it is possible Ulric's did as well." If Ulric was back on this world, danger was imminent. "My brother was in the other bubble, and I am aware that his failed centuries ago. He is supposed to be back here now." What Quade would not give to see Ronan again. To see all of his brothers.

She swallowed. "This is all crazy."

It must seem so, although she would have to believe her own eyes at some point. He patted her arm, wanting to touch her. Needing to touch her. "My new brother Ivar was somehow able to visit me briefly, and he left me some supplies, but I can barely remember what they were, or the news he shared. It has been centuries." There had been pictures, right?

She glanced his way. "I'm sorry you were alone for so long."

Ah, she was truly a sweetheart. "I am sorry you did not know your heritage and that the humans hurt you." Someday he would pull the entire story of her childhood from her, and then he would seek vengeance. For now, they required safety and shelter. "If we could find my family, we would have more knowledge than we do right now."

"We can search on the Internet when we get to Wyoming." Her voice was weary. Somehow sad.

He did not know what the Internet meant. More importantly, he did not know how to offer comfort. Even before enduring centuries alone in hell, he was not an emotional male. But he wanted to try for her. What words should he use? Eons ago, he would have vowed to protect her and their children through eternity, but they were not to mate, so he could not promise her such. "I am sorry that I killed those males in your vicinity." That was the truth, at least. "I wish to shield you from violence." It was his duty and his right.

"I can handle violence," she muttered. "Well, maybe not that kind of violence. I did see part of the fight. You punched right through that guy's throat. Are you like a specially enhanced fighter or something?"

"Yes." That seemed to be the truth, as well.

"What was he talking about when he said I wasn't mated?" she asked, watching the swirling white outside and not looking at him.

Ah. It was time they discussed this topic. Just being near her in the Jeep shot desire through him until every inch of his skin ached. Until his body pulsed to a tune he could not place but wanted to find. He looked down at the branding on his palm. "When immortals mate, it is forever. A demon's marking appears on the palm—mine is K for Kayrs—when he meets his mate. The brand is transferred during sex and binds the two forever." To him, it already felt as if they'd been bound for a millennium. For her, time probably felt different. He could sense her desire and interest in him, but he had no idea what the courting rituals were these days. Killing in front of her probably was not the correct path.

She coughed. "You said I'm a demoness. Saying I believe you, will I get the mark on my palm?"

If so, she would already have the branding on her hand. "You're half fairy, sweetling. They do not have markings, and since only one species is dominant in an immortal, I believe you are more Fae." Even though one of her eyes was a fathomless black, like a demon. He waited until she finally looked at him. "I wish that you would one day wear my marking, Haven. But that is not my path."

Chapter Six

The motel in Wyoming was off the Interstate in the middle of nowhere and barely had cable television, so hopefully they were in the clear for now. Quade was once again in a hot shower, and in the living room, Haven drew frantically with charcoal, her soul crying out for oil paints. She'd have to find a store but couldn't drive until she got some sleep. Even so, right now, she couldn't quit drawing. She had gone nearly twenty-four hours without sleep, without dreaming. A part of her was afraid to close her eyes.

If Quade's world had exploded, where would she go in her dreams? Nowhere? Was it possible? Were those crazy night travels over?

After his declaration that he could never mate her, which she hadn't asked for anyway, they'd driven silently for hours, until finally he'd fallen asleep. The violence she'd witnessed seemed far away, as if she wasn't really there. Every instinct she possessed screamed that she should be frightened of him and that she should run and now. But she was just so damn tired. Besides, violence was easy to escape from.

Just as she'd done when her parents, in her early years, had tried to exorcise the demons from her. Turned out she was part demon. A sob, slightly hysterical, escaped her as she drew, not seeing the paper. She'd been removed from her adoptive parents' home at the age of fourteen after another failed exorcism and put into foster care. That hadn't gone well either. After two years, she'd escaped and run north.

To Mark's Mountain, a wonderful commune of people living off the land. There she'd fallen in love with a man named James. Everything had been perfect.

She picked the apples off the ground and placed them gently in her basket, humming happily at her new name. Haven. She'd chosen it because she'd finally found one. No more drugs and no more attempted exorcisms. Though she might not be normal, here, she was loved.

Daisy, her best friend, laughed and ran by, heading for the blackberry bushes. "Incoming," she whispered on her way, disappearing quickly.

"That one is bruised," James said, leaning over her shoulder and smelling like the trees around them.

She turned and brushed her lips across his cheek. "We all have a few bruises." Happiness bloomed inside her like the sun. She never wanted to leave this place.

"True." He kissed her cheek and moved down the trees, reaching up for laden branches.

Her breath caught as the real sun touched him, turning his blond hair almost to gold. When he pivoted and smiled, showing even white teeth, her gaze caught on his impossibly blue eyes. "How are you even real?" she whispered.

He rolled those eyes. "You know my story."

Yeah, but he didn't know hers. Not even half of it. "You were a rich kid, your dad got caught in some bank scam, and he went to jail." Somehow, fate had brought James to the mountain. He was nineteen and she seventeen, but that was close enough in age. It was a world of no judgment. "You're perfect somehow."

A shadow crossed down the long row of trees, and she shuddered. A new member, one older than they, maybe in his thirties. The guy looked at her as if he knew her secrets, and she tried to avoid him every chance she got. His name here and now was Pierce, and it fit him. She couldn't help but wonder if her parents had hired him to find her. Why else would he pay such close attention to her?

"Want a boost?" James asked, looking up at a particularly fruitful tree.

Glee filled her. "Yes." She set her basket to the side and moved to him, enjoying every moment. He was so strong and sure, and his beauty mesmerized her. When he set his hands on her hips, desire warmed her. The good and true kind. Then he lifted her, and she scrambled up, climbing a tree as she hadn't had a chance to do as a kid.

"Don't go too high," James warned, keeping an eye on her.

She was suddenly young and free and uncaring. Laughing, she climbed higher, reaching for the top fruit. A branch cracked as a warning. Then, gravity took over. She fell, hitting branches, and landed on the hard ground before James could reach her.

He dropped to his knees, worry on his handsome face. "You okay?"

Pain pounded through her wrist. Tears pricked her eyes, and she lifted her hand. The bone stuck through the skin.

"Oh, shit," James said, holding her shoulder. "We need to go into town. See a real doctor." Worry pinched his lips together.

Town? No. She was seventeen, and her parents were still looking for her. Panic caught her, and she reacted without thought. Tingles rippled through her body and skin, going to the injury. The bone snapped back into place, and her skin slowly stitched itself up.

James backed away. "Wh-what?"

"I don't know," she whispered, looking up at him, her body shivering. "Honest. I don't know."

He straightened and seemed even further away. "I don't understand."

Neither did she. Looking around, her gaze caught on Pierce, who'd come a lot closer. He slipped his sunglasses up his head and studied her with light brown eyes. No surprise lurked there. Only satisfaction.

"James?" she asked, standing. When he took a step back and away from her, her heart broke into too many pieces to ever count. She'd run away the next day, before James told anybody and before Pierce made whatever move he had planned.

She'd been on the run for a decade. Unfortunately, she'd seen Pierce in her rearview mirror three times, so he was still hunting her. Why she wasn't sure. But he was always there, always just behind her, ready to pounce.

Her drawing became more frantic as memories blasted into her. The wetness of teardrops combined with the charcoal, messing up her lines, but she didn't stop. The entire world narrowed to her hands and the charcoal, even though her body was shaking. The noises she made matched the pained scratches on the paper.

Strong hands lifted her, paper and all, and carried her to the battered sofa. Quade set her on his lap; he was wearing the new pair of jeans she'd purchased earlier. "It is all right."

Those four simple words were spoken in that deep voice she dreamed about at night when she had nightmares about running from a terrifying past that was soon to catch her. Often, she'd tried to move toward that voice.

"Haven," he murmured.

With that one last word, she broke.

The paper and charcoals dropped to the floor. Curling into his hard chest, her knees next to her chin, she cried. All the frustration, all the fear, all the uncertainty came out in her sobs, and she couldn't stop.

He caressed her back, his voice a slow rumble of assurances that jumbled together into a comforting hum.

"I-I don't understand," she said, her eyes hurting as if they'd been stabbed with needles.

"I know." He brushed hair away from her wet cheeks, holding her easily, his body big and strong around her. "I do not understand either. Don't. I don't understand."

His use of a contraction drew an unwilling smile from her. She sniffed, her body spent, her mind buzzing. "I thought there was something wrong with me. *Everyone* thought there was something wrong with me." What other creature could heal itself with a thought besides a demon? The millions of lectures her pastor father had pounded into her, while she knelt and prayed until her knees bruised, ran through her head. How odd that he'd been right about that part.

Wrong about everything else.

The proof of Quade's existence and the Kurjans couldn't be denied. Even so, she wanted her pills. Wanted all of them right now to just make this go away. So she cried more, letting the sobs take her. How screwed up was she that she'd rather live a drug-induced falsehood than deal with a reality she'd always fought? Where was her strength? Did she have any?

Quade pulled her closer against his smooth skin. The hard muscles in his torso absorbed her sobs as if he wanted to take all of her pain into his body. Into his soul.

She couldn't fight him. Didn't know how. He was the first person in her entire life who saw the real her. She didn't even know who she was and she still doubted *what* she was. Quade Kayrs was as solid as the earth and probably as strong. So she let him hold her as she cried. Trusted in a way she probably never truly had, even with James. It was everything and too much but she couldn't stop. "You don't even want to mate me," she sniffed.

He held her tighter. "I would love to mate you, but it's not my destiny. I've vowed to stop Ulric, no matter what it takes, and my chances of survival are not good. I will not mate you to desert you."

Right. Nobody wanted to keep her. She rolled her eyes at her wimpy thoughts but let herself cry some more.

Until the tears finally dried up. There was no more water in her body. Her wet cheek rested against his pectoral muscle, and the steady beat of his heart filled her ear. "I'm sorry," she said, flattening her hand over the other side of his scarred chest.

One knuckle beneath her chin lifted her face so she could look into those deep eyes. Otherworldly aqua. "You have nothing to be sorry about." His touch infinitely gentle, he brushed more wet hair off her face. "I am sorry I was not here to protect you. That nobody was here to protect you."

So was she. Sure, she should say she didn't need protection, and maybe now she didn't. But she had. As a child, she'd definitely needed help. "That can't be your fault, Quade. You're a zillion years old, and you have been on a different world. I didn't even meet you until I was in my twenties." She'd seen his world, many worlds, but she hadn't met the man until her twenty-fifth birthday. Maybe fate had given her a present. Maybe not. Every time she trusted in her life, it turned out wrong.

"I will protect you now. We do not need to mate for me to take care of you." His gaze was earnest and somehow sweet.

She shook her head. "I'm all right. I've been taking care of myself for a long time." Her pity party was over.

"That is not right," he murmured.

The only thing she knew about Quade was what he'd told her. "Do you really think you have family out there somewhere? Are there other demons and, well, fairies?" She'd liked it when he'd called them Fae before. It sounded tougher, somehow.

"Yes."

She exhaled slowly, letting her body relax. The second she did, every inch of her became aware of every long, solid inch him. Of the rock-hard thighs she rested on. The ripped abs pressed against her rib cage. The impenetrable torso against her cheekbone. For a woman, she was petite at only five feet tall, and he made her feel even smaller. Delicate. She'd managed to live in Portland for almost a year, and she'd had the freedom to explore and cook and eat, so her curves had turned generous, and she'd enjoyed that.

But already she was losing weight, now that she was on the run again. Most women wanted to lose weight. Not her. She felt healthy and whole and secure with curves. Free.

And feminine. This male made her feel so much a woman. It was a dangerous trap to trigger, but she couldn't help it. She looked up again, meeting that dark gaze. "Quade."

He exhaled, the smell minty. Very. "Haven." His broad hand slid along her jaw and cupped her head. His gaze intently watching her, he slowly lowered his head toward hers. She sucked in her breath, her entire body growing still like the air in that quiet moment before lightning strikes the earth.

His eyes still open, he touched his mouth to hers.

Firm and sweet and minty and male. She blinked, and her eyelids closed. Leaning closer to him, she pressed her mouth harder against his.

His growl was a low roll of thunder to match that lightning strike. His lips moved over hers, seeking and exploring as if his mouth hadn't been used in eons. He took his time, gentle and firm, increasing the pressure by increments until the touches turned into a kiss.

A deep, hard, delving and demanding kiss.

Desire engulfed her in a sweet heat that made her limbs heavy. Colors flashed behind her eyes, images more powerful than any she'd ever dreamed, much less painted. She kissed him back, a moan spilling from her as she tried to get closer to him. Her hands curled over his robust shoulders, and his skin heated beneath her touch.

She shifted her weight, and evidence of his arousal prodded her thighs. Need swirled through her with sharp edges.

He jerked his head to the side, his chest shuddering with fast breaths.

She could only stare at him, stunned. What had just happened? Her body didn't even feel like her own. His gaze swung back to her, and his eyes had sizzled to an incredible bluish-green topaz. A color that she hadn't realized existed.

"This is real," he said, his voice guttural and raw. "You have to know. This is real."

She could only nod. It had to be. Right?

Chapter Seven

Quade's fangs began to drop, and he ruthlessly drew them back into place. The scent of her blood was so close, and the need to bite her, to taste her, nearly drove him mad. The female had been crying and vulnerable, and he would not take advantage. He might be an animal, but she could have been his mate if the fates decreed otherwise, and he would protect her. Even from himself. "Tell me why you cry."

She sniffled and a small smile escaped her. "You want to talk about feelings?"

"Yours, not mine," he said, amusement filtering through him. Such an odd and delightful feeling after so long in pain and hell. "Why are you crying?" He needed to know her problem so he could take care of it.

She plucked at a string on his flannel. "I've always felt wrong in my skin. Never at home. Like maybe I was possessed."

"You did not know yourself." With one knuckle beneath her chin, Quade lifted her face. She was lovely and had no idea. "You are strong and intelligent and magical." His people did not believe in magic, but the word fit her. "Not to mention beautiful and incredibly talented."

She rolled her eyes.

Ah. Not good at taking a compliment, now was she? "I will avenge the wrongs of your past. Whoever hurt you will cry much larger tears than yours." Not only the humans but whoever had left her with them.

She shook her head. "I don't want vengeance, but I do want answers. Who am I?"

An age-old question. From day one, he'd known his brothers and his family, and he'd known his destiny. He'd had that comfort, but she never had. She had no idea who her people were, and actually that might be a good thing. "I will find the answers you seek," he vowed. First, he had to find his own family. Then, if he did not like her people, she could make her way with his somehow.

Being this near to her made the brand on his hand hurt as if he'd touched burning metal stuck in embers. Her curvy body felt just right on his lap, and the urge to kiss her heated through him like a live wire.

Not mating her, when she was so clearly made for him, might be the worst hell of all.

She looked up, tears still on her lashes. "You said we couldn't mate because of your destiny. What is it?"

He weighed how much he could reveal. The vow he had taken included silence. "Seven of us created the world you saw to bind an evil Cyst who will probably return some day. There is a ritual that can kill him—it's the only way he can die—and I must be there to endure it. All seven of us must be there along with five others. Three Keys, a Lock, and the keeper of the location. I cannot tell you more." He brushed her soft hair from her face.

She leaned into his touch just a tiny bit. Barely noticeable, but he noticed. "You might live."

"Doubtful. The Fates require balance. A win and a loss." Usually. During the wars he'd experienced, usually everybody lost. To take Ulric out, to make sure he could not destroy this world, would be worth the ultimate sacrifice. Quade had trained since birth to do just that.

"You need Keys?" Her frown was adorable.

"They're females but that's all I know about them." It was doubtful any of the Keys had been found.

She pressed her hand against his chest, looking young and vulnerable. Female and soft. "Am I a Key?"

"No." He placed his hand over hers. "The Keys are marked as such and give off a certain aura." He doubted she understood those words. "You are powerful and unique all on your own." Which was definitely true. It was quite possible she was the only Fae-demon hybrid in existence.

Her pretty eyes were bloodshot and she yawned, hiding her mouth behind her hand.

He was not taking very good care of her. As gently as he could, he set her to the side and stood. "You must get some rest. It has been too long." Even he had slept in the vehicle while she drove. "Mayhap you will feel better once you awaken." He couldn't look at the bed. If he did, he'd have her on it, and that could not happen. So he had to get out of that room and hope she went to sleep for a while.

"Yes," she murmured. "I could use a nap."

The idea of her lying in the bed made his body jerk and harden. The marking on his hand pounded. Damn it. He backed away from her. "We have soldiers after us, and I need sustenance. I'll catch game."

She shook her head. "We can find a small store, probably one without cameras, tomorrow morning. All of the nearby stores are probably closed right now."

He needed to run. Hard and fast and flat out. "That will suffice tomorrow. For now, I will hunt." He had missed hunting. In the world he'd just left, he was the prey more often than not. He moved toward the door.

"Wait. You have to wear the socks and boots I bought you. And for Pete's sake, put on a shirt and that jacket." She stood, her eyes deep pools in her pretty face. She sniffed the air again. "Also, you're very minty. I mean, I liked kissing you, but did you..."

Heat climbed into his face. "I found your toothpaste."

She pressed her hands to her hips. "Did you eat the entire tube?"

Well, the first tube had been so delicious, he had figured another would not hurt. He shuffled his feet. "Maybe." It was not right that she was providing for him. He needed to provide for her. Surely he had currency somewhere in this world. "It tasted good."

She pressed her lips together as if trying not to laugh. The small gesture lifted his mood as nothing else could have. "You're not supposed to eat toothpaste, Quade. It'll upset your stomach."

"I've eaten rocks," he returned. In fact, he'd eaten things she couldn't even imagine in his quest to live. At least now he understood what he'd been living for. A better and safer world for her. "I will not eat your toothpaste if we acquire more. Just brush with it." Seemed like a good waste of something delicious, but he owed her that much at least. "For now, I will hunt and then find rocks so we can strike sparks to make a fire."

Her mouth opened and then shut quickly. "I have a lighter in my bag. That makes fire faster than rocks. Are you sure you can't wait until tomorrow morning?"

"If I wait, I'll have those clothes off you in seconds," he said, giving her honesty. "We both need space."

Her light eyebrows rose. "You're confident."

"Yes." It was good that she saw him. "I am." He was regaining himself. He turned toward the bathroom and stopped at her startled gasp, looking over his shoulder. "What?"

"Your back." Her eyes had gone even wider.

Oh. He cocked his head. "You haven't seen my back?" He hadn't worn many clothes in her presence, but apparently she had only seen his front.

"No." She inched toward him and ran her hand down his back and across the marks on his torso. "Tattoo?"

"I am one of the Seven." The words resonated with power. "Each of us undergoes a ritual that makes a shield of our torsos, fusing the bones so that they cannot be pierced. Ever." As one of the Seven, he had a duty to this world. "My first task was to keep Ulric in his bubble by protecting mine so he could not move through it to return home. Now I must find out whether he is here. Then I must help to kill him before he can cause irreparable harm."

"What is the Seven?" Her caress slid along each fused rib in turn.

He closed his eyes as desire pooled hard and fast in his groin. "There are seven of us who endured a horrific ritual to become brothers, bonded in blood and bone. Two of us stayed in the bubbles and five more worked on this world to fight the Cyst and prepare for the future. I do not know who has survived all these years." Centuries ago, he had been visited by a new member of the Seven. Hopefully, Ivar was still alive. "I will return shortly."

She swallowed. "Your last name. Kayrs?"

He nodded, not turning to look at her. If he turned, he'd take. All of her. It was too early for that and she was too fragile. "Yes."

"I'll get on the Internet and see what I can dig up." She stopped touching him, and it was like losing the light after a long imprisonment in the dark.

He had no idea what she meant. "All right. Now I will put on the boots and jacket, as you wish." It had been so long since he'd worn anything on his feet, it took a while to find his balance once he put them on. An idea struck him. "Do humans still trade for game or hides?" If he earned currency, he could buy all the mint toothpaste he wanted.

"Not really. Not here, anyway," she said.

He donned a shirt and then buttoned up the red flannel jacket that was just a bit too small. Not bad at all.

She reached in her bag and brought forth a light green cylinder, snapping it. A flame appeared.

His eyebrows rose and his chest filled. "Fire in a cylinder. Fantastic."

She handed it to him and waited patiently as he flicked it several times, fascinated by the small flame. "If you start a fire, it has to be away from this motel. We don't want to draw attention to ourselves."

Smart. His female was smart. He smiled. "I will bring you cooked meat."

She lifted a hand. "No, thanks. I'm not hungry."

Yet she had not eaten. He would bring her something to eat whether she liked it or not.

Then he moved to the entry and ventured into the cold, shutting the door behind himself. He stilled, listening for threats and then smelling for them. No enemy was anywhere near. He couldn't even sense an immortal, any immortal, in the distance. Good. His sweet Haven would be safe for now as he did what he needed to do.

It was time to hunt. Animals first and the enemy next.

He had returned. This world had better be ready.

Chapter Eight

The kiss had nearly detonated her entire body. Haven planted a hand against her abdomen and tried to quell her rapid breathing. She'd hidden it well enough from Quade, but holy burnt sienna in a tube. The man could really kiss. It might be a good thing he didn't want to mate her, because every time she looked at that marking on his hand, she kind of wanted it. Deeply. When he shut the door behind himself, the atmosphere in the room changed. Mellowed.

She gathered up her drawings, not surprised to find many featuring Quade. A couple featured a young girl of about seven years old with direct eyes and angled features. Haven had drawn the girl many times through the years, although they'd never met.

Didn't mean they wouldn't meet soon.

After setting the room to rights, and repacking their bags in case they had to make a quick exit, Haven stretched out on the bed and tried to relax every muscle in her body, head to toe. She dropped into sleep before reaching her ankles.

For one second she was on a beach in Hawaii, and then a force dragged her through a portal to another place.

This world was different. She stood on a mushy red round thing that kind of looked like a mushroom, surrounded by pitch-black liquid that rippled into the distance, propping up similar mushrooms. The sky was gray with a couple of faraway suns. The silence was painful as if everything held its breath—as if a predator awaited. She shivered in the cold, and instantly popped through another portal.

Her lungs seized and her head screamed. Pain filled her face, and then she dropped onto purple grass, rolling several times to catch her breath.

This place was new as well. She looked up to see tall trees, bare of leaves, their razor-sharp branches dripping with icicles. One teetered and dropped, slicing her arm and sticking into the ground. Pain welled, and she grabbed the wound, sitting up. She had to get out of there.

"Quade?" In the past, she had been able to follow his voice somehow.

"This way," a deep voice called. "Safety."

A creature screeched from atop the trees, the sound bone-chilling. Then another scream, this one more of a high-pitched laugh. She shivered and ducked, trying to make herself smaller. Should she run into the trees? Or not move? Maybe whatever it was had horrible eyesight.

"Hurry," called the male voice from a world away. Or maybe several worlds away.

She turned and leaped away from the trees, tunneling through portal after portal. Something tried to grab her, and she fought it off, getting tumbled around again.

Finally, she landed on a heated rock, and the wind whooshed from her lungs. She coughed, partially rolling to her side, sucking in air. Wheezing, she stood and looked toward a deep forest made up of tall trees the color of blood. Deep and red. A monster howled in the distance. She looked for a way out, and a portal opened near the trees. She inched toward it, seeing blue swirl around inside.

Cold clashed against her skin.

She paused, and some type of force pulled her closer. "Haven! Help me."

How did he know her name? It wasn't Quade. The voice was deep and hoarse. "Now!" The air pulled her, heating and chilling, hurting her skin. She fought it, scrambling, biting her lip. Every instinct she had yelled at her to run. Gasping, crying, she turned and fell onto the rock.

She woke up, her hands slapping at the air. God. She gasped, sitting on the bed, her gaze darting around the innocuous motel room.

Safe. She was safe. For now. She looked down at her injured bicep to find it was just a scratch. It had felt a lot worse in the dream. Was it a dream? But there was the scratch. What had just happened? She bit her lip, thinking through the journey she had taken. What had been in that final portal? If Quade was right, and she could really somehow journey to other places, that was a bad place. She almost hadn't escaped. Or was she really nuts, in desperate need of the pills Quade had thrown away?

For the moment, she might as well see how much trouble she was in right now. No way would she go back to sleep.

Reaching for her bag, she secured her trusty old laptop. The motel promised free WiFi, so she connected easily, somewhat surprised that it worked. First, she researched the police officer in Idaho, and found the guy was out of the hospital and still having press conferences about the attackers. Well, press conferences online on the station's Facebook page, so the rest of the world probably wasn't tuning in. Good. Her shoulders relaxed.

Then, she caught sight of one of the three comments, and her skin froze. She clicked on Pastor Jack and went to a different page—her father's church.

Oh God.

She swallowed rapidly. So the Internet was not the sinful exercise he'd first preached. Her picture, the last one she'd had taken at fourteen, was over to the right with a big missing tag beneath it. Next to it was the composite drawn by the police officer with a question mark beneath it and the words: *Is this our missing daughter?*

Her stomach heaved.

Why were they still looking for her? Surely they were glad she'd been gone for so many years. Unable to help herself, she clicked through the photos, pausing at one of her parents in front of the church. Her dad's brown hair was now sprinkled with gray, and her mother looked smaller than ever in her plain cotton dress and no makeup. Her lips smiled, but her eyes looked stark. Lonely. A pang hit Haven.

It had been twelve years, and it still hurt. Her mother had shown her kindness, even love, but she'd always followed her father's lead—except for one time when she'd stood between them and tried to protect Haven. She'd gotten punched for that. Nobody had wanted to face Pastor Jack's wrath. In the pictures, his brown eyes looked serious and stoic. "You'll never find me," Haven whispered, clicking out of the website.

She took several deep breaths. Okay. She was fine. Safe and away from them. How had they sensed that there was something different about her? Exactly what kind of gifts did she have that she'd never explored? Besides being able to fix a broken bone quickly. She conducted a quick search on demons and fairies and just found the expected fanciful or frightening websites. Enough of that.

Then she typed in *Quade Kayrs*.

Nothing. No articles, websites, or social media. So she typed in the Kayrs name.

Also nothing. She apparently needed more information about Quade's family. She tried to research the Kurjans, the Cysts, and other worlds, but nothing came up. Finally, she pulled up the email address that she used with the art dealers who sold her art. Her address was a series of numbers and fun names that had nothing to do with her.

Several emails requested more art to sell, and a couple mentioned sending payments to her account in Texas. Good. She was running out of money. The Portland gallery owner passed on requests from three women she'd met who weren't what they seemed, which was why she'd run from Portland. They were off, and they wanted more than art. What, she didn't know. She conducted a quick search on their names: Promise Williams, Grace Cooper, and Faith

Cooper. Nothing startling. Academic papers by Promise and Faith; photographs by Grace. Nothing more, and yet . . . something was there. Were they members of her father's church?

Who could she trust in this weird new world? Closing the email account, Haven ran a quick search on her name to find her art reviewed in several places. Mostly good. Then a website drew her with fan fiction stories about little girls named Haven and Hope. They were fairies and demonesses and lost but having adventures, and there were misspellings and grammatical errors that somehow made the stories all the more charming.

She couldn't breathe.

Some of the details, like her memory of picking apples, were too close to reality. She scrolled down, and a picture of a girl came into focus. The same girl she'd drawn.

She sucked in air. Okay. This was a trap, but she wasn't sure how. So she clicked on the contact form at the bottom, and a live screen opened up to the side of the story.

"Hi." The little girl's eyes were a fathomless blue. "You're Haven."

Haven swallowed. "You must be Hope."

"Yep." The kid smiled, revealing a missing front tooth. Her light brown hair was in twin pigtails, and she had cute dimples. "I've been dreaming about you for a long time. We put up the stories so you'd call me. Me and my friends Libby and Pax wrote them."

Haven looked wildly around the motel room and then back to the screen. "Who are you?"

The little girl wore unicorn pajamas, and a small light illuminated her from the side. "I'm Hope. I already told you that."

Haven shook her head. "Do your parents know about this? Who are they? Where are they?" What was happening?

Hope rubbed her nose. "No, they don't know. I haven't tole them because you're my fairy. I think. It's been hard to find you, so I don't know for sure. But we can be friends, right? I have another friend I don't tell nobody about anymore, because I'm not supposed to see him. But I see him in dreams. You and me can be Internet friends."

"What do you know about me?" Haven whispered.

Hope's nose wrinkled. "Not enough. You're Haven, a fairy, a demoness, and you're running. But that's all. I dunno if you're good or bad, but I think good. We can't tell each other about where we live or nothin' until we know each other. Okay?"

No. Not at all. None of this. "Are you a fairy?" Haven asked, her mind reeling.

Hope snorted. "No. My aunt Mercy is a fairy. Do you know her?"

"No." Haven leaned toward the screen. This was beyond crazy. "Where is she?"

Hope studied her. "I can't tell you that. Everything's a secret." She sighed a long-suffering sigh. "It's so boring. Where are you?"

Haven licked her lips. "I, ah, can't tell you." What if somebody was using the kid to get to her?

Hope nodded. "'Zactly." Her eyes widened. "My mom's coming. Gotta go." She clicked off.

Haven stared at the blank screen. What the hell was that all about? She was so far down the rabbit hole, she might never get home again. Not that she had a home to begin with.

The door opened, and Quade strode inside. "I brought you a leg to eat."

Hysteria at his words and the entire situation finally took her, rumbling up in a chuckle that turned into a full-out laugh. She snorted and wiped her eyes. "It's not me, Quade. The entire damn world has gone crazy."

He shrugged. "Aye. I can see that."

Chapter Nine

Hope Kyllwood-Kayrs shoved the tablet beneath the covers and rolled over, pretending to be asleep. Her mama walked inside the room and kissed her forehead and turned off the light before shutting the door. Hope waited several minutes before sitting back up. "Mama is gone."

Paxton, her best friend, pushed out of the closet where he'd been hiding. A bruise covered his already strong jaw; he said he'd gotten it training, but he didn't wanna go home. "I heard you talk to the lady on the Internet."

Hope nodded and tugged the covers open so Pax could climb in. She was seven and he was now eight years old, and she used to be scared at night. Now it seemed like Pax was having nightmares a lot, so she tried to get him to sleep over when his daddy was out on patrol and wouldn't know. "I told you I'd meet Haven soon. I've been dreaming about her a lot. Maybe she'll be my fairy or a sister of Fate or somethin'." Hope was a prophet: one of three. Sometimes Fate told her what was gonna happen, but she never got the whole story right.

"Maybe." Pax snuggled down, his black hair sticking up all over. "I think you should tell your daddy about the Internet fairy. We can't trust people not in the Realm."

The Realm was a group of vampires, demons, shifters, witches, and now fairies who worked together. Well, usually.

"I dunno," Hope murmured, turning on her side to face him. "She seemed kinda sad and alone. Her name is a good one, right?" "Yeah, but we don't like the Fae a lot. I mean, we like your aunt Mercy, but the rest of them are kinda crazy." Pax scratched his chin. "Mercy is crazy but in a good way."

Yeah, that was kinda true. "I wanna ask Drake if the Kurjans know about Haven, but I don't want to tell him information," she whispered. She and Drake used to meet in dreams, and they were friends, but since he was a Kurjan and she a demon-vampire, they were supposed to be enemies. Since she was the only female vampire in the entire world, she figured she could change that.

It was probably her destiny or somethin'. She laid her face on her hand. "I can't get to the dream world no more, Pax." She hadn't wanted to tell him because he'd be glad, but she had to talk to somebody. "I've been trying for a bunch of nights, and it's like the world is closed." Her green book, the one she couldn't read yet, was there. She had to get to it somehow.

Tonight Pax's eyes were all blue. Sometimes they were blue and sometimes silver and often both. Tonight, they were the blue of a midnight sky without a moon. "I'm sorry, Hope."

She blinked. "I thought you'd be glad."

He shifted beneath the covers. "I'm not glad for anything that makes you sad."

Sometimes his words made sense when nothin' else in the world did. She was glad they were best friends. A knock on the window made her jump.

Pax slid from the bed and snuck to the window to open it. "Libby's here," he whispered, holding out a hand to let their other best friend in.

Libby scrambled inside, her blond hair in twin pigtails. She was a feline shifter, but she couldn't shift yet. "I can't sleep," she whispered, helping Pax shut the window before scampering over and sliding into the bed on the other side of Hope. "The wind is whispering a lot, and I don't get it. Any of it."

Sometimes the wind talked to Libby. Fate talked to Hope. But so far, nobody talked to Pax.

He moved back into bed. "Should we do somethin'?"

Hope sat up and pushed the covers to her knees. "I have an idea. I've been workin' on it, but I didn't wanna make you mad. You know, there's a power to three."

Libby sat and moved over. "Yeah. We learned that in meditation the other day." Libby's mama wanted her to meditate because she sometimes got a little wild, which seemed normal for a shifter. But meditation was fun for Hope, so she was glad to have Libby there.

Hope nudged Pax to sit up and move over until they formed a triangle.

"This is a bad idea," Pax grumbled, crossing his legs. His feet were huge for his small size, and his belly still kind of rolled over, but he'd been working hard at training.

Hope took his pudgy hand and then Libby's, surprised at how much bigger Pax's hand was than theirs. Once they all held hands, she closed her eyes. "I think I can do this. We have to find out why the dream worlds are gone."

"Fine," Pax muttered.

Hope concentrated really hard on reaching Drake across time and space. Nothing happened. She imagined her dream world and tried to put herself there. Nothing happened. Finally, Libby started to squirm.

Hope opened her eyes. Her stomach hurt. What if she never got back to the dream world? Her mama and daddy had met in a dream world and then saved this world from a terrible war. She was certain her future fate lay in a dream world, too.

The tablet dinged beneath the covers. Maybe her fairy was calling again. She dove and grabbed it, clicking on the video chat. Her friend Drake's face filled the screen, and he backed away, his eyes a lighter green than normal. With his dark hair and almost regular eyes, he could nearly pass for a pale human. "Drake," she whispered. "How did you find me?"

His dark eyebrows rose. "I read the story about Hope and Haven and clicked on the link."

Libby winced. "We should probably take that down now."

Hope rubbed her nose. "You were Internet searching for me?"

Drake paused a second before answering.

"He was looking for Haven," Paxton said quickly. "Not you. Right, Drake?"

Drake ignored him and stared at Hope. "What happened to the dream world? I can't get there."

Tears almost filled her eyes but she stopped them. "I don't know. I can't get there, either."

Drake's chin lifted. "If the other worlds are failing, maybe Ulric is coming home. My people have been waiting for him."

Hope sighed. Drake thought Ulric was a good guy, and her people thought him a bad guy. Maybe everybody was wrong and he was just an okay guy. "Do you think if his world fell apart that all the worlds fell? Like dominoes?"

"Maybe," Drake said, wiping dirt off his chin. Where was he that it was still daylight? They never told each other. "About this Haven in the story you put up online. Have you met her? Is she with you?"

Paxton shook his head. "We don't share, Drake. That's the deal, remember?"

"Hope? Haven factors into our mythology, too. Have you met her? Is she still alive and well?" Drake's eyes darkened.

Man, he used big words for a kid only eight years old. Hope nodded. "I talked to her, but that's all I can say. She's safe."

"Good." Drake looked relieved. Then he glanced over his shoulder. "I have to go," he whispered. "Here's my email address if you ever want to talk." He rattled it off, and the screen went dark.

Hope pulled the comforter back up as the three of them snuggled down in her bed.

Libby yanked her hair out of the ponytails and threw the bands across the room. "Do you think he wants Haven to be safe?"

"No," Pax said.

"Yes," Hope said, punching Pax in the arm. "I told you we can trust him. Him and me are going to bring peace to the Realm and the Kurjans someday. That has to be why we're meeting in dream worlds. Or at least, why we used to." She had to get that green book back, though.

Pax shook his head. "Enemies are enemies because they're enemies." He played with a string on the comforter. "If Ulric's bubble broke, then maybe it broke all the bubbles? If the dream worlds are like bubbles, that is. I don't understand any of it, really."

Neither did Hope. Not yet, anyway. "If Ulric is back, then so is Quade, and we'd know about that." She'd heard all about Quade by listening to the grown-ups when Ronan had returned to Earth and everyone learned about the Seven. Two of her uncles, Garrett and Logan, were now part of the Seven. Was Quade back? If so, why hadn't Fate told Hope? "I'm so tired of Fate not telling me enough," she muttered.

Libby cracked her knuckles. "At least now you can Snapchat or email Drake if you want."

Yeah, but that was boring human stuff. "I guess."

"Is Fate a person?" Libby asked.

Hope shrugged. "I don't think so. She's more an imaginary creature who just visits me in dreams sometimes. I think she's in charge of the prophets. Or of talkin' to us."

"Or you're just psychic and your brain makes your visions easier to understand by pretending that Fate is a lady who talks to you," Pax said sleepily. "That's probably more likely."

Maybe. Hope's eyelids started to get heavy.

Libby giggled. "I hope we don't get in trouble for this sleepover. I kinda like sneaking around."

Pax snorted. "Don't be dumb."

Libby leaned over Hope and smacked Pax in the arm. "I'm not dumb."

"I know," Pax said, rubbing his arm. "I'm sorry. But think about it."

"What?" Hope asked.

Pax yawned. "Your daddy is the leader of the whole demon nation, and your mama is the smartest female I've ever met except for mine before she died."

"Yeah, so?" Hope asked.

Pax stretched. "They know exactly where we are and what we're doing right now. I'm sure your mama has already called Libby's and tole her that you're staying the night. They know everything."

That was probably true. But their parents didn't know everything. Hope let her eyelids close and wished she could enter the dream world again. There was trouble coming, and nobody saw it, even her. She felt it in those quick seconds between being awake and being asleep.

The end of the dream world was just the beginning.

Chapter Ten

It had to be close to dawn, and still Quade could not get Haven to go to sleep. She said she'd slept while he hunted, but dark circles bruised the skin beneath her eyes.

Stubborn female. He refocused on his task. Laptops were truly amazing creations. He used his index fingers to type in more letters for a search, but nothing on his family appeared. They could not find anything else on the little girl Hope, either. The story she'd written was intriguing and probably dangerous. The child sounded like a psychic, and he had never trusted any of that ilk.

Haven was much quicker finding the darn letters, so he'd had her type for a while until she'd started yawning more than typing. Now she sprawled on the bed, watching that television. How odd that people now watched a box for entertainment.

He glanced over at a man giving a rose to a woman in the television. "Roses are nice."

"Yeah." Haven glanced at the clock and back. "This is a rerun from last week, and I didn't see it. I didn't know they'd show it twice." She looked up. "You haven't slept. Do you want the bed?"

"No." He felt restless at the thought of being in that bed with her and not touching, but their bodies required sleep to stay strong. Eating two deer earlier had given him additional strength, and he was finding it increasingly difficult to stay away from Haven with the bed so near. In addition, the idea of the Internet was running through his brain, and he was not understanding how it all worked.

One of the women on the television started crying because she did not get a rose.

Haven sighed. "I liked her and thought she'd win."

"It's a game?" Quade turned more fully to the screen, attempting to use contractions and sound modern.

"Kind of. It's dating in the social media age. All of the women show up and then at the end he picks one." Her voice was sleepy and arousing all at once.

Quade rubbed his now scruffy jaw. "Their fathers don't have oxen?"

Haven's lip curved. "Oxen? As in the guy with the most oxen gets his daughter off his hands?"

Man, she was cute when amused. He found himself wishing, for the first time in his entire life, that he was a humorous male instead of a killer. "Well, yes. With humans, anyway."

Her lips pressed together and she cleared her throat. "Then, no. Their fathers don't have oxen, so the women have to go on television and pray they get a rose."

"Humph." He studied the lovely woman on the bed. If he had any flowers, he'd shower her with them. "Why don't they pick their own roses?"

"Amen, buddy," she said, stretching. The material of her shirt pulled tight across her full chest, outlining very nice breasts.

He shut his eyes and then turned back to the laptop. "At some point, we need to explore your gifts," he said. It was his duty to train her to survive, since nobody else had.

She swallowed audibly. "I can't control them. Sometimes I just wander other worlds while I sleep."

A disturbance in the air outside captured his attention. His heart rate accelerated, and he sprang for the bags. "Something is coming." Grabbing her hand, he ran to the door and opened it to the snowstorm and darkness.

She kept his hand while slipping into her boots and peering outside. "I don't see anything."

Neither did he. He shoved his foot in the boots and led her to the vehicle. "I can't explain." But he could sense the danger. Warning vibrated against his skin, leaving the same kind of signature as a predator running across land used to in the world he'd left behind.

A light cut down from the sky.

He reeled back, shoving the female behind him. The *chop, chop, chop* pounded through the blizzard.

"It's a helicopter," she yelled from behind him. Pings echoed, and propellants hit the Jeep. She screamed. "They're shooting at us. Get in the Jeep."

He turned and scooped her up, opening the door and tossing her in before sitting and twisting the key as he'd seen her do. He slammed the door and pressed down hard on the longer pedal, speeding out of the lot. "Those were not arrows," he snapped, overcorrecting the wheel when he slid onto the main road. "What are they shooting?"

"Bullets from guns. Modern weapons. They're projectiles that burst apart in the human body. In all bodies." She frantically clutched the seat belt to secure it, looked over at him, and then began to undo hers.

"No." He held up a hand and sped up, even though visibility was at zero. "Keep on your belt." In case he had to jump out and fight, he couldn't be restrained. "How are they shooting from the sky?"

She hit her head back against the seat several times. "Ugh. You've been gone for so long."

At least she was finally believing him.

She gasped, looking at her arm. "I got shot."

Everything in him grew still. He looked over to see blood blooming from her upper arm. "Heal that."

"Heal that?" She looked at him, her eyes wide.

He nodded. "Now. It looks like a cut. Imagine it healing."

She winced but looked down at her arm. Slowly, it closed. "Holy crap," she muttered, gazing up at him, her pupils wide. "It's all true. Everything. I'm not human."

Finally.

More bullets impacted the road ahead, and he swung to the side, narrowly missing a large chunk of ice. "Yes. You have much to learn, but trust me, you will not be harmed." The world hadn't changed enough for him to allow her to suffer if he could prevent it. The horrible weather was actually a blessing. He craned his head and looked up to see a craft hovering above them, swinging in the storm. "It's a Jeep in the air. Flying." What the hell? How in the world?

"Yes. Close enough. Those are enemies, and they have better firepower and advantage than we do," she said, sounding like a soldier.

A different rhythm set in from the opposite direction, and more lights shone down.

"Shite," he muttered. "There are two air Jeeps."

"Helicopters," she corrected, her hand braced against the dash. "We can't outrun them on this deserted road, Quade. It's impossible."

The lights picked out the Jeep, but no more bullets came from the second helicopter. The sound of explosions echoed all around them now. Were the helicopters fighting with each other? Quade settled into battle mode and drove off the road and down the snowbanks toward trees lining a winding river.

"What are you doing?" Haven bellowed, reaching up and grabbing a handle above her window.

"Getting to safety." The Jeep flew into the air, and he twisted the wheel to avoid trees, going as deep into the forest as he could. Finally, he hit the brakes and slid several yards, slamming up against a sturdy pine. "Grab only what you need. Right now."

The fight grew louder behind them.

She unlocked the belt, yanked her purse over her head, and donned the backpack. "We'll have to go deeper into the forest and away from the river. Hopefully, they won't be able to land anywhere in this storm."

He jumped out, grasped her arm, and swung her onto his back. "Hold on." Now, finally, they were on his battlefield.

* * * *

This couldn't be happening. Haven wrapped her arms around Quade's neck and clamped her thighs against his hips, holding on with every ounce of strength she had. He ducked his head and ran so fast, even the trees became a blur. If she'd ever needed more proof that he wasn't human, he gave it to her right there and then. No wonder he'd caught two deer with his bare hands earlier.

The world around her lightened as dawn finally broke with snow falling softly now. Yet the wind picked up, almost gleefully.

Ice and snow slashed her face, so she ducked and pressed her nose against his neck, protecting herself. His speed increased, if that was somehow possible. Water and more ice splashed up, and she looked down to see the river. He was running full bore through an icy river. "Trees," she whispered. They needed cover.

"Soon. Trying to mask our scent just in case." He ran for minutes more and then finally jumped out of the river and into the trees, moving so fast that branches dropped behind them.

Her arms and legs began to ache, but she held on tighter. If he could take the pain of running through huge snowbanks among trees, she could handle muscle distress. The cold grabbed her, even though his body was like a heater. She closed her eyes and let him carry her away.

A howl echoed through the forest.

His words came clearly to her ear. "Damn it." Ducking his head, he ran faster. Branches cracked against his chest, but he paid no heed. Snow burst all around them from his rough steps. His sudden skid to a stop had her crying out against his neck.

She lifted her head.

He swung her around and set her against a tree, his head swiveling in every direction. "He's circled around." Quade's body vibrated and an aura of threat all but poured off him.

She gulped, unable to breathe, trying to peer through the blistering snow. "Who?"

A figure stepped out from between two trees, naked and panting. She blinked several times. "Pierce?" This was where he finally caught up to her? And he was *naked*?

He smiled, revealing abnormally long canines. "It has been too long, Haven. I've been hunting for you forever." His eyes gleamed a translucent copper through the snow. "The TV picture of you gave me a starting place, and once I caught your scent, it was finally my chance."

The sound of bullets from the helicopters came closer, and she shook her head. "You couldn't have jumped from one of those and caught us." What was he? She pressed against Quade's side. "I don't understand." None of this made sense. Quade shoved her back behind him.

"You have one opportunity to walk out of here," Quade growled. "Turn and leave. Now."

Pierce's smile widened. "Oh, vampire. I don't know you and I don't care if you carry the Kayrs marking. I'll give you one opportunity. Leave the demoness and don't look back."

"You know," Quade said, almost conversationally, "I'm getting real tired of nobody knowing who I am. It's enough to give a male issues."

Haven's mouth dropped open. "You're joking? *Now*?"

Rapid fire sounded above them, and chunks of hard snow fell from treetops. Quade angled away from her, his body one long line of intense threat, his red flannel covered with ice, snow, and sticks. He was looking for an opening.

Maybe she could help him, since Pierce's gaze hadn't left her. So much satisfaction colored his face that nausea made her dizzy. She pressed against the tree. "Pierce? How did you know I'm not human?" They had to get out of there, but she needed answers. "Was it a coincidence we met?"

"Of course not. Your parents hired me to find you," he returned, seemingly undisturbed at being naked in the storm. "Then when I met you, I knew you were for me. Of course, they'll still pay me to bring you back first."

"Why?" Her voice shook.

He shrugged and began to crouch. "You are your father's life work, I believe. The man truly believes he has to rid you of a demon." His chuckle wafted steam through the falling snow. "Ironic, no? What else are you, anyway? I've been dying to know."

Her voice wouldn't work. Was her being part Fae some kind of anomaly? She attuned herself to Quade, noting every subtle movement. "Can't you tell what I am, Pierce?" she asked. "Surely, if I were meant for you, you'd know." Could she keep his attention?

"Not true." Suddenly, Pierce switched focus. "If you make a move, vampire, I'll shred you." When he lifted a hand, claws slid out of his fingers as if he were anime on a screen.

"Hybrid," Quade corrected. "I'm a vampire-demon mix. We eat felines for supper."

Haven jerked, and her throat closed. Claws. Real ones. "Wh-what are you and why are you naked?"

Then everything happened at once. Quade charged and Pierce dropped to all fours and changed into a cougar. A full-fledged, bigger than normal animal. He leaped at Quade, his claws swiping.

Haven screamed, her body going ice cold. She looked frantically for a weapon, but the two were already grappling across the ground, biting and clawing. Quade caught the cat beneath the jaw and flung it toward a tree. Pierce, if it was still Pierce, impacted and bounced off. The tree cracked all the way up and then fell in the other direction, landing hard and throwing up yards of snow.

Pierce pivoted and leaped at Quade, clawing down his neck. Blood sprayed across the white ground.

Haven shoved her way through the thick snow, trying to reach him.

More bullets sounded from above, and she looked up, catching her breath. As if on the same course, both helicopters lowered to just above the tree line. The storm tossed them around, and Mother Nature howled. They fired on each other, and one pitched dangerously.

Then the other copter burst forward, and they impacted each other with a horrible crunch of metal on metal. Fire blew out of the first one. Metal and debris rained down. A piece hit Pierce in the shoulder and knocked him to the ground. Blood burst into the air. Steam rose.

Quade hauled her against his chest and started to run, fast and hard, through the trees. She yelped as her stomach lurched. "Let me down." Blood flowed from wounds across his neck and torso, covering her coat. "Quade. You're injured," she yelled, trying to struggle.

"Quiet," he barked, his body partially folded over hers as he ran even faster. An explosion rocked the trees behind them, and metal slammed down to the ground. "Just hold on."

She did so, having absolutely no choice. It occurred to her, more clearly than ever before, that the most dangerous thing out there, the deadliest anywhere, was the male she was trusting with her life. And he wasn't giving her a choice in that. Not by a long shot.

Chapter Eleven

Quade ran well into the morning hours, holding his mate, trying to stem the blood flowing from his neck. The wild game he'd eaten earlier certainly helped, and the female's fear focused him as nothing else could have. She shivered, even in his arms. "We need shelter," he muttered. He'd crossed his own path several times, trying to shake the shifter in case he was strong enough to follow.

She pointed to a building in the far distance. "That's an abandoned barn. We can get inside and look at your wounds, at least."

He wasn't pleased that his neck still bled, and soon he'd need to eat again. At least the storm was gathering more force, making it difficult to follow them. Ducking his head against the cutting wind, he ran across frozen ground to a dilapidated building with crumbling wood covered in ice. He gently slid Haven between two boards and followed, instantly grateful to be out of the wind.

She moved to the center, which was covered with hay. "Did you sense anybody following us?"

"No."

She took a deep breath. "The helicopters were fighting each other. Maybe one of them was an ally of yours?"

His temples ached. "Maybe. We could not take that chance. But perhaps my brothers are still alive. Ronan and Jacer. If they are, and they saw the Kayrs marking on the television, they will be searching for us." He looked around the small empty shelter. "We can't stay here long."

She frowned, studying the blood frozen on his flannel jacket. "You haven't stopped bleeding?"

"No." He pressed a hand to his neck and tried once again to send healing cells to the injury. "I might need to hunt again. Now."

She wiped snow away from her eyes. "Wait a minute. You're half vampire. Does that mean you take other people's blood and can turn them into vampires?"

"We can't change anybody into anything other than what they already are. As for biting, yes, but only in extreme situations like fighting or sex." His neck hurt like a raw wound, and even his blood felt chilled. He needed to regain his strength before fighting again.

"Does blood heal you?" she asked, unzipping her coat, her green eye darker than usual.

"I am not discussing this right now." He moved for a slat and peered out into the storm. Nothing.

She grabbed his arm and jerked him around. "The hell you're not. If I'm really part demon, then I must have pretty strong blood, right? Why not take some of mine and heal yourself?" She shook her head. "I can't believe I just said those words. Seriously. Life is weird." She poked him in the chest. "But I'm right, and you know it."

"Absolutely not." He let his natural growl take over the hoarseness in his voice.

Her chin lifted, and a lovely pink crossed her high cheekbones. "There's something wrong with my blood? Because I'm part Fae?"

"No." No doubt her blood tasted like salvation and sex. Both of which he'd love right now. "I am a Kayrs soldier, a leader of the most dangerous beings on this or any world. I will not take your blood, which you will need if we're attacked again." How could she even suggest such a thing? They were on borrowed time, and no doubt one of the many groups pursuing them would catch up again at any moment. "You need to be at full strength."

She tossed her head, and that blond hair flew all around. Snow dropped to the hay. "I need you to be at full strength. Have you thought of that?"

Stubborn. Sexy and stubborn, she was. "You make a good point," he allowed. Truth be told, he'd never taken either a demoness's or a fairy's blood before. No doubt it was a potent blend, and considering she'd brought out his mating mark, it would affect him more strongly than any other. But they hadn't mated, so perhaps not. He did not know.

She stepped closer to him, meeting his gaze. "Come on. You know you want it." Her voice was a low croon and a strong challenge.

His nostrils flared, and he caught her scent. Wild and free with a hint of oranges. The craving took him, right to his soul. "Haven. You do not know of what you speak." His first job, his only job right now, was to protect her. She should understand that fact.

"Yes, I do." She slid her hand up over his chest and tilted her head, exposing the gentle column of her sweet neck. "We both need you at your best. It's possible one of those helicopters was full of allies, but maybe not. At the very least we have two forces after us, and maybe three."

She sure did analyze a shitty situation well, and she knew how to spot a male's weakness and use it. It hurt him that she'd had to develop that skill through life. "One taste of you won't be enough," he said, giving her the truth.

"That's all you get for now," she retorted. "Take enough to heal yourself but leave me whole. We're going to have to run again soon."

"You will cease this bossiness," he snapped, his blood beginning to burn for her.

"Not a chance." She leaned even closer. "Come on, big boy. Take a bite."

* * * *

If there was one thing Haven Daly had perfected and honed through life, besides her art, it was the ability to survive. Without question, if there were men out there who changed into cougars in a heartbeat, she needed Quade at his very best to fight. If her blood could fix him, he could take whatever he wanted so long as she remained strong enough to run.

And he wanted her.

Lust glittered in those eyes that were rapidly turning to the mystical topaz of the Caribbean Sea right before a storm. His desire and need heated the air around them, and she couldn't help but respond. Not only out of self-preservation, but out of a curiosity that was rapidly sliding into a craving.

"Quade," she whispered.

His tortured groan rippled through her body to land in her abdomen.

"This is insane," he muttered, brushing her hair away from her shoulder as if he couldn't help himself.

"Insane?" She partially turned to meet his gaze. "We're being chased by creepy dudes with helicopters, a weirdo who can turn into a wildcat, and who knows what else. We're in a crappy old barn, it's freezing, and we're both getting turned on. We left insane several miles back. This is—I have no clue what to call this. But bite me, take my blood, and let's figure out our next move."

A dark scruff covered his rugged jaw, making him look even wilder than she knew him to be. "I'm glad you can keep your sense of humor in this type of situation," he said.

"I'm not laughing," she retorted, stretching her neck more. "You are still bleeding." Drops were falling onto her shoulder. "Stop being a jackass and bite me."

"Fine." He swept her up so quickly, she yelped. "You've never been bitten before, so we don't know how you'll react." He kicked a bunch of the dry hay against the most intact wall and then dropped to sit, cradling her. "I've never taken blood like yours, so likewise, this is an experiment."

He felt warm and hard around her, and doubts crept in. "Will it hurt?"

"Yes."

Figured. "Okay."

He rocked her, extending his long legs and crossing his boots. "If you were more demon than fairy, you'd have fangs, too."

"Fae," she replied automatically. "Sounds tougher. Like a magic force instead of Tinkerbell." Adrenaline flooded her system, and her muscles tensed.

"Relax." He massaged her shoulder, sending warm tingles down her body. "The points are blade sharp, and the pain will only last for a heartbeat."

Right. Said the guy who had the fangs. "Pierce. Back there. He turned into a cougar."

Quade paused, apparently willing to let her stall now that doubts were creeping in. "Aye. He's a shifter. There are feline, canine, and multi, which are all bears, I believe."

Reality crashed down on her. Unbelievable. "What? No dragons?" She tried for levity.

He winced.

Her torso straightened. "There are dragon shifters?"

"They're a secret." Quade shifted her in his arms, settling her to straddle him, her thighs bracketing his. "At least they were back in my day. I visited their island off Ireland long ago. The floors of the castle were made of crushed diamonds."

Her eyes widened. "Diamonds. Real ones?"

Amusement tipped his firm lips. "You like diamonds."

"Who doesn't? Anything that sparkles, really." She shifted nervously. "We should probably—"

"Yes." He gently grasped her chin between his thumb and forefinger, rolling his wrist and tilting her head. His nostrils flared, and his entire body hardened beneath her. Those deadly fangs dropped low.

She shivered at the sight. A full body roll that moved her clit over the obvious bulge in his jeans. She jerked as electricity zapped through her lower body. Then she closed her eyes, wanting to hide some of the emotion assailing her.

His chest moved, and pain lanced the spot where her neck met her shoulder. Then warmth. He drank from her, and she could feel her blood flowing, but no pain. Only sparkles of pleasure inside her at a level she hadn't thought possible. Need and want combined so fast she gasped.

She pressed her hands against his impossibly strong chest, digging her nails into the wet flannel. Closer. She had to get closer. She sighed, more of a whimper, and rubbed against him. Her nipples hardened and her clit pounded. So much. It was too much.

His hands gripped her hips and he drank more. Rolling up from his chest came a growl different from any she'd heard before. Deep and hoarse—almost a battle cry. His head lifted slightly, and he licked the wound, numbing and closing it. She felt his tongue *everywhere.*

His unrelenting grip still on her chin, he turned her to face him and licked the remaining blood off his lips.

She tried to think through the havoc and hunger in her body and fell back on flippancy. "What do I taste like?"

Instead of answering, he lowered his head and kissed her. This time there was no exploring or tentativeness. He kissed her deep and hard, commanding a response. All male and all strength, he consumed her, his thumb increasing pressure on her jaw until she opened her mouth so he could sweep in and take.

And for the first time, he *took.*

Everything he wanted and then more.

Her blood thickened and heated, and she leaned into him, overcome. Desire assailed her, making her want on a plane way beyond the physical. There was only the male holding her and what he could do. At the moment, he could do anything. She gasped and rubbed against him, needing relief in a way that felt desperate. She found none.

His grip on her hip tightened, and he pulled her closer, right over that ridge.

Against all odds, against all reality, she exploded into an orgasm so powerful she completely stopped thinking. There were no sights or sounds. Only the rippling pleasure that took her away for several moments. She wrenched her mouth free, her breath heaving, her body coming down.

Finally, shocked, she met his now completely topaz gaze. Helpless. She was helpless to say or think anything.

His eyes glittered and his jaw was set hard, a muscle ticking visibly in his throat. "Ask me again. Your question." His voice was so hoarse the words were garbled.

She swallowed and tried to force out words. "Wh-what do I taste like?"

"Mine."

Chapter Twelve

Ronan Kayrs kicked a piece of smoldering metal against a tree, his head aching and his broken bones slowly stitching themselves back together. "Son of a fucking bitch," he snapped. The main body of the crashed chopper was still in flames, sputtering in the unrelenting snowstorm. Even though he was immortal and could not die, surviving a helicopter crash hurt like no other pain imaginable. They'd all been out cold for at least an hour, maybe more, as their bodies repaired themselves enough to allow consciousness to return.

Adare O'Cearbhaill, his face pale as the snow beneath his natural bronze skin color, threw his shoulder into a tree and snapped the bone back into place. He grunted, the sound filled with pain, before turning around. Blood poured from his left ear, no doubt from the head wound that still showed pieces of skull. "That was Quade. I know it was."

Ronan's limbs itched with the need to run and find his brother, although at least an hour had gone by since the crash. Maybe two. While he and Quade were biological brothers, Adare had become a brother to them both during the ritual of the Seven and was as desperate to find Quade as Ronan.

The third member of their helicopter disaster ran toward them, blood still spurting from his shoulder. "Just scouted over the ridge. The Kurjan chopper went down, and I can see three survivors.

They're in same shape we are. Want to fight?" Logan Kyllwood, the youngest member of the Seven, was always up for a fight. Even with an obvious broken arm and what looked like a compound fracture of his femur.

"Jesus. Heal your leg and stop running on it," Adare said, always grumpy. "While you're at it, you look ridiculous with that unicorn tattoo on your face."

Ronan snorted. "More like macabre." Blood and grit slid in rivulets over the sparkly animal.

Logan rolled his eyes and dropped to the ground, trying to extend his leg. "My sister painted that, and for a five-year-old, I think it's amazing. In fact, her sitting still for ten minutes was a miracle."

What was amazing was that the three Kyllwood brothers, some of the most dangerous demons in the world, had a little sister named Clarissa because their mama had re-mated a deadly witch enforcer. Since their mama was slightly nuts and robbed banks for fun, the little sprite was probably going to wreak havoc her entire life. This was just the beginning.

Logan's bone snapped into place, and he let out a growl. "We going to fight, or what?"

Ronan grimaced at the sound and tried to send healing cells to his ruptured liver. "Let's call this one a draw and all live to fight another day. We radioed for backup, and I'm sure the Kurjans did as well. I'm more interested in catching up with Quade. If that was Quade." He hadn't gotten a good look through the storm.

"Has to be," Adare argued. "You saw the marking on the television set. It's Kayrs."

"Yeah, it was a Kayrs marking. Doesn't mean it was Quade." Ronan hated to get his hopes up. Snow piled down from the disturbed trees, landing on his head. He shook it off and winced as his broken clavicle protested. There were just so many healing cells he could use at one time.

The snow finally quenched the fire in what was left of the helicopter, leaving black smoke continuing to rise from it.

Logan grimaced and another bone cracked audibly in his leg. "What I don't understand is why Quade, if it is Quade, is with the female. We've been chasing Haven Daly for months. How is he with her?"

"I don't know," Ronan said, his ribs rattling as one sliced through a lung. "But we know from her paintings that she has drawn or painted him through the years, so they have a connection. If the marking appeared, she's his mate."

"Think they've mated?" Adare asked, wiping blood off his lip.

Ronan shrugged. "Hell if I know." He'd give anything to have his brother back and whole. "Last time Ivar saw him in his hell world, which was months for us and centuries for Quade, my brother was mostly insane." There was a possibility that if the male they'd seen running was Quade, he had kidnapped the female and she'd need saving. The woman had had a hard enough life as it was. "We need to find them before the Kurjans do, either way."

Logan knocked his head back on the tree. "Is it just me, or do you two smell shifter? Cougar?"

Ronan lifted his head. "My sinus cavity is still cracked. Can't smell a thing." If an animal was around and wanted to remain hidden, it definitely wasn't an ally. "The shifter nations don't know about the Seven or the bubbles or Quade." All they needed was another wildcard in this disaster.

A cut along Logan's jaw slowly mended. "I'm telling you. I smell shifter."

Another helicopter hovered low, and Benjamin Reese dropped from it to land next to Ronan, spraying snow and pieces of metal in every direction. The male was large, even for a hybrid. He smiled and clapped Ronan on the back. "You wrecked our best helicopter. Dumbass."

Ronan coughed and shut his eyes against the pain. "Benny. For God's sake."

"Sorry." Benny surveyed the group. "Holy shit. This is worse than you said. No wonder you couldn't chase after your quarry.

I've called in backup to pick up the wreckage and try to track the male and Haven Daly. In addition, I haven't alerted the Realm. Yet."

The Realm was a coalition of immortal allies.

"They won't like this," Logan muttered.

"Then let's not tell them," Benny said, his fathomless eyes sparkling. "You can keep secrets from family, right?"

"Yeah," Logan sighed. "I agree. Let's keep this fuck-up among the Seven, only. The Realm is already uneasy about us."

Considering the male was talking about his blood family, it was a surprising comment, but he was right. Ronan nodded. "Let's get up to the main road so the helicopter can pick us up. We need to return to headquarters and now."

Benny, who'd been with the Seven since the beginning, placed a much gentler hand on Ronan's shoulder. "Why do I smell shifter?"

"Told you," Logan muttered.

Benny switched topics again. "Was the male with Haven Daly our Quade?" Hope glimmered in his powerful eyes.

"I think so," Ronan said, not wanting to give Ben false hope. Every time they thought they had tracked down Quade and failed, the massive hybrid sank into a furious darkness even Ronan couldn't penetrate.

"It makes sense," Benny said. "There's no other explanation for the Kayrs marking plus Haven Daly, who has painted Quade somehow. Since she's a fairy-demon mix, something she might not even know, she probably can move through dimensions with her mind like we did during the Seven ritual. It's him, Ronan."

"My money?" Adare limped toward Logan. "The air is different and something is in the wind. We all sense it. The world has changed, and it's time for the Seven to act, my brothers. Ready or not."

Ronan grimaced as Benny tugged him up the hill toward the road. "True words," he muttered.

* * * *

After a short helicopter ride and taking some of Ben's blood, Ronan felt his head finally stop pounding as they stepped off the craft right outside headquarters. "Ben, you tasted like bourbon." Benny released him and shook snow out of his long brown hair. "Whatever. It's the good stuff, so don't complain."

They were running out of mountains because their headquarters kept getting blown up, but Ronan liked this one. Set in Utah, it was a hundred acres of forest land nobody could reach by car. They'd been building for months, and the interior was finally ready. Logan jumped from the copter and tapped his ear communicator, his arm still at an odd angle. "We have a serious problem."

"Don't we always?" Benny asked, turning and leading the way through the thick snow to the hidden doorway.

Ronan followed, still trying to heal his liver. He stepped inside a cave, surrounded by rock full of copper ore. If the humans even suspected what was there, they'd arrive instantly. For Ronan, the sparkly rock lent comfort and a healing energy.

The outside door closed, leaving them in darkness, with only the copper lighting the space.

Five seconds later, the opposite wall smoothly opened into a sheer rock hallway. Logan gave the commands, and the booby traps disengaged.

Hopefully. They hadn't completely gotten those under control yet.

Ronan held his breath and walked down the hallway past the trigger points, finally expelling his breath as he reached relative safety and the first communication room, which held three wide screens and a multitude of computers, laptops, and consoles. Most weren't functioning yet. "Where's my mate?"

As if on cue, she hustled out of a far doorway, bandages in her hands. "Who's injured the worst? This time?" she asked, her intelligent gaze already running over him, top to bottom.

He hardened instantly. "I might require assistance," he allowed.

She rolled her eyes. "Does anybody need stitching up?" As a neurosurgeon, she often came in handy after fights.

"I think we're all healing on our own," Ronan admitted, his body settling as she reached him. Her scent filled him, soothing the beast inside that needed to find his brother. "We think it was Quade."

Mercy O'Malley Kyllwood ran out of a second doorway, her dual-colored eyes wild and her red hair up in a spunky ponytail. "This is a disaster. A complete and utter shit show of a disaster." The petite fairy reached her mate, and Logan instantly settled an arm around her shoulders to stabilize her.

A rock dropped into Ronan's gut. "What's happened now?"

Mercy turned toward him, her blue eye sharpening and her green eye darkening. "We can't get off this world. Fairies. All of us are stuck here. There's no path to other worlds anymore." Panic painted pink across her delicate features.

Ronan blinked. Fairies were the only species, usually, who could teleport to other worlds. The ritual that had taken him, Quade, and Ulric to other worlds had bent the physics of this one in a way that could've been catastrophic. "You've checked with all your people?"

"Yes." Now she paled. "We have seven people off world now, and we can't reach them. They might never get back." Her voice rose.

The Fae nation was small in number; only somewhere between fifty and seventy fairies were alive today. They couldn't afford to lose any.

"What does this mean?" Ronan asked, looking around the wide room. "Where is Promise?" Ivar, another member of the Seven, had mated a brilliant woman named Promise, who was an expert in physics and their resident genius. As a human, she'd been one of the best physicists in the world; now that she was a mated immortal, she was *the* best.

"She and Ivar are working in Florida with the Fae nation right now," Mercy said, bouncing in place.

That left Garrett Kayrs as the sole missing member of the Seven. He was Logan's age, unattached, and worked continually to keep the Realm from getting pissed off at them. Since his uncle was the King of the Realm, his job wasn't an easy one. "Garrett is at Realm headquarters?" Ronan guessed.

"Of course," Benny said, loping down the hallway. "I'm starving. I'll get food going."

Mercy clapped her hands. "Everyone concentrate, damn it. Forget food. We have to find that Haven Daly, since it appears she's the only one who can travel to other worlds without her body leaving this one. She's our only chance."

They'd been hunting for the woman for months, but with no luck. She knew how to run and hide, that was for damn sure. Ronan looked at Adare. "If the fairies can't jump, then the paths between worlds are gone. That can only mean one of two things."

"Agreed," Adare said as he leaned against a rock wall, favoring one leg. "If Quade's bubble broke, then it might've messed up the entire system, or whatever you want to call it."

"Quade is here," Logan said, his broad face smoothing into a smile.

"Maybe," Ronan said grimly. "Or it's Ulric. The bursting of his bubble would create the most chaos."

Adare turned to limp down the hallway toward the kitchen. "My guess? One or the other burst, which means the end is coming soon," he called back.

"It's about damn time," Benny bellowed from somewhere up ahead.

Ronan looked down at his quiet mate. He'd hoped to have more time with her before facing the ultimate evil. For now, he had to find his brother. "Logan, let's call Garrett and have him reach out to the feline shifter nation to see if any of their people were in the area tonight. Then bring up satellite feeds for Wyoming."

They had to get to Quade before the Kurjans did.

Chapter Thirteen

Energy and power sizzled through Quade's veins like he'd been shot full of fire. Haven's blood tasted like pure spice, and when she came undone, it was all he could do not to lay her down and finish what they'd started. He'd meant what he'd said. She was his. There was no question in his mind. In his heart. What the hell was he going to do about that fact?

He looked into her dual-colored eyes, which were wide with surprise as she remained on his lap. His hand flexed on her hip, and he relaxed his hold, releasing her chin at the same time.

The wind whistled outside as darkness began to descend along with more snow.

Her gaze dropped to his neck. "You're healing."

"Yes." Faster than he would have thought possible. His healing cells felt as if they'd doubled in size. Maybe tripled. "Are you all right?"

Crimson colored her face. "I'm fine."

He couldn't help a smug smile. "That was to be expected, Haven." Maybe. He had no clue, but why not reassure her?

"Right." She uncurled her hands from his shoulders.

A sound thrummed from the sky outside. "Damn it." He set her aside and jumped to his feet, moving for the crappy wall and peering through gaps in the slats.

She joined him, squinting. "That's a commuter airplane."
Backing away, she shook her head. "How far do you think we
ran? Is it possible we're all the way across Wyoming? Maybe into
South Dakota?" Turning, she paced to the far corner and back,
seemingly talking to herself. "I don't know how to calculate the
distance. But that was a commuter plane—a large carrier. There's
an airport not far away."

He tried to keep up with her ramblings. "You're talking about
territories." That much he understood. An airplane had to be what
he'd just seen, considering it had been in the air. "What are you
thinking?"

"Well, it was landing, so we're probably only about fifty miles
away. Are you up to another run?"

He nodded. At the moment, he was up to anything, and getting
out of the small space was imperative. His cock kept trying to
jump through these odd pants called jeans, and after one kiss, he
wanted more of her and right now. "I would like to run."

"Okay." She smiled, and his heart lifted. "Follow that plane."

Fair enough. He held out his hand, and even though she hesitated
a second, when she placed her palm in his, against the marking,
his heart settled. "Do you wish to take a plane?" It was probably
like driving a Jeep. He swung her around to his back, and she
settled into position.

Her snort was cute. "No. But airports have long-term parking,
and that's the best place to steal a car." She tucked her nose into
his healed neck. "I have cash, so we can drive somewhere and
find another crappy motel. Maybe we can get some hot showers
and a whole night's sleep."

Hot showers were truly a miracle of this time. He lifted his
head and scented the air, not smelling any other immortals. A
couple of deer frolicked a few miles away, but he would have to
eat later. Pushing out of the building and into the snowy evening,
he ducked his head and started to run.

Fast. Even faster than before. Her blood was stronger than even
he'd guessed. How could he get her to see the power in being

immortal? She appeared strong and confident as a human—but she was not human.

They reached the airport in a shockingly fast time, and he set her on her feet.

"Okay." She smiled and took his hand, blinking snowflakes off her eyelids. "This storm sucks, but that's good, because the security cameras will have problems. The key to stealing a car is to act like you're supposed to be there. Be casual."

If this was akin to stealing oxen, the humans would be out for blood. Not that humans concerned him. "All right," he said.

They walked up and down aisles of vehicles of all different sizes and colors, finally reaching one at the end covered in snow. "This is an older SUV I should be able to hot-wire," Haven said, reaching for the door. "We might have to break a window."

"Huh." Quade grasped the handle and ripped the door open, careful not to take it all the way off.

She smiled. "Nice." Then she ducked in, yanked blue and red strings down beneath the steering wheel, and started messing with them. "Get in the other side." Leaning over, she reached to unlock the door.

His mate was rather handy, he had to say. He hustled around, and by the time he'd sat and shut the door, she'd started the engine. "Do I want to know how you can steal other people's vehicles?"

"No." She drove sedately out of the lot and pushed bills into a wide metal box. "These old fashioned fee machines are only in rural airports. Good thing we don't have to use credit cards," she murmured, driving slow until they reached a somewhat major road.

He wanted to drive, but she had stolen the car, so it probably was not his right. He reached for her laptop. "Why don't I do some research while you drive, and then we can change places?"

She increased their speed. "You can't get on the Internet here. There's no connection."

He frowned and paused in the middle of reaching for her bag. "You said the Internet is in the air. Air is all around us."

She sighed. "Just trust me. You can't get online until we reach a motel with a WiFi connection."

How the hell did that make sense? He sat back and crossed his arms, watching the white world speed by outside. "I would like to drive."

"In a while." She bit her lip, leaning forward to stare into the storm.

He huffed. "Is there something wrong with the skies? I have never seen so much snow. It hasn't stopped."

"Strong winter," she said. "We're in the mountains, but now we're headed south, so it'll get better." She switched lanes and put the outside lights on bright. "Quade? I do have a question."

"Good." He wanted her to know more about her people.

She swallowed. "You said the marking appears when a demon is with his mate?"

"Yes." His pants grew tight just talking about mating her.

She worried her bottom lip. "What if that's not it? I mean, you've been by yourself for a million years in a hell world, and I'm the first female you've even touched in that long. What if your marking appeared just because of that?"

He frowned, his temples beginning to ache. "That is not how matehood and markings work, Haven." He had heard of markings being forced onto hands with arranged matings, and he had also heard of unused markings disappearing after a long time. But that was not this case. "You came to me across time and space—more than once. It was you and your voice that saved me. If you think we're not true mates, you're not as smart as I believe you to be." It was as gentle as he could be with his response, although he was more confused than ever. Why would Fate give him this female he should not mate?

She drove quietly for several moments. "I really need to paint, Quade. This has been too much, and I can feel the absence of the pills I was taking." Her voice was soft. Thoughtful.

He did not understand the compulsion, but the urgency behind her words caught him. "Then we will find you paint." After the hot showers. He hardened even more, and the unused marking on his palm burned as if he'd touched a fire. She would be an interesting mate.

The idea of her with somebody else clawed pain through his torso, beneath the skin.

There was a time he'd accepted the fate of dying alone on that horrible world. This was another chance to live a different life, one he had not even dared to dream about before. The female had saved him, and now he would save her. How could he not mate her?

* * * *

Haven watched Quade's strong hands on the steering wheel as he maneuvered expertly through the darkened night. Snow continued to fall, and the wind blustered. It was probably after midnight, but they had to keep going and put more distance between themselves and all enemies. "Just stay on this road for as long as you can," she whispered, her eyelids heavy.

He didn't answer, his attention somewhere else.

She shut her eyes and let the heat blast across her, trying to relax her shoulder muscles. Even so, the sight of him remained stamped behind her eyes. Strong and handsome and outside this world. There was no question he was dangerous and coldly deadly; she'd seen him kill. Easily. That casual violence frightened her, no matter how well she hid it. If he turned on her, if he wanted to harm her, he'd win. Yet when he'd asked why the women on the show didn't just pick their own roses, he'd taken a piece of her heart. Maybe more.

For years, she'd dreamed of him. The first time she'd visited him in that place, she'd felt oddly as if she'd finally found home. What did that mean? Just because she liked him, and just because he could bring her to orgasm with a bite, didn't mean they were destined to be together forever.

Forever never lasted.

Right now he was lost and bewildered, yet still dangerous. What would he be like with his feet underneath him? Once he found his family, would he lose that aura of calmness? Of gentleness?

She'd known tough guys before, and he was the toughest she'd ever seen. Ever since she'd turned sixteen, she'd made a conscious decision to avoid danger. To avoid circumstances where she wasn't in control.

Bit by bit, he seemed to be taking over, even without understanding the world around him.

Her breath quickened, and she exhaled slowly, counting to twenty. Once and again. She had to stay calm. After breathing calmly for a while, she slipped into an uneasy sleep.

She was seven years old, and she'd just drawn another picture of one of her dreams. Her mother had taught her to draw, and it was a good memory to keep. Until the frightening drawings came into being. This one was a scary one with monsters and a lot of fire with ice. Her mother was trying to hide the drawing just as her father came in the door. They both cringed against the counter.

He was tall with thick brown hair and round glasses. His eyes hard, he took the picture. For several moments, he just looked at it. Then he sighed.

His sighs were bad. Always.

She was Mary then, and she knew the name didn't fit her. "I'm sorry," she said.

He looked at her, and a part of him seemed sad. "I knew when I saw your eyes. One black and one green. If we save you, when we save you, both will be green."

Oh no. He wanted to save her again. Her legs shook, and her belly hurt. Last time there had been no food and tons of praying with water being thrown on her. She'd gotten so hungry and tired, but they wouldn't let her sleep until she couldn't help it. "Mama?" she asked.

Her mom stepped toward her but stopped when her dad turned to her. "Call the assistant pastors. We'll need help this time."

In the dream, she cried out and waved her hand, and unlike what had really happened, a portal opened near the door. Still in little girl form, she jumped through it and landed on that heated rock.

Looking down, she could see that she was herself again. This was now and not a flashback to her crappy childhood. She stood, and a wicked wind battled her, nearly knocking her down. The same portal with swirling blue opened, beckoning her. She tried to back away, but its pull was too strong. She screamed.

"Haven!" Quade called.

She jerked awake to find his hand over hers. Had he said something? Had he called her back to the car? She pulled free and sat up, pushing hair away from her face. It was dawn, and she caught sight of a leaving Denver sign. She must have slept for hours.

"Bad dream?" he asked.

"Yes," she said. Another reminder about how physical strength won way too often, but she'd escaped this time, unlike when she'd been a child. She had to regain control. "It's my turn to drive."

"Your hands are shaking." He sped up and passed a semi as if he'd been driving for decades.

Her heart was beating too fast, as well. "I'm fine."

"No."

That one word nearly sent her fist toward his face. She was a peaceful person, damn it. "You are not in charge." He didn't answer. For some reason, that ticked her off more. "Quade," she snapped.

"Tell me about your dream." He slowed down and switched to the right lane. Snow still fell, but it had finally lightened to flakes they could see through.

"Why?" Her body felt thousands of years old.

He tilted his head, staring out at the icy road. "Well. You've been to my hell. Take me to yours."

A part of her hated how well he saw her. The other part, well now. That one wanted to tell him everything. Her fingers twitched with the need to pick up a paintbrush. "As we get close to some smaller towns, I want to pull off the Interstate and buy art supplies."

They wouldn't find the best oils and canvases, but at this point, she didn't care.

"As you wish." He increased his speed. "I need to eat again, too." He looked her way and glanced at her healed neck. "So do you." The spot where he'd bitten her still tingled, and it took every ounce of stubbornness she possessed not to touch it. Worse yet, she wanted him to bite her again. "We'll find you a steak somewhere," she muttered.

His chuckle wasn't comforting.

Chapter Fourteen

The toothpaste beckoned to Quade from the bathroom countertop. Fresh mint. His stomach growled, and he toweled off after a long, hot shower, shaking out his hair. It fell just below his ears and was starting to curl. He'd shaved again, and his jaw still felt foreign to him. He reached for the tube and downed the lovely paste, humming as he did so. Then he tried to fold it up so it didn't look like he'd just eaten half of it. He failed.

Mint coated his throat and made his mouth tingle.

He drew on a pair of dark jeans Haven had purchased for him in one of the small towns they'd passed through on the way to a place called Nevada. This motel was in a deserted area surrounded by scrub grass and tumbleweeds. The sign on the place didn't have the M, so it was just an otel.

The room had one bed, and he was at his limit of sharing rooms with her with just one bed. Although neither one of them had slept in a bed yet during their trip. They'd slept in vehicles the entire time. No wonder his neck ached.

But that pain was nothing compared to the raw pulse of his mating mark. He stared down at it and glared. It was not just his vow that kept them from mating. She was still getting used to the idea of not being human. Becoming a mate would be too much. Especially for her.

She seemed to have a need for control, and in his world, mates were protected. Things couldn't have changed that much during the years he'd been away.

He strode out of the bathroom. "I was thinking. Maybe we could contact my family the same way that little Hope contacted you? I think—" He stopped short at seeing Haven.

She was on her third canvas, her brushstrokes wild and strong. Paint flecks covered her shirt and her chin. An old sheet she'd purchased from a secondhand store protected the dubious carpet, and two other paintings already rested against the far wall by the door. A half-finished bottle of whiskey sat on the narrow table next to her.

He moved for the closest painting, which portrayed three stunning women, all different, wearing modern clothing and standing on what looked like a front porch. "Who are they?" he asked.

Haven stopped mid-stroke and turned, pointing with a brush covered in deep purple. Her pupils were a little unfocused. "Promise Miller, Grace Cooper, and Faith Cooper."

The Cooper women had similar jawlines and noses. "Who are they?"

"I don't know." Haven sighed and dipped the brush into another bottle. "They showed up at my place in Portland, and my guess is that they are part of my father's church. He often gets members to do his bidding."

"Humph." It was odd to think of a human hunting a demoness. Things had certainly changed. Quade moved to the next painting and saw a solitary figure surrounded by ice and fire. The landscape was unfamiliar and seemed far away. Dark tones and harsh brushstrokes lent an ominous feel to the entire canvas. "Who is this?" His voice roughened.

"I wish I could tell you." She kept painting, her movements rapid. "I just saw him and had to paint him."

Did she have some sort of psychic ability? She'd seen the women in real life, apparently, but not this male. "It's Ulric," Quade murmured. While the male's face couldn't be seen, Quade sensed his identity. Somehow. "Is he in this place right now, or did you envision this earlier?"

"I don't know." Frustration colored her words. "I see and I paint. It's that simple."

Nothing was that simple. Quade slipped his thumbs into his front pockets and prowled barefoot on the sheet to peer over her shoulder, careful not to disturb her. She smelled like spice, paint, and whiskey.

His body chilled. The painting she was working on featured seven figures, and he was in the middle. His brother Ronan was next to him, with Ivar the Viking next. Benjamin Reese and Adare O'Cearbhaill were on his other side, both of whom were original members of the Seven. Next to them stood two younger hybrids whom he did not recognize. His brother, Jacer, and his old friend, Zylo Kyllwood, were nowhere to be seen.

"I can't stop painting these," she said, drawing a deep background of black and blue.

He breathed deep, trying to calm his emotions. Were Jacer and Zylo dead? Did Ivar tell him that once? He couldn't remember. Or was this a vision of the future? Considering Ivar was in the painting, and Ivar had taken the place of his deceased brother years ago, Quade did not want the answer to that.

Jacer and Zylo could not be dead. He hadn't survived that hell world to be here without them. He reached for the whiskey, tipped back his head, and devoured all of it in long gulps. The burning liquid mixed with the mint in his belly, and he grimaced.

She ceased painting and leaned back, stretching her neck. Then she partially turned. "Are you all right?"

"Yes." His voice sounded like he'd eaten sharp claws. "I am... fine." That was the word she'd used earlier. "Have you ever painted something that has not come true?"

She shrugged, her gaze thoughtful. "I don't know. I paint a lot of scenes I dream about, and I don't know if they're real places or not. Or if they were places or will be places. Same with people."

She scratched her cheek, leaving a streak of orange. "I drew that girl, Hope, fifteen years ago, and she wasn't even born yet." Her brows furrowed. "This is confusing me."

Him, too. He moved toward the small kitchenette in the corner. "Is there any chicken left?" He apparently required a lot of food to regain his muscle mass. When he didn't find any chicken, he opened another bottle of whiskey and tipped it down.

"No." She set the brush down and moved for the laptop set on the bed, wobbling slightly. "That's some strong stuff. I hadn't realized until right now." She pressed a hand to her head and then opened the laptop. "Let me check my bank account in Texas. I had to use a credit card at the last stop, so if we're going to use an ATM, we should do it in the morning before leaving town." She glanced up. "Um, the bad guys can possibly trace credit card and ATM usage. Cash is always best."

Trace? "How?"

She bent her head and started typing. "I don't know exactly how, except to say that every transaction leaves a trail. We need cash, so we'll have to use an ATM." Her eyebrows rose. "There's an email from that gallery in Portland. Maybe I sold another painting?" Her voice rose with hope.

He should probably figure out how to make cash in this new world.

She gasped and sat back, her face turning pale. "Oh, God."

* * * *

Haven's chest started to ache as she read the email from the gallery owner. "The woman says that my mother has been trying to find me because she's very ill." She stared at the email address inserted as a contact point. If she clicked on it, could she be traced? She wasn't sure how the Internet worked.

Quade set a hand on her shoulder. "Click on it."

She swallowed and did so. "I don't owe that woman anything." Except Allison had taken care of Haven as best she could. She'd provided love and good food and even stories at night—and once she'd tried to defend Haven. When her father wasn't around, her mother was nice, even kind. Haven sent an email asking for an update. There was no response. She sighed. "If they answer, we'll figure out what to do." She'd used a secondary email address, and it listed her home as being in North Carolina, so how could it be traced? She shut the laptop and turned to view the chaos of the room. Paint was splattered all over the sheet, but at least she'd protected the crappy furniture. Her head spun, and she pressed her palm against her forehead.

Just how much had she drunk?

She rarely drank alcohol, but today had seemed to call for it. She couldn't get those kisses and that orgasm out of her mind. Her body had been on high alert, the *I want another orgasm* kind, all day. It was driving her crazy. Was there some biological bond between them because of that damn mating mark? There had to be a reason beyond the obvious—that he was the sexiest thing on two feet in any world.

The wind rattled against the cheap windows and the wall heater hummed loudly, lending a sense of seclusion and intimacy to the room. Her mind wanted to shut down for a while, but her body was wide awake and ready to play.

"What is that?" Quade asked, quick strides taking him to a canvas hidden behind the television console. Partially hidden.

"Nothing." Haven jumped up and tried to intercept him.

He kept moving and grasped the edge of the painting, tugging it out. Paint smeared against the furniture, but the scene was clear enough. "It's a graveyard," he murmured, lifting it to see. "Who is Mary Agnes Lockship?"

Dang it. The words were barely discernable. Her stomach tilted.

"Me. That was my name before."

The atmosphere in the small room changed as tension spread through it, stopping her lungs. He gently, deliberately, set the canvas down and turned to face her.

She took a step back out of instinct.

With his legs braced, his scarred chest bare, and his eyes a glowing greenish-blue, he looked like a predator more dangerous than even those in her dreams. Muscles, hard-cut and strong, contoured his upper arms and roped neck. His chin was up, his chest out, and his lips in a firm line. "You are not dying."

"Everybody, even immortals, dies at some point," she countered, her voice soft as she angled herself toward the door.

He cocked his head. "Am I scaring you?"

She swallowed, every sense heightened. Just the sight of him triggered a strong reaction inside her. Add in that gravelly voice and his deadly nature, and fear was certainly one of the emotions. Desire, the other, and that was scaring her even more. "I'm not frightened," she lied.

One of his dark eyebrows rose. "Why did you hide the painting?"

Why? Pure instinct. "You seem to have some sort of misplaced idea that you're responsible for me." She hadn't worked out the thought process before, and the words spilled out of her. "I figured you wouldn't like the idea of failing if I died."

"You were correct." He crossed his arms, bunching his biceps. "About all of that."

She licked her lips, and his eyes flared. "I'm not into the whole alpha male thing." Not true. Her body was all in. She never should have drunk half a bottle of whiskey. Four steps forward, and she could have her mouth on that hot male skin. "Sorry."

"Alpha male thing?" He rubbed his cleanly shaven jaw. "Explain."

"That. That order," she burst out. "I'm not into guys who think they're in charge and are all *grrrr.*"

He frowned. "I'm not all *grrrr.*"

This was getting ridiculous.

"But I am in charge." His voice, although gravelly, was reasonable and not irritated. "Surely you understand that fact."

She shouldn't say it. Nope. Not now. "Don't call me Shirley."

He blinked. Once and again. "I was not—"

She held up a hand. "I know. Old joke. Sorry." The room spun just a little, and she settled her feet more securely in place. "Listen. We need to get a couple of things straight."

His frown deepened.

God, that made him even more sexy. How was that possible? "Listen. I'm fairly certain that painting was symbolic. I'm Haven now, not Mary Agnes. So don't worry. We're in this together for the time being, and with the close quarters, things are getting out of hand. I don't want to mate you, but if we continue like this, we should have an understanding." She was rambling now. Turned on, irritated, emotional, and maybe a little scared.

"What should I understand, Haven?" His eyes darkened to an even deeper green that was definitely not human.

That voice. Low and dark and so gritty, her skin got flushed and sensitive. She cleared her throat. "You want me, I want you, and it's getting more difficult to ignore that fact." The orgasm the other day had been just the beginning, and she knew it. "In today's society, it's called sex with no strings." Would he think she was some kind of slut for suggesting it? Women in his time probably still wore chastity belts.

"No strings?" He took a step closer, bringing warmth and tension with him. "I had no intention of tying you up, sweetling."

Heat rolled through her body from head to toe, landing right in her center. "It's an expression," she babbled. "Means sex with no expectations."

He reached her then, sliding a hand through her hair to cup her jaw. "Ah, Haven. Not a chance. I have a multitude of expectations."

Then he kissed her.

Chapter Fifteen

Even the torture in his former world didn't hurt this much, Quade thought. His mate had just offered sex with no strings, and he wanted strings. A whole lot of them. Even so, he couldn't help pressing his mouth to hers. She had no idea how expressive her beautiful eyes were, and he could relate to the turmoil in them.

His body was on a slow flame that was burning from within and had been since the first time she'd touched him, back on his old world, when he thought she was an angel, come to take him home.

She was no angel, but she was definitely his home. He sank into the kiss, and she sighed, opening her mouth to give him what he wanted. More. He tried to be gentle and tamp down the fury that had caught him at seeing a painting of her gravestone, but he was rougher than he intended when he lifted her against him, forcing her head back with his kiss.

Her moan spurred him on. He walked her back to the bed and followed her down, his groan mixing with hers when he finally covered her. Her nails dug into his shoulders with a small bite that shot straight to his cock. He lifted up and paused as both of her eyes turned a translucent yellow, almost gold. He'd heard tales that a fairy's could turn a third color, but he'd thought the rumors exaggerated.

Not even close. She was stunning.

She blinked and her smile was like the sun after a storm. "You have paint on your chin."

His jeans were too tight, and his body on fire, but he returned her smile. "So do you."

Purring, she caressed his shoulders and chest, tracing each of the four lines above his heart. "What kind of beast scarred you like this?" she whispered, her hardened nipples outlined beneath her light shirt.

"One I hope you never imagine," he said, palming the side of her smooth face and enjoying her soft skin. "The swipe should've taken out my heart, but with my bonded torso, it only scarred my skin. I was in a weakened state at the time." He still did not feel at full power, but he was getting there.

She leaned up and nipped his bottom lip, wiggling her butt and widening her legs. "Do we have a deal?"

"Of no strings sex?" he asked, an unwilling smile tugging his lips this time.

"Yes." She smoothed her palms down his flanks and around his waist to his back, her touch sweet torture.

"No." He punctuated the word with a hard kiss. "I want strings."

A muted pink spiraled across her cheekbones. "Oh. Women in your day probably didn't like sex, huh? Engaging in it before marriage was wrong?"

He snorted. "Those rules and marriage itself are human constructs, not ours." He'd lived four hundred years before going to the other world, and he certainly had never pretended to be a monk. He'd been with plenty of females as well as a couple of human women in his time. "You know you're not a woman, right?"

Her eyes flashed back to green and black. "Excuse me?"

"You're not human. You're a female Fae with a hint of demoness." With her body beneath him, he was losing his train of thought. How quickly could he get her clothes off? Pretty damn fast, if he wanted.

She swallowed. "You're not a man?"

"No. I'm a male." There was nothing human in him. "Immortals are just different species from humans. Not better or worse. Just different." How strange it must have been for her to be raised as a human when she wasn't even close. "Regardless, what we're doing means something to me, and I will not walk away afterward. Tell me now, and I will go for a run in the snow." Though nothing would ease this craving he had for her. Only mating her.

Her frown was adorable and made him want her even more. "Let me get this straight. You've been in a hell world for centuries upon centuries, and you haven't had sex in that long, and you would blow me off?" She sounded more surprised than angry, and that was a good thing.

He didn't understand the idiom, but he caught the meaning behind it. "Haven," he muttered.

Her lips, slightly swollen from his kiss, pressed together. "You don't want me?"

Oh, for hell's sake. For answer, he rolled his hips, pressing his fully engorged and aching cock against her sex.

Her eyes morphed to the translucent yellow again and widened. Pink burst full on across her entire face this time. "Oh. You feel huge."

"I am," he agreed.

Her startled laugh wrapped around his heart and squeezed. "We have to work on this confidence issue you're having," she said dryly—if a bit breathlessly.

He could smell her arousal. Sweet and pure with a hint of spice. The animal inside him, the one that had allowed him to survive for so long, stretched wide awake with a growl of its own. He was vampire, part demon—a lethal combination. His mate was beneath him and she was offering herself. He would be insane to refuse her.

"Quade." Her voice had that timid quality of somebody trying to be gentle. "I'm not the forever kind. Yes, I believe you now that I'm not human because that feels right and finally makes sense.

I'm a loner. Staying with someone else for any period of time doesn't work for me."

If she liked her life, why did she sound so sad? "Are you trying to protect me? From your inevitable death?" The idea kind of pissed him off. Nothing was predetermined, and he would make it his business to save her.

"Maybe." She shrugged, and her breasts bounced nicely. "I'm the only human, I mean *being*, that you've seen in a zillion years, and somehow, I helped you to leave hell. I think you're reading a lot into our being together because of that."

Fear. There it was. Deep in those golden eyes. "Ah." She was lying to herself as much as to him. Her life had sucked so far, so of course, she pushed people away. Did she not know her value? Nobody had ever shown her that she was valuable, now had they?

How should he prove her value? Did he take what she offered and show her afterward? Build a bond, a stronger one, through their physical connection? Or did he prove himself by refusing, waiting until she wanted more—wanted what she deserved, which was everything? If nothing else, he could give her honesty. "I do not know what to do," he admitted.

Her smile was a siren's call. "That's easy, then. Do me."

* * * *

Haven caressed the dip in Quade's lower back, stopping just before his butt. His arousal was obvious, and she moved against him, wanting more. Wanting to forget reality and just get lost in all that muscle and heat. "Let's get swept away, Quade," she whispered.

His eyes softened and filled with acceptance. Finally. He was on board. "Ah, sweetling. It is fine to use sex to escape or to regain control." His large hand was gentle as he swept her hair back. "But control is mine. You should learn that now." Then he kissed her, his body pressing her into the mattress, his hands sweeping down her rib cage to draw up her shirt.

Cool air brushed her before she ducked and let him remove it. The tank top and built-in bra she wore soon followed, baring her to him.

His smile was sweet and ravenous. "You're beautiful." Lowering his head, he kissed each nipple reverently.

Shivers took her, zapping right to her clit. She dug both hands into his thick hair. "Fast and wild," she said, wanting him inside her.

He smiled against her breast and sucked a nipple into his mouth, toying with the other one. "No," he murmured around her nipple.

"Yes." She lightly tugged on his hair.

His teeth enclosed her nipple.

She froze.

He released her without biting and looked up, his gaze impenetrable. "Don't forget, I have fangs. You don't give the orders here." Then he lowered his head and went back to playing, torturing her with kisses, licks, and soft nips.

This showed a new side of him, one her mind didn't like. Her body moved of its own accord, rubbing against him and feeling every touch as a low pull straight past her abdomen. He kept playing, moving between her breasts and down her abdomen, nipping along each rib as he went.

It was as if he wanted to touch, to brand, every millimeter of her, not missing one spot on the way down. Levering himself up on his knees, straddling her, he looked like one of those old marauders from years gone by. Powerful and primitive. Her breath caught, and her blood quickened.

Keeping her gaze, his eyes a turbulent aqua, he drew off her jeans and underwear with one smooth motion. She gasped and then smiled. "You seem to remember your way around a woman."

"Let's test that theory." He inhaled deeply and a low growl rumbled up from his chest.

This was too much. She wanted fast and crazy and forgetful. Not intense and thoughtful. "Quade—"

He flattened his hand across her entire abdomen and then dipped down, kissing her square on the clit.

She arched against him, sparks flying through her lower body. His wide shoulders nudged her thighs farther apart, exposing her to him. He turned his head to the side. Slowly, intently, he sank his fangs into her inner thigh just as he slipped one finger inside her. Sensations, pain and pleasure, crashed together inside her. She shut her eyes, arching against him, her fingernails digging into the bedspread on either side of her hips. He drank deeply and then those fangs retracted, almost in slow motion. As if he wanted her to know he'd made his mark.

The finger inside her found a spot she'd only read about, and she bit her lip to keep from begging for more. This was too much, and she wasn't getting lost. He was keeping her in the moment and with him. She moved restlessly, reaching for his hair again, and tangling her fingers in the thick mass.

He chuckled against her, his generous mouth around her clit, providing some pressure. Not enough. Not nearly enough, and he knew it.

She almost pulled his hair again and then remembered the fangs. The ones so close to her most sensitive parts.

"Haven." His voice shot vibrations through her sex that nearly sent her over.

"What?" She opened her eyes, exasperation in her voice.

He lifted his head and caught her gaze. "You feel lost yet?"

The bastard. "No," she snapped.

"Good." He slid another finger into her, and she was wet enough that it didn't hurt. "You taste better than any dream I've ever had."

She couldn't handle sweet right now. He was totally controlling her reactions, even her mind, and fighting his sweet side was beyond her. "I'm getting a little bored." She was such a complete liar.

His smile flashed a surprising dimple in his left cheek. "I'll choose which challenges I'll rise to, little one. That one isn't close to tempting me." He lowered his head again and licked her, taking his time. "This, however, is very tempting." Humming softly, he continued playing, his fingers driving her mad and his tongue teasing her clit.

She gyrated, her body sweating, need driving her higher and higher. Her thighs began to tremble, but she still couldn't quite reach the pinnacle that was so near. "Quade," she moaned, not caring any longer who was in control and who wasn't.

Coils of energy bunched inside her, sparking in every direction. "All right." He paused and looked up at her until she focused on him. "You are worth waiting for, Haven Daly. Someday, when you're ready, your heart will be mine."

His words barely computed, but her heart warmed anyway.

He twisted those fingers inside her, sending electricity along every nerve. "For now, your pleasure is." He lowered his head and licked her, finally nipping at her clit with enough pressure that she exploded.

She cried out, her eyes shutting. Sparks of color, wild and free, shot behind her closed lids. She rode the orgasm, her body tense, until she finally dropped and went limp.

He placed one final kiss on her sex and moved up her body, nibbling on her neck. "You are stunning, my little Fae-demon."

She couldn't move. Her entire body was limp and satiated. Maybe forever. Yet guilt took her. "What about you?"

"I'm fine," he said, licking her neck. "Might go for a run, though."

Her laptop dinged.

He stiffened. "What is that?"

She pointed somewhere in the direction of the computer, and he reached for it on the bed table, opening it by her head. She had just enough energy to turn and look. "That's the email we contacted." Right now, it was difficult to concentrate.

He clicked on it, propping himself on one elbow.

A picture of her mother in front of Pierce, the bastard feline shifter, came up on screen. The shifter had claws to her throat.

"Well, shit," Quade muttered.

Chapter Sixteen

Quade increased the pace out of the small town after Haven had used a machine called an ATM to get more currency. They'd stolen a smaller car this time. Christmas decorations and pretty lights twinkled all around, making the area near the machine almost cheerful. She'd had him park around the corner so his image would not be captured on the camera in the money machine. Letting her out of sight, even for those few moments, had increased the anxiety he'd felt ever since seeing that video of her mother earlier.

Haven moved with silent efficiency, her face pale, her brow furrowed. She'd also placed a green contact in her black eye, making her look different.

He wasn't fond of the green contact.

She swallowed and looked out at the clear night. It had finally stopped snowing. For now.

He did not know how to reach her or what kind of words would give comfort. "I will rip out the shifter's throat as soon as we get there," he offered.

She turned and just looked at him.

Were those the wrong words? "You do not have to watch," he added.

Her face scrunched up, making her look cute and a little lost. "I figured it would always come down to another fight with the pastor, but a part of me thought I might be able to run longer."

The sadness in her voice pissed him off even more. "Tell me again what exactly the shifter said."

She sighed. "Just that he was hired by the pastor, my sucky father, and will exchange me for my mother. It's pretty simple—at least that part of it. What I don't know is why I'm rushing to rescue her."

For the first time, he could see the lonely little girl she must have been. "She was the only mother you ever knew. She was kind to you at some point, right?" When Haven nodded, he continued. "Then it makes sense you want to help her, especially since the immortal world has now impacted hers. You are from the immortal world."

She turned back to looking out the window. "Why do you think I ended up with humans?"

His heart hurt for her. "I do not know, but we will find out." In fact, as soon as he found his family and got her to safety, he was going to seek answers. He was certain that if anybody in his world knew about her, they would never have left her with humans, especially not people who thought she was a human as well. How confusing it must have been for her.

The human family had guessed wrong about her. He did not know what went into an exorcism, but he would find out. Already he knew he'd be out for blood afterward. That was fine with him. "I wish I could give you answers right now, but trust me. You will have them," he added.

She breathed in and out several times, deep breaths, apparently in an effort to calm herself. "We still haven't slept in a bed."

He chuckled, surprised by the amusement he felt. "For me, it has been lifetimes, so I do not know what I'm missing." However, he wasn't taking very good care of his mate, and that had to change. She required sleep, in a bed. "Why don't you sleep now? We have a long journey, if I understand your map." The day before, they'd purchased a map in one of the little towns decorated for the holidays.

She bit her lip. "I don't think I could sleep right now. We should come up with a plan of what to do when I get home." Her shoulders hunched. "I mean, when we get there. It was never home."

The fury he'd kept banked broke out. He cleared his throat. "We will park this vehicle a safe distance away, and I will go in and get the woman you thought was your mother." He added the clarification on purpose. "I will bring her to you." After killing that shifter who wanted his mate.

Haven rolled her neck. "I assume Pierce will be expecting shock and awe."

Shock and awe? What a wonderful expression. He'd keep that one with him for sure. "Then that is what the shifter will receive."

"Okay. It could be a trap, so I'll lay out a false trail for us on the Internet, using ATM's, that will look like we're headed north," she murmured. "Also, I'll do a few google searches about Canada and border crossings and rent a motel way away from us."

If that made her happy, then he was fine with her precautions. That was simple.

"I'm going too," she said.

All right. Not so simple. "You have not trained to fight." He increased the vehicle's speed over the icy roads and drove past two long trucks with pictures of fruit on the sides. "Your survival skills are admirable, but fighting is something else." When it came to enemies, human or otherwise, he was the fighter, not her. "This subject I will not relent on." It was only fair to be honest with her; he knew she'd appreciate that.

She snorted. "Right. Relent. Bite me."

"I already have," he retorted easily, turning toward her. Could she possibly be that stubborn? One quick look at her chin, and he had his answer. Definitely stubborn. "In a fight, you would be in the way."

Her shoulders went up. "Excuse me?"

He frowned, trying to remain logical and not lose his temper. "Yes. You do not know how to fight. This will be a fight. So you stay out of the way." How was that a difficult concept?

"According to you, I'm a Fae-demon. Shouldn't that heritage give me skills?" There was a hint of sarcasm in her words that poked at him.

"Sure, if you had spent your life training, which you have not. It appears your skills lean more toward the psychic and teleportation." He looked over at her, seeking words that wouldn't start a fight. "You will not accompany me to rescue that woman."

Her eyes flared. Nope. Not the right words. "Listen, Ace. Whatever little bug told you that you were in charge just got squashed. This is my situation, and you're invited along if you behave."

Behave? Huh. "I said no."

Her smile was a little mean. "It's a new world, buddy. Women have equal rights, and we choose our own paths."

"In my time, females always had equal rights, and they always chose their own paths," he returned. It was nice humans had finally caught up. "However, females also were not stupid. If they were not fighters, they did not venture into fights." How fucking easy was it to understand that simple fact? "Mates have a responsibility to stay safe. Without them, a soldier like me loses everything."

"We have not mated," she snapped.

"Apparently, that was my mistake," he snapped back.

"Whatever." She hunched into herself and turned away, fuming silently. Then calming. Finally, after accomplishing all of her plans on the computer and about an hour into the night, she fell asleep.

He reached into the back seat and grabbed the jacket she'd purchased for him, draping it over her. He'd tried to make his way tentatively in this new world, and perhaps that had been his mistake.

His approach would change. Now.

* * * *

Haven awoke outside of Los Angeles, still on the Interstate. She lifted her head and yawned. "I slept for hours."

"Yes." Quade's grip on the wheel showed his knuckles to be white. A horn honked behind them, and he jumped.

Shoot. "Dude. You've never driven in traffic." She reached over and patted his arm, which was tight with tension. "Pull over in that fast-food place parking lot, and let's switch. It's okay."

He turned toward her, his eyes bloodshot and that muscle ticking visibly down his neck. "I need food. Before I find Pierce."

Of course. She looked around. They were in a small suburban town outside the city. "Pull over at that coffee shop. They'll have WiFi, and I can get on and figure out where we are and how to get food." There had to be an organic place with decent food he'd eat. When he'd stopped, she reached for the laptop and quickly typed. "We should get a phone, maybe." But those were expensive and easy to trace. Did burner phones connect to the Internet? She'd have to do a quick search.

He turned off the engine and stretched his back. "Should we steal another vehicle here?"

This one they'd stolen several states back, so she shook her head. "No. We should be safe for a little while." She connected and then did a quick search. "There's an organic takeout restaurant two blocks over. Let's go there, and then we're about thirty minutes away from my parents' house. I'll drive."

He stepped out of the car and stretched, his T-shirt riding up to reveal those ripped abs. She scrambled over the console and moved the seat up. When he took her seat and shut the door, he shook his head. "Amazing. How many vehicles there are on the streets. How many people are alive today."

His tone held something she couldn't identify. Frustration? "We'll find your family, Quade. Even though there are more people, there are ways to communicate across the world that we didn't have before."

"I should be able to jump through time and space to where home was," he muttered. "I keep trying, but that ability is gone." He sighed. "I'm lighter here and stronger, though."

"Could be the difference in gravity?" She started the car and pulled out of the lot. "Every planet or place is different. I can try to explain gravity later." It only took her a couple of minutes to reach the organic restaurant, which was next to a bank. "Stay here for a few minutes, and I'll get food and more money from my account. We should stock up on cash since we've now left yet another trail, which will hopefully confuse anybody looking for us, and have to get out of here as soon as we get Allison." Nothing in Haven could call the woman "Mom," even though she wanted to save her.

Quade tapped his long fingers on the dash. "There are so many stores. Is there one that sells weapons?"

Her chest heated. Why hadn't she thought of that? "Yes. We don't have time to do background checks for a gun, but we could buy knives. We just passed an outdoor sporting store." She had a credit card she only kept for emergencies and never used; since they were leaving a trail right now, this would be the time to use it. Then she'd pay it off and discard it immediately. "I'll be right back."

Minutes later, she returned with several sandwiches, cash, and two burner phones from a small shop down the way. "These have Internet but not a lot of memory or minutes, so we'll just use them if necessary." She clicked one open and immediately found the Internet. Going to her email, she found a link and clicked on it.

Pierce came up. "I was beginning to wonder if I should just kill her."

"Don't. I'm hours out, but I'm coming," Haven said, her stomach aching. She angled away from Quade so he couldn't be seen.

Pierce frowned. "Where's the hybrid?"

"Back in Denver," she said. "He didn't think saving a human was worth it, and I disagreed, so I had to take off."

"Well, then." Pierce smiled. "Good to hear. If you're not on this doorstep by nine tonight, I'll rip pieces of your mother off one by one. No matter where you are, you can get here by then. I'll be waiting." He clicked off.

She shut the phone to keep from using any more data.

HERO'S HAVEN

117

Quade's eyebrows rose. "He did not believe you."

"I know," she breathed. "But he might still think there's a chance I'm alone."

"Right." Quade reached for the bag of food and demolished two steak sandwiches in moments. "Let's go to the knife store and buy weapons, and then we can discuss this mission and your place in it."

She'd wondered if he'd given up his ridiculous notion that she would not help rescue Allison. "Thanks," she said, accepting the sandwich he offered her. "I assume you spent the night thinking that maybe somebody has to be there to get Allison out while you and Pierce fight with knives and claws." The poor guy really needed to sleep, didn't he? At some point? She wasn't stupid enough to think she could fight Pierce on her own, but what if Quade needed backup? She was a scrapper and might be able to help.

He sighed and reached for another sandwich. "No. That is not what I spent the night thinking about."

She blinked. No, she shouldn't ask. She really shouldn't. "What did you think about?"

His gaze was deep in the afternoon light. "That we need to be more careful. When I tasted you, I wanted nothing more than to brand my mark into your flesh."

She coughed, even as desire uncoiled inside her at the worst possible time. "Um, I have to be willing to mate, right?"

"You were," he said, his confidence obviously back.

She couldn't find a retort because there wasn't one. When he'd had her on that bed, almost begging, she would've agreed to anything. Apparently, he knew it.

Chapter Seventeen

Knife stores were impressive places, and he had thoroughly enjoyed choosing the right weapons earlier in the day. Quade felt more centered with the large blade at his waist and a smaller one tucked into his boot. He would certainly need to gain employment to earn cash and repay Haven once he got her to safety.

After scouting the area for an hour, he stood behind a tree staring at a pristine white house with blue shutters and a brown but still manicured lawn. The winter breeze ruffled his hair, but it was nowhere near as chilly as it had been up north. "That's where you grew up?"

Haven nodded, her gaze stoic as she looked at the house. More blank than stoic. "What if Pierce has a bunch of other cat shifters with him?"

"Now you worry about that?" Quade muttered, looking down at her.

She shrugged.

"Lions have prides, but cougars are usually loners," he said. Well, years ago they had been loners. Although times might change, the nature of a beast usually did not. "If this one actually works for humans, then I doubt he is affiliated with any others. Only a loner, a mercenary, would work for humans, especially on a job hunting down a female." Or was Pierce interested in Haven for himself? "Do you understand the plan?"

She looked up at the stars beginning to dot the darkness above them. "Yes. You go in, start fighting, and then I try to get in the back door and find Allison."

He didn't like it, but she'd had a point earlier. "When I've found my family, there will be no missions of this type together," he warned her. When he found his brothers, he'd have backup.

She rolled her eyes.

"Your face may stick like that," he said, recalling his mother's warning. He pressed a hand to his chest. She'd passed on, along with his father, in a war far before he underwent the Seven ritual. How he missed her, missed both of them. His longing for his brothers assailed him and the world tilted again. "Damn it." He ground a fist into his eye.

"What?" Haven tugged on his arm. "What's wrong?"

"Nothing." He shook his head. "I get dizzy once in a while."

She patted his arm. "It's probably the different atmosphere and gravity—or something scientific like that. Take several deep breaths."

He did so, and the world righted itself. "Okay. Come with me to the fence line."

She nodded, taking out a smaller knife they'd purchased for her, her face set in delicate yet firm lines. They crossed the street, and his boots gained purchase on the wet grass.

Then hell descended faster than a whip through the air.

A helicopter suddenly came into view, this one without any warning, and soldiers dropped from the sky on black ropes. His gaze narrowed, and he caught sight of several Cyst members, their long white braids glowing in the night. Panic and fury ripped through him.

He grabbed Haven around the waist, pivoted, and tried to run back across the street.

A shot was fired above his head, hitting a wooden pole with wires extending out from it. Sparks flew. He ducked, spun around, and set the female behind him. A figure, the largest one, disengaged from the rope and stood, legs braced.

Quade blinked. Once and again. Memories grabbed him from a long-ago war. He'd fought this asshole before. "Xeno," he muttered.

The Cyst general smiled and his yellowed fangs glinted. "Quade Kayrs. We thought it was you but couldn't be sure."

Haven peeked out from his side. "Holy shit," she muttered.

Anger distracted Quade, and he shoved it away; he needed to find an escape route. The remaining soldiers fanned out in perfect formation, forming a shield that made running impossible. "Let the female go, and I'll go with you," he offered.

Xeno snarled. "We want the female as much as you, Kayrs. We'll take you both, and you will lead us to Ulric. Now."

So the bastard hadn't appeared yet. Quade forced a smile. "He's dead. His entire world imploded, and I saw it happen. That's how I was knocked back here." He hoped that was the correct usage of the word "knocked." The power of an oncoming fight flowed through his veins, sharpening his focus. "Things have changed if you're working with a cougar shifter. Have the Cyst become that desperate?"

Pierce walked out onto the porch, a gun in his hand. He looked at Quade, at the Cyst, and then the remaining soldiers. His eyes widened, and he jumped back inside.

Xeno chuckled and motioned for one of his soldiers to take the house. "A cougar shifter? This world has not changed that much, my friend." He shook his head, and his eyes glinted a sharp purple. "We tracked you from the female's bank records and realized you were headed here."

Of course they weren't working with a shifter. Damn it. The ATM and credit card trail had led the Cyst here so quickly? This new world made it hard to fade away—except for his family. Quade drew the knife from his waist and calculated the distance between them. If he took Xeno down fast enough, would the other soldiers attack, giving Haven a chance for freedom?

A female scream came from within the house and then the sound of breaking furniture. The cougar would give the Cyst soldier a good fight.

Haven turned and bunched her muscles to run for the house. Quade grabbed her arm and halted her in mid-stride. "No."

She struggled against him. "I have to help her."

Hopefully, the human was going out the back door or hiding. "You will stay here." How could he get her to safety?

Xeno watched them with narrowed eyes. "Apparently, the matehood isn't going well." He tilted his head and scented the air. "Oh. No matehood yet." Those eyes started to glitter. "Well. Then she's up for grabs, huh?"

Quade didn't like the idiom. His heart rate increased, and he took a step toward the enemy on the oddly quiet street. "You and I fight. You win, we go with you. I win, and you let the female go." No way would they let him go free, and he knew it. He was outnumbered, but he could decapitate Xeno and at least two others before being taken to the ground. Probably. The world tilted again, but he kept his expression fierce.

Xeno lifted a glowing green object, similar to the ones at the outdoorsman shop called guns. But those had not been green. "This fires lasers that turn to metal upon hitting flesh. I have no problem shooting you both and taking you in unconscious. Make up your mind. Pain and coming with us, or just coming with us?"

"I've never seen a green gun," Haven whispered, her voice shaking.

Quade had no doubt the weapon would perform as promised. "How seriously does a bullet incapacitate the body?"

"Dunno," she whispered. "They kill humans easily, but I don't know about you. Or apparently, me."

It appeared bullets would slow and harm him but not take off his head. There was only one choice. "I'll rush him, and you run as fast as you can back to the vehicle."

She tugged her arm free. "I'm not leaving you."

"Obey me." Ducking his head, he charged.

Xeno fired, and a projectile shot through Quade's upper arm. He howled in fury, running faster. Haven ran by him in a blur, heading for the house. Damn it.

In an instant, his velocity changed.

Vehicles sped in from both sides of the street, screeching to a stop. Doors opened and soldiers jumped out, guns firing and knives already being thrown. A body tackled him to the ground and rolled him behind one of the huge black vehicles. He punched, fighting, turning and stopping cold when his vision cleared. "Ronan."

His brother, aqua eyes dark, grabbed him in a hug. "You're alive."

"It's about damn time," Quade muttered, hugging back quickly. Then he drew them both up behind the vehicle. He focused on the moment. Later there would be time to feel.

Ronan handed him a gun and leaned around the side of the vehicle, firing rapidly. Return fire pinged off metal, ricocheting into the nearby fence.

Quade ducked and sucked in air to run to the house.

Ronan pivoted, stopping him with a full-body impact. "Stay the fuck behind the vehicle."

Quade shoved him. "My mate ran into the house." Only silence came from the interior now, and his legs bunched with the need to run.

Ronan shook his head. "Give me a minute to clear the way. You'll just get shot. A lot." His brother wore all black, and his hair was tied at the neck. He looked healthy and whole and deadly, and he matched Quade's six and a half feet of height.

Quade's gaze met aqua eyes a shade lighter than his. Memories of their childhood, of their friendship, of their becoming part of the deadly Seven all ran through his mind faster than a hiccup. He clapped his brother on the shoulder. "I missed you. For now, start firing at those bastards while I run. Stop me again, and I'll take off your head."

Ronan shoved him back. "Give me a minute." He ducked and shot the gun, which released several laser bullets at once.

Quade ducked his head and charged, running across the street toward the home. Pain lanced into his leg and arm, but when the lasers hit his chest, they bounced off uselessly. The Seven torso shield, created in blood, bone, and pain, apparently trumped current weapons.

A bullet sliced across his neck and he dropped to the ground, rolling and coming up quickly. He clamped a hand over the blood spitting from the wound, sending healing cells there immediately. He leaped over the curb and onto the lawn while the firefight continued behind him.

He'd just reached the porch when he was hit by a tackle from behind that sent him face first into the wooden steps. Pain exploded across his forehead, and he turned, his knife already out. The Cyst soldier sank fangs into his already damaged neck, and Quade howled, stabbing furiously with the knife. The blade bounced off the soldier's back. He was wearing some type of armored vest.

Switching his aim, Quade stabbed for exposed skin.

The knife pierced beneath the Cyst's jaw and the bastard ripped his fangs away, taking a chunk of Quade's neck with him. He spit it out.

Quade punched him in the eye, following up with a second punch to the nose. Taking advantage and ignoring the blood now streaming from his neck, he rolled them over and straddled the asshole, his strength superior in a way it hadn't been centuries ago.

He punched and punched, breaking every bone in the soldier's face before finally plunging the knife right through the throat to embed it in the wooden porch floor. The Cyst's eyes widened and then closed. "I'll take your head later," Quade muttered, stumbling to his feet, his neck open and exposed to the chilled air.

Lowering his head, he stomped up the stairs and tried to dispel the dizziness swamping him. Blood flowed down his side from several wounds.

With a whisper of sound echoed, Ronan stood at his side, bleeding from a wound beneath his right eye. "Fight's over. Xeno got away, but we killed several of the others."

Quade nodded and kicked open the front door. He moved in with his brother at his side.

Overturned and broken furniture littered a living room that smelled like a marsh. "What is that?" His eyes watered and he covered his nose.

"Bleach," Ronan said, stepping over the remains of a glass vase. "Used for cleaning. Way too much cleaning."

Bleach sucked. "Haven?" Quade ran to the next room, which held a table and a bunch of china, and looked around, seeing no one. Panic grabbed him around the throat tighter than the Cyst had. He moved through the next doorway to a large, sparkling kitchen. Blood covered a middle island, and Haven's adopted mother slumped unconscious by a cupboard, her face bruised.

Quade reached her and felt her neck. "She's alive." He ran out the back door, following the scent of shifter that ended at an oil spill where a vehicle had left marks in the dirt. Another quick search of the grounds came up empty, and when he returned to the kitchen, the woman was stirring but was disoriented.

Ronan looked at him, his gaze concerned. "I need you to update me."

Quade leaned a hand on the counter as the world spun around him. His mate was out there somewhere, and he was bleeding out. "Tear this place apart for any hint as to where the father is." Pierce had promised the pastor he'd deliver Haven, so that was where they'd go. "As for her?" He pointed to the woman who had failed to protect Haven. "She comes with us."

Ronan nodded. "We don't have a choice. If she saw us or any immortals, we have to interrogate her and reach an agreement."

Quade didn't much care what happened to the woman. He made it as far as the refrigerator before the darkness finally claimed him. His last thought before he hit the floor was that his brother was there to catch him. Then, blessed unconsciousness.

Chapter Eighteen

Haven had taken a blow to the head the second she'd run through the front door, but she'd seen Allison try to jump in front of her and save her. Then there was nothing. She awoke, lying on the wooden floor of a cramped room with the sound of the ocean coming from not too far away. She blinked several times and pressed a hand to the lump above her left ear. Swollen but not bleeding. Where was she? "Quade?"

No answer.

Her legs wobbling, she stood and looked around. Garden tools lined one wall, while a planting table had been pushed to the other wall. She was in a garden shed?

Turning, she realized she'd been lying against the door. She twisted the knob, but nothing happened. Yanking, she tried to force the door open, but it was somehow secured on the other side. Probably with a padlock. Her stomach lurched and twisted, and she swallowed several times to keep the bile down. Her head hurt and her vision was still fuzzy, but she had to get out of there.

Was Quade all right? There had been bullets flying, and he'd never been shot in the head before. The biting mark on her neck pulsed just enough to ground her.

The ocean became louder, and the smell of soil and salt filtered around. She moved over to the garden tools and grasped a trowel and a three-tine soil rake. Keeping the weapons steady, she knocked against the walls, looking for a weakness.

Where was Quade? Had he survived the fight outside her old home? And where was her mother?

The door opened, and moonlight filtered in, outlining Pierce. She pivoted to face him. "You hit me."

"Was necessary." He looked her over. "You won't win in a fight. Put those down."

"No. Where are we?" The only way out was through him, so she'd have to take it. She angled the tines so she could aim for his eyes.

"Pretty beach house owned by one of your father's flock." Sarcasm and amusement mixed together in the shifter's tone.

Figured. "Faith, Grace, or Promise?" she snapped, fully aware she was hesitating to attack.

His sandy-colored eyebrows rose. "None of the above. Some guy name Joe, actually. He's totally into this whole exorcism idea."

Her knees weakened at the thought, followed by a healthy dose of anger. "Do they know what you are?"

"Of course not." He snorted. "They don't know what you are, either. I took the job for money and then found you."

She swallowed loudly. "You've been chasing me all these years for money?"

"Oh, no. I've been chasing you for me, because I knew you were special. I've finally figured it out—you're part fairy." A low purr came from his chest. "Do you have any idea how unique you are? How unique your offspring will be?"

Offspring? "Not a chance in hell, buddy." She tried to remind herself that she had powerful immortal blood in her veins, but she felt more vulnerable than ever. Could a normal Fae-demoness fight a shifter and win? Why hadn't she been taking karate lessons her entire life? "How much money am I worth?"

"To these idiots? A million," Pierce said. "He really thinks it's his calling, the greater purpose given to him by God, the Big Guy, to rid you of this evil. The pastor is obsessed, I'm telling you."

She drew back. Her father had apparently grown his church admirably. "That's a lot of money."

"I'll split it with you. Be a good girl, come out, go through the silly human exorcism, and we'll run off to the Bahamas." Pierce pivoted to the side.

The spit in her mouth dried up. "I am not going through an exorcism ritual." Her voice shook.

"Come on, demoness. They can't really hurt you." He shrugged a strong shoulder. "They can cause pain, but it's a million dollars. What wouldn't you do for a million in cash?"

"Go through an exorcism," she snapped. Obviously. But at least she had him talking. "Did you kill my, um, mother?"

"No. Knocked that bitch out, though. She can definitely talk. Would not stop praying." He shook his head. "No wonder you're half nuts, being raised by those two. I'll make you a deal."

She paused in planning her attack. How far were they from Quade? Was he okay? If so, he'd be on his way. She knew it. "Deal?"

"Yeah. Go through the ritual, we take the money, and I'll come back and kill him for you." In the moonlight, his canines glinted with sharp edges. "Or I'll teach you how to kill. Could be a prelude to some pretty damn good sex."

Oh, she hated this guy. "Animals aren't my thing, *shifter*." She made her voice as haughty as possible.

He threw back his head and laughed, apparently not insulted in the slightest. "Spoken just like a demoness. Stuck up and sexy. I have no clue what a fairy sounds like, but probably the same. They love money, you know."

"What about Quade?" she asked, trying to sound nonchalant. "Did he survive?" She held her breath, waiting for the answer.

"I have no clue. The Cyst and the vampire soldiers were fighting it out to the death, and I got you out of there. You are definitely going to thank me for that later." He gestured with his arm. "Let's go, fairy."

Vampire soldiers? Would that be Quade's family or friends? Warmth filled her heart, surprising her. He'd tunneled right in there, hadn't he? She narrowed her focus. The shifter seemed to be a pretty selfish guy. "You know that the Kayrs marking appeared on his hand and that he considers me his mate, right?"

"I saw the drawing." Impatience crept into Pierce's tone.

"He'll kill you. I saw him punch through a Kurjan's throat once in a fight, and that was back when he hadn't eaten in centuries. If he gets his hands on you, he'll rip you apart." She was trying to scare the shifter, but the words held so much truth, she shivered. "Let me go, and I'll make sure he doesn't hunt you down."

Pierce's chin lowered. "I'd normally take that deal. But you're worth the risk, pretty one. Now come out here so we can get this over with. The humans won't give me the money until after the ritual, so let's do it. I'll take you on a nice shopping trip afterward."

She was immortal. A Fae-demon blend of pure adrenaline and strength. Keeping those facts in mind, she ducked her head and charged, swinging wildly with the garden tools.

* * * *

Quade kept quiet in the back seat of the large SUV as it drove away from the fight, his neck hurting nearly as fiercely as his chest since Haven had disappeared. Ronan sliced open his wrist and pushed it his way. Quade shook his head.

Ronan growled and grabbed his arm. "We need you strong to find your mate. Don't be an ass."

Quade settled and took the wrist, sucking deep and taking blood. His injuries began to close instantly, and power, the ancient kind, rippled through his veins. "Thank you." He turned to face his oldest brother and forced a smile. Everything inside him was jumbled up with Haven's abduction, but he'd waited for this moment for millennia, fearing it would never happen. His chest heated and warmed. He reached over and yanked Ronan close for a hard hug. His brother. It was a miracle and one he'd never even hoped for. "I missed you."

Ronan hugged him back. Hard. "Me too."

The soldiers in the front seat stared straight ahead, looking for threats.

Quade finally settled. Together again with family. With Ronan, the only person in existence who understood the solitude he'd withstood in a hell world so far away. He cleared his throat and leaned back. The painting Haven had completed ran through his head. He didn't want to know, but he had to ask. "Jacer." Their middle brother had always been the stable, calm one of the three, and his wisdom was needed right now.

Ronan's eyes filled with pain. His mouth opened, but no words emerged. Finally, he shook his head.

Quade took the kick to the solar plexus and breathed out, pain engulfing him. He'd known, but having Jacer's death confirmed was agony beyond description. "He lived a good life?" His voice cracked at the end.

Ronan's smile was sad. "Aye. Mated and had two boys, but all are gone. One of the boys was very busy and had five kids."

"Five Kayrs brothers?" Quade asked, his voice hushed. Incredible. Anybody with vampire blood only made males, so they'd be five brothers. "All still living?" He knew better than to feel hope, but right now, sitting with his brother, he couldn't shield himself.

"Yes. All five are living and a few have kids already." Ronan nodded, fully understanding Quade's emotions. "When I came back from the bubble, I was shocked to know we had family left. They're good soldiers, and our great-nephew is the King of the Realm. Name is Dage."

Sounded like a good name for a king. "They know about the Seven?" There had been a blood oath of secrecy when the Seven were made.

"They know some but certainly not all," Ronan said. "We got into a bit of trouble and had no choice but to reach out to the King of the Realm. We needed two new members, and the king's nephew, our great-great-nephew, is one. You'll meet Garrett soon."

The painting came into focus in Quade's mind again. "Zylo Kyllwood died as well?"

Ronan straightened. "Yes. How did you know?"

"Long story. Who took his place?" How odd that there were two members of the Seven Quade had never met.

"His great-nephew. A badass named Logan Kyllwood. The kid mated a fairy." Ronan shook his head. "Hey. I'm mated, too." He held up his hand to show his branding mark, which was faded since it had obviously been used.

Quade's mouth dropped open. "You have mated?"

Ronan shifted his weight, his cheeks coloring. "Yes. I figured I'd take the time I'm allowed and enjoy it fully. Hell. Maybe we'll win the final ritual."

Quade shook his head. "The vow, Ronan." His body ached.

"We didn't vow to be alone," Ronan countered. "Just to give our lives in the end if necessary. I will adhere to my vow."

Quade exhaled slowly. He couldn't let his brother leave a mate alone for eternity. "Ronan," he muttered.

Ronan grinned. "Her name is Faith, and you'll love her."

Quade's head jerked. "Faith? A brunette with pretty eyes?"

"Yes." Ronan frowned.

"Friends with a Promise and sister to Grace?" Quade recalled that other painting. "They contacted Haven a while back."

Ronan nodded. "Yes. We found her and figured she'd lead us to you. But she's smart, Q. She's evaded us for months. Impressive, that."

Yes, his mate was impressive. And missing. Quade looked into the darkness outside.

"We'll find her." Ronan clapped him on the shoulder as if he couldn't stop checking to be sure Quade was real. "The mother says she doesn't know where the father is, and I believe her, but we'll find them. We have the Realm computer experts already dealing with satellites and cameras on the way, and we'll locate her soon. Trust me."

"I do," Quade said softly. He trusted his brother more than anyone else on this world. "There's so much…"

"Me too," Ronan said, squeezing his shoulder. "All the words, me too."

Quade grinned. "I hope you're better getting the words out with your mate."

"I'm okay," Ronan snorted. "She usually knows what I mean. So do you."

"Aye," Quade said, finding the moment surreal. He was with his brother, and he was home. There would be time and space to grieve for those he'd lost later as well as to rejoice with those who had survived. Right now, all he could think about was Haven. "I should have forced her to remain back in the vehicle."

"Based on my research, she seems a rather independent type." Ronan motioned to the drivers, and they pulled up next to a helicopter. This one was black with twin propellers up top. "These days they want more than oxen and land. They want love and all that stuff, and they're not willing to compromise."

Quade stared out at the innocuous-looking helicopter. Love? After a life of hell, he wasn't sure he could manage that feeling. But he could offer protection, and apparently, these days it was more necessary than ever. Life was dangerous, more so than before. With this new technology, even humans could be a threat. "Love is just a word."

Ronan snorted and covered the sound with a cough. "So you say."

Quade jumped out of the SUV and stalked toward the beast, his stomach pitching violently. He'd been through hell dimensions, teleporting wildly during his quest to become one of the Seven, but even then, he hadn't flown in the air.

A male jumped out of the front, a laptop in his hands.

Quade stopped cold.

The stranger had sizzling gray eyes, black hair, and Jacer's jawline.

"I know," Ronan murmured. "Quade? Meet your great-great-nephew, Garrett Kayrs."

Garrett held out a hand. "Great-great-uncle."

Smart-ass. Quade drew him in for a hard hug. "You look like my brother."

Ronan snorted. "You should see the kid's father, Talen. He's a dead ringer for Jacer." Ronan cleared his throat. "He did not, however, inherit Jacer's good disposition and calm manner."

"Neither did I," Garrett said cheerfully. "My uncle Kane is probably the closest in disposition to your description of Jacer. You'll meet him at some time, I'm sure."

Family. Quade swayed and then caught himself. He wasn't alone any longer.

Ronan edged closer. "You okay? It took me a while to get accustomed to the gravity here, and I was in a coma for seven years. Your mind has to be spinning."

"I am fine," Quade said, nodding at the laptop. "Have you found my mate?"

"I'm on her trail," Garrett confirmed. "We traced her through town to Malibu by hacking into bank, store, and traffic cameras. Then we lost her, but the techs at home are hacking into governmental satellites right now to pick up her path."

Quade swallowed, his nerves fraying. "Good."

Ronan gestured him inside the dark beast. "Let's go. We can continue searching from the air."

Quade sucked deep and nodded, taking a step forward. It would take time to heal if this thing crashed. "Who is flying?"

"I am," Garrett said, reading his computer screen. "Don't worry. I only hit buildings half of the time."

"Wonderful." Quade jumped all the way in.

Chapter Nineteen

Haven slashed Pierce across the neck and down his torso with the tool, spinning and aiming for his eyes. He roared and stepped back. She jumped out of the shed and looked around. A wood and glass house was perched down the path with a wide deck facing the ocean, and a trail led in the opposite direction around a stone wall. She turned and started to run along the rock-strewn path away from the house. On one side was a cliff; on the other, pointy trees.

Pierce moved silently, securing her around the legs and taking her down hard.

The air whooshed from her lungs and she coughed, momentarily stunned. He flipped her over, straddling her and looking down, blood dripping from his neck.

She slapped him, punching him in the stomach.

He shifted his weight and pressed his knees against her upper arms, effectively trapping her. He was heavy and strong, and anger glinted in his catlike eyes. His canines elongated beyond his lips, looking like they could tear her apart. Easily. "That all you got?"

She bucked and struggled but couldn't dislodge him. Frustration brought tears to her eyes, and she blinked them away. "You are such a dick."

"And you suck as a fighter." He wiped blood off his cheek, and his skin slowly mended. His eyes filled with a light she didn't much like. "I can see we're going to have some fun together as you learn your place." He pressed harder with his knees, and she bit her lip as agony shot down both arms. "Some females like pain, and I'm thinking you're one of those bitches. Do I have it right?"

The ocean crashed far below as his words registered in her brain. "No. You have that wrong." Why couldn't she have some cool ability like being able to melt his face off? She struggled again but couldn't get her hands free. "Why have you been chasing me?"

"Money and sex, of course. Aren't those the primary reasons for everything?" He glanced down at her breasts. "I'm not saying I haven't taken many side jobs over these years, but I've always kept on your trail. Someday, I knew we'd be here. You under me."

Was the guy crazy? Were cougars insane with stalker urges? She fought harder, but he was too strong, and she finally stopped, her breath panting out furiously.

"Mary?" That voice straight out of her nightmares came from the porch.

She went still, her body going ice cold.

Pierce cocked his head. "Interesting. You're afraid of a human but not of me."

Not true. They both were terrifying. "Get off me," she snapped, her voice shaking just enough to tick her off.

He rolled to his feet, grabbed her arms, and yanked her up. "You know you can't die, right? Well, unless they take off your head, and I'm not going to let that happen," he whispered, dragging her toward the porch.

She jerked free and walked forward, her chin held up. If it was possible to be cold to the soul, she was right now. The chill spread out, causing her limbs to tremble. "You've aged," she said, reaching the porch and studying the man she'd once called Father. He was still ramrod straight and tall, but his brown hair had thinned and grayed. Though his hawklike eyes were still sharp, the hands holding the well-worn Bible had a few dark spots.

He turned his attention to Pierce. "Thank you. I can't imagine the difficulty you must have had facing a demon."

Pierce stepped up to her side. "Some demons are sexy, Pastor. You have no idea."

"I do not wish to know." Her father rubbed the frayed cover on the Bible. "Your eyes are both green. Contact?"

"Nope. The devil left me, Pastor," she said, letting sarcasm bubble over. "That means our business is concluded." Adrenaline flooded her again, and her breath heated as her body screamed to run.

"Take it out," he ordered. "If you don't, I'll do it for you. Neither of us would like that."

"I remember how you don't like to touch," she murmured, studying him for the first time without fear. He was just a man. Just a human who had never shown her love. Never shown her attention, even before he'd decided she was possessed. She blinked hard, and the contact flew out. Score one for the Fae-demoness. "Better, Pastor?" She'd never think of him as her father again.

He took a step back.

Triumph filtered through her. "You know the moron next to me can shift into a cougar, right?"

The pastor shook his head. "You're insane."

Pierce snorted. "The more you call me names, the more I like you." He brushed her hair off her shoulder and rubbed his knuckle along her jawline. "How silly, Pastor. Shifters? Maybe she is crazy."

She turned in an instinctive move and kicked him square in the side of the knee.

Pierce's leg buckled, and only catlike reflexes keep him from falling. "You're going to pay for that later, I promise you." His snarl was so bestial, it was astonishing the pastor didn't see the shifter in him.

The pastor cleared his throat. "I've studied and prepared for years, Mary Agnes. I can save you. Please, let me."

She frowned. He truly believed his baloney. "I am not possessed, Pastor. Never have been and never will be." Pierce grabbed her arm, and she tried to pull free, but his grip tightened. Before she really started fighting, she had to know the truth. "My parents. My biological parents. Who were they?"

The pastor shrugged. "No clue. You were left at the church, and at the time, I thought you a gift from God to make my Allison happy. I was wrong."

"You still are," she said, squaring her feet. "I'm not going through another one of your stupid rituals, so you might as well give up now." Telling him the truth wouldn't help this situation any, and if she showed him how quickly she could heal, he'd think his suspicions were confirmed. She could probably take him, but the shifter next to her was strong. She couldn't battle them both.

"I was hoping you'd agree to be freed after all this time." Sorrow lightened the pastor's brown eyes. "I've studied and learned. This ritual will be painful, but I think it will work. Only you or the demon will survive."

The words slashed through her. She bunched her fists to start fighting. "You're crazy. This isn't happening."

The pastor sighed and nodded at Pierce. Before Haven could turn, he clocked her in the temple, his fist harder than a rock. She went down, fighting the darkness, and hit the ground a second before she was swept into unconsciousness. The last word to tumble from her mouth was Quade's name, and then, nothingness.

* * * *

Quade plastered his hand against the side of the craft as it rose into the air. His stomach dropped and remained on the ground below. He sat on a long bench against the side of the craft, the kid was up front, and Ronan sat across from him in a chair next to the still open door. "You get used to it," he said.

Quade looked up front where the kid was driving. Anybody younger than a century was a kid as far as he was concerned. "Is there a driving age?" he asked, trying not to throw up. This craft would get him to his mate, so he'd endure the possible drop. How safe could a vehicle in the air be, anyway?

Ronan grasped the laptop from up front and drew it back. "Garrett is flying, not driving, and he's one of the best pilots around." He reached for the door and shut it. Silence descended. "This craft is a Realm specialty, hence the silence inside so we can talk. It can't be traced or followed, either."

Garrett, wearing some odd headset, glanced over his shoulder. "I stopped being a kid when I was a kid."

Yeah, his sizzling gray eyes hinted that he'd seen some shit. If nothing else, becoming a member of the Seven would age a male horribly, even if it didn't show on the outside. Quade nodded. "Understood. Just don't crash this thing."

Garrett grinned. "No promises." He turned back to all of the dials and blinking lights, pressing on a couple.

Ronan flipped open the laptop, stood, and sat next to Quade. "We've traced her to here." He pointed to a location near an ocean. He typed quickly. "We should have another update in a couple of minutes from the Realm techs. They're excellent." He sat back, a solid form in a turbulent world.

Quade stared at the opposite side of the craft, grateful the door was closed. "How did Jacer die?" The words surprised him, but he couldn't let go of the thought that his older brother was gone.

Ronan grimaced. "Let's deal with one thing at a time."

Quade clamped a hand on his brother's strong forearm. "He wouldn't have gone easy. How did he die, Ronan?"

Shared pain filled Ronan's eyes. "The Cyst got to him during one of the wars."

Quade's chest seized as if he'd been punched. He breathed through the pain. "Did Xeno kill him?" Xeno was the head of the Cyst sect, and Quade should've killed him earlier that day, damn it.

"No. Omar did, but I'm sure Xeno ordered it done," Ronan said, his tone hoarse. "I already killed Omar. Xeno is next."

Quade nodded. Omar had been a Cyst general and a spectacular fighter, although he'd been rumored to be insane. "Good job." It was fitting that Ronan had killed Omar. Quade would continue avenging his brother by going after Xeno once Haven was safe.

The female had to be safe. He closed his eyes and knocked his head back on the hard metal. "I failed her."

"No, you did not," Ronan said, his tone weary now. "We were in a fight, and there was no way you could get to the house before being taken down by bullets. Shifters are fast and crafty."

"We're better," Garrett said, dropping the helicopter several feet in the air. "We'll get your mate back, Quade. We're almost there."

Quade forced down the bile caused by the sudden descent and opened his eyes. "Do we know what kind of force they've amassed?"

"No." Ronan clicked several keys, his gaze scanning the screen. He straightened.

Quade tuned in to his brother's mood. "What?"

Ronan looked up, his jaw hardening. "Once we had the location, the Realm techs hacked into Pastor Lockship's computer."

"So?" Quade said, his instincts humming.

"The pastor has been studying exorcisms for the last decade and has even traveled across the globe in search of different methods. The one he has studied the most is called the Tewazni Method, created in the early fourteen hundreds by a group of zealots."

Quade stiffened. He didn't like that word. "Zealots?"

"Yeah." Ronan shut the laptop. "They believed that pain was the only way to exorcise a demon. They used fire and whips until the subject either died or the demon left the body." He shook his head. "It's crazy. Much like the burning or drowning of so-called human witches years ago."

Dull blades cut a swath beneath Quade's skin, and his heart rate picked up. "They're going to light her on fire?" He leaned forward. "Garrett? How close are we?" They had to arrive in time to save her. "I didn't tell her she could die by fire." It was rare and horribly painful, but immortals could be burned to death. Beheading was easier, but he'd heard stories about wars gone by and the torture of fire that ended lives. "They could kill her, Ronan."

Garrett leaned back. "We're almost there. I don't know where we can land, but I'll get you as close as I can."

Quade jumped up and swept the door open, looking down. The ocean was on one side and cliffs on the other. Large homes dotted the cliffs, and whitecaps sprayed up high from the water. His head spun, and he lurched.

Ronan grabbed his arm and yanked him back. "The dizziness will last awhile," he yelled over the wind. "Just sit. We'll be there soon."

Quade couldn't breathe. He'd felt fury often in his lifetimes, but fear was rare. Knowing Haven was in the hands of zealots and guarded by a shifter, one faster than he'd ever seen before, tunneled a hole of terror through his being.

He had to get to her in time.

Chapter Twenty

Haven came to in the middle of a circle, surrounded by fire. She lay on her side, curled up on a wooden floor, her legs to her chest. Somebody had removed her clothing and placed her in a thick white gown that covered her from neck to ankles. The cuffs around her wrists were too tight. Slowly, she sat up, her vision hazing.

She was in some sort of room, a library with many shelves, all of them empty. The entire room had been cleared of objects, but was full of people. The long gown made her feel vulnerable in a way her jeans and sweater had not.

Figures sat on the outside of the fire, several feet back. She could make out the pastor, three men, and two women. "Pierce?" she croaked, her throat aching.

"He went to the bank to check his accounts," the pastor said, sitting across from her, a tattered book in his hands. "I know he is interested in you, but I think it's the demon he wants. Once we save you, Pierce will be gone. I'm sure of it." The pastor opened the book.

"That isn't the Bible," she whispered, her neck aching.

"No," he said.

She looked at him, her head hurting from the blow. Her chest ached in a way it hadn't for a long time. "You're supposed to be my father," she said. "Supposed to protect me." Supposed to love her, but he'd never come close. So why did his behavior still hurt?

"I am trying to help you." He patted the book.

"What is it?" She gave up right then and there her last remaining dream that he might really be her father or care about her. That would never happen, and it was time to completely let it go.

He held the book as if it was something precious. "This is an ancient text that will save you, Mary Agnes." He looked down and started to chant in a language she had never heard before. The other people around the circle did the same.

She snorted and wiped a tear off her heated face. "You're chanting? Seriously?"

The pastor lifted his head. "Ignore the demon. He will try to stay with her."

Haven rolled her eyes and looked for a way out. She felt a little off, and not just from the smack to the head. Though coming down from the pills had been easier than she'd expected, she still felt sluggish. She rubbed her neck, feeling the indent left by Quade's fangs. He'd bitten her, which meant they'd shared blood. Would that give her any extra strength?

Probably not. She kept him in her head, anyway. What would Quade do? The smell of chemicals filled the smoke that rose through a wide-open skylight in the ceiling. The smoke blocked out the moon and the stars. She herself angled to the side so she could study the burning rocks placed in a ring around her. Who knew what chemicals covered them? It'd hurt like hell, but she could jump through the flames. Even if she landed on a rock or two, the burns would go away.

As she began to stand, a whip cracked across her arm, cutting the material of the white gown. Pain encircled her wrist, and blood welled to tarnish the white. Swallowing, she turned to find one of the men holding a whip. The other men, except for her father, stood, also holding whips. She looked in turn at each of them. If she stood, they'd strike. The women continued the chant, their bodies swaying as they sat, their eyes wide. She focused on the pastor. "What? The chicks don't get whips, too?"

"Get out, demon!" he yelled, holding up his palm to face her.

She rubbed the fresh cut on her arm. "There's no demon inside me, you dumb fuck."

A whip cracked, slicing across her cheekbone. She yelped and scrambled back. Blood dripped down her face, and she willed the pain away. The sensation of her skin stitching itself together itched.

One of the women screamed. "The demon healed her."

Three whips struck simultaneously, cutting her chin, shoulder, and foot. She cried out, the pain coming from every direction. They attacked again, and she turned, grabbing the end of one whip and pulling with all her strength. The man fell flat onto the burning rocks and released the whip, screaming and scrambling back. Blisters instantly sprang up along his face and hands and he sagged back against the wall, whimpering.

She jumped to her feet. "Now I have a whip, assholes." Swinging, she nailed the second man across the chest, splitting open his shirt. Blood arced toward her. She might not have extra strength, but she definitely had beyond-human speed.

The pastor stood, his hand still out. "No more, demon. Come out. Let her free."

"I am the demon, damn it," she yelled at him, no longer able to keep quiet. A whip cut across the back of her head, and she fell to her knees. Partially turning, she waited, and the second her attacker struck again, she captured the whip and pulled. He released it, and she fell to the side, her elbow colliding with a burning rock.

Agony roared up her arm. She whimpered and scampered to the middle of the circle. Then she stood and turned toward the last guy holding a whip. "Wanna try it, asshole?"

He was around thirty years old with blond hair and blue eyes. Thin with large hands. He swallowed, his Adam's apple bobbing. "I just want to save the girl."

She sighed. "The girl doesn't need saving." Well, she wouldn't mind a little backup. Pain wasn't her thing, and if she passed out again, who knew what they might do to her. What if they cut off her head so the imaginary demon could get free? Then she'd really be dead. "Now. You all get out of the way, let me run, and I won't destroy you." Maybe they'd believe her.

The pastor finally stood and set the book aside. "It's too late. I'm so sorry." He nodded to the women.

The two women stood, drawing large squirt bottles from behind their backs. In unison, they pointed the nozzles and aimed at Haven. Liquid flew through the fire, increasing the flames and then covering her. The flames crackled and popped, much brighter and higher than before. Even hotter.

The liquid hurt her exposed skin. What the hell kind of chemical was it?

She took a deep breath. The only way out was through the fire. With the chemical on her, how badly would she burn? There was no choice.

Pivoting, she turned and leaped into the flames.

* * * *

Quade looked down—way down—at the porch of the large house and held on to the side of the craft, his legs bunched. Black smoke and particulates billowed from a hole in the ceiling, and panic seized him. "There's fire." The smoke seemed odd.

"Wait." Ronan grabbed his shoulder from the other side of the helicopter's open door. Wind swept the vehicle, and they swung in the air. "If you jump now, you'll break both your legs and probably most of your body." He leaned to the side. "Get lower, Garrett," he bellowed over the blustering wind.

"I'm trying." Garrett pushed some lever, and they went lower. He struggled with the stick in front of him, sweat breaking out on his forehead.

"What is wrong with the smoke?" Quade yelled.

Ronan shook his head. "Probably an accelerant of some type. The fire will burn hotter."

Hotter? Haven was in trouble. He had to go.

"I...can...get...lower," Garrett grunted. "Then meet me half a mile to the north. There's a front lawn there big enough to land this thing."

Quade couldn't wait any longer. He pushed off and fell several stories, hitting the porch and dropping, then rolling instantly. Pain lashed up his legs, but no bones broke. A second later, Ronan landed next to him, emitting a harsh grunt. He dropped and rolled in the other direction.

Screaming came from inside the house.

Quade leaped up and ran through the doorway. Glass crashed all around him, cutting his face and neck. He hadn't realized it was a glass door. Shaking off shards, he kept going, running past a sparkling kitchen with plates of fruit set neatly on the countertop.

Two women ran out of a far doorway, screaming, smoke billowing in their wake. He shoved past them. Unnatural smoke burned his nostrils and throat, irritating his lungs. Whatever an accelerator was, it fucking hurt.

He barreled through the doorway, and the entire room was filled with the smoke. He ran into Haven's father, who was trying to run out, grabbed him by the neck, and threw him into the nearest wall. The asshole crashed to the ground and bounced twice, out cold. "Haven!" Quade bellowed.

A scream from below the smoke, down on the floor, had him dropping into a slide.

He reached her and everything inside him fell silent. Her right arm was burning, her body convulsing.

"Quade," she moaned, blisters upon blisters singeing her beautiful skin. He grabbed her arm and patted out the flames, trying to pull them away from her and onto him. Every time he smothered an area, the fire lit up again.

Grunts sounded from a brief fight behind him, and then Ronan crouched next to him.

"Can't get fire out," Quade coughed.

Haven went limp, blissfully out cold.

Ronan attacked the fire starting on her legs, soot covering his face and his eyes watering. "It's the chemicals. Get her outside," he yelled over the roaring flames.

Maybe into the ocean? Could he stay conscious with her if he jumped off the cliff? Ignoring the searing pain, Quade lifted Haven and turned to run through the house and outside, toward the cliffs.

"No," Ronan yelled, right behind him. "Soil not water. Use dirt."

Quade leaped off the porch, his heart thundering as he set his mate on the ground and frantically started digging with his hands, flinging the soil on her arm and down her right leg. Ronan dropped next to him, also digging and then patting the dirt into her.

Terror seized him, and Quade worked faster, fury commingling with desperation until his movements were faster than even he could believe. "Haven," he yelled. "Hold on. I've got you." The house exploded behind him, and he crouched over her, protecting her from flying debris and glass.

The fire finally subsided on her arm, so he moved down her abs while Ronan worked on her legs.

Sirens sounded in the distance. He recognized their sound from a television show, but he couldn't stop yet. Even if the humans arrived.

He finished with her just as Ronan tamped out the last of the fire near her ankle.

White material, burned black, was embedded in her burned skin. Blisters covered her arm, and most of her hair was a mass of dirt and soot. Apparently, she'd protected her head and left side from the accelerant, so hopefully her brain wasn't injured too badly.

Quade sat back, staring at her, the anger inside him ballooning into a raw rage and a driving need for revenge. First, he had to get Haven to safety. Being as gentle as possible, he reached under her and stood, lifting her.

Her soft moan of pain cut him to pieces.

Ronan stood, his gaze as hard as Quade had ever seen it. "Let's get her to a hospital, and then we'll go hunting."

Quade turned to look at the house. "Her father is dead." Most of the humans, except for the two women who'd escaped, were dead. He didn't much care about them. But the shifter. He was going to bleed and soon. "I want to know everything there is to know about Pierce the cougar."

"Agreed." Ronan rubbed the burns on his right arm, and his hand was black with burned skin from snuffing out the flames on Haven. The wail of the sirens grew more urgent. "Let's go. This way." He jogged down the path along the ocean.

Quade followed, holding Haven as close as he dared, careful not to jar her any more than was necessary. Another explosion and then several more bellowed behind him, and he crouched over her, increasing his speed.

They reached the helicopter and jumped in.

Garrett looked over his shoulder at Haven, and his face turned pale. "Holy shit." He turned and quickly pressed a series of levers and flashing lights. "We'll have to take her to Realm headquarters and the hospital there."

Ronan's lips pressed together as he shut the door and turned to sit. "Do it. We'll deal with the fallout later. She's all that matters."

Quade settled back, not liking how limp she was in his arms. "Fallout?"

Ronan wiped soot from his eyes. "Yeah. The Realm doesn't know you're here on Earth. They haven't exactly decided to support the Seven and might take a stance against us at some point. This may force their hand faster than we'd like."

Quade's entire body thumped with pain and burns. "Because of the ritual?" The entire purpose of the Seven was to participate in a ritual to destroy Ulric, if he ever reached home again. The problem was that the ritual might also end the entire world.

Ronan nodded, his gaze weary and filled with pain. "One thing at a time, brother."

Quade looked down at his wounded and barely breathing mate. The Realm had better not fuck with him right now.

Chapter Twenty-One

Haven came to with a scream, trying to roll away from the pain.

"Stop." The command came harsh and fast from above her. Quade. She knew that voice.

"You came for me." The words burned her throat, but she didn't care. Sucking in air, wincing as her lungs shrieked, she forced her eyelids open to find herself cradled in his arms. In a helicopter?

He looked down, burns covering his neck and jaw, soot all over his face. "Yes." Gently shifting his weight, he drew a burned and scabby wrist to his lips and dug his fangs in. Then he pressed the cut to her lips.

She shook her head and then winced as the world dropped away. Take blood? She'd never tasted anybody's blood. The liquid burned her already burned lips, and she cried out. He pressed harder, not giving her a choice. Tears filled her eyes, feeling like acid. She wanted to fight him, but her limbs weren't working. The pain was too intense. Without any choice, she opened her mouth, and his pressure decreased.

The liquid scalded her damaged tongue, and she whimpered, shutting her eyes again.

His hold tightened a fraction around her and then loosened. "Take the blood, Haven. When the liquid warms your belly, imagine healing cells going everywhere your body hurts. This will help you. I promise." His voice was pained and hoarse.

She didn't have a choice. As soon as the liquid heated her stomach, she tried to imagine a little army of cells marching along her skin and inside her lungs to take away the pain.

Darkness came again, and she willingly let herself go unconscious.

She came to again, being carried by Quade through a wooden archway with dawn breaking outside. Snow fell lightly across her face. "Where?" she croaked, her lungs feeling marginally better.

"I've got you. You're protected. Now concentrate on those healing cells," he ordered, his voice firm.

Now who was bossy? She wanted to make the joke, but her eyes hurt and she had to shut them again. Her mouth still felt as if she'd been branded with an iron, and her throat was raw, so speaking seemed stupid. Instead, she imagined those little cell soldiers and tried to direct them to her throat and mouth. "My mother?"

"Safe. Not here."

The second she felt tingling along her lips, she passed out again.

When she awoke for a third time, she lay in a hospital bed with soft sheets covering her. A soft hum and a low beeping sound came from behind her. Slowly, carefully, she opened one eye.

Quade sat slumped in an oversized chair, his eyes closed, odd tingles popping the air around him. Raw burns covered his lower face and neck, and his T-shirt was charred. Soot and dirt were matted in his hair and covered both hands, while most of his jeans had been burned away to leave his legs visible.

He hadn't left her. Not for a second. She could trust him. At that thought, her heart just turned over.

She allowed her other eye to open. Slight pain stabbed into her skull from the light, but she rode it out, breathing more easily than she had earlier.

"Well. Good morning. Or rather, evening. It's almost midnight." Sparkling blue eyes set in a classically beautiful face came into view. The woman wore a white lab coat and had her black hair secured messily at the top of her head. Her eyes were full of intelligence and kindness. "I wondered if you were going to join us."

Haven looked around the plush hospital room. "How long have I been out, Doctor?"

"About twelve hours," the doctor said, leaning over and staring into her eyes. "Call me Emma. How are you feeling?"

"Like I've been burned alive," Haven said, swallowing over a dry throat.

Emma handed her a glass of water with a straw. "You're healing nicely, truth be told. Quade gave you blood, and then he gave me some to test, and it's potent stuff." Her eyes gleamed. "Different from other members of the Seven who have let me study them."

Haven looked down at her bandaged arm. "I must look horrible."

Emma nodded. "Blistered and burned, definitely." She looked toward the monitors. "But your heart rate has stabilized, and your breathing is much better than it was even an hour ago. Your body will heal vital organs first, from within, and then your skin. Judging by the rate you're going, I'd say you should feel much better in a few hours."

She felt better already. Much. "Is Quade's blood stronger for me because of the, well, I mean..." A flush worked its way beneath her damaged skin and hurt. A lot.

Emma smiled. "Because of the mating mark? His blood might be more potent for you because of that, but his blood is different regardless. Probably from living and dying in a different atmosphere for so long. Or maybe from fighting and surviving for eternities. Who knows? I haven't had a lot of time to study immortals."

Haven took another sip of water, relaxing when the liquid cooled her throat and didn't burn. "You are human?"

"I was. I mated a vampire, my chromosomal pairs increased, and now I'm immortal. Pretty much, unless I'm beheaded or burned to death." Emma reached for a tablet on a metal counter and typed, reading off the monitors as she did so. "My mate is part demon as well, but I think he still denies that fact sometimes." She hummed, her smile softening. "He's fun that way."

Mate. The term sounded so natural coming from Emma. "It's true, then. Humans can't be turned into vampires or demons?" Haven asked.

"Nope." Emma set the tablet back down. "There are enhanced humans who have psychic, empathic, telekinetic, or other gifts who can mate with immortals. Current theory is that we're a different species from human but close enough."

Haven tried to stretch out her injured hand, but the pain stopped her. "You checked my blood?"

"Yep."

Haven focused on the doctor, her breath catching in her throat. Tingles wandered down her arms. "And?"

"Fae with a mutation of demon." Emma leaned closer, her eyes lighting up. "It's fascinating. One species usually takes over, the other is a mere mutation. Kind of like having green eyes, which are just mutations of blue."

Quade stirred and opened his eyes, flashing a deep aqua. "Please stop calling my mate a mutant, Queen. I'd really appreciate it."

* * * *

Quade sat up as the healing cells finished on his neck and worked their way down his arms and up his face. He'd been sleeping for hours, healing, but had known the second Haven had awakened. Listening to her talk with the queen had entertained him briefly.

Haven's eyebrow rose. "Queen?"

Emma shrugged and felt for her pulse. "I mated the king."

Haven's mouth opened and then closed.

Quade smiled, sharing her surprise. "It's a new world to me too, little one." In his time, queens acted like queens instead of doctors. Emma wore jeans and tennis shoes beneath her white lab coat, and she had been working nonstop to heal Haven and study their blood since Quade had arrived. "Emma? Shouldn't you get some sleep?" He'd called her Queen Kayrs once, and she'd nearly snapped his head off. So, Emma it was.

"Agreed." Dage Kayrs strode into the room, power and tension coming with him. The King of the Realm moved like a deadly predator, and the light in his eyes did nothing to dispel that impression. He moved closer to the bed, and his hard face softened. "Well, hello there. How are you feeling?"

Haven stared at the king, her eyes wide.

"She's better," Emma said, releasing Haven's wrist. "The healing powers of the Fae are impressive, and there's probably something in her blood that will help me cure human diseases. At least one."

The king slid an arm over Emma's shoulders and kneaded her neck. He towered over her by at least a foot, yet his touch looked gentle.

Haven turned from them to Quade. "Kayrs. So that means..." Confusion clouded her eyes, more visible in the green one.

Quade nodded. "I'm the king's great-uncle."

"You look the same age," Haven said, her voice hushed.

The king barked out a laugh. "You're not going to age much either, our new fairy friend."

"Fae," she said, the correction automatic.

Amusement tilted the king's mouth. "So I've heard. Fae it is."

Haven looked at Quade. "Now that you're back, does that mean you're, well, the..."

"Hell no," Quade said.

Dage's eyebrows rose. "It's yours if you want it. Maybe you should think about it."

"Not a chance," Quade muttered. He was never made to be king. Plus, his duties to the Seven, hopefully far in the future, would probably end his life. Hopefully very far in the future.

Emma chuckled and patted Dage's flat stomach. "You keep trying, but nobody wants to be the king."

"Humph," Dage muttered, his gaze cutting to Quade.

Quade gave a slight shake of his head. This was not the place to discuss the Seven or the Realm's untenable position. It would greatly bother him if he became enemies with these relatives he'd just discovered, but his vow to the Seven and their duties was absolute. Even if the Realm declared war on them.

Dage's eyes turned a deep silver, just as Jacer's used to do. "Yet people keep forgetting that I am the king."

Quade felt for the male. Now that the Seven had inducted Garrett, a nephew Dage had no doubt helped to raise and train, the king was in the middle of a mess. As king, he owed the other species and members of the Realm his allegiance, and he did not owe the Seven anything. Especially since they might be a threat to the world at large. "You wish to talk now?"

Dage shook his head. "Tomorrow will be soon enough. You might want to take a shower first."

Quick footsteps came down the hall, and a tall boy of about six years old skidded into the room. "Dad? Can I stay the night with Uncle Garrett? We're in the middle of a chess tournament, and we're even." The kid had black hair, blue eyes, and huge hands. It took only one look at him to see that he was definitely the king's son.

Dage straightened. "What are you still doing up?"

The kid rolled his eyes. "Beating Uncle Garrett at chess." He bounced back on dark tennis shoes. "Please?"

Emma moved forward and patted a cowlick above the boy's ear. "Hunter? This is your Uncle Quade and Aunt Haven."

Apparently, the queen thought the mating a foregone conclusion, although that couldn't happen. Could it? Still, Ronan had mated, which was an immense shock. Amusement took Quade when the kid moved toward the bed, taking a good look at Haven for the first time. His small shoulders went back. "Who hurt you?"

Oh, definitely the king's kid.

Haven blinked. "It's a long story."

The kid lowered his chin, and power emanated from him in waves. "Have you been avenged? I will help."

Haven's smile showed delight. "You're sweet, but I'm a Fae-demon blend, my new friend. I can avenge myself."

The kid tilted his head to the side, studied her, and then turned to shake Quade's hand. "You took care of her?" Definitely a Kayrs male.

"Yes." Quade solemnly shook his hand. "Hunter?" he asked.

"After my father, Hunter Garrett Kayrs," Dage affirmed. "Garrett is named after him as well. One of my brothers is named Jase."

The name slid to Quade's gut and punched. These were Jacer's descendants. His chest warmed with pleasure this time. "It's a pleasure, Hunter."

The kid had a good handshake. "Nobody is named after you because we didn't know you existed." The kid's expression turned earnest, and he leaned in as if confiding a secret. "But don't worry. Now that we know you're around, I'm sure somebody will have a little Quade. It'd be a cool girl's name."

Quade smiled, taken with the guy. "Thanks. Once you're king, you can make everybody use my name."

The boy snorted. "Ha. I'm a scientist and a soldier, not a king. Uncle Garrett will be king someday, when Dad decides to take a break, and everybody knows it."

Garrett was one of the Seven. How could he do both?

Hunter turned back to his parents. "So, can I hang with Garrett? Just for the night?"

Emma nodded. "Sure. Just don't lose. He gloats when he wins too much."

The boy made a happy hop toward the door. "I know. When Hope beat him last month, he pouted all day. Didn't even want to train outside for a while, and it was snowing." He shook his head and ran out the door.

"Hope?" Haven asked, tentatively.

All eyes in the room returned to her.

Dage stiffened, his face going blank. "Yes, Hope. Why?"

Haven swallowed and looked toward Quade, obviously seeking reassurance.

He stood, moving to her side. "Why do you ask?"

She eyed him and then looked back at the king. "Is Hope a cute little girl with blue eyes and pigtails?"

Emma's smile disappeared and Dage looked more menacing than ever. "Yes. Why?" he asked.

Quade's shoulders kicked back.

Haven's chin lifted, and she faced the king squarely. "I think I've met her. She contacted me through an online chat."

"Damn it," Dage muttered. He looked over at Quade. "Well. I guess it begins, then."

Chapter Twenty-Two

Haven let the soothing *beep, beep, beep* of the machines calm her breathing. The queen had ordered everyone out of the room, saying it was past midnight and her patient needed sleep. It was nice to have a moment to herself. The window to the right of the bed was unshaded, giving a beautiful view of the snow and the frozen lake outside. Christmas lights twinkled from many of the trees, illuminating the armed guards who patrolled on a set schedule.

So she was back in the mountains somewhere. She hadn't thought to ask earlier.

A dim light was still on in the corner, and one of the buttons near her would turn it off if she decided she wanted darkness. Instead, she lifted her hand to stare at her fingers. They were burned and blistered. Taking a deep breath, she imagined blue-filled healing cells flowing through her system. In her mind, healing should be a blue color. Then, in front of her eyes, her thumb slowly healed, the burn turning from red to pink to a healthy peach color.

Wow. Just wow.

Her eyelids fluttered shut, and exhaustion took her. *Within seconds, she was flying through time and space, flowing through places she'd never seen. It was like when she used to visit Quade but her travel was faster somehow. She panicked, trying to control the flight as she'd learned to do.*

Nothing.

She was thrown through portal after portal, through ice and heat and something wet. She shut her eyes and tried to concentrate.

There was nothing to grab onto.

Then there was light. She landed on a ball of wax, stuck, and then was sucked up through the yellow sky. She tried to grab on, tried to focus the way she'd done before, but Quade's voice was missing. There was no anchor. She rolled out of another portal and smashed into a tree, a slim one, so she grabbed on with both arms.

Resting her head against bark that smelled like licorice, she sucked in air, trying to get her bearings. "I am not here," she whispered, chanting the words several times. "Wake up, wake up, wake up."

The wind strengthened and shrieked around her, throwing leaves with sharp edges. One cut into her cheek. Pain spread through her face, and she pressed closer to the tree, which had started swaying dangerously. She should be able to control this.

The wind lifted her legs, pulling so hard her shoulder popped. She cried out, her hands flailing, as she was dragged up and out. Over and over, spinning, she tumbled through darkness as if going the wrong way. The force continued to haul her around with no mercy.

Finally, she landed on her back on the rock where she'd been before—during the last dream. Hard.

Gasping like a landed trout, she turned to stare up at the reddish sky. The rock was warm and felt steady, so she took several precious moments to regain her breath, which had been knocked out of her lungs. The air smelled like sulfur and something else. An odd smell. Lemons? But not fresh ones. Moldy lemons.

The scent made her gag.

She forced herself to sit. The shadows between the red trees had darkened. Was it nighttime here? She flattened her hands to feel the warmth. The rock was ten or so feet across and round with jagged edges. She inched toward the end and looked down. Way down. She could only see mist and air. She gulped and crab walked back to the middle of the rock. What if she fell?

Could she die in this weird world while sleeping safely back in that hospital bed? If she could get cut or injured, as she'd been before, it made sense that she could die, too.

She closed her eyes and tried to force herself awake.

Laughter rumbled, and she jerked, opening her eyes. The bluish portal swirled again by the trees. The wind picked up.

"Come here, fairy," the voice yelled from way beyond the portal. A male voice. Strong and hoarse.

The hair on the back of her neck stood up. "Who are you?" she yelled into the void.

The wind caught her as if it had hands, pushing her toward the edge. She fought but moved forward anyway, inch by inch. She could either jump toward the void or drop into all of that mist. Her nails dug into the rock, and she screamed, shutting her eyes.

"Fairy. Wake up." A small hand shook her arm from far away.

She turned at the last second and jumped into the mist, hitting a portal and springing wildly away. There wasn't any sense of control, and she struggled, trying to stop herself. She slammed up against a stone wall and cried out, waking up.

"Nightmare?" A little girl bounced on her bed, shaking her arm.

Haven blinked and sat up, pushing hair out of her face. "Yes," she gasped, her ears ringing from that collision with the wall. Where had she been? Had it just been luck that she'd hit a portal when she'd jumped into the mist? Why had the portal led to a damn wall? Her hands shook, so she slipped them beneath the covers. Sweat dotted her lip, and she brushed it off on the blanket. The smell of strawberries wafted around her. Had somebody washed her hair? Made sense. She focused. "Hi."

"Hi." The girl smiled, revealing a gap in her front teeth. "That was a bad dream. I have them sometimes, too. Are you okay?"

No. Not at all. Haven swallowed. "Yes, thank you." She had to get out of there, but where could she go? She couldn't avoid sleep forever.

Hope patted her blanket. "I knew you were my fairy and were good."

Haven's hands shook. "Shouldn't you be in bed?" It was a dumb question, but she was finding it hard to concentrate. Her head was starting to pound.

"Yep." Hope nodded, her blue eyes twinkling. "Mama said I could stay with Uncle Garrett and my cousin Hunter tonight in the main lodge, where Uncle Garrett has a suite, and they both fell asleep watching a movie. Hunter was cranky because Garrett won at chess."

"Are we in the main lodge now?" Haven tried to keep the room from spinning around. It didn't make sense that the child could leave the building with all of those soldiers outside.

"Yep. You're on the main floor and the suites are up those stairs." Hope leaned toward her. "Cool eyes."

"Thanks." Haven liked not wearing the contact with other people, for the first time ever.

Hope nodded. "My Aunt Mercy, who mated my Uncle Logan, is a fairy, too. She has one green eye and one blue one. Very pretty."

Haven straightened. "Is that normal for a Fae?"

"Yep. Also, demons have black eyes, which is probably why one of your eyes is black. You're a little bit demon. Not a lot. Kinda like me." Hope rocked back and forth. "I'm a little bit vampire and a whole lot of prophet, too. But we don't talk about all of that yet because I'm not old enough." She pulled Haven's nearly healed hand out from under the covers, her grip surprisingly strong. "I need your help."

It was difficult to keep up with the switch in topics. "Sure. What can I do?"

Hope sighed. "I need to get back to my dream worlds. Can you help me?"

Absolutely not. Dream worlds held monsters and stone walls that could cause concussions. Or worse. Haven's damn head still ached. "Dream worlds? Have you traveled other places in dreams, too?"

Hope nodded. "Yes. Not exactly like you have, but there is one world I got to visit, and my book is there. Can you help me get back there?"

"I don't know how." Haven gave the little girl the truth. "I only had a little bit of control in those dream worlds, as you call them. I'd go from place to place and end up wherever the compulsion wanted me to. A couple of times, I thought I heard Quade, and I tried to twist in his direction." Now she had no control. None whatsoever. "There are things out there that can hurt you, Hope. Maybe you shouldn't go into the dream world."

Hope sighed. "You sound like a grown-up."

Heavy footsteps sounded down the hallway, and Quade strode in with another man just as tall. The second guy had the same jawline and facial structure as Quade.

"There you are," the other guy said, plucking Hope off the bed. "Your mom would kill me if I lost you." He tickled the little girl, and she giggled, swatting him. He paused. "Hi. I'm Garrett."

"Hi." Haven wasn't going to be able to keep all these huge, way too sexy males straight. Most of them seemed to be related to Quade, and the Kayrs genes ran strong and masculine, no question about it. "I'm not sure how you're related to everyone."

Garrett winked, his gray eyes an odd metallic hue. "Quade is my great-great-uncle. Older than dirt. You should probably find somebody younger than this old man. Just sayin'."

Quade nudged him in the side. "Go back to playing with the kids, young Kayrs."

How cute. Garrett had ticked him off. Haven forced a smile, even though she wanted to crawl under the covers completely and just yell at the universe to leave her alone. Or maybe cry a little, but she'd done enough of that. She wasn't usually a crier.

"Fair enough." Garrett swung the little girl onto his shoulders.

Hope grinned at Quade. "There's mint-chip ice cream in the kitchen. I'm thinkin' you'd like it."

Quade blinked. "Like toothpaste?"

"Better," Hope whispered.

Man, the girl must be psychic. Haven studied her.

Garrett grinned and headed for the door.

Hope turned at the last minute, right before Garrett had to duck to get through. "I hope you keep Ulric from coming here."

Quade jerked and partially turned. "I tried, sweetheart. How do you know about Ulric?" he asked.

Garrett paused, looking up at his niece. "Hope?"

The girl shrugged. "Fate tells me stuff. And I wasn't talkin' to you, Uncle Quade. I was talkin' to my fairy." She patted Garrett's head. "Giddyup." The two disappeared down the hallway.

"Well." Quade moved to the bed and studied her face. "We'll have to follow up on that later, right?" Concern and a darker look glimmered in his immortal eyes.

She nodded. "Thank you for saving me from the pastor and his church." Without Quade, she would've burned to death.

"Always." He took her good hand. "I don't know how to say this, but your father—"

"He wasn't my father." She shoved down emotion until she could deal with it when she was alone. "Dead?"

Quade nodded.

She should feel something, shouldn't she? "My mother? I mean, Allison?"

"Safe house for now," Quade said. "We think she saw the Cyst or vampires, and she needs to promise to keep that a secret. Right now, she's demanding to see you to make sure you're all right, and I'm not ready to appease her."

Haven shuddered. She didn't have time to worry about Allison right now.

Quade couldn't answer the main question plaguing her. Why was she traveling through worlds again, and where did that swirling blue portal go? She couldn't go to sleep again until she discovered the answers.

He studied her, his gaze intense. "You are all right?"

"Not really." She had to trust somebody in this crazy new world, and since he'd actually traveled through portals, maybe he could help. So she told him everything, hoping against hope that he'd have words of wisdom. When she'd finished, his jaw was hard and his eyes stone-cold.

"Bloody hell," he muttered.

Wonderful.

Chapter Twenty-Three

"Well. This is odd," Ronan said, sitting next to Quade in what was called a conference room. It was well past midnight, and the brothers faced two other brothers across an ancient oak table. Dage and Talen Kayrs—their great-nephews.

Quade had trouble keeping his gaze off Talen.

Ronan nodded. "I know. Spitting image of Jacer."

"I wish he were here right now," Quade muttered. He focused on the king. "Jacer was the calm and rational one. He'd know the right thing to say."

A hint of a smile played on Dage's lips. "Just like you, Talen. Calm and rational."

Talen's golden eyes glittered. "Yep. That's me."

The soldier looked like he'd rather just shoot them both and get back to bed. But Quade had to admire how he flanked his brother.

Dage cleared his throat. "I'm sorry about Jacer. I can't imagine losing a brother. Not at all."

Quade tilted his head in acknowledgment. "Thank you for treating my mate. She's doing much better, thanks to your mate." Could this be any more stilted or awkward? He hadn't been around people in so long, he sat back and let Ronan take the lead. The tension in the small room was making his fist ache to punch somebody, and these guys were family. Possibly enemies, but still family.

"Good," Dage said. "I heard your conversation with Haven about her moving through portals. There isn't much doubt she's being pulled toward Ulric."

Quade stiffened and his ears grew hot. "How did you hear my private conversation?"

The king's eyebrows lifted. "I have the room bugged."

Quade's chest filled. He did not understand the language, but he got the gist. The existence of Ulric was a secret, damn it. "You were eavesdropping."

"Expertly," Talen said, his smile more threat than pleasantry.

Quade growled. While he could understand their need to gain knowledge, especially since the Seven had been a secret for so long, he did not appreciate his mate being used in such a way. The king had stepped too far into Quade's business. "The bugs will be removed." As soon as he figured out what bugs were. If they were really bugs that somehow had learned to record and communicate, he would step on them all.

"Back to Ulric," Dage muttered.

Ronan looked toward the door. "If we're discussing Seven business, shouldn't Garrett be here?"

"My son is busy," Talen drawled, anger now glinting in those primal eyes.

Ah. Couldn't blame the male. Quade wouldn't want his kid going through the Seven ritual—either of the rituals. The one to become a Seven or the one to end it all. "Isn't that Garrett's decision?"

Talen angled his head toward Quade. "No. My son is none of your business."

"Your son is now my brother," Quade returned, his chest heating. "Whether you like it or not." The second Garrett had survived the ritual; his torso had been forged, he'd become a brother, even if Quade had been worlds away at the time. This was all so weird. He looked at Ronan. "You couldn't find someone outside the family to join the Seven?"

"Amen," Talen muttered.

Ronan sighed. "No. Only ten percent of males who tried the ordeal survived, as you know; it turns out certain bloodlines have a better chance. A much better chance." He leaned toward Quade. "Science is a whole new thing—you won't believe it all." He cleared his throat. "Garrett made his own choice."

Talen crossed his arms. "Since you're here, Quade, I'm assuming Ulric is also back home and tucked in with his people?"

Quade glanced sideways at Ronan. Wait a minute. Had Dage already known about Ulric and the Seven rituals?

Ronan's jaw hardened. "We had to share some of the information, but so far, we've kept it to the vampires. The other nations don't know, right?"

Dage's jaw flexed. "Right. However, I'm King of the Realm, which includes many other nations. It goes against our agreements and treaties for me to keep such information from the heads of the other nations, some of which are family to me. To you, too."

Quade shook his head. He had been gone a long time, but the existence of the Seven was to have remained secret. The changing of the rules did not sit well with him.

Talen leaned forward. "What happens once you're all in the same place?"

So the vampires didn't know the details.

Ronan spoke first. "Our first duty is to take out Ulric, whose goal is to kill all enhanced females. That much you already know. I don't need to remind you that both of your mates are enhanced females, do I?"

The atmosphere heated as if a fire had been lit all around the room.

Talen's chin lowered. "Is that a threat?"

"Of course not," Ronan countered. "It's a fact. We've told you this about Ulric."

"Yet you haven't given us enough details," Talen said, his voice a low growl. "If he's an enemy, and he's here, we don't need your help taking him out."

Aye, Quade liked these new family members. A lot. Even though they used bugs to listen in on his conversations. "You don't understand the reality of who Ulric is and who we've become," he said softly. "The ritual of the Seven bonded us in blood and bone, by misusing the laws of the world in a way we cannot explain. Ulric did it first, using the blood and bone of enhanced women to shield his entire body."

"It's called physics these days," Ronan told him. "Fascinating stuff."

His brother was getting sarcastic, which meant punches would soon follow. Quade wouldn't mind a good fight. He continued, "Ulric cannot be killed from the outside. His body, his entire body, is impenetrable."

"Then how do we kill him?" Dage growled.

"*You* don't," Ronan said simply. "We have the knowledge to end him, and soon we'll have the power. That's all I can tell you."

For a moment, Quade thought Talen would lunge across the table. He braced his legs just in case.

Dage held up a hand, halting his brother. Temporarily, anyway. "The repercussions of what you've done, and the laws of physics you've fucked with, are already creating ripples."

Probably true.

Talen focused on Quade. "Can you teleport?"

"No," Quade admitted. "Not since I've returned, but I assume the difference in what you call atmosphere and something called gravity might have something to do with it. My ability will return."

"And you?" Talen asked Ronan.

"No. Not since I returned and was in a coma for seven years. But I, too, will regain my ability."

Dage crossed his arms, mirroring Talen's pose. "Oh yeah? Well, guess what, assholes? I can't teleport any longer either. No demon or hybrid on this earth who could teleport before can do so now."

Quade sat back. "What are you saying?"

"I'm saying that whatever happened to the world you concocted affected this one," Dage said, his silver eyes morphing to blue.

"When you messed with laws you never should've messed with, you caused more problems they even we understand."

Quade looked at Ronan.

Ronan's nostrils flared. "Our abilities wouldn't have changed. So, the paths have. There used to be paths we used and now we can't." He shook his head. "I don't understand the physics of it, but we'll get Promise Williams on it right away."

Dage's glare grew even harder. "I spoke with the Fae leader, and according to her, the Fae can't teleport off this world or in it any longer. That ability is gone for all of us." He leaned forward, his gaze intense. "Now. Demons could teleport from one spot to another on this planet only. Fae could go to other places, and they're the only ones who could. So guess what I have in my infirmary. Right now?"

Quade froze.

Talen answered first. "Well, King, you have a Fae-demon hybrid. The only one, as far as we know, to ever exist. If anybody can fix this, it's going to be somebody with the ability to teleport on this world *and* out of here. That's who you have."

Quade's fangs elongated. Dage had it all wrong. "The person in your infirmary is my mate. No way in hell do you have her." Although he hadn't mated her, her safety was on him.

Dage met his gaze full on. "Not true, and you know it. However, as you might remember, mates often end up with each other's gifts."

"Your point?" Quade snarled.

"His point?" Talen leaned back. "One of you is going to solve this problem. Right now, she's our best bet. You want to be the one? Stop dicking around and mate her."

The king held up a hand. "Think of it a different way, perhaps."

Quade's chin lowered. He didn't give a fuck that these guys were family. He was about to take Talen down and see if Jacer's descendants had learned to fight or not. "In which way?" he growled.

Dage's eyes, although hard, held a sympathetic light that actually pissed Quade off more. "I listened to your conversation. Haven said she's being pulled through dimensions against her will, and she has no control. She has to sleep at some point. Even immortals can't go long without sleep."

Quade's jaw ached from grinding his teeth. "Your point?"

The king exhaled. "You were always able to control your jumps here on earth. Right?"

Quade nodded.

"So mate her, get her gifts, and maybe you can go off world and kill Ulric," Dage said. "At the very least, mate her and give her the ability to control her jumps before she ends up on Ulric's world or wherever those damn portals go."

A part of Quade had hoped the portals were all gone. That there was no way he'd have to leave again, ever. But now that the portals had hold of Haven, now that she was being pulled, probably toward Ulric, he had no choice.

Ronan turned toward him. "If you mate her, you might be able to go with her when she's pulled."

Quade's chest heated. A mate. "She'll be left alone when—"

Ronan nodded, cutting off the rest of Quade's sentence.

"When what?" Talen snapped.

When Quade gave his life at the end, as he'd vowed to do. As the entire Seven had vowed to do. He'd discuss the rest of this later with his brother, when there weren't snarling relatives or bugs around. He pushed his chair back and stood. "I need to go for a run. I will think. While I am running and thinking, you will get rid of the bugs."

"Will we?" Talen drawled.

"Yes," Quade snapped, bombarded by too many emotions to think clearly. "I must go." He strode for the door.

"Hey, Great-Uncle," Talen murmured. "If you want to spar, we have a hell of a gym."

At the moment, Quade wasn't sure he'd leave a sparring partner with his head still attached to his body. "I will return." With that, he exited the room, walked out of the lodge, and started to run in the snow along the lake. As fast as he could.

Mating Haven? Every time he looked at one of her paintings, he saw her soul. Her clean, good, kind, strong soul. He knew his emotions were ruling his mind, and he couldn't let that happen.

Mating seemed the only logical solution to the problem. Now, to convince her of that fact.

Chapter Twenty-Four

After her second day in the hospital room, Haven was healed. Head to toe, no burns, bruises, or aches. While she was exhausted from refusing to sleep, her body felt whole again. It was astonishing that she'd had this ability her entire life and had only used it accidentally the one time. She looked at Quade as he escorted her up the stairs to his suite after a quiet dinner in her room. He hadn't eaten very much. "Do you remember bumblebees?" she asked, her healthy body reacting to his nearness. The guy smelled so damn good.

He nodded, his gaze preoccupied. "Aye."

"They say, scientists that is, that bees are too heavy for their wings to be able to hold them aloft. But bees don't know that."

He led her down a wide hallway with thick wooden polished floorboards. "Your point?"

She shrugged. "I'm just wondering what other gifts or abilities I have that I've never used. Besides healing myself, that is." She looked up at him when he stopped in front of a tall oak door. "How much did your blood help me?"

He finally focused on her. "Quite a lot, according to the queen. Ordinarily, burns like that would take at least a week to heal, even for the most seasoned warrior. There's something odd about my blood. Makes sense, really."

She shifted her feet, her skin tingling. Why was he acting so distant? Did he plan to leave her here? It was a nice place, but it was time to go figure out her problems on her own—as usual. "You said Allison is safe. Where is she?"

"She was taken to a safe house and will remain there until we know the danger has passed and that she'll agree to stay silent," he said.

Then Haven had done her duty. She shoved aside her emotions for now. "I need to paint, Quade. Or at least draw."

"I thought you might." He pushed open the door and gestured her inside a comfortable-looking suite with a living area, stone fireplace, kitchen, and three doorways. He pointed. "Guest bathroom, master bedroom, and this." Taking her hand, he led her beyond a deep sofa to the third door and opened it.

The smell of oil hit her first, followed by turpentine. She stepped inside a room that had been converted to a painting studio. A wide window across the entire north wall let in a perfect amount of light. Canvases, paints, and brushes had been lined up on a well-worn table in the corner, while sheets had been taped down to protect the floor. She moved toward the far wall, where several of her finished paintings had been stacked. "How?"

Irritation crawled across Quade's expression. "The king raided your storage unit outside of Portland and had your art brought here." He cleared his throat. "I spent much of the day going through the paintings, and I recognize a few of the places you painted." His voice deepened. "You have incredible talent."

She shared his irritation. "They found my storage unit and just took my paintings? How rude of them."

"Amen to that."

She turned around, feeling small and vulnerable surrounded by the white canvases and sheets. Her body was healthy, but the lack of sleep was throwing her off-kilter. "I haven't agreed to stay here, Quade."

No expression indicated his feelings. "I am aware of that fact. But staying here makes sense. You still have a shifter on your scent, and while the pastor is dead, we don't know how many people in his flock have committed themselves to finishing what he started. If he believed he was sanctioned by God to this duty, this crazy task of ridding you of evil, then they probably are true believers, too. I've seen religious obsession before. Morons." Quade held up his palm. "And there is this."

The marking drew her somehow. Warmth spiraled through her belly, surprising her. They'd grown closer as they'd run away from trouble, but now he had his brother. His family. She was a Fae-demon who didn't know how to be a Fae-demon. Didn't even know what that meant. The only thing she knew was that all of the women, females, she'd met here so far, including Emma and her sister, were beyond brilliant. She hadn't even finished high school. "You could probably be the king if you wanted, Quade."

He exhaled, his gaze roving over her face, his eyes softening. "My path is a different one, sweetling. Even if I weren't bound by my Seven vows, I do not have the temperament to be king. I'm a soldier." He glanced at the snowy, moonlit lake outside. "I must ask you a question."

Her breath caught all funny in her chest. "What?"

"Can you awaken yourself when you're traveling through the dream worlds? Have you tried?"

She coughed, hiding the heat flushing up into her face. What had she expected? A mating offer, because he'd discovered he'd fallen in love the last week? God, she was a moron. She wasn't even in love herself. Sure, she liked him and wanted him. A lot. But that wasn't love. So why was she feeling disappointed in his question? "Yes," she answered, hurriedly. "I think I did the first time, but last night, I couldn't."

He walked past her to the window, facing out. The moonlight illuminated him, showing his power and his strength. Long muscles lined his back and stretched down his legs. He'd filled out since returning to this planet and eating somewhat regularly. "Have you slept since last time?"

"No." Her face heated. "I'm thinking Fae-demons don't need as much sleep as humans."

"You do not." He turned around. Framed in the window with the moon shining over the lake, he looked immortal. Unreal and handsome and primal. Sexy. "You will need sleep soon."

A pit opened up in her stomach. The idea of going back through those jumbled worlds, of finally seeing what was pulling her there, sent anxiety through every nerve. "I know."

His dark eyebrows lowered. "I'm not much for talking."

The guy looked so earnest, she hid a smile. "Okay."

"My brother, Jacer? He talked a lot. Easily." Quade scrubbed a rough hand through his thick hair, ruffling the mass. "I was always more one for action, and words elude me. Even more so here and now when half of the words and all of the idioms do not make sense."

Where was he going with this? "You're catching on quickly." Her head ached from lack of sleep, but she could handle a little pain.

"Thank you." He slid his hands into his faded jeans, his thumbs out. "I can talk to you. Well, more than most."

Special. Without trying to, he made her feel special in this crappy world. She warmed and, this time, she let her smile show. "I'm glad."

He shuffled his feet, looking big and wide and strong—like one of those superheroes in his borrowed jeans. "Only one out of ten males who undertook the ritual to become one of the Seven survived."

Her head jerked. Those were horrible odds. "Did you know that fact before or after you underwent the ritual?"

"Before." He waved the question away. "Death was always expected. During the ritual, then during the horrific jump though time and space and worlds to reach the one where I kept vigil, and finally during the centuries I endured to keep Ulric imprisoned." Quade's eyes took on a faraway look for just a moment before his focus returned to her. "It was unthinkable that I would return home, but even so, I vowed to give my life in the last ritual. The one that destroys Ulric for good—and saves countless others."

It was nice he was confiding in her, but she was having trouble understanding his reason for doing so. Maybe he needed reassurance? Tough guys wouldn't seek that from other tough guys like his brother. "Well, think about it this way. You didn't die during the ritual, during the jump through worlds, or during your time keeping Ulric from escaping. Maybe you won't die during the final ritual." She kept her voice light, but the thought of his dying, really actually dying for good, passed a heavy shadow over her.

His lips tipped up in a rueful smile. "That is doubtful, but I appreciate the hopeful sentiment. My point is that any mate I take would be left alone for eternity after my death. Mating is forever. Any mated immortal who touches another has a horrible reaction like an allergy."

That was just freaking weird. Even so, she got it. She held up a hand. "I'm well aware you don't want to mate, and I'm not asking for that." Now sex, she wouldn't mind. It had been a long time, she was feeling a lot of tension, and he was the hottest thing she'd ever seen. Plus, she liked him. A lot. Probably too much, but sex with him would be worth the emotional hit. "You don't need to worry about mating with me, Quade. I'm not a forever type, anyway."

"I am not good with words," he muttered. He exhaled. "I like you."

Delight bubbled through her as if she was a teenager with a crush, and she didn't even try to quash it. Such an unfamiliar feeling. She chuckled. "I like you, too."

He ducked his head, his lips twisting. "Yeah, about that. You know only a part of me, and I've been dizzy and not quite myself. I'm not usually so...congenial."

She couldn't help the laughter that burst out of her. "This has been you *congenial*? The last week?" She'd seen him kill everything from Kurjans to humans to deer. He was cranky, bossy, and often on such high alert that she felt the tension in her own bones.

"Yes." He scratched his neck. "I do not know how to be other than what I am."

Okay. She shook her head and leaned forward. "Quade? Are you trying to proposition me?" Man, he was cute. Also sweet.

"I am trying to warn you." The words burst out of him. "Give you what's called a heads-up nowadays."

A heads-up. If he got any cuter, she'd just jump him right here and now. "You're giving me a heads-up that you're who you are and I have not seen all of you."

"Exactly." Relief lightened his expression.

"I consider myself warned." She could just stare at him all day, but her hands were starting to twitch with the need to paint. Was he going to ask her out or not? Did immortals just date? Go to movies amongst the humans? Or was there some odd ritual she hadn't learned about yet? "Is there a reason you're warning me?" Maybe she should just ask *him* out. While their fling might be quick, it'd be explosive. He'd brought her to orgasm twice, easily, and they hadn't even had sex yet.

"Yes. Of course." His shoulders went back. "You need all of the truth before we mate."

She opened her mouth, but no sound emerged. Huh? What? Okay. What? "Mate?" she croaked. "Are you joking?"

"No." He nodded as if satisfied with a job well done. "Not joking. You know the truth. We shall mate tonight, then."

Again, no words. Her lips tried to form a couple, but no luck. She cleared her throat. "We are not mating." That word. The images it conjured had her breath squeezing in her chest and her thighs tightening. But this was a subject for her brain, not her body. Thank goodness. "Not a chance. No forever. But we can have right now," she added quickly.

"Oh." He ground a palm into one eye. "How I wish for the days of oxen and arrangements."

This was getting too odd. "Why don't we talk tomorrow?" She really needed to start painting.

"We are mating tonight," he said, dropping the hand.

"No, we are not."

"Yes, we are." He crossed his arms, looking pretty damn intent.

She shook her head. "This is nuts. Did you sustain a head injury? I mean, another one?"

"I do not think so." He rubbed his temple. "I have given this thought. All day. Mates take on each other's talents, and you need mine to survive traveling to your dream worlds and keep control in them. I might get yours and be able to accompany you. In addition, even though my survival is in question, I would like to leave children behind. Maybe have a time to know them."

"Whoa." She held up her hands and took several steps back. "Now wait a minute." They'd gone from liking each other to mating to children way too fast. "Quade. Come on."

"Think about it. You are terrified to sleep, and even if you stay awake for a couple of nights, at some point you will succumb. Do you believe you'll survive your next journey?" His voice roughened and he held up his palm again. "I do not know about fate, but this mark means something. You saved me and I will save you."

"Quade—"

"Think about it." Long strides ate up the space between him.

His masculine scent washed over her a second before the heat from his body enveloped her. Her knees wobbled.

She swallowed.

Moving slowly, he lifted her chin with one knuckle until her gaze met his unfathomable one. He leaned down and brushed her mouth with a soft kiss.

Yearning ran through her faster than a thought.

He released her, satisfaction glittering in his eyes. "When you have finished, you will reach the same conclusion as I. We will be mated." He turned and strode to the doorway. "I'll give you this night." Then he was gone.

She swallowed, her mind spinning. Almost in a dream, she moved for the nearest paintbrush.

Mate?

Chapter Twenty-Five

"And she's a fairy and a demon and she's my new friend." Hope wiped jelly off her mouth and ducked her head to catch the peanut butter from her sandwich before it fell on her jeans. Red and green lights surrounded the Santa display across the kitchen counter, and Christmas music played from speakers she couldn't see.

Her mama looked up from a laptop on the other side of the island. "I only met her briefly. She's just out of the hospital and apparently she needs to go paint or something." Twinkling lights from the trees lining the road to the lake glittered across her white T-shirt. "Although I'm quite curious about the places she has been—in her head. I wonder if it's like my dream world or yours?"

"Yours blew up," Paxton reminded Hope's mom.

Her mom grinned. "I'm well aware of that, and I'm hoping Hope stays out of hers until she's a grown-up."

Paxton drank down all of his milk and then picked up his second sandwich. He had another bruise on his neck, and when Hope's mama had taken a look at it, her blue eyes were worried. "Yeah. That's a good idea," he agreed.

Hope huffed out air. Paxton always took her mama's side, but that was probably because he missed his own mama so much. She was a demon who'd died in the last war, and his dad, a vampire, didn't seem to be around much, and he never, ever smiled.

The front door opened and soon Hope's daddy walked through the living room to the kitchen. He wore dark pants and a T-shirt and had a gun strapped to his leg.

"Zane." Her mama raised her head for a kiss. "Why are you armed?"

"Janie Belle," Hope's daddy said, kissing her mama. "I was at Realm headquarters and just walked back." His eyes twinkled as he winked at Hope. "The lake is frozen thick enough to skate, kids. Maybe later today?"

Paxton hopped on his chair. "That'd be awesome, Zane." He stumbled over the name because he always wanted to add a "King" before Zane since her dad was the king of the demon nation, but he didn't like to be called King.

Her dad grabbed Hope and swung her around, making her giggle. She put her hands on his shoulders, laughing.

"Cutie?" He set her gently down and then dropped to his haunches so they were eye to eye, even though she was on a tall stool. Her daddy was so big. "Honey? I was at the Realm and right now, all of us who can teleport are unable to do so." His green eyes sizzled. "I have to ask, are you visiting that dream world you're not supposed to go to at night?"

She pouted. Why couldn't she visit her dream world and her Kurjan friend Drake? "You and Mama had a dream world and you saved this world," she reminded him. Why did grown-ups always forget the important stuff?

"I know, sweetheart." Her daddy patted her knees. "But that wasn't the question I asked you."

She rolled her eyes and sighed. Seriously. Grown-ups. "No, I can't get into the dream world." She looked over at her mama, who should understand because she'd had dream worlds too when she was young. "My book is in there. I have to get back."

Her mama frowned. "What does this mean?"

Her daddy stood. "Nobody knows. But we'll figure it out." He turned to Paxton. "I heard you did an amazing job in archery the other day."

Paxton puffed up like he'd been blown full of air like a balloon. "Thank you."

Her daddy's face stayed the same but his eyes narrowed. "What happened to your neck?"

Paxton turned red and rubbed the bruise beneath his jaw. "I was playing with shifters, and they're faster than me. Lions."

Hope frowned. "You said it was demon kids."

"Both," Paxton said, putting the rest of his sandwich on the plate. "I'm fine, Zane."

Her dad rubbed his jaw, which had a shadow. "If anybody hurts you, I want to know. Your dad has been...sad since your mom died, right?"

"We all are," Paxton said, looking at his plate.

Her dad looked at her mom and then back. "Is your dad maybe having a rough time of it? Maybe taking it out on you, accidentally?"

"No," Paxton said, even his ears turning red. "I'm just clumsy and not good at training." His phone buzzed from his pocket, and he almost jumped out of his chair. "I hafta go. My dad is back." He jumped off the stool and all but ran to the door. "Thanks for lunch." He was out into the snow in a second.

Hope watched him go. Wow. That was fast.

"Hope?" her mama asked. "Has Paxton said anything to you about his dad?"

"No," Hope said, her stomach starting to hurt. A daddy wouldn't hit his own kid, would he? That didn't make sense.

Her dad took a phone from his back pocket and pressed a speed dial number before putting it against his ear. "Max? Yeah. I want full surveillance on Paxton Phoenix, the eight-year-old? On him and his dad, especially." Her dad waited and listened. "I'm aware he's a vampire. If he so much as snaps at that kid, I want to know about it. Right." He slid the phone back into his pocket.

Janie's eyebrows rose. "You're talking about a vampire soldier, not a demon. Why don't I call my dad?"

Zane shook his head. "Talen has enough to deal with right now, and Max will clue him in, anyway. Paxton's mom was a demoness, and her son is my responsibility. The kid is a little clumsy and still learning to train, so he might be telling the truth. Or he might not. I will find out."

Hope nudged the rest of her sandwich away. Pax had tripped and fallen over nothing the other day, so she knew he was clumsy, but he was getting a lot faster and stronger. She also knew he didn't like his dad much. She reached for her daddy and another hug. They were gonna help Pax, no matter what.

* * * *

Quade spent the entire night and most of the next day educating himself about modern technology. The weapons room had been his first stop, and he'd enjoyed shooting lasers into targets. The Realm had every kind of weapon imaginable, but even after spending time with automatic weapons, he felt more secure with a knife in his boot.

For several hours, he'd learned about the status of the various species on Earth. So far, only the vampire and the demon leaders were aware of the existence of the Seven, and neither seemed particularly pleased about the situation. If the witch or shifter nations found out about them, there might be conflict. Okay. There would definitely be conflict. That was why it had been so important to keep the secret.

It was out now.

The marking on his palm had pounded for hours, and as much as he tried to ignore it, his thoughts wandered to Haven often. Way too often. He'd given her enough time to make a decision.

Ronan finally caught up to him when he was sitting on a thick wooden bench, looking at the darkening sky over the lake. Little lights came to life along all of the trees. "Hey," Ronan greeted him as he sat. "You haven't slept in twenty-four hours, and don't give me bullshit that you don't need it. I remember waking up back here and trying to get my bearings. Sleep and protein helped."

Quade eyed the thick ice on the lake. The cloud cover was thin but enough to waft snowflakes down. His other side, where Jacer should be, felt cold. "There's too much to learn to sleep." He hadn't conquered computers or the history of the world so far, although he was feeling marginally better and more centered.

Ronan leaned back and kicked his legs out, scuffing up snow. He took a deep drink of what smelled like whiskey and then handed over a large bottle. A very large one. "We need to get to Seven headquarters as soon as possible. If Ulric's world has imploded and he's here, we have work to do. If it hasn't, it will, and we need to get ready."

"Affirmative." Quade took several deep pulls of the alcohol, and warmth infused him. He coughed and looked at his brother. "Has the king agreed?"

"No. They want us to stay here." Anticipation lit Ronan's eyes, as he took the bottle and drank. "We might need to make a break for it."

Quade grinned, his blood speeding up. "Teach this younger generation that technology has flaws?"

"Yes." Ronan chuckled, handing the booze back. "While I miss the ability to teleport, we won wars without technology. In ways these descendants can't imagine."

Quade's chest warmed, and he took several more drinks, letting the liquid numb him. Sitting with his brother, discussing strategy, brought him finally all the way home. He'd never thought to see Ronan again, and here they were. It felt right. "For the first time in so long, I have hope. A little. Not a lot." He snorted.

Ronan chuckled. "Yeah. I get that. The final ritual is pretty daunting, but it could be years away. Why not enjoy the now?"

"And prepare," Quade said quietly.

Ronan lost his amused look. "Definitely. So, in that vein, I was thinking."

"Always a dangerous proposition," Quade drawled.

The smile flashed again and then disappeared. "I know you. I know what you have planned and why you're so hesitant to mate Haven."

Quade stiffened. "I'm hesitant because the final ritual will end in bloodshed and not a rose ceremony."

Ronan frowned and then shrugged. "No. You're hesitant because if you gain her ability and can jump through worlds, you might be able to jump to Ulric's. Even when you and I were maintaining our vigil over his bubble, we couldn't cross over from our worlds to his. Now you might have the chance."

Quade looked back toward the lake, which was now shrouded in darkness. "We have new weapons at our disposal. Devices we couldn't even imagine back then."

Ronan clapped him on the shoulder. Hard. "Ulric can't be killed from the outside. Only the blood of the three Keys has the poison necessary to stop his heart. Even then, we don't know how the final ritual works."

"Three Keys and the Lock," Quade murmured.

Ronan stiffened. "You've met Hope. The Lock."

"Yeah. She's cute and little and sweet." He shook his head. "If there's a way to keep her from participating in the ritual, from even having to be the Lock, shouldn't I take it? Take a bomb or laser weapon or something into Ulric's world?" If he did, he would not return, and Haven would be left a widow, alone, for centuries. "We took a vow, Ronan. I will satisfy it."

Ronan's head dropped. "We will both satisfy our vows, brother, but only when it comes time for the final ritual. Your dying in Ulric's world makes no sense, and besides, we can't take weapons when we teleport. We're strongest working together as the Seven, and we will plan together as always." He looked over, snow landing on his dark hair. "In the meantime, why not grab happiness with both hands right here and now?"

Quade nodded. "I have already decided to mate, yet I am sorry for the eternity she will be alone after I am gone." Perhaps there would be a good stretch of time before they found Ulric. "She's lonely already." Which was the absolute truth.

Ronan cleared his throat. "Well, okay. Here's the thing. There's now something called a virus, like an illness, that can be injected into a mate to negate the mating bond."

"Bullshit," Quade said, partially turning and scattering snow.

"It's true." Ronan held up a hand. "So far, the virus has only been employed on those whose mates died a long time ago. It has never been used in a mate whose partner is still alive. We don't know if it'd work under those circumstances."

Quade shook his head. "Why the difference?"

Ronan shrugged. "Nobody knows yet. Perhaps once a mate dies, and time goes by, the mating mark and chromosomal pairing disintegrates, making it possible for the virus to run its course. That's the queen's hypothesis, and it works for me."

What the hell were chromosomal pairs? Quade was starting to greatly dislike this new world. "So you are saying that if I die, Haven could one day mate another?"

"Yep." Ronan kicked back again, staring at the dark lake.

Somehow, that did not make Quade feel any better. He tipped back the rest of the alcohol, taking it all in and letting the warmth spread through him. Haven was his, damn it.

Chapter Twenty-Six

Haven swayed on her feet as she finished cleaning her brushes. Her eyes ached from being open too long, and her shoulders felt as if she'd been moving boulders all day. It had been at least twenty-four hours since she'd slept, and her body wanted to shut down.

"That's beautiful," Quade said, leaning against the doorjamb. Snow dusted his thick hair and dark T-shirt, molding the material to his hard-cut chest. A shadow covered his jaw, and his eyes had turned a deep aqua with a hint of more green than blue.

She didn't have the energy to be startled. How long had he been watching her? "Thank you." Turning, she stared critically at the oil painting of little Hope with her big blue eyes and cute pigtails. The girl was surrounded by pink trees, a wide beach, and a winding river with rocks in the middle. A green book was open on a rock, reflecting the sun.

"Where is that?" Quade murmured.

"I don't know." Haven set the brushes back into place. "Hope said she had a dream world, and my guess is that this might be it?"

He loped closer to the painting and studied the forest across from the beach. "The trees are lovely, but these shadows between them, are…"

"Ominous," Haven said. She shivered and rubbed her arms to warm up. "I know."

He moved to the next painting, which was of him standing in front of the window, this time shirtless. The scars across his heart were darkened, and his eyes had turned pure green, with no blue. Her body had hummed the entire time she'd been painting him, and sensual colors made up the background in swirls of deep red and blue with a splash of purple. Even now, as she looked at it, her heartbeat picked up, despite her exhaustion.

He partially turned to face her. "This is how you see me?"

As sexy and dangerous and strong? "Yes." Her chin lifted. "I'm not ready to mate." She probably wouldn't ever be. She didn't believe in forever...with anybody.

He finished the turn to face her squarely. "You need sleep."

"Yeah." She was half-asleep already, and denial didn't seem worth the effort. "I thought you might want to sleep with me." She'd been able to think about nothing else since painting his damn face. Every time he was near, and even when he wasn't, he seemed to fill her mind. Or maybe her body. Either way, she was tired of fighting it.

He tilted his head, his eyes nearly turning the color of the ones in the painting. The atmosphere swelled and heated. "Just sleep?"

She smiled and her face grew warm. "No. We're both consenting adults, and we're attracted to each other. You know as well as I do that we're going to act on that attraction again, so why not tonight?"

His gaze sharpened even as a small smile played across his generous mouth. The one she wanted on her again. "You make the situation sound so logical and planned." He ran a broad hand through his thick hair in a gesture she was becoming familiar with, even though she didn't know exactly what it meant. "You want me to keep this to myself." He held up his palm.

Her entire body heated this time, just from looking at the mating brand. "Yes. Definitely keep that to yourself." She still hadn't figured out how the thing worked, but she believed him that mating was forever. Arousal slid through her, and she tried to quell it. Unsuccessfully. "If you're next to me in bed, maybe you can awaken me if I get caught in the dream worlds again."

Was she really trying to talk him into sex? For Pete's sake. "Or not. Maybe it's a bad idea."

"Oh, it's definitely a good idea." He pushed off from the doorway and held out a hand for her.

Well. Okay then. Her knees wobbled a bit as she walked toward him. Because she was tired. Yeah. That was it. She slid her hand into his, rubbing her palm against the mating mark. Desire slammed through her so fast she partially bent at the waist.

"You are exhausted," he said, misinterpreting her reaction. Releasing her, he pivoted and swept her up.

She bounced once and settled against his rock-hard chest, desire blooming across every nerve inside her. This was too much.

He carried her through the suite to the bedroom, where he set her gently on her feet at the edge of a bed big enough for several people. Well, several humans. It was probably the exact right size for him. She looked up, unable to stop touching him. She sighed inside, where he couldn't hear, at finally allowing herself the freedom to run her palms across his chest and down to his abs, counting each one. Truly incredible. "I don't want you to think that I'm, well, too forward?" Had she ever been this awkward and turned on at the same time?

"I don't." He cupped the side of her face, the brand hot against her skin. "At some point, you will have to stop running from the inevitable. For the moment, I will humor you, but we will be mated. If you want to be logical about it, as it appears you do, mating me will give you skills to maneuver the dream worlds. Maybe even give me the skill to go in your place."

She shook her head. "Nothing is for sure."

He leaned down and kissed her nose, the muscles beneath her hands vibrating as he schooled himself to gentleness. "You will need to confront your fears, and I will help."

The words took a second to register and then she leaned back, her neck prickling. "Oh, Quade. I have a lot of fears in this new world I've discovered. You are not one of them."

His quick smile flashed a hint of fangs. "No? Then you're not paying attention."

He leaned down and kissed her, forcing her to swallow a quick retort. He tasted like mint. A lot of it. Then he went deeper, his mouth on hers, his body leaning over hers, and she forgot all about anything but him.

* * * *

Quade lifted Haven onto the bed, removing her shirt in one motion and revealing her full breasts. Too many impulses gathered inside him—need, lust, anger, patience—and he ignored them all as he finally kissed his woman. Down by the lake, he'd made the decision to mate, and once made, it was absolute. Her mouth felt soft and sweet beneath his, and when she moaned and kissed him back, his head nearly came off his body.

She tasted of oranges and woman and everything he never thought he'd have again. He'd give her time to reach her own decision, but the world pressed in with a sense of urgency that quickened his movements.

"Your shirt," she said against his mouth, tugging on the hem.

Releasing her mouth, temporarily, he pulled the material over his head and dropped it to the floor.

The sound she made as her palms met his chest shot right to his balls. She sat all the way up, and those soft hands went to the clasp of his jeans.

Electricity zapped down his spine, and he took a step back, making quick work of the remainder of his clothing. He stepped free, nude and aroused.

Her eyes widened.

He would've laughed, but desire had become a pounding hunger that had to be appeased. Gentle. He had to be gentle. She lay back and shimmied out of her leggings, which were splattered with different colors of paint. Her hands went to her underwear, and he dropped to his knees, stopping her. "Let me." His voice was so hoarse the words were unintelligible.

She paused and then rested her hands on the bedcovers.

He tucked his thumbs in the sides of the flimsy pink panties and drew them down her legs, kissing her thighs and knees as he did so. Then he levered himself up and placed a kiss right where she wanted it.

She jerked and sighed.

Her taste spurred him on, and he licked her, brushing his whiskers against the tender skin of her thighs. They trembled around him, and he smiled. He was hard and ready, but he'd hurt her if she wasn't prepared. So he licked her again, taking his time, enjoying this slice of heaven after being in hell for so long.

Her body tightened, and an orgasm rolled through her, much faster than he'd expected. He prolonged her waves, licking her, finally letting her body ease onto the bed.

Then he maneuvered his way up her, enjoying the flush across her chest and face. "That was quick."

She grinned, the smile slightly lopsided. "Let's hope I don't say that."

Cute. His palm hurt as if he'd been stabbed with a hot poker, but he tried to stay in the moment and enjoy it with her. "You won't." He hoped. It had been centuries for him.

This moment was so intimate and sweet, he should find some words to say.

She cupped his jaw with both hands, sliding her palms along his whiskers and up to his hair to tug him down. His lips met hers, and she kissed him, her thighs widening and making more room for his hips.

He returned the kiss, his cock prodding her entrance insistently without his conscious intent. "Haven."

"Quade." She moved against him, her hardened nipples scraping across his chest. "It's just sex. It's okay."

Nothing was *just sex* with her. How could she not see that? "All right." Reaching down, he grasped her hip and pulled her off the bed. Then he penetrated her, going slowly, pausing several times until he could feel her relax around him. She was so small, he had to fight every instinct he owned not to shove all the way home.

Around him, she felt like heaven. Hot and wet and so tight. To feel such intense pleasure after lifetimes of pain and hell humbled him. Pulled much more from him than he was ready to give.

He withdrew and then thrust back in, holding himself back, going as slow as possible.

Her legs rose, and her small ankles crossed at his back, pushing at him.

"You're going to kill me," he groaned, dropping his forehead to hers.

"What a way to go." She twisted her head to lick his neck and sink her teeth into his earlobe.

Ecstasy spasmed through him, from head to toe, electricity zipping up and down his spine. He gritted his teeth to remain in control, going still momentarily until he could breathe again without coming. Okay. He had this. She tightened around him, caressing his length, gripping him with an immortal strength.

Sometimes he forgot her lineage.

He groaned and pulled out of her, then pushed back in, his movements increasing in speed and strength, unable to stop himself. She dug her nails into his arms and held on tight, throwing her head back on the pillow. Her honey-blond hair spread out, filling the air with the scents of oranges, strawberries, and Haven. All Haven. Sweet woman with a hint of paint to her.

She arched against him, a moan escaping her.

He hammered harder, losing himself in the moment and in her. Haven. The marking on his palm burned its way up his arm to his neck, making his skin feel the flames.

She tossed her head to the side, exposing her neck. "Bite me, Quade," she moaned, meeting every thrust with one of her own.

His fangs dropped of their own volition. He released her hip and planted the marking on the bedcovers, far away from her flesh.

Then he grasped her other hip with the hand scarred by the Seven rituals, and struck, going deep in her neck and taking her blood.

She cried out, her body stiffening, and orgasmed so powerfully she gripped him tight enough to make him gasp.

He pounded into her, riding her waves, his eyes closed. Sensations of raw ecstasy, powerful and uncomfortable, edged through him, uncoiling with sparks of electricity as he shoved inside her one last time, held tight, and came.

He rode the most powerful orgasm of his life and then caught himself with his elbows before flattening her. His fangs retracted, he licked her wound clean, and then rolled over onto his back, panting wildly.

"Wait. We forgot protection and birth control," she said.

He exhaled. "Immortals don't need protection and can only get pregnant if mated."

She propped herself up on an elbow, her eyes the soft yellow of a golden sunrise. "Let's do that again."

Chapter Twenty-Seven

Three times. They'd had sex—to completion—three times. More than sex. There was nothing casual about sleeping with Quade, and she refused to lie to herself. Maybe to him. Not to herself. So what had that been? Too much. Definitely too much. She snuggled into his side, her body shutting down from exhaustion and pleasure. He smelled like the forest with a hint of mint. Had he eaten more toothpaste? She didn't have the energy to ask.

"We should talk," he said, caressing her arm.

"Hmmm," she agreed, her eyes closing. Tired. She was so tired. He may have kept talking, but she dropped into sleep, dreaming about paintings and colors and lakes surrounded by vampires.

Then she was walking along the beach in the dream world she'd painted. Was Hope around? She looked, admiring the pink trees and finally turning to face the rocks in the center of the stream. The ancient-looking green book was open in the sun, its weathered pages almost glowing.

What kind of book was it?

A noise, something of a crackle, startled her, and she turned to face the forest. The shadows lengthened and darkened. Her breath quickened, and she turned to run, but a force yanked her toward the darkness. She cried out, her arms scrabbling in the sand, but was dragged through the trees.

She landed on her back on soft green grass with a dull thud. Pain ached in her shoulders, and she sat up, groaning. The world spun around. Water bubbled amidst large patches of grass with a happy gurgle, and the place smelled like sugar cookies.

"Who are you?" The voice came from behind her.

Jumping to her feet, she spun around to see two women, both short, one blond and one red-haired. The blonde had one green eye and one blue eye, while the redhead had a brown eye and a blackish eye. "Who are you?" she gasped as the world tilted around her and then settled.

The blonde wrung her hands together. "I'm Juliet and this is Morgan. We're stuck here. How did you get here? Show us the path out."

Okay. This was weird. Haven rubbed her eyes. Nope. They were still there. "I don't know the way out." It was the truth. She focused her gaze. "Are you fairies?" The two different eye colors were a clue.

"Fae," they both said at the same time.

She nodded. "Totally agree about that." A chill washed over her shoulders, and she looked around, spotting a forest with deep green trees in the distance. "You guys usually are able to teleport from world to world, right?" It was the first time she'd been actually curious instead of terrified of this odd gift. Or curse.

Juliet nodded. "Yes, but when we all rendezvoused here before heading back home, we discovered we were stuck."

"We? How many of you are there?" Haven looked around to see a flock of birds with bright purple wings flying above.

Morgan studied her. "Seven of us. The others are out scavenging for food right now and will be back soon."

Haven's skin tingled, and the forest began to pull at her. She fought the sensation. "There's food here?"

"Not much," Juliet admitted. "There are berries and birds, but the birds are hard to catch. We can survive a few more days comfortably, and then we'll start to get emaciated. We might live for fifty years or so, maybe longer, but it's going to be painful."

"Very," Morgan muttered. *"Since you're here, you must know a way home. Let's get everyone back here."* Her eyes glowed, and she exhaled. *"Thank goodness."*

The pull grew stronger, and Haven hunched her shoulders to stay in place. "I can't control it," she grunted. "Don't know the way." She dropped to her knees and dug into the grass, fighting full on now. Her hair flew back into the wind, and she arched.

The wind lifted her, and she screamed, blowing across the grass and into a portal in front of the trees.

She swirled around in nothingness, her head aching, her body bruising. Whatever portal was using her wasn't meant for people, anybody, to travel through.

For the first time, she landed on her face. Pain exploded across her forehead, and she sat up, wiping away blood. Damn it. She was back on the hot rock. Turning, afraid to look, she saw the swirling blue portal. "I am so tired of you!" she yelled, standing with her legs braced. "Enough of this bullshit. What the hell do you want?" Anger flushed through her, even though her entire body felt like it had become a smoothie in a blender.

The portal widened and started to pull at her.

She grunted and fought. This was like a fucking bad 1950s television show. "The graphics aren't even that good," she bellowed, beyond angry. And terrified. But anger felt a lot better than fear, so she went with it.

Last time she'd jumped into the abyss below her and then awakened safely in her bed. She was inching toward the side when a force much stronger than before lifted her off her feet and whisked her through the portal. She screamed but only silence echoed.

Pressure moved in, cracking at least one of her ribs. Pain forced the air from her lungs. When the pressure lessened, she bunched her muscles, prepared for the fall.

This time, she landed on a squishy blue ball, bounced several times, and settled onto her knees facing a far shore across pitch-black liquid. Something swam beneath the surface, leaving ripples. She held her breath, staying completely still.

A figure strode out of the trees at the shoreline, his strip of white hair contrasting with an eerie red sky. Light-blue veins showed beneath his too-pale skin.

The ball wobbled around her, and she didn't dare stand. "Ulric," she said quietly. Yeah. She'd figured this would happen.

He wore some sort of animal hide, his fangs out, his eyes a deep, swirling purple. "I've dreamed of you." His voice was a low baritone that easily crossed the distance.

"Ditto." She wanted to stand to face him, but no way did she want to fall into that black murk. A splash sounded behind her, and she jumped, wincing as her broken rib protested. She set her forearm against it to ease some of the pain. "You must have some serious power to pull me here."

"Yes," he said. "I have tried for years, but only recently have I felt you coming. I have sensed your presence."

Probably because Quade's world had failed. "I'm not helping you get back," she said.

His smile was the most chilling sight she'd ever faced. "Yes, you are." Bubbles rose from the water, and a massive silver head began to rise.

Haven screamed.

* * * *

Quade shook Haven, the blood roaring through his veins. "Wake up."

She sat up, sucking in air with a painful wheeze.

He sat and turned to face her, kicking bedcovers out of the way. "Hold on. Take a deep breath. You are safe." His heart thundered. Holding her shoulder, he reached to the side and turned on the light before facing her. His body went cold. Deep purple bruises covered her forehead and her bottom lip was bleeding. "What the hell happened?"

She winced and pressed a hand to her rib cage. "Broken," she grunted.

Fury heated his torso, and he forced it away. For now. He gently took her other shoulder. "Look at me."

She gasped, the sound pained, but her gaze met his.

"All right. Breathe with me and imagine sending healing cells to your rib cage." There might be other damage, but the ribs were the easiest to fix first.

She took several shallow breaths, her green eye darkening to almost match the black one, her lips pursed as she concentrated. Tears filled those eyes, but she did not make a sound.

What the hell had happened? He had been sleeping right next to her and had had no clue she was in danger or pain. Should he not have felt something? He kept his grip light and caressed her arms, checking for broken bones or obvious bruises. No lumps and no cuts. Good.

The sound of her ribs clicking back into place would plague him for decades. She gasped, her eyes widening, her body jerking. "Ouch," she snapped.

Quite an understatement. He wiped blood off her lips. "Do an inventory of your entire body, from head to toe, and see what is injured." He kept his voice low and soothing, when he really wanted to swear and yell. Loudly. But that would not help her, and she was all that mattered right now. "You can do it."

She shuddered but did as he said, a couple of tears sliding down her damaged face. "I think I'm okay."

"Fix your face, then," he said quietly, holding both of her hands. "You can draw strength from me." He would give her blood, but she needed to learn how to heal herself quickly if possible, and she was succeeding at the moment. "There are bruises and a cut. Probably some internal damage. Fix it all."

This time she shut her eyes, and tingles popped in the air around them. The bruise across her forehead slowly shifted from ugly purple to yellow to a barely there discoloration.

"That's all I have." She opened her eyes and dark circles appeared beneath them.

Healing could be exhausting. It was the middle of the night, so he shut off the light, gathered her close, and settled them both beneath the covers. "Tell me," he said, spooning her. "All of it."

Her body was cold against him, and she shivered but told him about her journey. He held her, his mind considering different scenarios. He was a soldier and had an enemy to fight, but getting to that enemy was the problem. In addition, if Ulric had the power to pull Haven to his world, he'd soon have the power to gain his freedom. While Quade was itching for the final fight, so far, according to Ronan, only two of the three Key females had been found. In addition, Hope Kayrs-Kyllwood was still a child and not able to choose her own path as the Lock yet.

So Ulric had to remain contained.

Haven wound down, her voice lost. Quade held her closer, somewhat surprised when she let him. "When you were traveling, did you get any sense how to stop the portals from pulling you? To close them all for good?" he asked.

"No." She yawned. "I didn't have a sense of anything except trying to fight the pull, which I couldn't. Do you think there's a way to stop or end all of the portals?"

There had to be. "Yes." He needed to get inside those worlds with her to figure out how, but first, he required more information, and that was not to be found at Realm headquarters. "Go back to sleep, and I will watch over you and remain awake."

"No way." She shook her head. "I don't need more sleep. Maybe ever." She sighed. "But I do need to somehow rescue those Fae. They're running out of time. If it's possible to stop this type of teleporting, we need to bring them home first. How do we do that?"

"I do not know." But he believed the answers were to be found at Seven headquarters. It was time to escape the Realm, whether his great-nephew the king liked it or not. "You do understand that we must mate now, correct?"

She stiffened.

Ah, hell. "You have to learn to trust somebody someday," he said, as gently as possible. "I cannot give you forever, but together, we could save the world."

She snorted. "That's quite a proposal."

He thought so.

She scooted from the bed and stood, wrapping a blanket around her to cover her nudity. "Listen, Quade. This was more than I anticipated, and I need time to process all of it."

Sweet little Fae thought she could run from emotion. Fear drove her, and considering her childhood, he could understand. He had patience to give her, but unfortunately, not time. Time was not on their side nor on that of those lost Fae females. "The decision is yours, Haven Daly. I believe you will decide to give yourself to me, and I will protect you for as long as I am able."

"Whoa." She took several steps back, her hair a wild and sexy mass around her bare shoulders. "I'm not giving myself to anybody." One hand waved in the air while the other clutched the blanket to her chest. "I may decide to mate you if that's the only way to save those people, but that's just a working arrangement." Turning, she strode into the bathroom and shut the door.

He cocked his head. "That's not how a mating works," he murmured. More importantly, that was not how he worked. If they mated, she would be one thing above all others.

His.

Chapter Twenty-Eight

Quade walked out of the bathroom after a hot shower and another shave to find Haven packing their meager belongings in a bag.

"I want to bring some of the paints," she said, looking around the room. "Maybe one canvas, if possible? We can leave the finished paintings." Her nose wrinkled, and she focused on him. "They'll keep the paintings, right? Not burn them out of anger or anything?"

"Right." Quade couldn't imagine Dage Kayrs burning those works of art for any reason. "Are you ready?"

She lifted her chin and sniffed the air. "Minty." Her nostrils flared. "Quade. Tell me you did not eat another tube of toothpaste."

He shuffled his feet and moved to throw borrowed jeans into a bag. They were his now. "I did not."

"Quade?" She drawled his name out this time.

His ears heated. "I just had a little." It tasted so good, why didn't everybody eat some after brushing?

"That's it. We are finding you some candy today. You can't keep eating the paste—it's not good for your stomach. More importantly, I need toothpaste to brush every day, and it's getting harder to steal from people. Will we have time to go to a store today?"

He finished with the jeans and borrowed shirts, turning around. "I do not know. This is the first helicopter I've stolen."

She gulped. "Your brother knows how to fly?"

Quade kept his expression stoic, when he really wanted to wince. A lot. "Yes. Ronan can fly." But Ronan had only been back on this world for a short time, so how had he learned the skill? It was doubtful, it truly was. But Quade trusted Ronan, and there was no alternate way out of the Realm. Hopefully, Dage wouldn't have them shot with bullets. Could bullets hurt a helicopter? Probably not. Yet Quade had learned about missiles the other day, and surely the Realm had some of them? "We will be fine, as you say."

"Humph." She tiptoed into the living area and past it to gather paints.

He followed. "Leave the canvases. The paints you can put in your pack, but if we leave with a canvas, they'll know we're not going for a stroll." His brother had planted the seed that Haven had trouble sleeping and Quade often took her for strolls outside in the snow to tire her, so hopefully, anybody seeing them would think that the case. He doubted the king would be fooled so easily, but often members of his family had blind spots when it came to family.

Haven reached him by the door. "This is probably a huge mistake."

He nodded. "Aye." He reached past her and twisted the knob, not surprised to see Ronan waiting against the wall.

"You ready?" Ronan asked.

No. "Yes," Quade said, looking down the empty hallway. Silence filled the lodge at this time of night. "What is your plan for the patrolling guards?"

Ronan's eyes gleamed a dark green. "I've memorized their patrol movements, and we can time it just right to reach the helicopter bay without being spotted. The weather has cooperated, giving us another blizzard. It will be tough flying but even tougher following us." He motioned them down the hallway. "There will be two guards standing post at the building, and we'll have to knock them out. No killing."

Quade had no intention of killing an ally. "Is there a way to follow a helicopter these days?" he whispered, following his brother to the back door.

"Yes, but I'll fly low and stay off radar," Ronan said. "Don't worry. I've got this."

Quade tried to keep from challenging the assertion for Haven's sake. He didn't want her worried. "You have been practicing flying?" He had to ask.

"Sure," Ronan said, sliding open the back door to the wide deck with its stairs leading down to the lake.

Wind, ice, and snow instantly pelted them, and Quade stepped in front of Haven to shield her. "Stay right behind me." Nobody was going to believe they were out for a stroll in this storm. "Stick to the building and the shadows," he whispered.

Ronan nodded, edging along the quiet building to the trees lining the lake, where he partially turned and maneuvered between trees, forging a path with his legs as he went.

Quade reached behind himself and grasped Haven's hand, pressing it to his hip. "Hold on to me."

She did so, tucking her hands in his jeans pockets. "This is crazy," she whispered, barely audible above the wind.

The wind smashed snow against his face, and he ducked his head. The female was not wrong. Should a helicopter even fly in this kind of weather? Probably not, but it made sense to go now, so another helicopter could not follow. Still, he didn't want to die in a damn crash.

They walked for about two miles before the landscape changed from trees to a wide meadow covered in hard black material. Much like the roads. He hadn't learned the names for everything yet. Two large metal buildings stood silently on the other side of the black field.

"We want the second one." Ronan crouched by a tree and pointed.

Quade could barely see though the storm. "All right." His blood pumped faster, and energy flowed throughout his body. He was ready for a fight. Hopefully, the Realm soldiers would live up to his expectations.

Ronan looked over his shoulder and up. "This might make us enemies with the Realm. With family."

"That is inevitable, I believe," Quade murmured. "Either way, we've come too far to turn back. Let's go the rest of the distance." There was nothing for them here at Realm headquarters; if he was going to save Haven, he needed the resources of the Seven, which had to be kept confidential. "Haven? Stay behind me." Lowering his head, he jogged through the falling snow, reaching the first building and listening for heartbeats.

Two faint ones came inside the other building. Made sense. Why protect the place from the outside when it was warm and dry inside?

Ronan made a hand signal and ran across the front of the first building.

Quade nodded and followed him, staying low, remaining silent. They reached a small door, and Ronan opened it, letting Quade leap inside first.

A guard turned and fired.

Quade ducked, rolled, and came up with an uppercut to the male's jaw before taking him down to the ground. The fight was short-lived, and soon the young vampire was unconscious. Quade turned to see Ronan dispatching the other guard while Haven stood in the doorway, her eyes wide.

Six helicopters, shiny and long, filled the massive building.

Ronan pointed to the closest one. "Get in. I should be able to open the hangar door from inside."

Quade motioned for Haven. "Was that too easy?" He'd expected a much more exhilarating fight.

"Yes. These guys are definitely newbies and young." Ronan shrugged. "The king probably thinks that nobody is dumb enough to try and fly in this storm."

Quade stumbled and then righted himself. Apparently, he was dumb enough.

* * * *

Haven clutched the arm strap as the machine rose into the air, swinging wildly. Her stomach rolled over. This was crazy. Was anybody immortal enough to survive a helicopter crash? From the pallor of Quade's face across from her, he was wondering the same thing.

Ronan sat up front, whistling, punching different lights. The copter swung a hard left and tilted. "Oops." He righted the craft.

Snow piled up on the front window, and ice crusted the bottom of it.

The air was freezing, and when she breathed, puffs of steam filtered around her head. "There has to be heat," she whispered.

"There's heat," Ronan called back. "I just don't know what button to push." He pushed a green one, and the nose of the craft dove swiftly down.

Haven yelped and held on tighter.

"My bad." Ronan righted the craft, but it still swung dizzily in the storm.

Haven tried to breathe through the panic, but she went light-headed anyway. "I think I hate your brother."

"Me too," Quade grunted, white knuckling the padded bench on either side of his hips. The helicopter rocked and his head knocked back against the side of the craft. He winced and swore. Loudly.

"Just hold on," Ronan snapped. "I've got this."

They were so going to die. Or at least crash. Haven bit her lip, tasting blood. "If I'm knocked unconscious, I might not be able to stop from going other places." If she had mated Quade, would he have been able to go with her? They had plenty of theories but no proof. "We need information. Now."

"That's why we're on this flying death trap." He said the words loudly enough that Ronan surely heard.

She tried to concentrate on anything but the fact that the storm was more powerful than the helicopter. "I don't know much about vampires and fighting and all of that, but it seemed like this was too easy."

Quade's eyes had darkened to a deep aqua with more green than blue. "Agreed. I just said the same thing to Ronan."

Ronan glanced over his shoulder. "You think the king let us take this puppy?" The copter pitched, and he quickly looked back at the night outside, fighting with the wheel.

Haven gulped down panic. "Maybe. What do you think?"

Quade leaned forward and turned toward his brother, grabbing a hanging strap while he did so. "Can this machine be traced? Like with cameras?"

Man, he was learning about modern society so quickly. Haven tried not to move too much.

Ronan nodded. "Sure. They definitely want to know where Seven headquarters is located. That's why we're not going there right now." He yanked the wheel to the side and they spun.

Haven's stomach lurched. The copter banked sharply, and she set her head back, closing her eyes. It was okay. They were okay. This wasn't crazy. Oh, this was fucking crazy. "Where are we going?" she yelled.

"Rendezvous with Adare," Ronan said. "We'll leave this at a halfway point and go with him."

Not a bad plan. "Who's Adare?" Haven asked, not that it mattered. She'd do almost anything to be on the ground.

The copter dropped several yards suddenly, and Quade hit his head on the ceiling, landing back on the seat with a sharp growl.

Haven kept her hold on the strap, trying not to scream.

"Adare is a member of the Seven," Quade said. "From the beginning. A brother of mine."

The helicopter pitched violently. "That's it," Quade bellowed. "Put this fucker down. Right now. Out of the storm."

Haven nodded wildly. "Agreed. It's two against one. Put this down on the nearest street or meadow or farm." She didn't care at this point.

A flash of light came from the ground below. Ronan jerked the wheel, but it was too late. A missile hit the back of the craft, spraying fire in every direction.

Quade bellowed and leaped for Haven, throwing her up front and following quickly, settling them both in the copilot's seat and securing a chest belt over the two of them. He wrapped his arms around her middle, holding her tight, his feet braced against the floor.

"Shit." Ronan fought with the wheel. Warning alarms blared from every direction, and all of the lights flickered. The craft swung around and around, while freezing air and wind swept from the gaping hole in the back.

Haven sucked in air, her body trembling. The copter spun crazily. She grabbed onto Quade's arms and tried to brace herself for impact.

"Don't we need the rest of this thing?" Quade yelled.

"Yep." Ronan fought hard, sweat dripping down the sides of his face. "Hold on. We're going down."

The engine droned, complaining through the storm. They hit branches first. Snow scattered and the front windshield cracked. Another series of hits from branches, and the glass shattered.

Haven held tight and shut her eyes, trying to protect her face. Quade's arms lifted, and he covered her as much as possible while holding her in place. His head smashed against the metal side so loudly the *thunk* sounded over the alarms and whipping wind.

The helicopter pitched, nose down, held aloft by the branches of tall trees. Way too tall trees. For the briefest of seconds, the entire world seemed to hold its breath. Oh, they were going to die. Haven screamed.

"Damn it." Quade unbuckled the belt quickly and grabbed her arms. "Hold on tight, little Fae."

She yelped and fought him, but he was too strong. He flung her out of the craft and straight at the nearest tree. She grabbed a snowy branch and fell, scrambling for the next one. Her hands found purchase and then her feet. She clung, breathing wildly, pants of air whooshing out of her.

The branches holding the helicopter cracked and then gave. Snow billowed up, and she couldn't see what happened. Had the brothers jumped out in time? The copter pummeled to the ground and hit so hard that snow flew up the several stories to where she clung desperately to the branches. The metal crumpled with a resounding crunch.

"Quade!" she screamed. Holding tight, she swung herself to a lower branch, scrambling down as fast as she could. Many branches had been sheared off by the falling helicopter, so she had to jump several times. Finally, she reached the ground, her legs sinking into the snow up to her thighs.

A noise to her right had her partially turning to see a cougar quickly morphing into a full-blown male shifter.

"Hello, Fairy," Pierce said, right before he hit her temple with a jagged rock.

Chapter Twenty-Nine

Quade came to flat on his face in the ice. He groaned and turned over to see snow falling hard. An answering groan came from his right, and he partially turned to find Ronan sitting against a tree with the helicopter on fire behind him. They'd both leapt through the windshield at the last second, clearing the helicopter before it hit the earth nose first. "Haven," he called.

Nothing. Damn it.

He took a quick inventory, finding eight broken bones, a skull fracture, and some liver damage. Sending healing cells to the broken bones in his leg, he waited until a crack sounded before trying to stand. The pain focused him, but he swayed while slugging through the thick snow to his brother. "You okay?"

"No." Ronan took the offered hand and stood. A thick gash across his cheek revealed his bone and teeth. It slowly started to stitch itself together.

Quade looked up in the trees. Where was Haven? "How long do you think we were out?"

Ronan glanced at the burning metal. "Not long. The fire won't last. I'd say fifteen minutes, tops."

A scent wafted through the snow, and Quade lifted his nose, trying to identify it. What was it? He moved around the tree and caught a full dose. Shifter. "Damn it." Sending healing cells to his liver and head, he pushed through the thick snow to where he thought he'd tossed her and looked up. This close, her scent lingered as well. Oranges and Haven…and blood. The metallic smell nearly dropped him to his knees.

Ronan staggered up next to him, leaving a red trail of blood in the snow. "I smell cougar. You don't think that asshole you told me about shot us out of the sky, do you?"

Quade looked frantically around, trying to catch another scent, but smoke and the storm made it impossible. "Where are we?"

"Still in Idaho, I think," Ronan muttered, leaning against a tree. "We didn't get very far in this damn storm." Pain and healing energy, the angry kind, radiated from him.

Quade had to find Haven. Rage shot energy through his body, through his blood, and he let it loose, needing the power. The healing cells had already taken care of his liver and head, so he sent them to other injuries, but they slowed, turning sluggish. He needed protein and blood, but so did Ronan. Sucking in a deep breath, he ignored the storm and concentrated, turning slightly to the right. "They went this way. Can you keep up?"

"Of course." His brother pushed off the tree. "We'll get her back. Shifters are fast, but so long as we keep his scent, we'll catch up." The wound on his face started to mend, but only part of the skin stitched together. "Let's go." He shoved his way between two trees.

A noise caught Quade's attention. A buzz of some sort. He partially turned to see lights cutting through the trees in several different places, bobbing up and down. "What is that?"

Ronan turned. "Who is that?"

A machine roared into range, black and red, on some sort of skis.

"Snowmobiles," Ronan explained, panting out air. "The Realm boys must've tracked us."

The machines maneuvered expertly between the trees, their high-pitched buzz increasing in strength as they drew nearer. He peered through the snow, seeing white. Strips of white braided down the side. "Shit. It's the Cyst." Shoving Ronan, he ducked his head. "Run."

Ronan tucked and started running full out, scattering snow as he went. Quade followed, ducking and dodging between trees, moving in a zigzag pattern. They instinctively went deeper into the forest where the trees were thicker. Soon the sounds of the snowmobiles slowed and then ebbed.

Finally silence.

Quade kept running, his ribs aching, his still damaged arm pounding in pain. The Cyst were on foot now. He couldn't hear them, but he could sense them. How had the Cyst found them? His mind filled with Haven. Where was she? Was she okay? Rage was white-hot inside him, and he needed it. The idea of her in danger sped up his feet, and he ignored the pain. There was no pain. There was only Haven.

His mate.

He almost barreled over a snowy cliff, but Ronan grabbed him and yanked him back.

Shit.

He turned and stiffened as three Cyst prowled out from the trees. In the storm, with their white hair and too pale faces, they blended in with the snow. Even their uniforms, this time, were white. They moved with strength and grace, obviously well trained.

"Where's Xeno?" Ronan sneered, moving to stand alongside Quade.

"You'll see him soon," the soldier to the far right said, his eyes glinting through the swirling snow.

Okay. Guy to right was the leader. He'd need to be taken out first.

The same soldier looked around, lifted his head, and smelled the air. He frowned. "Where is the female?"

"What female?" Quade asked, bracing his feet. He could barely scent Haven, and she was his mate. The storm was finally assisting him. But she'd been taken by that bastard Pierce, and the longer Quade waited, the fainter her scent would become. He did not have time for this.

The far left soldier frowned, his white eyebrows slashing. "Do you smell...shifter?"

Quade cut Ronan a look. There was no way these guys were working with a shifter, so now he had two enemies on his ass? "Why did you shoot us down?"

The leader shrugged. "We knew you were at headquarters and would have to leave the Realm, so we just waited."

Quade stepped forward, his chest heating. They could've accidentally decapitated his mate in that wreck. "You just waited and shot down the first helicopter you saw?"

The leader grinned. "Sometimes you have to roll the dice."

What the hell did that mean? Quade's ribs finally cracked back into place. "If you'd shot down the King of the Realm, war would ensue again." That much he knew.

"The King of the Realm wouldn't be flying out in this storm," the leader countered.

That was a good point. So, was Pierce monitoring the Realm or the Cyst? How the hell had he gotten to Haven so quickly?

The middle guy finally spoke, stepping forward. "The Seven is weak when fractured, and we knew you would have to regroup soon. Plus, you're still a big old secret to most species, right? I bet you didn't even tell the king about all of your mission."

He wasn't wrong.

Quade bunched his legs. "Now." He leaped forward just as Ronan did the same, tackling the soldiers into the snow.

* * * *

Haven jerked awake, surrounded by something warm and soft. She blinked, sitting up on a bed, pushing a flannel blanket down to her waist. "What the holy hell?"

Pierce stoked a fire on the opposite wall of a square wooden cabin, then stood up and stretched his back. "The storm got too bad for me to run in human form, and I can't carry you in cougar form, so we're sitting it out for a short while. I need a break." He frowned. "You're heavier than you look."

Her head jerked and she sat straighter. "I most certainly am not."

"Sorry." He held up both hands in surrender.

The room spun crazily around her. "Dude. You have got to stop hitting me in the head." She pressed a hand to her pounding temple and tried to ease the pain. There was a lump but no blood. Healing cells were already fixing the problem. She was getting pretty good at this.

He shrugged, his chest bare, his legs in dark sweats. "Again, sorry. But I have to make you see that we're meant to be together. I've been pursuing you for years."

She looked around the small room. Bed against the wall, kitchenette with no fridge in far corner, and two chairs between the bed and the fireplace. "Where are we?"

"Cabin in Idaho. I've kept it close to Realm headquarters and figured they'd take you to the hospital there after the fire. I was trying to figure out how to infiltrate the facility. When there was a helicopter crash, I investigated. Don't you see? It's fate I found you tonight." He reached for a photo album from a table in front of the sofa and hurried toward her, holding it out. "I don't have many pictures of you, but I keep several of these in different locations."

Her hands shook, but she took the album and flipped open the front page. Photographs of her as a child, some with the pastor and some from what appeared to be child services files, filled the first several pages. Then photocopies of her art taken from the web. She swallowed. "You have more than one of these?"

"I have tons. In every place I go." He gingerly sat at the edge of the bed, his brown eyes earnest. "You'll see that we belong together. I've dreamed of you my whole life, and I've been trying to reach you for so many years."

She couldn't breathe. All right. "You're not very good at stalking."

"You're excellent at running and hiding," he countered, his chest puffing out.

She shook her head, wincing at the ensuing pain. Memories of the helicopter crash slammed through her brain. "Did Quade and Ronan survive the accident?"

Pierce's eyes darkened. "That hybrid isn't your business. Even if they did survive, they'll be useless for years. You need a real male. Me."

How delusional was he? "You left me with the pastor to be whipped and burned," she snapped.

He winced. "I didn't know that was his plan. But there's a silver lining." His eyebrows rose, and he reached out to grab her hand. "I have the money he paid me. We can go anywhere and do anything. Together."

Was Quade all right? She had to get back to the wreck or at least call Realm headquarters and beg the king to go find him. Quade and Ronan could be buried beneath burning metal right now. Couldn't burns kill a hybrid? Panic threatened to choke her, so she took several deep breaths. The pain in her head began to dissipate. "Do you understand how crazy you sound?"

Pierce's hand tightened over hers. "Don't you get it? We're both alone and have always been. Together, we have somebody. I knew the first moment I looked at your picture, when the pastor hired me, that you and I made each other complete."

Do not feel sympathy for this nut job. She gently withdrew her hand. "You don't have family?"

He shrugged. "Just parents and two brothers. Other than them, I'm alone."

That wasn't alone. "Do they know about your obsession with me?"

"Not really. We keep our business separate, and until now, you were business. Now that we're together, I'll take you to meet them." His smile made his eyes glimmer oddly. Was that what crazy looked like?

Yes, he was nuts, and she could use that. "I, ah, need time." To get the hell way from him.

He clucked his tongue. "We should mate and get all of that settled, just in case the vampire survived the crash. Or is he more demon than vamp?"

Mate? Oh, hell no. "I don't know. How do you tell?" She shifted toward the edge of the bed.

"You can usually just sense it. Like you're more Fae than demon, but I can see both in you." He drew the photo album closer to his chest as if it was something precious. "I'm full-blown cougar. Our kids will be an interesting blend."

Right. She set both feet on the floor, gratified that her socks and jeans seemed to have dried. There were still a few wet patches on her shirt, but she wasn't cold. "Do cougars get a mating mark on their hands?" She stood and checked out her legs, making sure all her bones were in the right place.

"No. We just have sex and bite deep." He stood, his head tilted. "You know there's nowhere to go, right? The storm is a whiteout. Can't see a foot in front of your face."

Yeah, but she didn't want to be in the bed any longer. He was bigger and most likely stronger, definitely faster than she. But she was smarter. Without question. "I, need to use the, ah…"

"Oh." His expression lightened. "Door to the right of the kitchen. It isn't much, but at least it's attached."

She swallowed and strode past him, looking for weapons. There wasn't even a knife block on the counter. She found the door and pushed it open, finding basically an outhouse. She shut the door and leaned against it. No window, no escape route. Okay. She'd have to strike fast and hard.

She used the facilities and then stepped out into the kitchen.

He waited by what looked like a battery-operated hot plate. "Are you hungry?"

"Yes." She grabbed the nearest object, a cast-iron pan, and swung it as hard as she could at his head.

At the last second, he pivoted, ducked, and charged. "You'll regret that," he roared, knocking her back into the cupboard.

Chapter Thirty

Laser bullets that turned into metal upon hitting immortal flesh fucking hurt. A lot. Quade took the impact to his back from the guy behind him, punched the guy in front of him in the throat, and then turned to charge. He hit the soldier square on, grappling with him over the icy ground and landing at the edge of the cliff.

They both realized their position at the same instant.

The Cyst's purple eyes widened, and he scrambled to shove Quade off him.

Quade slapped the gun from his hand, rose up on his knees, and shoved the Cyst as hard as he could. The soldier slid in the ice and snow, going over the edge and bellowing a panicked cry. Landing was going to hurt.

A knife slashed into Quade's neck from behind, and he turned, yanking it out at the same time. Blood welled from beneath his jaw and pain exploded in his head.

Growling, he stood, bracing his feet to keep from falling on his face. Out of the corner of his eye, he tracked Ronan fighting with two Cyst over by the tree line. When had the fourth guy appeared? How many more were there?

The soldier in front of him reached for a gun at his waist.

Bellowing, Quade ducked his head and knocked the bastard into a tree. Snow and ice pummeled down, covering them both. He swung hard and fast, sending the gun spinning into the dark forest.

The soldier punched him in the neck wound.

Quade's vision turned red and then black. He swung out instinctively, nailing the Cyst soldier in the nose. It cracked, and the soldier snarled.

Grunts came from the fighting trio in the trees. Quade's eyes cleared, and he punched the Cyst in the mouth, breaking several teeth. Pain flashed along his knuckles, so he punched again and again, going for speed rather than placement.

He advanced on the soldier, following him into the trees, ducking and dodging blows while landing his. He'd spent centuries fighting, and even a soldier as well trained as this one didn't have his speed. Or strength. Quade's legs weakened from blood loss, but he ignored the pain, striking repeatedly until the Cyst dropped to his knees.

Blood covered his pale face and long strip of white hair, even spotting the braid that reached his waist.

The Cyst lunged up with a blade that had been hidden.

Quade tried to jump back, but the blade ripped into his right leg, cutting deep. Blood poured from the wound, and he instantly sent healing cells to it, ignoring the damage to his throat.

Hisses and growls came from the forest, and he partially turned to see the two Cyst advancing on Ronan, who was bleeding profusely from his neck and arms. Glass from the crash was still embedded in the back of his neck, and bright red blood dripped to the snow. He dropped to one knee.

Hell.

Quade grabbed for the bloody knife in his leg just as the Cyst did, and they struggled, their hands slipping on it. Quade partially turned, steadied himself on his injured leg, and side-kicked the Cyst in the head. He fell to the side.

Ronan bellowed.

Quade partially turned to find one Cyst holding his shoulders and the other slicing at his neck.

Fuck.

Quade ripped the blade free of his leg and plunged it into the soldier's neck in front of him as the guy tried to rise. He twisted, partially tearing through the entire neck. The soldier dropped to the snow, blood pooling around him.

Panic clawed at Quade, and he drew on it for energy, leaping across the clearing and tackling the guy with the knife in his brother's neck. The soldier turned at the last second with the knife and tried to stab it beneath Quade's rib cage.

The blade cracked and dropped uselessly to the ground. "Impenetrable torso, asshole," he muttered, his fangs dropping. He slashed them, quick and deadly, into the enemy's neck, ripping and tearing, grunting like an animal.

The Cyst's blood burned his lips and mouth, but he drank deep, taking the nourishment along with the pain. The soldier fought him, slashing with claws across Quade's lower jaw, but he held tight, draining the bastard.

Rain and snow battered him as the blizzard increased in strength. He tossed the unconscious Cyst to the ground and struggled to turn. "Ronan?" he croaked.

Ronan was on his knees, his fangs in an unconscious soldier's neck. The Cyst's head was partially off, with a knife still sticking out beneath his ear. Ronan sucked deep, and color exploded across his face. His neck slowly started to mend, blood mixing with the pelting snow. He threw the Cyst to the ground. "We don't have time to take their heads." Struggling, he leaned over and grabbed a device from the soldier's pocket, tore the back off, and threw a small object into the forest. "Let's take the snowmobiles." His eyes were unfocused, but he stumbled to his feet.

The trees and snow whipped around Quade, making him even more dizzy. Could he really drive one of those things right now?

Ronan reached him, and they helped each other through the trees. "They'll have more backup coming soon. We have to move. Fast. Can you still scent her tracks?"

Quade caught a slight whiff of oranges. "Barely." They had to hurry.

* * * *

Pain exploded across Haven's shoulder blades from the wooden cupboard. She dropped the pan and fell on her butt.

Pierce grabbed her hair and swung, tossing her end over end toward the sofa. Her scalp screamed.

She hit face first, turned, and faced him. "You are crazy," she gasped, rubbing her aching nose.

"You tried to take me out with a pan." He picked it up and set the heavy iron on the cupboard. "I'm starting to think you don't like me."

"I *don't* like you," she exploded, grabbing the sofa to haul herself to her feet. "You're crazy. Obsessed. Are there any immortal shifter loony bins? I mean, do they exist?"

He frowned and crossed his arms. His blond hair had red highlights that glowed from the fire, and his eyes had turned a lighter brown, nearly honey. "I am not obsessed. My people believe in fate, and I know we're fated."

When he said it, the whole thing sounded crazy.

But when Quade had said it, she'd felt all hot and bothered and kind of happy. Interesting. "Does it bother you any that I don't want to mate you?" she asked, rubbing her aching scalp. He'd pulled her hair, darn it.

Pierce's mouth tightened. "You're just scared, and that makes sense. You've had a rough childhood and don't trust easily, and you have walls like a Scottish castle around your heart. Don't be frightened."

"I'm scared to mate Quade, not you," she snapped before giving herself time to think.

Pierce smiled. "That says a lot, don't you agree?"

Yeah. It did. Quade could hurt her, and not just physically. The truth smacked her like another blow to the head. "You're right," she murmured. "I am afraid to trust and even to love." Plus, she couldn't control Quade in the slightest. He was more of a control freak than she was, and that was definitely saying something. "I'm afraid of you, a little bit, because you're asshat crazy. But I'm afraid of Quade…" She trailed off, her mind spinning and not just from continual brain trauma. "Because he could break my heart."

"Your heart is mine," Pierce hissed.

She hadn't even known she still had a heart until she'd met the hybrid. "He says he can't love." That was risky, then. She wasn't the type to take a risk. "What if he's just forgotten how?"

Pierce snarled, his canines elongated. "I'm not here for a therapy session, and I'm not your damn shrink."

She waved a hand, her mind spinning. "I'm figuring stuff out here. Just hold on." She paced to the fireplace and back. Sure, Quade wanted to mate her and gain her gifts, but partially that was just to save her. "Does he feel obligated because of the mating marking on his hand?" she muttered.

"Hello!" Pierce snapped. "I'm standing right here."

If Quade felt obligated, then that wasn't good enough. She wasn't risking the defenses she'd built around herself just to help him fulfill a responsibility. Pausing, she looked at Pierce. "Forever is just forever, you know?" What if things didn't work out? What if…

"You're not concentrating," Pierce said, his hands fisting at his sides.

"I am concentrating," she countered, pacing again. The fire gave off a nice glow, but adrenaline was attacking her body, and it was difficult to think. "What if he ends up not wanting me?" Everyone in her life had decided she wasn't worth it.

"Damn it." Pierce smashed his fist against the counter, and the old wood shattered. Shards stuck into the wall and dropped to the floor.

"I know." She held up a hand. "I'm an adult, and it wasn't my fault crazy people adopted me. It wasn't my fault that whoever left me with them did so." The words and logic were one thing, but her heart felt otherwise. "I'm accomplished. I make money from doing something I love." Painting kept her sane. She'd been on the run for so long, she hadn't had time to just stop and think about what she wanted from life.

Survival wasn't enough.

She stopped by the fire, letting the crackling flames heat her chilled bones. "I'm not a risk taker. There has been too much risk thrust upon me." Every time she went to sleep, she risked not coming back. How insane was that? She was so tired, and her body hurt. Her head hurt. But sleep was a mistake. It was a miracle she hadn't entered that horrible portal the last time Pierce had knocked her out. The memory of Quade's kiss, of their incredible night together, heated her faster than the fire. "Being safe might not be enough any longer."

"You are not safe." Pierce ground out each word.

She waved a hand. "Oh, I know that. But maybe it's time to take a risk. He did offer to mate me, and he seems to like me. Said so himself." She bit her lip. "Could it be more? I've never felt like this with anybody, even my earlier crush."

"Damn it." Pierce lowered his head and charged, the claws of one hand extended.

Haven reached behind her, grabbed the fireplace poker, and held it up. He ran right into it, impaling himself. Blood welled from his lips, and he clutched the handle. He dropped to his knees, his eyes wide. When he pitched forward, she scrambled out of the way.

His face hit the wooden floor with a satisfying thud.

The poker extended out of his back, and nausea rolled through her stomach. "You'll live. I think."

A high-pitched engine roared outside, and a second later, Quade kicked the door open, jumping inside. Blood covered his neck and torso, and his eyes were a deadly black. Even so, he looked big and strong and fierce with the wild storm behind him.

She put her hands on her hips, facing him. "We have *got* to talk about this whole mating thing."

He looked around, grabbed his bleeding neck, and pitched forward onto the floor. Out cold. Ronan stumbled in behind him, also holding a bleeding wound, looked around, and then dropped to his knees.

She frowned. "Well." That was a lot of blood. "Glad you two survived the crash."

Ronan chortled, and blood bubbled from his lips. Painstakingly, he took a phone from his back pocket and dialed. "Adare? Come get us as soon as possible," he muttered into it, his body swaying. "I think we're ninety miles or so south of Realm headquarters. There are two snowmobiles, a cabin, and a fire." He dropped the phone, smiled at her, and fell sideways. His eyelids shut and his body relaxed with a sigh as unconsciousness took him.

She studied both males and then sighed. "This is some rescue."

Chapter Thirty-One

Quade came to in a bed with the sound of a roaring fire crackling in his ears. Tingles cascaded through him, finishing the job of healing all his injuries. He opened his eyes to see Haven across the room, drawing furiously with charcoal on a pad. His tension eased. She was there, and she was fine. He looked around.

Stone walls lined with copper and silver, stone floor, weird-looking fire. No smoke. The bedroom just held a bed and one sturdy yellow chair by the fire, where Haven drew. He partially sat up, and the blanket fell to his bare waist.

She glanced his way. "Hey. You're all healed. How do you feel?"

He took inventory. The Kurjan blood had helped, although the damn stuff had burned his throat and then stomach the entire time. "Well." He narrowed his gaze at the fire. "What is wrong with that fire?"

"It's electric." She set the pad aside, and he took a moment to study her. Dark circles bruised the delicate skin beneath her eyes, and her mouth appeared pinched.

His heart rolled over. "You're afraid to sleep." How long had it been for her? Definitely too long.

Her hand shook when she brushed her hair back from her face, highlighting her delicate bone structure. "Yes."

He blinked, surprised by the admission. Instinct whispered that he should not press her. "Where are we?"

She shook her head. "Underground at Seven headquarters, and I have to tell you, it's kind of a disaster." She leaned forward. "We nearly had our heads taken off when we entered the mountain because the booby traps misfired, and then all the computers went down, and there was yelling. A lot of yelling." She shuddered. "This is one of many bedrooms, and there aren't any rugs or anything yet. But the fire is nice. Well, the fake fire."

Irritation clawed along his skin. "They've had centuries to create a nice, safe headquarters. What in the hell has been happening?"

She shrugged, her eyes glimmering, each reflecting a different shade from the fake fire. "I don't know, but I did hear something about headquarters blowing up a lot. You and Ronan were taken to different rooms, his mate checked you both out, and then you were asleep for hours." She scrunched her nose up. "Any chance you're hungry?"

His stomach growled as if in answer. His heart warmed, too. She was too shy to venture out on her own? Sometimes her sweetness took his feet out from under him. "I'm starving. Shall we explore and find food?"

She hopped from the chair. "Definitely."

He stood and let the bedclothes fall, glancing down to see he was nude. "I don't suppose anybody left clothing."

She pointed to a pile on the other side of the bed. "Faith brought some of Ronan's clothes for you earlier. Jeans and T-shirts. Nothing fancy." A pretty pink filtered across her face.

"After the night we shared, you've seen it all." He grinned and strode for the clothing, his body feeling almost centered. Not quite, but as close as he'd gotten. Perhaps it was being inside the earth this way, or maybe it was because his mate was safe and close enough to touch. "You mentioned talking about mating." He drew a shirt over his head.

She cleared her throat. "You remember that, huh?"

It wasn't something he was likely to forget, even if he had been bleeding out. "Yes." He drew on the jeans, frowning at seeing several holes in the legs. "Ronan's mate gave me faulty clothing?"

Haven chuckled. "No. Frayed jeans are the style now. People pay extra for those holes."

What an odd world he'd returned to. "All right." He took in her black leggings and soft pink T-shirt. "Yours do not have holes."

"I'm not wearing jeans." She wiped charcoal down her pants. "I think you'll like Faith. She's a neurosurgeon. And I met Ivar's mate, Promise. She's a famous physicist."

What was that tone in her voice? Something was off. Quade took her hand. "You're a famous artist."

She snorted, but her smile was genuine. Good. He'd said the right thing. "Promise has some theories about the portals and Ulric, but she wanted to figure it all out and wait until you'd awakened before telling us."

"I'm awake." Quade led the way out of the room into a wide hallway with smooth walls. "Where are the booby traps?" He wasn't sure what those were, but since they cut off heads, he needed information.

Haven skipped to his side. "They're in the walls, but only when you first come in the mountain. There aren't any back here in the living quarters. Or rather, the sleeping quarters. Ivar said there would be bigger suites cut into the rock, but he didn't say when. Or how, for that matter."

They reached a wide room with some type of screens on the walls, but they were blank. Nobody was around. He continued past the room to another hallway, sniffing out food. Finally, they reached what appeared to be a kitchen of sorts with a long counter, several appliances he didn't recognize, and many round tables surrounded by yellow and green chairs. "Where is everyone?" he muttered.

She shrugged. "It's late at night. You slept all day, so everyone is probably sleeping. Logan is on his way from a safehouse with Allison, the woman who was my mom, because she won't agree to keep silent until she sees I'm okay. That may be true or not. But he won't be able to land in this storm." Moving toward a tall box, she opened it and drew out what appeared to be sliced meat.

"I'll make us sandwiches." She yawned and tried to cover the action with a hand.

"Okay." He looked along a stone counter and found bread. Already sliced. Amazing. "After we eat, we need to talk about your getting some sleep." His female needed to keep up her strength, even though she'd made quick work of the shifter. "Good job with Pierce, by the way."

She rolled her eyes. "Thanks. I asked Ivar to contact Dage and have somebody pick Pierce up and get him some help. The guy really needs it."

"He needs to have his head removed," Quade countered, taking out slices of bread. "I'll take care of that once we figure out what's happening with the portals." It was the least he could do.

She made the sandwiches and handed him two, moving to one of the tables and taking a seat. "I don't want him killed, just helped. He seemed more lost than dangerous to me." She took a bite and hummed, chewing thoughtfully as he pulled out a green chair and sat.

He ate half of his sandwich in one bite. "Let's talk about mating. Now."

* * * *

Haven nearly choked on her ham sandwich. She finished chewing and swallowed. "Do you believe in love?"

"No." He reached for the second sandwich she'd placed on his plate. "Maybe young girls feel it, but most of us gave up emotions like that a long time ago." His eyes were a burnished aqua in the dim light, oddly reflecting the silver in the walls around them. "I believe in duty and commitment. Family."

She'd never had family. Not really. "I think I believe in love. Maybe it's just for other people, but I do believe in it." She felt more for him than she'd ever felt before, but she didn't know how to define the sensation. She liked him and she wanted him.

Everything inside her wanted to trust him. She cleared her throat. "Did you know that there's a new virus—"

"Yes." He cut her off, his chin lifting. "That is not a possibility. If we mate, you will not take a virus. There is no out. You must understand this before you make your decision."

Haven swallowed. Faith had explained that the immortals, especially the older members of the Seven, were dead set against the virus or anything that messed with a mating bond. She'd also said that no mate who hadn't been widowed and alone for decades had ever taken the virus, so there was no way to know if it would work in other circumstances. "I'm just saying—"

"That is nonnegotiable," he said, finishing his sandwich.

Her vertebrae stiffened until her posture was probably as good as it would ever get. "This is not your way or the highway."

He frowned at the expression. "This is absolute."

She was about to let him have it when a shadow crossed the door.

Quade looked up and then slowly stood. "Adare."

Haven turned. Adare stood in the doorway, his dark eyes expressionless. He had black hair that reached his shoulders, a wide chest, and an aura of strength. "Quade. My brother." The brogue was masculine and deep. Thick and from the Highlands, or what she imagined the Highlands would sound like.

Quade met him halfway and they hugged with the sound of two bucks locking horns.

Emotion swam through the room, clogging her throat. She could feel it.

Adare pulled back first, his hand remaining on Quade's shoulder. They stood eye to eye at six and a half feet. "I never thought to see you again."

Quade nodded, flashing a quick smile. His eyes looked misty. "Me either. It is good to know you are well."

"You, too." Adare clapped Quade hard on the shoulder. "So good."

Quade drew him to the table. "This is Haven. Haven, this is my brother Adare."

Apparently, all of the members of the Seven shared brotherhood. Must be nice. She held out a hand, and the giant gently shook it. "Hello."

"Hi." His brogue lessened. He looked to the side. "I did not mean to interrupt."

"You didn't," Haven said, beginning to stand. It was obvious the two needed some time, and she could use some private minutes to think about what Quade had said. She hadn't expected him to be so unbending.

A woman stomped into the room. "Damn it, Adare. Did you tell Ivar I'd changed my mind about returning to Chicago?"

It took Haven a second to recognize her. "Grace Cooper," she murmured. The woman was a world-class photographer and had been with Promise and Faith when they'd visited her in Portland. She hadn't realized Grace was staying in the mountain.

Grace paused. "Hi, Haven. Sorry about this and about everything. We'll talk later, but right now, I need to yell at my mate."

Quade stepped back. "Mate?" His voice went low and gritty with what sounded like incredulousness.

Adare sighed. "Yes. Mate."

"Not really," Grace piped up, her eyes glittering. "Long story. I was in a coma, we mated with just a bite and brand, and now it's over. We've never had sex, will never have sex, and that's the end of it. So I'm done with you deciding anything for me."

Haven cleared her throat. "I thought sex was a necessary component—"

"Usually," Grace muttered. "But my case was different."

"Aye. I saved your damn life," Adare said, his jaw looking harder than the stone around them.

Grace glared. "Thanks, but that doesn't give you rights over me forever."

"The hell it doesn't." The Highlander crossed his arms.

Haven swallowed and edged toward the door.

Grace threw her hands up in the air. "I am so done with you." She turned on lovely beige boots and stormed out, leaving instant quiet.

Haven coughed. "So. I think I'll go draw for a while. Ponder life and figure things out." She didn't wait for acknowledgment from either male but just took her leave.

Immortals had some serious drama.

Chapter Thirty-Two

"Come this way," Adare said, strolling out of the room and stalking down the hallway and beyond the place with all the screens. "If anything spins out of the wall at you, duck. Fast."

Quade grimaced but followed, impressed when they ended up in a cave for a few moments. Then an outside door opened. "Why is headquarters not better fortified?"

"We keep having to move." Adare stomped out and strode through heavy snow toward a stand of trees. "There's a place beneath a tarp."

Quade ignored the snow falling all around. At least the storm had lightened. He followed Adare between two trees and then stopped, cold. A wide greenish-brown swath of material had been stretched between several trees, protecting the ground from the snow. Several tree stumps had been placed around a firepit, and a fire was crackling, the smoke going out to the side and mingling with the snow.

Ronan looked up and grinned. "How's the neck?"

"Good." Quade paused at seeing the fourth person at the fire. "Benjamin." Benny Reese had been his friend as long as Adare had. When Benny stood, they hugged.

"It's good to see you, man," Benny said, clapping his back with hands bigger than the lily pads that covered the ponds of his youth.

Quade hugged him back, joy making him feel lighter than he had in eons. "Are you still crazy?"

"So they say." Benny released him and retook his seat, grabbing a stick to poke the fire. "So. The four of us. What's left of the original Seven."

Quade drew a stump closer to the warmth and sat next to Adare. "Yes."

Ronan pulled a bottle from the side of his chair and lifted it to the fire. "To those of the Seven we've lost." He took a deep pull and passed the bottle, waiting until they'd all drawn a drink. Then he cleared his throat. "And to our three new members. May the strength they've shown in surviving the ritual carry them forward with us." He drank and the bottle passed again.

Quade took a deep pull and let the alcohol heat his body. It tasted like the whiskey from his younger days. "I've met Ivar in my dream world and Garrett at Realm headquarters. I have yet to meet Logan."

"He's leaving Fae headquarters with his mate, Mercy. They'll pick up that Allison woman who didn't do right by your mate, and then they'll be here when the storm ebbs," Benny said, his gaze on the fire.

Quade looked at the ones he'd begun this journey with, so long ago. "We were not to take mates."

Benny held up both hands. "Hey. Don't look at me. I'm free as a bird and twice as wild."

The idea of Benny ever mating was laughable, to say the least. Not only was he half-crazy, even for a hybrid, but he had always liked his freedom. Quade couldn't imagine him settling down with one female.

"I'm not really mated," Adare protested. "I had no choice. Grace is a Key."

Well, hell. Quade hadn't caught that. It made sense that Adare had mated her. He turned to Ronan. "And you?"

His brother kicked back, extending his long legs toward the fire. "Faith is my mate." He looked up, his eyes a darker shade than Quade's. "Sometimes it's really that simple."

Quade frowned. Nothing was ever that simple. Especially in their lives.

Ronan had their father's jawline, and even relaxed, it was hard. "She's my heart and soul. How could I not mate her and spend what time I have with her?"

Quade warmed to the idea, while Adare looked puzzled and Benny made gagging noises.

"Knock it off." Ronan tossed a snowy pine cone at Benny's head. He then focused on Quade. "What about you? The mating mark has appeared."

Quade's shoulders relaxed. He held his hands out to the fire, warming his palms. "I lost my heart and definitely my soul—too long ago to fathom." Was it possible to regain both? Did he deserve to have either? "Haven cannot navigate the portals and worlds on her own, and if Ulric gets ahold of her, he'll force her to bring him home or kill her." Quade could not let that happen.

Benny cut him a look. "That's the only reason?"

Quade hunched his shoulders and then forced himself to relax. "That's not a good enough reason?" He paused. "Speaking of which, how did a Fae-demon hybrid end up with humans in the first place?"

Ronan shook his head. "You're not going to like it."

"I already dislike it. Now give me the truth," Quade muttered, relaxing now that he was back with family. Damn, it felt good to be with his brothers.

"Fine." Ronan picked up another branch to poke in the fire. "The Fae have lived off world for so long, none of us knew when there was some sort of explosion that killed many of them. The remaining Fae were old—very old. They had a lab with genetic samples, and they created twenty new, young fairies, including Mercy, who has mated Logan."

"Huh?" Quade asked.

"Oh." Ronan winced. "Yeah, well, it's possible to take samples from people, put them together, and make a baby on a plate. Those cells then have to be put into a female for development."

Quade's mouth dropped open. "Are you jesting with me?"

"No. Human science has progressed much in the last few centuries," Ronan said. "As it turns out, the Fae had a genetic sample from a demon, and they used it once to create Haven. Then there was some turmoil and they had to leave our world again, and they didn't think they could take her."

Heat burned through Quade. "They created her and then abandoned her?" That was unthinkable. Truly so.

Adare shook his head. "That's the story. It's crazy, and we don't like the Fae nation much, although our contact is usually with the younger folks who didn't know any of this. Mercy was appalled that Haven had been abandoned."

Quade swallowed. "Who were Haven's genetic donors?"

"No clue," Adare said. "We'll probably never know that fact."

Ronan leaned toward him. "If you want to give her a family, give her yours. I'd love a sister."

Quade kicked snow off his boots. It was the least he could do.

* * * *

Haven wandered along a crystal-clear white shore where diamonds sparkled from the sand. Beauty surrounded her, and she let the warm sun wash over her skin. The ocean lapped toward her, its color a deep, warm purple that was inviting instead of frightening. Even the whitecaps seemed cheery.

She had fallen asleep. She'd tried so hard not to shut her eyes, to keep drawing, but she must've lost the battle.

Still, this was nice. Peaceful. If her nighttime journeys went like this every time, then she'd love to sleep. What would it be like to truly journey to places like this on purpose, as the Fae could? Well, as they used to be able to do.

Without warning, the ground opened up, and she fell.

She screamed, reaching for the sand, but a hole closed over her. Trying to curl into a fetal ball so she could roll, she fought the forces around her, dropping out of a sky and landing on her knees. Pain ripped up to her hips, and she gasped, looking around wildly.

Soft green grass, bubbling brooks, nearby trees. Oh. She'd been here. She stood, wincing as her legs protested, but nothing was broken. "Hello?" she called out.

The two women from before limped out of the forest. Their skin had sunk into their bones, and most of their hair was gone. She gasped. "What happened to you?"

Juliet still had a little blond hair on her head, and she squinted as if she couldn't see. "Haven? It has been years."

Haven's stomach lurched. "It has been days."

"Not here," the other woman sighed. "Time moves differently."

Haven calculated the distance to the trees. "We have to get you out of here. What if you held my hand?" It couldn't hurt.

"I'd try anything," Juliet murmured, leaning on her friend for support. "All seven of us are still alive, but we're fading fast. Or slow, but it feels way too fast."

Haven moved nearer to the women, walking alongside the little brook. She was mere yards away when a gust of wind slammed her to the side. She faltered and regained her balance, only to be pushed again. Yelping, she fell toward the brook and went right through, spinning around and around.

Landing on the heated rock didn't surprise her this time, although it still knocked the wind out of her. Gasping for air, she pushed to her feet.

Ulric waited on the shoreline, blood on his mouth. "Stop fighting me."

She edged away from the drop-off, her heart thundering and her legs trembling. "What's your plan?" she called. "Seriously. I want to know."

"It matters little what you want." His voice carried easily over the distance. "You will take me home, or you will die."

"What if I don't know how to take you home?" She looked for the swirling blue portal, but it seemed to have disappeared now that she could see Ulric. Had there been two worlds that now were combined? That's how it looked and felt. "This can't be good," she muttered. What if another world collided with hers? She glared at him. Wait a minute. He was closer than he'd been last time. Was the rock moving nearer to his shore?

His fangs glistened. "Oh, you can take me home. I guarantee it." Raising his hands, he flattened his palms toward her like a mime in a pretend box.

The rock started to move through the thin air. She lost her balance and dropped to one knee, holding on to the coarse surface. The stone tilted.

She screamed.

"Haven. Wake the hell up," Quade ordered.

She opened her eyes and gasped for air, sitting up in her chair in the underground bedroom. Quade knelt before her, both hands on her shoulders, his gaze an intense blue barely tinged with green. "I'm okay," she mumbled.

He tightened his hold. "Did you see Ulric?"

"Yes." She told him about the entire journey, and by the time she was finished, her body had stopped shaking. "We have to save those Fae people. They looked terrible." Every second that went by might be a month for them. Or even more time than that.

Quade's jaw clenched. "You might not want to save them when you hear the truth. I just found out that they created you with genetic material and then abandoned you because you were part demon."

She blinked. "They created me on purpose?"

He nodded, his expression grim. "Yes. Then they left you with humans. It's unforgivable."

Her body warmed. "Do you know who donated the material?"

"We will never know, according to my brother," he said. "I will try to get you more answers, but that may be all we'll ever learn. I promise the Fae will not go unpunished."

"It's okay," she said automatically, ignoring the sputtering hope inside her. Yeah, she'd thought maybe she'd find family in this immortal world, but she'd always been alone, and that was okay. Tears pricked the backs of her eyes because she was tired. No other reason.

He gently wiped a tear from her cheek. "If you mate me, you'll get a brother- and sister-in-law, not to mention all of the Seven members. We're family."

She forced a chuckle. "I don't need family."

"Fine, but you do need to mate. It sounds like Ulric will reach that rock soon, and you are unprepared to fight him." Quade brushed her hair back from her face. "Belonging to me will not be so bad."

The sudden heat that statement brought to her extremities was one she had to ignore. He was not turning her on. She was a modern woman, a Fae-demoness, no less. "Your language is archaic," she said.

"I am archaic," he said quietly. "I mean the words that I say."

She'd never belonged to anyone or with anyone. The sense of belonging that some people seemed to have intrigued her as much as it had eluded her for so long. For hours, before falling asleep, she'd drawn with her pencils, thinking about Quade. About mating him. There was only one possible decision, and she'd already made it. "I am willing to mate you to handle this problem with Ulric and the lost Fae, but I'm not promising forever."

"If we mate, I'm taking forever," he said, threading his hand through her hair and effectively trapping her head. "You need to understand that and right now."

This side of him, so confident and arrogant, drew her in a way she'd have to examine later, because she should be ticked off. Instead, her breath quickened and her body heated. Her thighs ached. "We'll see." She leaned in to kiss him, and he met her more than halfway, his mouth firm and his kiss hard.

He leaned back, keeping his hold. "Say yes."

She looked at him, immortal and so damn strong. "Yes."

Chapter Thirty-Three

The simple word changed him. In front of her eyes, he widened, ancient power shimmering in his eyes. Warning ticked through her, but it was too late. Everything inside her knew it on a level she'd never be able to explain. She told herself mating was the only way to save those poor Fae members and maybe stop Ulric.

But she was struggling to breathe for some reason.

"Don't be afraid." Quade cupped her jaw, his palm rough against her skin.

"I'm not," she said automatically. It wasn't like they hadn't already slept together. This just seemed so big, somehow. "Quade? I don't think I'm meant for forever." The words rushed out of her, and she couldn't stop them. "I don't want you to expect, well, everything and be disappointed."

A dimple flashed in his right cheek. "I do expect everything, and I will not be disappointed." Ducking his shoulder, he lifted her from the chair. "I can get what I want from you, sweetling."

Her eyebrows rose and she slid an arm around his neck. "Is that a fact?" What exactly did he want? Besides everything.

"Aye." He set her down on the bed and gently lifted her shirt over her head.

Cool air brushed over her skin, but she flushed, instantly hot. "What do you want?"

He removed her tank top, which was also acting as a bra, his eyes flaring as her breasts were released. "Honor, loyalty, obedience."

No love? The words ticked through her. "Wait a minute. No obedience." She wasn't a dog, for Pete's sake. "Your time has passed, my friend."

"My time is apparently now." He yanked his shirt off with little care, revealing that hard and damaged chest. "All the time I have, before the final ritual, I will devote to making you safe. We will start with the dream world, and then this world. That I vow to you."

Nobody had ever really given a crap whether she was safe or not, so it was tempting to fall right into his plan for them. So tempting. What would it truly be like to be the center of somebody's world? Even temporarily? She unbuckled his belt. When had he gotten a belt? "Your words are nice, but the underlying assumptions beneath them are bothersome." Making her point, she released his zipper.

He sucked in air, and his ripped abdomen rolled. "No assumptions. Just facts."

No complete sentences, either. She smiled and reached for him, humming at his thick length. The guy really was gifted. "Okay, Ace." She caressed him, and the growl that rumbled from his chest shot right to her core. "I'm not the obedient type. You should probably learn that now."

He lifted her by the arms and settled her back on the bed. "Perhaps nobody has taught you." Humor glimmered in his unreal eyes along with a healthy dose of hunger.

She rolled her eyes. Energy coursed through her, sparking her blood and making her nerves tighten. Rolling, she came up the other side of the bed, her breath quickening. "We need to get this settled before the mating." Her chin went up at the same time his lowered, giving him a predatory look fiercer than any animal. Her legs bunched to run.

He cocked his head. "What are you doing?"

"I'm not sure," she admitted, edging toward the end of the bed. "The whole agreement, like we've signed on the dotted line, just seems off." None of this made any sense, but she went with her instincts, as usual.

He angled her way. "I have no problem taming you, if that's what's troubling you."

Her eyes widened. "Seriously. Dude. We have to talk."

An alarm blared insistently through the underground facility, and the entire mountain rocked. Quade instantly zipped up and tossed her a shirt. The mountain bucked again, and an explosion sounded somewhere deep in the rock.

She struggled to get the shirt over her head.

He grabbed her hand and ran for the door, shoving her behind him as he looked into the hallway. Smoke filled the area. "We have to get out of here." Holding tight, he stepped gracefully into the hallway and started running toward the computer room.

She held the shirt up to her mouth, trying to keep smoke out of her lungs. Her eyes watered, but she ran with him, stopping cold at the kitchen. Flames poured from a room beyond the computers.

Benny ran out, a shirt over his face.

"Are we being attacked?" Quade barked, just as Ronan ran from the sleeping quarters, his chest and feet bare; Faith and Grace were behind him.

"No." Benny bent over. "We were wiring explosives, and one went off." He grabbed a fire extinguisher, turned, and shot the white mess toward the flames. They sputtered out.

Ivar rushed out from one of the rooms and instantly dropped into a slide by a computer. He typed in several keys, and a whoosh of air sucked up all the smoke into black grates on the ceiling. "I put the ventilation system in first this time." He coughed, his eyes watering. "What the hell, Ben?"

Benny wiped soot off his chest. "We need protection in place." He winced. "Sorry."

The last person in the entire world who should be playing with explosives was Benjamin Reese. Quade angled to the side to view the damaged room. One entire wall had blown back several feet, revealing another vein of copper. The grate in the ceiling above him opened, dangling from one side.

"Damn it," Ivar muttered, glaring up.

Benny wiped soot off his face. "I guess we'd better clean this up."

Quade turned and brushed soot out of Haven's hair. So much for his smooth romantic moves. "Why don't you go wash up, sweetling? I'll help here."

Her eyes were wide and soot covered her nose, but she nodded and retreated, keeping an eye on Benny. Then she turned and jogged down the hallway.

Benny coughed. "I hope I didn't interrupt anything."

Quade was going to kill him.

* * * *

Haven's body ached from too much arousal too fast, and the adrenaline rush from the explosion hadn't helped much. However, her mind was pleased with the reprieve. She stepped into the stone-walled enclosure, looking up at the rain-type showerhead extending from the rock. Hot water poured out with impressive pressure.

Even if the Seven had skimped on computers and bedrooms, the showers were luxurious. She smiled, humming softly as she stepped under the spray. Steam rose around her, but the copper veins still glowed.

A whish of sound caught her attention, and then Quade stepped around the corner and into the shower, soot covering his bare chest. He was nude and fully aroused.

She jumped. "What in the world?"

He smiled and reached for the soap. "We're finishing our discussion."

"Wh-what discussion?" She slid to the side so he could wash off the soot, her gaze caught by his powerful hands over that incredible chest.

"Our mating." He set the soap down and tugged her closer. The smell of mint wafted through the steam.

She slid her hands up and over his soapy chest, unable to prevent herself from touching him. "Did you eat more toothpaste?"

"No. Just brushed my teeth." When she held his gaze, he lifted one large shoulder. "I may have eaten a little."

She smacked his chest. "I told you to stop doing that."

"I know." He retaliated for the punch by jerking her closer, his mouth taking hers. He kissed her long and hard and deep, his big body curling over her, his hold absolute. When he finally lifted his head, she could barely breathe. "Haven. You're the one." He tangled his hand in her wet hair and tugged just enough to send electric tingling along her scalp. Then he kissed her again, his mouth claiming, his tongue possessing.

She leaned closer, a moan sighing up from her chest.

He traced kisses down her neck and nipped the spot where he'd bitten her before.

She shivered, biting her lip. Pleasure rippled from his mouth, straight to her core. He flipped her around, and she gasped, planting her hands on the smooth stone wall.

"Keep your hands there." His voice was raw. Hoarse and commanding. His erection brushed her butt, and he reached around her, both hands soapy and playing with her nipples. He rolled and teased, having her panting for more in a minute. Then his hand slid down her belly and he parted her, rubbing across her clit.

Her knees nearly gave out, and she dropped a hand to steady herself.

The smack to her butt had her crying out. Heat spread out from his palm, slamming right to her core.

"I told you to stay there." He grasped her hand and raised it next to the other one, one large foot kicking her legs farther apart. "Let go again, and you won't like the result."

She shut her eyes and a shudder took her. "Quade." This was a new side to him. Just how much of himself had he been holding back?

His fangs sank into her neck, in and out, and he licked the wound clean, sending electricity to her breasts. He'd marked her again. He tweaked her nipples and one hand slid down. She sucked in breath, holding it, her body on the precipice. Chuckling, he slid one finger inside her and then a second, crisscrossing them until she was ready to beg.

An orgasm uncoiled inside her, taking her breath. She rode it out, her body shaking, and rested her cheek against the wall by her hands.

The wildness in him, the barely controlled movements, spurred her on as nothing else could have. He palmed her, his hand grinding against her still firing clit. She cried out, pleasure and warning mingling in her head.

He placed his hands over hers on the wall and slid them down, bending her over. Flames licked along her skin. Then he penetrated her, going slow, just his body taking hers. His fingers curled over hers, and she held on like her life depended on it.

Just as he'd embedded himself fully, he pulled out, setting up a hard and fast rhythm that forced her onto her toes. With his hands over hers and his body taking hers, she couldn't move. "Quade," she breathed.

He leaned over and nipped her shoulder. Was he going to bite her? He shifted his angle, prodding a spot inside her that shot streaks of white behind her closed eyes. She rose, fast and hard, for that edge she'd only found with him. Her body tensed, and her thighs trembled. She cried his name as an orgasm bore down on her, taking everything she had.

She panted, her eyes wide on the rock wall. It took her a second to realize he was still hard inside her. She blinked.

He released her hands and withdrew, flipping her around. "This way." Lifting her easily, he impaled her against the stone, his gaze capturing hers.

She grabbed his shoulders, curling her hands over. Her thighs clamped onto his hips on their own. He grasped her pelvis and tilted her so he could go deeper.

Then he started to pound. Hard and fast and deeper than she would've thought possible. His eyes were a deep midnight with no green, fathomless and powerful. His jaw was hard and his concentration absolute. He held her aloft, controlling their movements, controlling them both.

His fangs dropped low.

She spasmed around him, and he growled.

Fast as lightning, he struck, his fangs digging deep in her neck. Pain lashed into her and she threw her head back, crying out as he continued to hammer inside her.

The orgasm uncoiled inside her, fast and hot, and she climbed toward it. Sparks flew along her nerves and she stiffened, digging her nails into his skin.

Heat flashed along her hip and buttock, spreading fire through her flesh. She cried out and fell over, coming so hard she could only hold on to him and trust that he'd hold her. His thrusts increased, faster and harder, until his muscled body jerked with his own release.

She gasped, her body going soft with exhaustion. He lifted his head and a smile tugged at his lips. "Hello, mate."

Chapter Thirty-Four

For the first time since leaving his hell world, Quade Kayrs was settled. Full on, in control, back in this world. Settled. After the mating, he hadn't let Haven get much sleep, keeping her busy in bed all night. She sat next to him in the computer room, eating a bowl of cereal, the bite mark on her neck evident for all to see.

He brushed a thumb across the bite mark, hiding a smile when she shivered.

She looked at him, her green eye lighter than usual. "Knock it off." But then she smiled and returned to picking the marshmallows to eat out of her cereal. Why didn't they just make the cereal with only marshmallows?

Promise Williams, Ivar's mate, cleared her throat up by a screen. They'd filled her in about Haven's abilities and what had happened the last few times in the dream worlds, and she'd done a bunch of math for a while. "Okay. So, here's what we think we have." Ivar sat next to her on a computer, and right now, it was just the four of them. Adare and Benny were out scouting, and Ronan and Faith were still in bed. Grace was nowhere to be seen, and Logan and Mercy would soon arrive with Haven's human mother.

Quade was not looking forward to meeting that woman.

Promise typed on a laptop, and a series of numbers came up on the screen. "So, what I think is happening is that when Quade's world imploded, energy released by its destruction ricocheted across other worlds, much like a rock skipping across a stream."

Quade studied this female of Ivar's. Spirally black hair, lovely dusky skin, intelligent brown eyes. She managed to put modern science in a way that made sense, and he appreciated being able to follow her logic. She wore dark pants with a pretty green blouse, making her look feminine and soft next to the big-ass Viking, who was clearly in love. Ivar kept nodding and grinning as she explained. He was definitely not from the same era as Quade.

But every time Promise smiled or ran a hand down Ivar's arm, the male brightened. What would it be like to have that connection? To feel that closeness?

Had the ability to love been tortured out of Quade?

Promise tapped a silver cylinder and turned to point it at the screen, emitting a laser. A blue one. Quade stiffened and bunched his legs to cover Haven, but nothing exploded. Oh. All right. Lasers weren't only for blowing things up.

Good to know.

Haven chuckled, and he cut her a look. Smart-ass. She'd known exactly what was going through his head. His heart warmed. A little.

"So." Promise pointed at a bunch of numbers. "There must be something in demon DNA that allows you to teleport on this planet, and a marker in Fae DNA that allows teleportation off this world."

"To another dimension?" Haven asked.

Ivar groaned, and his head dropped.

Promise smiled. "Ivar?"

Ivar turned. "We can't travel to another dimension because we're three-dimensional beings. So we can only go to three-dimensional places, although it's possible we travel *through* other dimensions. We just don't land in them." He rolled his eyes and then turned back to his mate.

"Got it," Haven said, munching contentedly on another marshmallow.

Quade didn't understand what the numbers meant, and right now, he didn't really care. "The only question I have is whether or not I'll be able to travel with Haven in her sleep. Or even without her, now."

She stopped chewing.

Promise looked at the board. "I think so. Haven is the only Fae-demoness in existence, as far as we know, so she's the only one who apparently can travel without her body. It's a whole new level of science, and I'm just starting to figure it out. But since you've mated—and congratulations, by the way—you should gain her abilities." She pursed her lips. "Especially since you've already actually traveled to other places. In the same way there are pathways in the brain, I believe there are pathways through dimensions."

Ivar turned to face Quade, his blue eyes dark. "I've been thinking as well. What if Quade's world didn't completely implode? What if it collided or combined with others much like planets and stars have collided for eons? If Ulric's world combined with the other world or worlds, there has to be a way to keep him from moving again."

Promise nodded. "I believe that's what you were actually doing all those years in your own world. Ronan described how he moved magnets to change the polarization of his world, and I'm sure you did the same. What you were really doing was keeping portals from opening so that they would not allow Ulric passage."

Quade sat up. "Is there a way to shut all portals? For now, anyway?"

Promise's eyes gleamed. "I think so?"

Haven set her spoon down. "The rock, right? It's the rock I keep landing on. It has to be."

Promise's eyebrows rose. "Smart. Yes, I believe so. You describe the area as rock, trees, weird water, and drop-off cliffs. What if, as Ivar said, these all represent different worlds that have collided? In that case, I think the rock is the piece holding them all together. Blow up that rock, and there will be no connection to our world for Ulric to seek. We think. I mean, that's the best hypothesis I can offer right now."

Quade shook his head. "We've never been able to bring weapons when we teleport." He rubbed his chin. "Though I might be able to break the rock." He was stronger than ever before after his time in hell.

Haven grasped his arm. "If you break the rock while we're on it, you'll fall. We both will."

Ah. She hadn't completely figured out that he was going to go it alone, and as soon as possible. He captured her hand on his arm, flattening it beneath his. She was strong and healthy, and he planned to keep her that way.

Quick footsteps sounded down the hallway, and a petite female rushed into the room, bounding right up to Haven. "Hey. I'm Mercy." The fairy had one blue eye and one green, and her hair was a dark red with streaks. "You're Haven." She dragged Haven from the chair and hugged her, hard. Quade released her hand so she didn't fall.

They were exactly the same size.

"You're short, like me." Mercy pulled back, keeping Haven's arms. "I'm so sorry about what they did to you—I never had a clue. But now you're here, and we're together. We brought you a bunch of canvases and paints like Quade asked for. You have to help me save those Fae in Brookville. Can you do it?"

Haven looked shell-shocked. "Um. Yes?"

"No," Quade said. "Not without me."

* * * *

The world tilted around Haven and she took a step back, taking a look at Mercy. Another Fae. She wasn't completely alone, even though she was the only Fae hybrid. Truth be told, they looked a little bit alike. "I think I can get back there tonight when I sleep," she said, ignoring Quade.

Heat rolled from him, and she stubbornly kept her attention on Mercy.

Mercy sniffed the air. "Oh, you've mated. Wow. That didn't take a lot of time."

Heat burst into Haven's face. Her butt and hip still burned from the marking, though she'd looked at it earlier, and it truly was beautiful and wild.

Mercy laughed and patted her hand. "Don't worry about it. Most of us mate fast when it's real." She looked over her shoulder. "Speaking of which. That's Logan, my mate."

Haven turned and the spit in her mouth dried up. Next to a massive dark-haired male stood Allison, the woman who had acted as her mother for a short time. She looked tiny next to Logan, even in a thick light blue coat and jeans. Her brown hair was streaked with gray and there were many new lines on her makeup-free face. "Hi."

Allison hesitated, clasping her wrinkled hands together. "Hi."

Quade stood and placed a reassuring hand at the back of Haven's waist. He leaned in, his breath brushing her ear. "What do you want, sweet Fae? Time alone with her or do you want me to come with you?"

Haven let out a shuddering breath, warmed by his instant support. Did Allison even know the pastor was dead? "Time alone." She looked over her shoulder at Ivar. "Is there a bedroom for her?"

Ivar nodded. "Two doors down from you there's another room. It's not fancy."

None of this was fancy. "Thank you." Did Allison even know that these weren't humans?

Logan cleared his throat. "First, it's nice to meet you. Second, I've informed Allison about our research facility here, and that it's government-sanctioned and top-secret. She's agreed to sign an NDA."

Well. Haven nodded. "I understand." So, no telling the human about immortals. Not a problem. She'd never confided in Allison before, so why start now? She moved toward the woman, pausing next to her. "If you'd come with me?" Without waiting, feeling all eyes on her, she started down the corridor.

Allison quietly followed along, waiting until they'd reached the door before speaking. "I'm sorry. I'm so scared. You have to help me."

Haven tried to keep calm and pushed open the door to find a room with a bed and nothing else. "The bathroom is on the other side of the rock, and if it's like mine, it's pretty nice." She partially turned to face Allison. "They brought you here to meet with me, so I could get some sort of closure. I don't know if I even want that."

Tears filled Allison's blue eyes. "I'm so sorry. I believed in him. That he had a mission from God, and that he was right about you." She wiped a tear off her cheek. "You were so different, and it seemed like he was right. I did try to protect you. But not enough."

Haven recalled an image of Allison standing up to the pastor and getting hit once when she was younger. "I remember," she said slowly. "Kind of." That didn't mean she forgave Allison, but maybe she should try to do that. Wasn't forgiveness good for the one forgiving? Her temples began to ache. This brush with the past was too much.

Her body felt different since the mating, and her head was spinning. She wished, more than ever, that she had a relationship with this woman so she could confide in her. But it wasn't there. Her heart ached.

Allison leaned in. "Who are these people, really? I saw them fight, and I saw fangs." Fear shook her voice. "I signed the NDA, but they know I saw. Are they vampires?" She quickly crossed herself.

Well, shit. Apparently Allison trusted her, because she'd just given a reason why she could never return to her old life. Haven shook her head. "I think maybe the stress of the situation with the pastor got to you." She finally reached out and patted Allison's arm. "What happened was traumatic. Thank you for trying to stop the, ah, guy from taking me from your kitchen." She'd seen Pierce knock out Allison.

Allison grabbed her hands. "I tried. I really did. I am your mother." She looked around, her eyes wide. "I feel like these people aren't just going to let me go back to my life. Am I right?"

Haven swallowed, emotions fighting within her. She wasn't sure what to think—about anybody. "I won't let them hurt you." It was the least she could do, considering Allison had tried to protect her a couple of times. "Though you need to understand, I don't consider you my mother. We don't have a real mother-daughter bond, and it's not because I was adopted." She kept her voice gentle, but she needed to say the words. "You abandoned me and let him scare and hurt me. Some of the foster homes I was in weren't great, and I was on my own at fourteen."

Allison's head dropped. "I know." She sniffed. "I'm sorry. Maybe we can start over? Be friends?"

That was asking for a lot. Haven extricated herself. Was this closure? For the first time in so long, she could see a future without running and without fear. Well, maybe there would always be fear in this new world.

Allison released her. "We weren't completely wrong, were we?" She stepped into the rock room, looking around. "You're not human. None of them are." She turned, her expression more resigned than afraid. "Right?"

"Why don't you get settled in? Once you realize that you did not see what you thought you saw, you can go live your life." Haven wasn't sure of the rules of this new world, but instinct told her that the existence of the immortals was secret for a reason. She couldn't imagine Quade killing a human, but what were the options? "Get comfortable, and maybe we'll talk later." It had been over a decade since she'd seen Allison, and since then, she'd made her own life.

Allison nodded. "I would like to know who or what they are." She tilted her head. "You promised not to let them hurt me. Do you have fangs?"

"No." Haven backed away. "I wish."

Mercy called down the hallway. "Haven? The queen wants to talk to us."

Allison's eyes widened again. "You all have a queen?"

Haven turned to go. "Yeah. She's pretty cool. More like a doctor." She shut the door and hustled down the hallway, rubbing the bite mark on her neck. Life had gotten way too weird.

Chapter Thirty-Five

Haven reached the computer room, where the farthest monitor was smoking and sputtering. "What happened?"

Ivar slapped the flames out. "We're not ready to set up headquarters here yet, and the electricity went off." He glanced up, a burn healing across his chin. "I tried to hack into a satellite." He lowered his head and muttered, "I bet Gwen got the rose."

Haven paused. "She didn't! I saw a rerun the other morning. Jennifer got the rose."

Ivar frowned. "Seriously? She's such a wretch. Gwen is the sweet one."

"I know, right?" Haven shared a smile with him.

Ivar slapped the monitor. "I can't believe I missed it. We keep getting headquarters blown up. It's such a pain."

Quade strode down from the kitchen, a sandwich in his hand. "How did it go with Allison?"

"Okay." She wanted to burrow into his side; instead, she straightened her spine and remained in place.

His eyebrows rose and he crossed to her, hauling her close for a hug. "You don't have to be brave all the time." He dropped a kiss on the top of her head.

Her eyes stung and she batted away emotion, taking a deep breath of him. Mint and male and Quade. She settled for the first time since Allison had walked in. "I'm fine."

"I know." He kissed her again. "Want some of my sandwich?"

"No, thanks." She wasn't hungry. "Where's Mercy? She called for me."

"Here." Mercy bopped out of the kitchen with Logan on her heels, both holding grape sport drinks. Logan easily took her hand as they neared.

Quade stiffened and then relaxed. Interesting. Was he getting ideas from all the folks in love around them? Haven could relate. It was hard not to when faced with such happiness. Did he want love such as his brother had found? Or did he think it was impossible after the life he'd led?

She placed her hand over his heart and rose up to kiss him beneath the jaw.

Surprise flashed across his hard face, followed by pleasure. He grinned. "What was that for?"

She faltered and recovered by turning toward Mercy. "You were saying something about the queen?"

"Yeah." Mercy looked over at Ivar and the smoldering computer console. "Said to give her a call when we had a chance. Maybe it's about the missing Fae? She has connections we don't."

"Here." Ivar grabbed the nearest laptop, typed in several codes, and brought up the queen in her lab on the closest screen.

Emma looked up from a tablet. "Hello. Where are you?"

Ivar shook his head. "It's a secret."

Emma's dark hair was down around her shoulders this time, and her blue eyes were intense. But she wore her customary white lab coat over a T-shirt and jeans. "Whatever. We could find you if we wanted. Well, maybe."

Quade snorted. "Right. We stole a helicopter from you." Then he winced. "Sorry we crashed it."

Emma grinned. "Yeah. Dage isn't happy he let you go with one of his best prototypes and you destroyed it. You might not want to mess with him for a while."

Haven pursed her lips. "He let us take the helicopter?"

Emma rolled her eyes. "Did you really think two Realm soldiers would be that easy to subdue?"

"Not really," Quade admitted. "I take it the king wanted to track us and find our headquarters?"

Emma chuckled. "Yeah, and instead he ended up with a pile of destroyed metal." She cleared her throat. "His sense of humor is nowhere near as good as mine, just so you know."

Haven winced. Dage Kayrs hadn't seemed like a guy she'd want to piss off. "Tell him we're sorry?"

"I'll do that." Emma typed something on her tablet. "So, I wanted to talk to the two of you."

Haven shared a look with Mercy. Was there something wrong?

Mercy stepped forward. "What's happening?"

Emma typed more and read the screen. "I've been conducting tests on your blood, looking for chromosomal abnormalities that would explain your abilities, but nothing so far." Her brow furrowed. "There has to be something, but it might take me years."

Haven relaxed against Quade. "You're giving us an update." All right. She could handle that.

Emma looked up. "Yes, and there's more. I ran a DNA test with all of the Fae blood I've managed to acquire so far—meaning Mercy—and you two share a genetic donor."

Haven tilted her head. What? "Wait a minute. What are you saying?"

Mercy gasped, clapping her hands together. "Really? Are you sure?"

Emma nodded. "Yep. I don't know whether it was maternal or paternal, but you definitely share one donor. My guess is maternal, but there's no way to know for sure."

Mercy grabbed Haven's arms and yanked her free of Quade. "Sisters! We're sisters." Joy filled her face and she hugged Haven, jumping up and down. "Can you believe it? I always wanted a sister, and this is so awesome." She let go, her eyes sparkling.

Haven swallowed. A sister? A real sister? Emotion overcame her, and her mouth dropped open. She couldn't move.

Mercy's face softened. "Oh, Haven. This is a good thing. I promise." She leaned in and hugged her again.

"I know." Haven hugged her back. She wasn't alone. She had a sister and now a mate. She looked over at him, and he winked.

That simple gesture helped calm her better than anything else could have. A wink from a too-serious, dangerous, wild vampire-demon hybrid.

His sandwich finished, he extricated her from Mercy and drew her back to his side. "You okay? This is a lot."

It was a lot. The entire day—it was still just morning—had been overwhelming. Plus, her body felt different after the mating the night before. Her blood felt sluggish and her limbs tired. She cleared her throat. "Emma? I, ah, this is personal, but I was wondering if I should feel so tired after being mated." She might as well learn to trust her new family now.

Emma's lips twitched. "Yes. My research shows that mating takes a toll, temporarily, on the female of the pair right away. Don't ask me why, because it isn't fair. Considering you're a hybrid, I assume you'll feel better very soon. It's nothing like going from human to mated, believe me."

Quade leaned down. "You're not feeling well?" Clouds gathered across his expression.

"I'm well but a little tired," she admitted. "Thought I'd ask if it was normal." She looked up at his shadowed jaw. "What about you?"

"I feel great," he murmured.

Figured.

Emma set her tablet aside. "If you'll excuse me, I have a date with my niece, Hope. Something about a chess game." She smiled, and the screen went dark.

* * * *

Hope kissed her aunt Emma bye and crawled into her bed, taking out the hidden tablet. She typed online, and soon Drake the Kurjan came into view. She yawned. "Hi. You get into the dream worlds yet?"

His eyes were a deep green edged with purple, and he had a bruise across his cheekbone. "Nope. You?"

She shook her head. "What happened to your face?"

He rubbed the bruise. "We were training, and I didn't duck fast enough. Not a big deal."

It was too bad kids didn't have the healing cells that adults got. Hope rubbed her nose. Maybe Pax really was getting bruised in training, just like Drake. She wondered if one day the two of them would wind up facing each other on a battlefield. "Do you think we'll all be friends someday?"

Drake shrugged, showing a dark T-shirt with snapping turtles on it. "I don't know, but that'd be nice." He settled back against what looked like a wooden headboard. "I've never met a shifter, and that'd be fun. Or a witch."

"They're cool," Hope said, plucking at the bedspread.

He yawned. "Do your folks know we're talking?"

"Nope. You?"

He shook his head. "No, my dad doesn't know. My uncle Terre asked me the other day, and I told him no. He's my dad's brother."

She didn't know his daddy had a brother. "I have uncles, too."

"I know. Two of them are members of the Seven." Drake smiled, showing long canines. "We know stuff about you."

She rolled her eyes. "We know stuff about you, too. Like Ulric isn't coming home."

"Yes, he is." Drake leaned forward. "Now that Quade is on this world, Ulric is next."

Yeah, she'd figured he knew about Quade. "Ulric is a bad guy. You're a good guy, so you shouldn't like him."

"He's our spiritual leader," Drake countered, his jaw looking hard. "You don't know him, and we do. Maybe the Seven is wrong. Have you thought about that?"

"No," she burst out. "The Seven knows stuff." But sometimes, late at night, fate whispered in her ear that things were scary and could go wrong. She wasn't sure how, but she needed her green book and her dream world to fix things. She and Drake had to get back there.

A knock on the window had her jumping.

Drake stared at her. "Is the hybrid there?"

She'd told him about Paxton a long time ago, figuring they'd all be friends someday. "Yes."

"Tell him hi." Drake clicked off.

Paxton opened the window from outside and jumped in, his boots muddy. He gingerly took them off. "Whatcha doing?"

"I was talking to Drake." She set the tablet beneath her pillow.

"The Kurjans can trace calls like that." Pax shrugged off his snowy jacket and set it by the window.

She snorted. "They all know where Realm and Demon headquarters are, Pax. We have defenses in place, and you know it." In fact, Paxton was interested in defenses and had asked Hope's daddy to show him the missiles and how they worked. She wasn't as interested and would rather learn about people than missiles.

Pax jumped on the edge of the bed. "Did Drake try to find out more about the Seven?"

They weren't supposed to even know about the Seven, and maybe Hope shouldn't have told Pax. But he was her best friend, along with Libby. "Kind of?"

The window opened again, and Libby jumped inside, her blondish hair in pigtails. "Hi. Saw your dad outside and he told me I could use the door, but this is more fun." She shrugged out of her coat and boots, leaping gracefully across the room to land next to Paxton. "I decided I'm gonna be a spy."

Hope coughed and covered her mouth until she was done. "A spy? How cool. How do you do that?"

Libby shrugged, her brown eyes concerned. "Do you have another cough?" She shared a look with Paxton.

"No." Hope crossed her arms and then ruined it by coughing again. "Maybe a little one." She frowned at her friends. "It's no big deal." Except it was. Immortal kids didn't really get sick like human kids did, and she was immortal. The first and only female with vampire blood in her. So why was she getting sick like a human?

Pax grasped her hand. "Did you tell your mom?"

She shook her head. "Mom looks all worried when I get sick, and since it's just a little cough, I figured I'd just get over it myself." She didn't like it when her parents got worried and all quiet. "Do you think there's something wrong with me?" she whispered.

"No." Paxton's grip strengthened. "There's nothing wrong with you. Sure, you might get a little sick once in a while, but someday you'll get healing cells, so it'll all be okay."

Libby nodded, her hair tossing all around.

Hope swallowed. "What if I don't get healing cells?" She'd never had the guts to say those words out loud, but she was starting to worry.

"You will," Libby piped up. "Or I guess you could mate somebody and get his healing cells." She scrunched up her nose.

"Gross," Hope and Pax said at the same time.

Hope giggled. She was never gonna mate, so she'd have to figure out healing cells on her own. Boys were gross, except for Paxton, and they were gonna be best friends forever. He didn't want to mate anybody, either. Grown-ups were so weird.

Her friends jumped into bed beside her, and she coughed a little more.

Pax took her hand. "I promise you'll be okay."

She nodded. She had to be, right?

Chapter Thirty-Six

Haven spent the day painting in the back room with horrible light, but she didn't care. She needed time away from everybody to process the last few days, and the process of creating art on canvas soothed her. She painted the place Mercy called Brookville, the rock, Ulric, and different portals. At some point, Mercy brought her some soup, and she ate it before losing herself in her painting again.

"You got your way with Pierce," Quade said from the doorway.

She jumped, turning to see him lounging against the doorframe. "What?" She wiped her hands off on a rag

He shook his head. "I talked to the queen, and she said Pierce was committed to some facility. Can you believe it? These days we send crazy cougars to facilities and don't just cut off their heads?"

He looked so bewildered she had to smile. "It's the right thing. Maybe he'll get help."

Quade tucked his thumbs in his faded jeans as if he'd been wearing jeans his whole life. "If he comes after you again, I'm taking his head clean off. You need to understand that."

Kinda bossy and definitely sexy. She glanced at a painting of his face, eyes hungry, jaw hard. "I painted you."

He loped into the room. "I can see that." He looked around. "These are all of the places you can get to?"

Huh. She looked at the paintings, and saw they were all of the places she'd seen in the dream worlds. "I hadn't realized that." If they closed all the portals, would she still have subjects to paint? Sure. There were tons of possibilities on this planet, and if nothing else, she'd paint the sexy Quade Kayrs.

He looked over a depiction of the rock and Ulric. "Do you ever paint yourself?"

She coughed. "A self-portrait? Not really."

"If I could paint, I'd do you." He brushed hair away from her face, his touch soft. "It's almost nighttime. Mercy is on me to save those Fae, and I was wondering if you were up to trying?"

She nodded. "I've been thinking about it all day."

He leaned down and brushed a kiss over her mouth as if it were the most natural thing to do, and she leaned into him. "I don't know if I'll be able to join you yet. You have to promise me that if I can't, you'll wait for another time."

That didn't make any sense. "Those Fae don't have any time left, Quade."

He cupped her jaw, holding her in place. "You can't control the jump, remember? You might get them free, or you might end up with Ulric. Promise me."

Mercy appeared in the doorway, eating a chocolate Santa. "Has anybody decided what to do with that Allison woman? Christmas is only a week away. Shouldn't she be somewhere else? Somewhere not here?"

Haven paused. Apparently, her new sister wasn't forgiving. Nice to know. "What are the options?"

"The usual," Mercy said, walking toward a painting of Brookville. "Wow. That's perfect. I loved going there." She sounded wistful. "Hopefully, we can get there again."

Haven grasped her arm. "The usual?"

"Oh." Mercy ate off the Santa's arm. "We like to keep humans from knowing about us. We usually scare them into keeping quiet, and since nobody will believe them anyway, it's pretty easy to do. But there is an island off Ireland that the demons have sent humans to as well. Totally off the grid."

Quade reared up. "Fire Island?"

"No." Mercy frowned. "It's called Green Island. What's Fire Island?"

Quade shrugged. "Dunno."

Haven looked at him. Hadn't he said something about an island with dragons that was a secret? Interesting. She'd love to see floors covered in diamonds. She cleared her throat. "Who decides about Allison?"

"You do," Mercy said, finishing off the treat. "She's your connection, so you get to decide. I'm not calling her your mother."

"I'm not, either," Haven admitted. "I owe her something for trying to protect me as a kid, and for at least loving me a little. But it's been over a decade since I saw her, and I don't feel like I owe her a lot." Should she feel more than she did? She bit her lip.

Mercy patted her arm. "Yeah, that's what I thought. I'm totally with you, sister."

Sister. It was so odd to think about having a sister. Haven smiled. "I promise we'll try to get those Fae home tonight." No matter what Quade said, she was going to try to save them. For her new sister, if for no other reason. That connection mattered.

"That's good. Thanks." Worry darkened Mercy's eyes.

Haven swallowed. "Not for nothing, but why do we care if humans know about us? I mean—vampires, demons, Fae—we're all just different species." How freaking crazy it felt to say those words and have them make sense. "Why is everything such a big secret? I don't get it."

Mercy licked chocolate off her fingers. "Well, think about it. Humans would love to be immortal, and they'd probably go to war to figure us out and experiment. We'd go to war, end them all, and then we wouldn't have humans. So we're doing them a favor."

Quade nodded.

Haven exhaled slowly. "All right." There wasn't much of an argument to make against that logic.

"Well, then. I guess we should get ready for bed." Quade ducked a shoulder and tossed Haven over it, turning and striding out into the hallway.

Haven yelped and the blood rushed to her head. She smacked his back and chuckled. Apparently, they weren't going right to sleep. As he carried her, humming, she tried to relax into the moment. Happy times for her had never lasted, and it was difficult to take this night and just enjoy.

When he flipped her onto their bed and kissed her, she forgot all about relaxing.

* * * *

After a very energetic evening with Quade, Haven felt relaxed and exhausted. She fell into a deep sleep, and was soon wandering along a beach, enjoying the sparkling diamonds in the sand.

She leaned down and picked one up, turning to face the gentle sea. Hmmm. Okay. She was asleep in the good place. Now. She turned and faced the darkened forest. "Quade?" she called.

Nothing.

Okay. She walked along the shoreline, careful to stay clear of the real diamonds. Her feet were bare, but she wore leggings and a tunic. The sun warmed her, and she lifted her face and shut her eyes.

"Haven?"

She jerked and opened her eyes. Quade stood down the beach, his legs braced, his fists clenched. "Where are we?"

"It's a good place." She hustled toward him, her voice hushed. "You're here. Really?"

He looked around, scouting for threats. "Yes. Where are the Fae?"

"This isn't the right world." A chill from the forest swept over her, and clouds began to cover the sun. "Did I call you here?"

"I think so," he said, frowning at the clouds.

Had she been able to do so before mating him? She'd never tried. Quade cleared his throat. "This doesn't feel right. Wake up, now."

A cry in the distance alerted her. The Fae. "We have to get to them." She turned and started to run toward the forest.

"Haven, no!" he yelled, running behind her.

The ground dropped out beneath her again, and she spun around to grab his arm, but she wasn't fast enough. She tumbled end over end, her head hitting something solid, until finally, she landed on her side on soft grass. She blinked several times and sat up. Brooks bubbled around her, and the trees in the distance were taller than ever.

Quade. She could sense him. Back in their room, trying to awaken her. She fought him, needing to stay in this world. Huh. Who knew she could do that?

A portal opened, one with swirling blue lines. Ulric.

She fought the pull. "Hello? If you're here, hurry up." The pull from the portal picked up, along with the wind.

The seven Fae limped out of the trees, looking emaciated and pale. Five females and two males. They made their way to her, over patches of grass, helping one another move like elderly people. Juliet reached her first. "You came."

Haven braced her legs against the portal's pull. "Yes." Now what?

The blonde eyed the portal. "I don't think we should go that way."

"No." Haven struggled to stay on her feet, noting the other Fae weren't being pulled. It was only her? She recalled the time she'd spent on the rock. When she'd fallen off, she'd awakened. She looked frantically around, starting to slide on the grass.

Juliet grabbed her, but she wasn't strong enough to stop the pull.

Haven struggled wildly, but the portal drew her. She gasped and stared at the brook. Wait a minute. Biting her lip, going on pure instinct, she focused on the water. Slowly, it began to spin, turning a light green color. She swept her hand out, as if painting, and the water swirled faster. Power flowed through her, much like when she painted. "Everyone jump into the brook," she yelled, going with her instincts. "Trust me," she snapped when they hesitated. "You have nothing to lose."

Juliet nodded and grabbed Haven's hand. "Let's jump together."

This was either going to be a disaster or a triumph. Who knew what the heck was in that brook or how she'd changed the color and movement. The portal's pull increased in force, and Haven dropped to her knees, fighting with every ounce of strength she possessed. "It's now or never," she grunted, pitching forward and holding Juliet's hand.

The water was surprisingly warm. It enclosed her head, and she dropped down almost gently.

"Haven!" Quade shook her so hard, her teeth snapped together in the back of her jaw.

She sucked in air, sitting up, her eyes wide.

"What the holy hell?" he snapped, shaking her one more time for good measure. "You wouldn't let me awaken you."

She coughed and shook her head. "Are they here? Where are they?"

He jumped from the bed and yanked on a pair of jeans. "I was in the snow when you brought me back." He tossed her his hastily discarded T-shirt, and she pulled it over her head, running barefoot out of the room and down the hallway to the computer room.

Mercy and Logan were waiting.

"Well?" Mercy's eyes were wide, the blue one extra dark. "Any luck?"

"Don't know." Haven looked around, trying to feel for the Fae. Nothing.

"Outside," Quade said, motioning for Logan. "When I came back, I was by a river. Maybe water has something to do with it?"

Yes. The water. She'd somehow changed the water by pretending to paint. No wonder she needed to paint so badly all the time, especially when life got crazy. Shoes. She needed shoes. Haven turned to head back to their room just as the computers all buzzed.

Ivar strode out of the kitchen along with Adare, both eating what looked like chicken legs. He jogged for the nearest keyboard and typed rapidly. A woman came up on the screen. Blond hair, dual-colored eyes, regal bearing.

Mercy stood. "President. Hello."

President? Haven cocked her head to the side and studied the leader of the Fae.

The president nodded. "We have reports coming in from all different locations of Fae returning to this world. They're in bad shape, but they're alive."

Quade stepped up to Haven's side and slid an arm over her shoulder. "Where are they being found?"

The president focused on him, her gaze moving to Haven. "Different places that have significance to each of them, I think. Many by water."

What was it with water? Haven stared at the female, not sure what to think. Or feel. "Are you the one who had me created?"

The president's eyebrows rose. "I wondered if that was you. The elders made those decisions, and I didn't even find out about you until years later." She eyed Quade. "I heard that you were left to be raised by humans, and on behalf of the Fae nation, I'm truly sorry."

"That's not good enough," Quade said grimly, his voice beyond hoarse.

The president nodded. "I'm sure it is not." She smiled at Haven. "We hope you'll join us someday to meet your people. Most of us still living weren't involved when the elders created the youngsters, including Mercy. You might find people you like."

Mercy stepped up next to Haven, her face pale. "Have we found all of the missing Fae?"

The president nodded. "Yes. They're all getting medical assistance. But still, none of us can travel off world. Any luck there on your end?"

Mercy shook her head. "No."

Haven remained silent. Yeah, she could travel, but she had no control. It had been blind luck she hadn't been pulled through that final portal, and she knew it.

The president signed off, and everyone headed back to bed.

Quade took her hand. "We need to talk. Now."

Chapter Thirty-Seven

It took Quade several moments to recognize the feeling of frustration coursing through his veins. Anger, he was used to, and he was dealing with a healthy amount of that right now as well. He kept his mate's hand and all but dragged her back to their bedroom.

Once inside, she pulled free. "What is going on with you?"

It took him a moment to be able to speak without yelling at her. "I told you not to rescue the Fae on your own, and when I tried to awaken you, you wouldn't let me." Who knew she had that ability? She probably hadn't even known until she tried, and that just pissed him off more.

She put her hands on her hips. "I didn't have a choice. They were dying. I did what I could."

"Did the portal open?" he snapped, shoving his hands in his jeans to keep from reaching for her again.

She faltered and obviously thought about lying. A multitude of expressions crossed her face in rapid succession.

He growled low. "Don't even think of lying to me."

"Fine." The word burst from her. "The portal did open and try to pull me, but I somehow painted an imaginary portal in the brook and then convinced everyone to jump into the water, and we ended up back here. Well, I ended up here, and they ended up all over the world, apparently." She rubbed her eyes. "I wonder why. That's weird, right?"

It all was weird. "You painted a portal?" he growled.

Her teeth sank into her bottom lip. "I think I did. Maybe my skills have to do with painting. I mean, we jumped into the altered water and got free." She rubbed her nose. "I wonder if I could do something similar with Ulric."

She did not just say that. Quade quashed the temper rapidly rising in him. Do you not understand that Ulric will most likely kill you?" He forced his voice to remain level. The idea of her dying, of her being harmed by Ulric, shot energy through his veins that popped with an edge of pain.

She shuffled her feet. "I understand he's dangerous."

She couldn't imagine what an understatement that was. Quade shook his head, his control shredding. "You fought me when I tried to awaken you. Under no circumstances is that ever to happen again. Tell me you understand."

Pink blushed across her pretty face, and her chin lifted. "I'll do what I want."

He wasn't sure what his expression revealed, but she took a step back. A wise one. "You might want to rephrase that answer," he suggested, his entire body going hot.

She faltered but didn't drop her gaze. "It's my gift and I'll do what I want with it." Her voice didn't sound quite as sure this time.

He admired her courage, but her safety was his responsibility, and he couldn't fight both Ulric and her. "I understand you've had to be independent your entire life, and I'm making allowances for that fact, but your grace period has ended. This is a new world you barely understand, and I can't keep you safe if you don't follow my directions." He said the last through gritted teeth, and his jaw ached. He held up his hand, revealing the now slightly faded marking. "I made the situation very clear before we mated. You said yes."

Then, before his eyes, she changed. The shuffling stopped. She straightened and walked right up to him, her chin high and challenge in her gaze. "I said yes to mating, not to the rest of it."

Why was she challenging him? His vision clouded and he tried to push anger out of the way to think rationally. Nobody had ever fought for her, had they? Nobody had ever fought her. Not really.

Maybe things hadn't changed as much as he'd feared in this new world. He grasped her arms and dragged her up, lowering his face until his nose nearly touched hers. Irritation and something else lingered in her pretty eyes. Need and hope. That was hope. Anger gave way to the control he'd honed through the centuries, and he smiled. "You're mine, Haven. It's time you realized that fact."

Then he kissed her.

* * * *

Haven sucked in air, her head pushed back as Quade kissed her with an alarming strength. His hold was firm and his mouth commanding as he swept his tongue inside her mouth and took. Desire shot through her so fast her knees weakened, but she fought it and him, wrenching her mouth away.

His chuckle nearly sent her into an early orgasm.

She'd opened her mouth to say something sarcastic when he lifted her by the arms and tossed her right over his head. Her yelp carried through the room as she landed on the bed, bouncing twice. Surprise kept her immobile for several precious moments.

He turned, and his hands went to the button of his jeans.

Her breath heated, panting out, and she scrambled up on her bare knees, acutely aware that she wore only his shirt and nothing else. "We are not done fighting," she said, probably out of desperation. This need engulfing her couldn't be healthy.

"We'll fight nude." He paused on the button. "Take off the shirt."

Don't say it. She knew not to say it. "No." Yep, she'd said it.

He moved faster than a whisper, grasping the hem and ripping it over her head before she could blink. She knelt on the bed, fully nude, definitely aroused, and slightly pissed.

His jeans followed the shirt across the room, and he reached for her.

She slapped his hands and spun around, landing on the stone floor on the other side of the bed. No reason to make this easy for him. Anticipation flooded her, and she bounced on the balls of her feet.

"You do not want to play," he murmured, looking broad and deadly in the dim light. The scars across his massive chest showed his deadly determination to survive, and the look in his dark eyes was all control. Primal and dangerous but in control.

She liked that about him. Could she make his control snap? Was she that powerful? "Oh, I'm not playing," she whispered.

"Come here, Haven." The low command in his rough voice licked along her skin, zinged through her abdomen, and settled right between her thighs.

"No." She edged to the side, gauging the distance between the door and the bed. Yeah, she was nude, but if she could get past him, she'd win.

Nothing in her wanted to win.

But she had to give it a shot. Had to make him prove—what, she wasn't sure. But something.

"I would not," he rumbled, his stance set.

"I would." She ducked and ran, full bore, faster than any human.

He caught her around the waist, turned, and threw her back on the bed. This time, before she could roll, he was on her.

She laughed, grabbing his hair and pulling. Hard. For answer, he flipped her around and yanked her onto all fours, facing the wall, his fangs sinking into her shoulder.

Pain slammed into pleasure, and she tossed her head, her body quaking. Those deadly points retracted, and he licked the wound closed, reaching between her legs and palming her.

The sound she made, one of need and want, should've embarrassed her. But she was beyond caring. "Quade."

He played with her, one hand tangling in the hair at the nape of her neck, and the other caressing her folds. "You're going to learn to obey me."

She laughed, full on, the sound slightly pained. "Not in a million years."

He removed his hand from her sex, and she started to protest, when he slapped up. Hard and right on her clit. Sparks flew through her lower half, and she stiffened, her eyes widening. "Oh, you did not," she gasped.

"I did." He slapped her again, once on her clit and twice on her thighs, making her widen them.

Her thighs trembled. This was too much. She needed more. "I'll...never—"

Slap. Once and again.

She tried to drop her head, to just feel, but he kept her in place. "I'm immortal, damn it," she muttered, trying not to push against his hand.

"I'm stronger." He slipped a finger inside her, twisted it, and brushed that spot only he'd ever found.

An orgasm bore down on her, and she tensed, riding out the pleasure. Even so, she needed him inside her. Needed more. Needed all of him. "That all you've got?" she moaned.

"I have more." He grasped her hips and powered into her to the hilt.

She cried out, pain and pleasure mixing until all she could do was feel. She loved how literal he was, even though humor had colored his last statement.

He pounded in and out, drawing her hips back to meet each thrust. She dug her fingers into the bedclothes, holding on with all she had. The slap of flesh on flesh filled the room, and she closed her eyes, riding the incredible pleasure. A quaking started deep inside her and she caught her breath.

He stopped. Full on inside her, his grip tight on her hips, he stopped.

She gasped. "What are you doing?"

For answer, he reached around and tweaked a nipple. Not so gently. "Getting your attention."

"You have my attention," she moaned. "Now do something with it."

"I am." His breath brushed her shoulder, and he licked along the shell of her ear. "I have fangs, an impenetrable torso, and centuries of combat experience."

He felt so big and full inside her, and she needed him to start moving again. Now. "Okay. Now move."

He nipped her earlobe, his fangs ticking along her jawline. "I fight bad guys. You do not. Now that I have found you, I will not let you be harmed."

Found her? What was he saying? She partially turned her head and bit his lip. "Fine. Now start moving before I hurt you."

His eyes had turned a luminous green without any blue. She'd never seen them that color before, and just for a moment, she was transfixed. Then her body started to ache, and she was brought right back to the present. "I'll be careful, Quade." It was the most she could promise him. Then somehow, she gave him more. "I won't go without you again." He seemed to need the reassurance.

"Good." He levered back up, gripped her hips, and then finally moved with a speed and strength that left her breathless. He pounded inside her, and she stiffened as the sparks uncoiled. The orgasm took her, shaking her, sending ecstasy through her entire body. She cried out his name, holding him tight, then finally letting go.

He shook with his own release, his grip bruising.

The kiss he brushed across her shoulder as he withdrew was feather soft and somehow firm. "I'm glad we reached an understanding."

She chuckled, flattening on the bed, half-asleep. "You are such a dork."

"Dork?" He turned and spooned around her. "Is that a term of endearment?"

She bit back a laugh. "Yes. That's exactly what it is."

"Good." He kissed her head. "That was fun, Haven. You do not want to cross me again, however."

She smiled into the darkness. Oh, she'd definitely cross him again. But not tonight. Tonight, she needed rest. "I'll sleep light, and you do the same." She wasn't ready to face Ulric, though that time was coming.

She could feel it.

Chapter Thirty-Eight

How interesting that immortal bodies could still be a little sore. Haven stretched her legs as she walked to the kitchen, humming softly to herself. She'd finally gotten some uninterrupted sleep with Quade next to her after their wild night. Maybe sex was the key. She chuckled and walked in to find Allison sitting with a cup of coffee, staring deep into space.

"Um, hi," Haven said, pouring herself a cup.

"Hi." Allison looked up, her gaze stark. "I have to get out of this mountain. Just for a little bit? Get some fresh air?"

Haven nodded. She'd forgotten about Allison's claustrophobia. "There's a little area right outside where the guys have had a fire going." Quade had told her about the place the other day, but she hadn't felt the need to go outside. Her paints were inside. "I can walk out with you if you want." They should probably talk about the future, anyway.

Allison jumped up. "Oh, I want. Anything to get out of this place." She was probably only fifty-five or so, but she looked much older. Why was that? Wrinkles and sadness in her eyes?

Haven's heart thawed. "I know this has been difficult for you. I'm sorry." To go from believing implicitly in the pastor's worldview, to knowing there were vampires and demons on Earth had to have been tough. "Also, while I don't understand your love for the pastor, I'm sorry for your loss."

Allison turned. "You always were a sweet girl, Haven."

Haven. She'd called her Haven instead of Mary, the name they'd given her. Haven smiled. Maybe they could both make an effort. "Come on. Let's see if it's still snowing."

The mountain rumbled, and she grabbed the wall to keep from falling. When the rock had stopped moving, she walked out into the main computer room, where Ivar was swearing at a group of computers. "What was that?" she asked, her legs still shaky. "Where is everyone?"

He looked up, his frown deep. "Quade, Adare, Ronan, and Logan are digging deeper into the mountain with minor explosives because we're going to need more room. Mercy and Grace are taking photographs outside since the snow let up, and Faith and Promise are in my room teleconferencing with the queen about science stuff." He paused. "I have no idea where Benny is, but that's not unusual."

So the snow had stopped. Good. She wouldn't mind being outside of the mountain while they used explosives inside it. For goodness' sake. "Allison and I want to go out to the fire, if that's okay."

"Sure." Ivar looked past her to Allison. "The booby traps on the way in have all been diffused until I can get them under control. Don't go beyond the picnic area. The snow is deep and I think there are some wild animals around." He turned back to his computer.

Haven strode toward the outside door, borrowing a pair of blue boots and a yellow coat from a closet area. She tossed Allison another pair of boots and a coat.

Allison shrugged into the coat, catching her cross necklace and pulling it free. She buttoned up and then followed Haven outside, taking several deep breaths of the clean air.

Haven looked around. "I think the fire is this way." There was only one path, so she followed it, soon reaching an area protected by a tarp that had several log stumps surrounding a fire, which crackled merrily even now. The snow had been mostly cleared from the area, and she stepped over a couple of logs to reach a stump. "Is this better?"

Allison perched on a stump like a wounded bird, her hands clasped. "Much better outside." She sighed. Dark circles smudged her faded eyes. "What happens to me now, Haven? I obviously know something I'm not supposed to know. Are you going to let them kill me?"

"Of course not." Haven sat on a stump. "The deal is that you just don't tell anybody. If you did, you'd be considered crazy, anyway."

Allison looked out at the snowy trees. "I was wondering if I had gone crazy."

Haven could feel sympathy for the woman. She grasped Allison's hand and squeezed. "It's okay. You can live a normal life away from here so long as you don't tell anybody about what you think you saw."

Allison turned pale. "These people you're with—they're not godly. You have to know that, right?"

Of course they were. Haven released Allison's hand. "These are good people. You don't know anything about them."

Allison clutched the cross in her hand. "Not true. I know more than you think."

"Hey, Haven." Mercy kicked snow as she created a trail between a couple of trees, her dark red hair covered in snowflakes. "Grace got tired of me bugging her and went off to take pictures by herself. What are you two doing?"

Haven stilled and turned toward Allison. "What do you mean you know more?" What was she saying?

A broad male swept in behind Mercy and lifted her, shoving a knife into her neck in less than a heartbeat. Mercy gasped, and blood flowed down her skin to pool on her jacket. She clutched at the handle, panic in her eyes.

Haven jumped to her feet. Her stomach rolled over. "What the hell?"

The male was pale with red lips and wore a dark hat. He partially turned, keeping Mercy aloft, and revealed a white braid down his back.

Haven stopped breathing.

The guy smiled. "If I twist my wrist just right, I'll take off her head. Even the pretty fairy here can't come back from that."

Panic caught Haven around the throat. "What do you want?"

"You." He jerked his head. "Back the way the fairy just walked. Come with me, and I won't take off her head. Stop, run, or yell for help, and we'll see this pretty red hair on the snow within seconds."

Haven looked frantically around, but there was no escape. She couldn't let Mercy die.

Mercy coughed and blood welled on her lips. "Sister? Run. Run now," she croaked.

"No." Haven could barely breathe from her panic, but she walked around the fire. "Allison? Wait until I'm gone, and then run back inside."

Allison reached her side and smiled, patting her cross. "I'm coming with you. We'll get you right with the Lord if it's the last thing I ever do, Mary Agnes."

* * * *

Quade marveled at the small explosive, turning it over in his hand. Such a wonderful invention. Small rocks littered the ground around him, but the entrance to the hallway was nearly blocked by much larger stones they would need to break into pieces.

"Adare!" Grace Cooper rushed down the hallway, flinging herself around the bigger rocks.

Adare intercepted her before Quade could, halting her. "Watch yourself," the Highlander ordered, plucking her away from the stones still falling.

Her blue eyes widened and she gulped in air. "They got them. A Cyst. He stuck a knife in Mercy's throat, and Haven went with him." She leaned over, coughing wildly. "That Allison seemed happy to see him."

Everything inside Quade went still. He completely stopped functioning for just a moment.

A Cyst had Haven?

Logan burst out of the nearest tunnel, pieces of rock in his hair and dirt across his face. His eyes blazed an unreal green. "Mercy had a knife in her throat?"

Grace nodded, gulping. "I hid behind the tree so I could come tell you." Tears filled her eyes. "I wanted to attack, but then two more Cyst showed up, and—"

"You did the right thing," Quade said, already jumping into a run. Maybe he could catch them. The snow was thick, and Haven would try to slow them down. He hurried down the hallway, his hands shaking for the first time in centuries. He halted at the computer room.

Ivar looked up from his computer and pointed to the screen. "I hacked into a satellite feed. It's spotty and the picture is horrible, but I noticed the helicopter parked a few miles away."

The helicopter lifted into the air.

Rage filled Quade and he bit down until he could taste blood. "Can you track them?"

"Yes," Ivar said. The screens went black. He hit the console several times, and the satellite feed came back on. "I think. I'll try."

Logan ran into the room by the kitchen and returned with several guns and knives, tossing them over. "I'll fly. We'll have to take the copter we used the other day, and it's not for long distances. But we're going anyway."

Ronan and Benny ran out from a back tunnel, both covered in rock fragments. "We're going too."

Ivar stood. "If they've found us, we may be under attack." An explosion rocked the entire mountain. "We are under attack."

Quade nodded. "Okay. Logan and I will track the copter. Everyone else stay here and protect the mountain."

Ronan took one of the guns from Logan. "I'm going with you." He paused and looked back at Faith, who nodded.

"No." Quade clapped an arm over his brother's shoulder and gave him a hard hug. "Stay with your mate." Now he understood. He really did. If anything happened to Haven, his soul would be gone forever. "Protect what we have here."

Another explosion blew outside, and the grate in the ceiling crashed down, landing on several of the computers.

"Let's go." Quade turned and ran for the door with Logan on his heels.

They ducked low outside, not surprised to see a helicopter hovering above with missiles aimed at the mountain. Logan led the way through trees to another tarp-covered helicopter. He jumped inside, waiting until Quade had done the same. "This is going to be fast and hard." Logan pressed several buttons, and the copter hummed to life. The tarp slid away. "As soon as they fire another missile, we'll head up and out. They may shoot at us."

The machine wasn't nearly as nice as the one they'd wrecked just last week. Quade swallowed and gripped the nearest handle, his mind only on Haven. He had to get to her. "Do we have missiles?"

"Not on this thing," Logan said grimly. He punched a red button in front of him. "Ivar? You there?"

"For now," Ivar said with the sound of rocks falling around him. "They're moving west and staying low beneath our radar. Your best bet is to take them out in the sky before they reach their destination."

Logan shook his head. "Unlikely. We'll be lucky if this thing flies that far. Keep on them."

Another missile hit the earth.

"Now," Logan said, hitting several buttons and lifting instantly into the sky.

Quade's stomach dropped out from under him, and he turned to see the Cyst helicopter swing around. "Incoming," he snapped.

The Cyst helicopter started firing, and Logan tilted their craft, flying between trees and around a mountain. Quade turned to see if the Cyst copter pursued them.

It didn't.

"They want to take out the mountain," Logan said.

Quade's chest heated. "Will the others be safe?"

"Yeah. We have missiles in the ground and a self-destruct, which will probably be the way to go. There's an escape route out the back that was the first thing Ivar installed." Logan jerked the wheel and turned the craft toward more mountains. "I was just starting to like that place." His knuckles were white on the wheel.

"They'll be all right, Logan," Quade said, grasping the knife he'd taken. They had to be. "I never told her."

"Told her what?" Logan tilted again and then readjusted.

Quade was silent. If he got the chance to say the words, he only wanted to say them to Haven. He should've told her he loved her. He hadn't realized until he'd discovered her gone. Taken by the enemy. What if he never got the chance?

Chapter Thirty-Nine

It had started snowing again and soon the visibility was so poor that Haven didn't think they'd survive the flight. After a wild helicopter ride that ended with the beast setting down in a field surrounded by farmland, one of the Cyst soldiers hauled Haven through the snow and tossed her in a smallish barn. She rolled in the hay and came up in time to catch Mercy before she hit. "Okay. Take a deep breath." She grasped the knife handle. Should she take it out or leave it in?

Mercy grasped the handle and yanked it out. "Damn it, ouch." She slid down and sat in the wet hay, her hand covering the wound. Blood continued to pour through her fingers.

Bile rose in Haven's throat. She choked it down and turned to look around. The barn was square shaped with two empty stalls and no weapons. She rushed over to a stall and kicked a lower board several times until it cracked in two. Then she grabbed a shard of wood and rushed back to Mercy, dropping to her knees and slashing the sharp wood over her wrist.

Pain swelled along with the blood. "Here. Drink this."

Mercy's head fell forward and she winced. "Do you know what you're doing?"

"No. I'm new at this immortal stuff." Haven shoved her wrist against Mercy's mouth. "You're wounded, and I have immortal blood." She brightened. "That I share with you, so this should really help." She actually had family. Even though she and her sister were in danger of being beheaded, she knew a brief moment of joy.

Mercy drank and settled her head back on the wooden wall. She closed her eyes.

Haven set her hand down and sent healing cells to her wrist. "Feel better?"

"Your blood tastes a little bit like honey." Mercy reopened her eyes and moved her hand.

Haven leaned over, holding her breath as she watched Mercy's skin slowly mend itself. "It's working."

Mercy rubbed blood off her hand. "I told you to run."

"Would you have run?" Haven stood and moved to the door.

"No." Mercy joined her, moving slowly. "I used all my healing cells and your blood to fix my neck, and I don't have much strength left. If we get in a fight, I'm trained, but I won't last long." She nudged open the door and looked outside at the freezing snowstorm. "If you can run to safety, you have to. It's you they want."

Exactly. If they didn't have her, they'd kill Mercy. "I didn't find a sister just to lose her," Haven whispered, peeking out at the ice-crusted field.

The door was shoved open, sending her scrambling back, trying to keep her balance.

Mercy backed away too, staying by her side. "If we have to fight, go for the eyes. Always go for the eyes."

Haven swallowed, her legs shaking.

A Cyst soldier walked in—bigger than any she'd yet seen. He wore a black uniform with several medals across his left breast. Two other males walked next to him; both had long black hair tipped with red and oddly greenish-purple eyes. Finally, bringing up the rear, was a twenty-something blonde human with green eyes who walked next to Allison.

The woman stepped forward, looking them over. She wore brown boots, jeans, and a blue cashmere sweater. "Which one of you is Mary Agnes?"

Haven rolled her eyes. "Nobody is. I'm Haven."

"I'm Yvonne. You have seen Ulric, my intended?" The blonde's eyes gleamed in a way that seemed slightly off.

Haven glanced at Mercy and then back. "Your intended? The guy hasn't been in this world for centuries. And yes, I've talked to him. He likes it where he is and wants to stay there."

Mercy leaned toward her. "Supposedly in every generation there's a chick who thinks she's going to be with Ulric. They're all nuts, and they always die alone. This one will die all by herself as well." Her voice was loud enough for everyone to hear.

Yvonne smiled. "Very well. Do what you need to do to her, and I will go prepare myself for Ulric."

Haven faced Allison and tried to ignore the pain blooming in her chest. "I never thought you'd do something like this."

Allison clasped her hands together. "You don't understand. They're missionaries from God. They will help you."

Haven let go of any hope for a relationship with the woman. Allison had followed the crazy pastor and now had aligned herself with monsters in a lame effort to find God. Or maybe she just liked following charismatic nutjobs. "You're dead to me, lady." Finally, Haven released her entire past, feeling relieved and lighter than she'd ever been. No more confusion or vacillation. It was over, and she was free. "You really are crazy."

Mercy leaned toward her. "I could rip off her head if you want."

Haven stood next to her sister. "No. That's okay."

"Poke out an eyeball? Just one?" Mercy didn't seem to be kidding.

Haven coughed. "No." She looked at the Cyst soldiers. "I don't think her path will be an easy one."

Yvonne's shoulders went back. "You will bring my love back to me. I shall go prepare at the main house." She turned on her heel and returned outside with Allison at her side. Neither looked back as they ran into the storm.

Mercy snorted. "What do you think she does to prepare?"

Haven shivered. "Human sacrifice? An exfoliating body oil?"

"I was thinking probably a full Brazilian. She looked hairy to me," Mercy muttered.

"Enough!" the Cyst soldier snarled.

Haven swallowed, focusing on the Cyst. "I've seen you before."

"I'm Xeno, general of the Cyst." He looked her over. "I've never met a hybrid like you." He sniffed the air. "It's a pity you're mated."

How did they all smell a mate? That was a skill she hadn't learned. "How did you get to Allison?" Never again would she think of the woman as her mother.

The dark-haired guy, not a Cyst but one of those Kurjan guys, smiled. "Allison was easily convinced we were sent from on high to secure this world, and we promised not only to save you but to give her everlasting life in the world to come." He chuckled. "The cross around her neck was a homing device, which you probably already figured out."

"Who are you?" Haven snapped.

"Oh. My apologies." He gave a half bow. "I am Dayne, head of the Kurjan nation, and this is my brother, Terre." He nodded to the other guy. "The Cyst are our religious leaders, something like monks."

"And soldiers," Xeno said, flashing sharp fangs. "We have specific training that you will probably enjoy soon. For now, you will take us to Ulric."

Haven shook her head. "You don't know what you're talking about. I can't take you."

"Yes, you can. I've seen your paintings and know you've been to other worlds. You will take me. Now." Xeno moved to her and grabbed her arm. "If you like, we could cut off the other fairy's head to motivate you, but that just seems so unnecessary."

Haven held up her hand. "You really don't get it." She didn't want to tell him the full truth, but she couldn't let Mercy be killed. "I don't really travel anywhere. It all happens in my sleep. My body doesn't actually go."

Mercy nodded vigorously. "Not only that, but now none of us can get off planet. When Quade's world blew, it ruined all of our methods of transport."

Xeno looked down at Haven. "So you need to be unconscious to seek Ulric?"

Haven bit her lip. Well, crap. "No—" His beefy fist smashed into her temple, and she went down. Fast and hard.

* * * *

The blizzard was going to make them crash. Quade held on as Logan hovered the craft above the barn Xeno had entered. "What are you doing?"

"Hold on." Logan pulled on the wheel and jerked the helicopter around, sweeping the roof off the barn with the tail. Boards cracked and flew through the wild storm. The figures in the barn all looked up, and one of the Kurjans grabbed a gun from his waist and started firing it at them.

Alarms blared and the craft pitched wildly, spinning around on its own. Logan opened his door. "Jump for it."

Quade gritted his teeth and opened his door, looking down to see Haven slumped on the ground. He leaped into the air. Several bullets struck his neck and face, shooting pain through his skull. He smashed into the two Kurjans, knocking them to the ground.

Logan hit the Cyst soldier and they rolled in opposite directions.

Two more Cyst soldiers ran through the door, one swinging a sword.

Quade pivoted and kicked the guy with the sword, spinning and punching the second Cyst soldier while Logan grappled with another by the far wall. He flipped the sword into the air, grabbed the handle, and impaled the Cyst soldier through the neck to the wall.

One down.

Mercy hauled Haven out of the way and into a stall, slapping her face. "Wake up," she muttered.

Quade took a punch to his wounded neck and went flying, hitting the far wall and going through it. Snow and wind blasted him, and he shoved to his feet, running for the guy who'd hit him. He left a trail of blood in his wake.

The two Kurjans made a beeline for the farmhouse, and he let them go, concentrating on the force in front of him. Logan took one of the soldiers down, grabbing his knife and plunging it into the Cyst's neck.

Xeno ducked his head and charged, hitting Quade mid-center and throwing him back into the snow. They skidded several feet across rough terrain, finally coming to a stop. Quade punched up beneath Xeno's neck, and the Cyst punched down, cracking Quade's nose.

"You shouldn't be back here," Xeno roared, punching him in the eye.

Pain exploded in Quade's skull. He locked his feet around Xeno and secured him in a hold, twisting until they both rolled over. Blood flowed from him in too many places, and his strength ebbed, but he battled on. For centuries he'd fought, and he drew on that strength to punch Xeno in the throat as hard as he could. "I belong here," he snarled, his fangs whipping out.

"Ulric will return," Xeno growled, slashing across Quade's face with sharp claws.

When did the Cyst get claws? Quade twisted his head to keep his eyeball from being torn out. Pain ripped through his cheekbone to his skull, and he rode the waves, taking it into his body to make him stronger. He clapped both hands against the soldier's ears, breaking both eardrums.

The Cyst bellowed and drew a knife from his boot, flipping Quade over his head.

Quade landed on his knees and pivoted, kicking out and nailing the Cyst soldier in the knee. He went down, snow spraying. The wind and blistering snow attacked them, sticking in the blood pouring from multiple wounds. He swung around, and Xeno moved fast, slicing across Quade's neck.

Blood spurted, and Quade sent immediate healing cells. He bellowed, punching the blade out of his enemy's hand. The fight inside got louder. Was Logan doing all right? Too much blood was leaving Quade's body, and his legs weakened.

Haven screamed from inside.

Everything inside Quade went on full alert. He shoved pain to the abyss and punched Xeno in the throat rapidly, several times, trying to put his entire fist through.

Xeno stumbled back, spraying snow. "You will bring Ulric back." He grabbed his neck with one hand and reached into his boot with the other, bringing out a sharp two-prong knife. Even through the snow, the blade glinted.

"No." Quade braced his feet, sliding on the ice. "Ulric is never coming back. Even if he does, you won't see him."

Xeno charged, knife up.

Quade dropped into a slide, knocking the soldier's feet out from under him. Xeno fell, and Quade leaped over him, grabbing the blade and twisting at the last second. He used all the strength he had left to plunge the knife into Xeno's neck, separating it in two.

Straddling the Cyst soldier, Quade dug left and right, grunting until finally the Cyst's head rolled free of his body. Quade stood, taking the knife with him, and fought the storm to reenter the barn.

Logan finished decapitating the other soldier. He looked up, blood covering his face and neck.

Mercy helped Haven out of the stall, an arm beneath her shoulder.

Quade swallowed several times as the world tilted around him. "We have to get out of here. Fast."

Logan nodded. "They'll have reinforcements coming, but we should be okay as long as this storm holds. I saw a truck not too far from here. I'll go get it, and we'll drive as far from here as possible." He jogged out of the barn, leaving a trail of blood in his wake.

Quade moved to Haven, his entire body one long line of pain. He didn't have extra blood to give her. "Are you okay?"

She nodded, her face pale and bruised. "Yes."

He drew her into his side. "I love you. Thought you should know." Then he dropped to his knees, releasing her so he wouldn't take her down with him. They had to get out of there and now. He didn't have another fight in him.

Chapter Forty

Haven's head hurt like she'd been pounded by a hammer, and the rest of the group wasn't in much better shape. They drove the old pickup truck as far as they could until the storm made driving impossible. She perched on Quade's lap, trying to stem the bleeding in his neck with her hands. "You should take my blood."

"You can't afford to lose any," he murmured, his smile sweet. "I'm fine. You just heal your head when you can."

She hurt too much at the moment to heal anything.

Logan pulled behind an abandoned motel in the middle of nowhere. "We'll have to wait out the storm here." He parked and leaned to the side. "Stay put, ladies."

Quade stepped from the truck, and between the two of them, they removed the boards covering one dented metal door.

"Come on." Mercy helped Haven from the truck, and they struggled through the storm to get inside. Once inside, Quade secured the door. There were two mattresses without blankets, a rickety old table, bedside cabinets, and a dirty green carpet.

"Hold on." Logan ran into the bathroom and a horrible racket ensued. He returned with the bathtub, which he set by the window, opening it slightly.

Quade nodded, grabbed the furniture, and broke it into pieces.

Haven shivered and sat on the mattress. Her head swam, and she needed sleep. But she wasn't strong enough to fight the pull of that portal, so she had to stay awake. All of the fighting earlier ran through her mind, and she took several deep breaths to calm herself. Quade had said he loved her. Like really loved her.

Was it the stress of the moment?

She looked through the bed cabinets, almost shocked to find matches with the motel's name on them. "Hey." She tossed them to Quade.

He grinned, the sight macabre with the blood still flowing from his neck. He struck a match and started the old furniture on fire. The smoke went out the window, and the area began to warm up a little.

Logan plucked Mercy off the ground and cuddled her on the farthest bed. He reached for a phone in his boot and quickly dialed, leaving a message for the Seven to come get them as soon as the storm abated. He looked over. "It's going to be several hours, at least. If the Cyst or Kurjans come looking in the storm, it won't be hard to find us here."

Quade nodded and set the blade he'd taken on the bedtable. "I need to sleep to heal." He stretched out on the mattress and drew Haven closer. "We can take turns, so we can keep you from entering a portal."

"You first." She cuddled into his side, worried about the blood still coming from his wounds. "You need to heal worse than I need to sleep." But the room swam around her, and she sucked in air. "Ah, crap. I'm going to pass out again." She fought as hard as she could, but unconsciousness took her under.

She landed in Brookville, but the grass had turned brown, and the brooks no longer bubbled. Instead, they wound silently, so dark she couldn't see beneath the surface. The smell of cookies in the air had changed to the scent of dusty fields.

Her head hurt, her chest ached, and her stomach pounded. This wasn't good. The portal opened, spinning wildly, and the force was too much for her to fight.

She curled onto the burned grass. Why hadn't she told Quade she loved him, too? Now he was going to be alone, and that thought hurt even more than her body. She had to get back to him. She dug her fingers into the dry soil, holding on, her body shaking with the effort of fighting the pull.

Her legs lifted first, and she struggled, but the wind carried her up and through.

A hand took hers. She tumbled around and around, her head hitting something solid. Finally, she fell and landed on the heated rock. Her breath catching, she turned to see Quade next to her. Her heart leaped. "Quade." She jumped up and hugged him, holding as tight as she could. "How?"

He leaned back, his neck wounded even in this dream state. "I don't know." Gently, he slid the hair away from her face. Then he turned to look toward shore, and his shoulders went back.

Gulping, Haven saw Ulric standing mere yards away. He filled the space between two trees, his fangs just visible, his eyes swirling with deep purple of fury at seeing Quade.

Quade leaned down and pressed a kiss to Haven's mouth. "I love you, my little hybrid." Before she could answer, he grabbed her wrist and one of her knees and swung her around so quickly she had to shut her eyes to keep from throwing up.

"Quade," she hissed. "What are you—"

He flung her through a portal, and she landed in Brookville before spinning away again.

She woke up on the bed in the motel room, gasping for breath.

Logan and Mercy sat up on their bed, their eyes worried. "What the hell?" Logan muttered.

Oh, God. Haven turned and shook Quade, but he didn't awaken. "He's going to fight Ulric in the dream world. He'll never make it back." Panic attacked her, and she shook harder, but his eyes didn't open.

* * * *

Quade watched the portal close behind Haven with a sense of satisfaction. This might be the end for him, but he'd saved her. He set his stance and faced Ulric. After all this time, for a moment, all he could do was stare.

Something swam in the black murk between them. He glanced to the side, seeing nothing but mist. So, he had Ulric and a forest in front of him, black murk between them, and mist on the other sides. Just how many worlds had combined to make this moment right now? He crouched down and felt the porous rock. Hot and thick.

Ulric growled. "I can ride you out of here as easy as I could her."

The idea of Ulric touching Haven centered Quade, despite the blood still leaving his body. Fury and determination clawed through him, and his vow as a Seven rang through his head. Through his heart. He'd made that vow in blood and bone, and he would adhere to that promise to the very end. "You're never leaving."

Ulric smiled, his fangs elongating. "We both know that's not true. Whether it happens today or in the future, there will be a final ritual, and I will triumph."

Not if Quade took him out right here and now. The sacrifice of his life was worth it if Haven and his family could go on without the threat of Ulric. "What drives you to kill so many women?" Quade asked, trying to send healing cells to his damn neck.

Ulric smiled. "Purity must be enforced." His voice thundered through the air. "You've tried to contain me, and you cannot." He lifted his hands, and the black murk began to boil. The rock started to slide toward the shore.

Quade dropped to his knees. His instincts had been correct. The rock was the landing point, and it had to be destroyed. Gathering all his strength, he punched down as hard as he could. Pain rocketed up his arm, and he punched again, using his knees as leverage.

"What are you doing?" Ulric bellowed.

Quade continued hitting, fast and furious. His knuckles cracked and then his hands broke, but he kept punching. Shards of rock began to crumple. A large piece flew off and into the murk.

The rock started moving faster toward the shore.

Quade stood and kicked a large chunk of the weakened rock away. Then another and another. He had to bend down and punch some more, breaking all the bones in his arms up to his shoulders. But it was the only way to weaken the rock. As soon as he had a loose spot, he stood and kicked it away into the abyss. Soon he stood on a square patch of just several feet.

Roaring, Ulric leaped across the murk and slammed into him, taking him down hard. His head bounced on the rock, and sparks flew behind his eyelids.

Quade punched up into Ulric's jaw, and the remaining bones in his hand shattered.

"I'm impenetrable," Ulric snapped, clocking Quade in the side of the head.

Several portals began to open around them, swirling wildly, each with a forceful pull.

"Which one?" Ulric asked, hauling Quade to his feet.

"None." Quade ducked, lifted Ulric over his shoulder, and threw him back across the murk. The Cyst leader landed between the trees, his shoulders smashing into the trunks. With large cracks, both trees split in two and fell back, landing on several other red trees and taking them down.

"Stop!" Ulric bellowed.

Quade smiled, blood dripping from his lips. He punched the rock three more times, and pieces fell away into the mist. Only a small space remained.

He took a deep breath. One more punch, and the rock would disappear.

It was a good day to die.

* * * *

Haven stared in horror as all of the bones in Quade's arms, hands, and shoulders cracked and broke through the skin. His blood covered the mattress.

Logan rushed over and shook Quade's legs, trying to wake him up.

Tears fell down Haven's face. "He won't let you wake him up. He's destroying the rock to keep Ulric away." She wiped her face. What could she do? "I have to be asleep. I can bring him back." She'd done it once. She could to it again.

Quade shuddered and groaned next to her, bleeding out.

She looked up. "Logan? You have to hit me."

The warrior stepped back. "No way."

"I have to be out cold. There's not enough time to go to sleep. I can save him. Please." She pressed her hands to the wounds in Quade's neck, willing the bleeding to stop.

Logan's mouth opened, but no words came out. He shook his head.

Mercy jumped from the other bed, landing next to Haven. "I've got you, sister." She grabbed Haven in a headlock and pressed against her windpipe, cutting off her air.

Haven instinctively clutched at Mercy's arm, but her sister's hold was absolute. Darkness fell over her vision. She swayed, her breath gone. Then she went under.

She landed in Brookville for a second, dropped into a myriad of different worlds, her body shaken and almost torn apart. Finally, she landed on the rock and grabbed Quade to keep from falling into the mist.

His arms hung uselessly at his sides, bones sticking out. "What are you doing here?"

"Loving you. I do, you know." She grasped his damaged wrists as gently as she could.

Ulric yelled from the tree line, and the small piece of rock still existing began to slide toward him.

She sucked in air, looking wildly around. At least ten portals swirled around, each with different colors. One showed a clear brick wall on the other side. The one on the far left caught her attention. An energy hummed from it. Could she do what she had for the Fae? She sucked in air and waved her hand as if painting. The portal shifted slightly to the left and began to spin with yellow, pink, and blue hues. "I've been there. I've painted that." She grasped him harder.

Ulric leaped at them, and she whipped her hand free, sending the murk up in bars between them. Energy drained from her, and the sharp bars began to waver. There wasn't much time until they failed and Ulric would reach them. "Break the rock and jump toward the last portal," she gasped.

Quade looked down at her, his eyes a fathomless aqua. "I love you. Forever." Then he kicked down, and the remaining piece of rock shattered, falling into the abyss.

She bunched her legs and jumped.

They landed in a different world, one with bright yellow trees and spots of blue mushrooms. They hit a mushroom and bounced into another portal. The mushroom world exploded behind them, heating their backs.

"Shit." Quade grasped her hand. "Hurry. Don't linger."

She nodded and leaped for another portal, and this time, her back was singed as the world behind exploded. They went through several places, each blowing up a second after they'd left. Her back was blistered from the burns.

They landed in Brookville, and the grass was already on fire. She held her breath, grasped his wrist, and jumped again.

They woke up on the bed together, sitting up, gasping for breath.

"Jesus," Logan said, setting Mercy behind him. He looked them over. "You guys still you?"

Quade coughed out smoke. "I think so."

The door burst open, and Ronan and Benny stormed inside.

Benny looked around, his gun in his hand. "Holy shit. You guys look terrible. What did we miss?"

Chapter Forty-One

They arrived at the new mountain headquarters later that day after a wild ride in a Humvee through the storm and then a helicopter ride where Benny and Ronan argued who flew the best. Haven sat on Quade's lap, snuggled into his healing neck, after he'd taken blood from his brother and had already healed his arms. She'd tasted a little of Benny's blood, and her skin felt a bit too tight, but at least her head wasn't hurting.

Quade jumped out of the copter with her in his arms, his boots spraying both blood and snow. He looked around at the trees and the rough opening in the rock.

Ronan grimaced after he jumped out. "Stay out of Ivar's way for a bit. He's really pissed we lost another headquarters."

Benny snorted. "At least he's ordering furniture from Restoration Blues via the Internet that we don't have to put together. Man, I'm tired of putting together shit, so who cares if it costs a little more?"

Logan and Benny began to cover the helicopter with a white tarp that matched the snow and camouflaged it from above.

Quade set Haven down. "Is it safe to go inside?"

Ronan nodded. "Yeah. No booby traps yet. This headquarters is one Ivar started decades ago but abandoned because it's so close to Realm and demon headquarters. But there's no other choice now."

Quade settled an arm around Haven's shoulders, his jaw hard and his gaze scanning. "Have we secured the area?"

"Not completely. You and I can do a patrol now," Ronan said, focusing on his brother. "Faith is inside, setting up a medical area."

"Good." Quade dropped a kiss on Haven's brow. "I want you to go in and get checked by Faith. Just to make sure everything is okay." Snow started to fall and cover his dark hair. "I'll be in once this area is secure." His smile was sweet and just for her. "At that point, you can tell me again, now that we're not dying, how much you love me." He nudged her.

Mercy laughed and hooked her arm though Haven's. "I'll take her." Mercy tugged her toward the opening in the rock. "You totally declared your love and all that while you were about to die." She sighed. "That is so romantic."

Haven leaned into her sister. "I know, right? He said it first, just so you know."

"Very important that they say it first," Mercy agreed. She ducked and led the way into another underground cavern, this one lined with silver. "I love it when we're surrounded by silver."

"Me too." Haven stepped over loose rocks and kept walking farther underground.

They reached a central area littered with boxes and looked around. "Faith?" Mercy called out.

The pretty brunette poked her head out from an opening in the far rock. "This way. Is anybody hurt?"

"Haven hit her head but Benny gave her blood." Mercy tugged her along and they walked into a surprisingly clean room with a real examination bed and a counter full of medical equipment. "Wow. We're stocked."

Grace sat on the bed with her shirt half off, revealing a faded marking on her upper shoulder. She jerked the shirt into place and hopped off. "Here." She reached for Haven and helped her onto the table.

Haven frowned. "Grace? Why is your marking so faded?"

Grace shared a look with her sister. "We're trying to figure that out. For now, let's keep this between us. Just us girls."

That didn't sound good, and by the worried look in Faith's eyes, it wasn't good. "I promise," Haven said. The girls had to stick together, didn't they?

Promise walked in behind them, cotton balls in her hands. "I found these and figured they should go in here." Her dark eyes gleamed. "Just talked Ivar into taking us Christmas shopping tomorrow, if everyone is up to it. The weather is supposed to clear, and we can fly beneath the radar. Probably toward Montana rather than Realm headquarters, though."

Haven blinked. She had people to buy Christmas presents for—for the first time in forever. Her eyes stung.

"Oh." Faith frowned and moved to her, bending to stare into her eyes. "How badly does your head hurt?"

"It's fine," Haven breathed out, dispelling her emotion. "I feel a little odd after taking Benny's blood. Just kind of like I'm having a constant adrenaline rush."

Faith took her vitals. "Yeah. You should stick to Quade or Mercy's blood in the future. Benny is off, in general." She grinned. "Though don't worry. The effects shouldn't last long."

Mercy hopped. "Haven and Quade did the whole I love you thing in the nick of time, staring right at death."

Promise chuckled. "Oh, we've all been there. Did you warn her?"

"No," Mercy said. "Figured she'd find out on her own soon enough."

"What?" Haven straightened. "Warned me about what?"

Faith rolled her eyes. "These guys become a little, what you might say…"

"Bossy, overbearing, overprotective," Promise listed, ticking each off on her fingers. "They get a little over the top, and considering Quade had planned to die doing his duty and hadn't seen love in his future, he'll probably be a total pain."

Mercy rocked back on her heels. "It's totally going to be fun to see."

Haven looked at these women who had become part of her family so easily. Finally, she was home.

* * * *

"You okay?" Ronan asked, scouting along the tree line a mile or so from headquarters.

"Yeah." Quade like the new lingo and decided there and then to stop saying "Aye." Only Adare used that term any longer, and considering he was a Highlander, he should. "I didn't think I'd make it back, and I made peace with that."

Ronan passed, turning to face him, his eyes sizzling. "You did it, brother. I'm so proud of you."

Quade grinned. "We put that asshole back into his hole, didn't we?" He clapped his brother on the back. "It's good to see you again." Being without his brothers for so long had felt like being without a limb. Without all his limbs. They hadn't really had time to celebrate the fact that they were both alive again. They needed to properly mourn Jacer, with several bottles of whiskey, as well.

Ronan slung an arm around his shoulders. "Let's go back and check on headquarters." They walked in companionable silence until reaching the helicopter and entrance to headquarters.

Ivar moved out of the rock, looking like the Viking he'd once been. "Status?"

"We're clear," Ronan said. "For now. We need to put security measures in place as soon as possible."

Ivar's deep eyes gleamed an intelligent blue. "I'm glad you two survived and are here and everything. But this is it." He gestured around the small clearing. "We've blown up every mountain I ever thought of using as a headquarters, and we even blew up that high-rise in Denver."

Quade opened his mouth to ask.

Ivar raised a hand. "It's a building. We blew up a building."

Quade's eyebrows rose. "We won't blow this one up?" Hell. He couldn't promise that. Not really.

"Good." Ivar seemed to accept the statement. "The females want to go Christmas shopping tomorrow. You guys are welcome to join in, if you want to shop." He looked at the rock fronting the entrance, shook his head, and strode back inside. "This is going to take forever to get functional," he muttered, his words echoing back.

Ronan chuckled. "He's kinda fun when cranky."

Quade nodded and started moving toward the entrance. He'd been away from Haven long enough, and he had to know that she was all right. He nearly hit his head and had to duck for several feet of the tunnel until reaching a main room with boxes strewn everywhere. Ivar hadn't been joking. This place was nowhere near ready.

Logan and Benny came down the hallway, carrying a large pine tree still covered in snow.

"Christmas tree," Benny said, grinning.

Logan rolled his eyes. "I told you this one was too big."

It looked just right to Quade. "Where is the medical room?" He'd just finished asking the question when Haven walked out of an opening in the rock.

He reached her in seconds. "You are all right?"

She looked up, and her smile was the sweetest he'd ever seen. "Yeah, but I shouldn't take Benny's blood. In fact, it sounds like nobody should."

He shared her smile. "Probably good advice." Everyone was watching them, and his skin started to prickle. He took her hand and led her back down the tunnel to the outside. There he searched until he found a low outcropping of rocks beneath several trees. "Let's sit."

She waded through the snow and let him lift her onto a rock. "How are your arms?" She ran her hands down them.

Her touch set his blood on fire.

"They're fine," he said. "Ronan's blood helped." He leaned over and examined her forehead. "No bruise. You are all right?"

"Yes." She tucked her hands into his waistband. "So. I love you."

Yeah, he'd asked her to say it again. How stunning what power words could have. He leaned down and kissed her, going deep and enjoying every second. Her sigh into his mouth filled him. "I love you, too." He licked his lips. Maybe she was right, and he would be able to survive the final ritual. Finding love was a miracle, so why not believe in more of them? "I know you need to paint, and living underground isn't ideal."

She tilted her head. "I could do a studio with some sort of skylight. Like when Ivar had that vent in the ceiling of the other place?"

His body grew still. "You're saying you'll be okay staying here with me?"

She kicked out her legs, a pretty pink flush covering her face. "I'll stay anywhere you are. We can make this work."

So this was the third time she'd rescued him. He kissed her again, because he couldn't help it. "I love you, Haven Daly. While you're not human, you were raised as one. Would you like a human marriage?"

She chuckled, her eyes lighting up. "Is that a proposal?"

"Yes." Of course it was.

She leaned up and kissed him. "Then I say yes. I will marry you. Forever."

Yeah. For the first time, he actually believed in forever. Forever was theirs.

Chapter Forty-Two

Lights from the Christmas tree danced around the main center room and made the silver veins in the rock shine like diamonds. The entire gang had exchanged presents after a lovely breakfast cooked by Benny, who turned out to be a master chef. People had then scattered to attend to duties and make sure the facility was safe.

Haven led Mercy back to her suite, where another Christmas tree, this one much smaller, glittered from the corner. A bed was the only other furniture in the room so far. "I have something else, just for you," she told her sister.

Mercy hopped up on the bed next to her with a backpack over her arm. "Me too. Though I have to tell you, the charcoal drawings you did for each couple were a huge hit. I just love mine. Logan looks so sexy and dangerous in it." She sank to her knees on the carpet in front of the tree.

Haven had only had a week, so the framed charcoal drawings would have to do. "I'll make you an oil painting when I can." She sat next to Mercy. "I'd actually like you to pose outside for me sometime."

Mercy dumped out the bag to reveal a bunch of presents. She frowned. "I might have gone overboard."

How sweet. Haven eagerly reached for the first box and started opening. By the time she was finished, she had a sister mug, frame, keychain, bracelet, and even earrings. Her heart warmed and she hugged Mercy. She was the perfect sister, for sure. "Okay. I didn't go this crazy, but I did buy you something." She reached under the tree and handed over a package.

Mercy hopped in place and quickly opened it. "Oh, Haven," she breathed, taking out a pretty emerald bracelet with a sisters logo on it. "It's beautiful."

"I have a matching one." Haven held out her wrist and shook her bracelet. "Since we both have one green eye, I thought the emeralds fit." She had never met anybody who'd embraced her as Mercy had, and she wasn't sure how to express her emotions, but she wanted to try. "I'm glad we found each other."

Mercy slipped on her bracelet. "Me too." She leaned in for another hug. "You're the best sister ever."

There was no way either one of them could know that, but Haven leaned in to the love, anyway. "No. You are."

Mercy snorted and then looked up as Quade entered the room. She winked at Haven and then stood. "You two have a very Merry Christmas. Or what's left of it anyway." At the doorway, she paused. "You sure you don't want to come to demon headquarters and meet Logan's brothers? Zane and Sam are pretty cool, and their young sister is tons of fun."

"No," Quade said, his gaze warming on Haven. "We're staying here."

Haven grinned. That look in his eyes heated her from head to toe. "Yeah. Lots to do, you know."

"Whatever." Mercy rolled her eyes, her smile wide. "I'll find you before we leave." She disappeared.

Quade strolled over, lifted Haven off the ground, and sat back down with her in his lap. "I like the sisters mug." He surveyed the various presents and discarded boxes.

"Me too." She shifted on his lap and took a deep breath. Hopefully, he wouldn't think she was a dork. She'd already given him new jeans without holes and a bunch of clothes, pretty much depleting her bank account. "I have a couple more presents for you."

His eyebrows lifted. "Oh yeah?"

"Yeah." And from the boxes still under their tree, she wasn't alone in that. She pulled out the biggest gift. "This one first."

He kept her gaze and smoothly flipped open the lid. His nostrils flared, and he sniffed the air, angling to the side. "What is that?"

"Candy. All different kinds of peppermint, spearmint, and butterscotch." She caressed his whiskered jaw.

He plucked a mint from the box and stuck it in his mouth. A low rumble of pleasure came from his chest, and his eyes widened. "All for me?"

She chuckled, truly happy for the first time in her life. "Yes, Quade. All of the candy is yours." She sobered and shook off any remaining self-consciousness. "I also made you something else." Staying on his hard lap, she reached around the tree and pulled out an oil painting. The only one she'd had time to create.

He stopped chewing the candy. "Oh, Haven." His gaze flared. "You painted you for me."

She swallowed. "Yes. It's my one and only self-portrait." He'd asked if she ever painted herself, and she never had, but he had seemed eager to have a portrait of her. "Do you like it?" She looked over at herself, even though it felt a little weird. Her eyes glowed and she looked happy. "I painted myself thinking about you."

His chest moved. "It's perfect. You're perfect." He kissed her, his mouth firm and now very minty. "I love it. Thank you."

She relaxed. "You're welcome."

He reached under the tree and brought out several boxes. "These are for you."

She opened the first one, her eyes widening at the sparkly diamond bracelet. "Quade," she breathed. "This had to cost a fortune." Matching earrings and several rings were in other boxes. All huge diamonds. Then some boxes with rubies and emeralds and some stones she couldn't identify but sparkled wonderfully.

"Turns out I'm wealthy." He grinned. "My brothers invested our holdings through the years. You said you like diamonds, so I bought you some. You can have as many as you want." He slipped the biggest ring with a square-shaped diamond onto her ring finger. "You said you wanted to get married, and a ring goes with that commitment."

"Wow." She held her hand up to the light. Just wow.

He reached for the last box and opened it to reveal a choker necklace with emeralds and onyx stones lined up. "This matches both of your eyes." He secured it around her neck, the stones heavy and somehow warm. "Ah, perfect."

Nobody had ever accepted all of her this way. "I love you," she whispered, tears clogging her throat.

He smiled, her valiant, deadly, honorable warrior. "I love you, too." He kissed her again. "Forever."

Acknowledgments

Thank you to the readers who have jumped into this new era of the Realm vampires. I have many wonderful people to thank for getting this book to readers, and I sincerely apologize to anyone I've forgotten.

Thank you to Big Tone, Gabe, and Karlina: for their love, support, for making my life better every day.

Thank you to my eximious editor, Alicia Condon, as well as everyone at Kensington publishing: Alexandra Nicolajsen, Steven Zacharius, Adam Zacharius, Vida Engstrand, Jane Nutter, Lauren Jernigan, Elizabeth Trout, Samantha McVeigh, Lynn Cully, Kimberly Richardson, Arthur Maisel, Renee Rocco, Rebecca Cremonese, April LeHoullier.

Thank you to my wonderful agent, Caitlin Blasdell, and to Liza Dawson and the entire Liza Dawson Agency.

Thank you to Jillian Stein for the absolutely fantastic work and for being such a great friend.

Thanks to my fantastic street team, Rebecca's Rebels, and to their creative and hard-working leader, Minga Portillo.

Thanks also to my constant support system: Gail and Jim English, Debbie and Travis Smith, Stephanie and Don West, Jessica and Jonah Namson, Kathy and Herb Zanetti, and Liz and Steve Berry.

Finally, thank you to the readers who have kept the Dark Protectors alive all of these years. It's because of you that we decided to return to the world of the Realm.

Rebecca Zanetti teams up with fellow *New York Times* Bestselling Authors Kat Martin and Alexandra Ivy to create heart-pounding romantic suspense in

PIVOT

Coming soon!

As girls, they bonded over broken homes and growing up in foster care.

As women, they're fighting for their lives, and loves, once more. . . .

MERI
When Meriwether Jones takes her young daughter and runs from trouble in L.A., that trouble follows. By the time Meri reaches Spokane, she's out of gas, money, and ideas. Luckily, ex-cop Ian Brodie hires her to help him with his father's farmhouse, and they seem like the answer to each other's prayers. But Meri is keeping a dangerous secret—and Ian is in danger of losing his heart. . . .

MELANIE
That secret explodes when Melanie Cassidy spots two men trying to kidnap a young boy she tutors and responds by ramming them with her car. The last thing she expects is for the man she once loved, Detective Gray Hawkins, to appear and rescue them both. Now she has no choice but to trust him as they investigate the truth about a conspiracy of dirty, drug-trafficking cops—and the truth about their relationship. . . .

MICHELLE
After a rough youth, Michelle Peach was finally content in Portland—until two men broke into her home, threatened her, and sent her mentally unstable mom on a blackmail spree that Michelle has to stop. The last person Michelle wants to see is her ex, Evan Boldon, a former marine turned sheriff. But Evan misses the woman who walked away instead of letting him help years ago. This time he's not asking permission; he's going to put a stop to the trouble stalking Michelle and her friends—and win her heart for good.

Printed in the United States
by Baker & Taylor Publisher Services